STOLEN INNOCENTS

Addison Kline

For my sister, Leigh

PROLOGUE

July 22, 1974
Elkhart, PA
Forest of York
2:00 P.M.

UNDER THE CANOPY OF TREES in the Forest of York, sounds of laughter echoed into the sanguine summer air. Gwen O'Mara stood in her rose garden at 27 Caribou Road hanging clothes on the line as the summer wind blew her dress and tousled her wavy, blonde hair. She peered across the horizon, her gray eyes scanning the landscape to see where her three eldest daughters had gotten off to this time. She had told them not to wander far.

"Angie! Angie! You can't catch me!" yelled young Tiffany O'Mara at her sister as she ran through a thicket in the Forest of York. Her strawberry blonde hair whipped behind her as she raced from flower to flower. Angela O'Mara crouched her tiny frame to the forest floor as she inspected the tree that towered overhead. She pretended not to hear her older sister's taunts and continued to do what she pleased. She didn't have time for such juvenile pursuits. Angie's blue sundress fell just above her knees revealing scratches and scrapes that she had earned days earlier when she tried to climb the very tree she was inspecting today. Tried and failed.

"Angie! Didn't you hear us?" called Angie's other sister Misty-Lee from beyond the thicket.

Tiffany yelled, "She's ignoring us! That's because Angie's too slow to catch me!"

Misty quipped, "Tiff, you know Angie is the faster runner."

Tiffany's smooth lips curled up into a vindictive smile. "What do you expect from a tomboy?"

Somehow Tiffany always managed to make a sport out of proving that she was better than Angie at everything. Tiffany loved to taunt Angie and would go to great lengths to prove that she was the superior sister. Misty-Lee, though a much kinder and gentler soul than Tiffany, often played along if only to remain in Tiffany's good graces. Angie had tired of their childish games. She was much more interested in the white tree that loomed overhead. At age twelve, Angie didn't enjoy the same things as the other children and relished in the quiet that the forest provided. That, of course, did not apply on days like today when her sisters, Misty-Lee, age ten, and Tiffany, age thirteen, tagged along with her.

Angie continued to dig in the warm dirt with her bare hands. She was intent upon discovering what mysteries lay hidden just beneath the surface of the forest floor. Her pace quickened as she pulled the earth out of the hole that she created — until a little glint of silver caught her eye. Her heart began to race as she dug out the treasure that was buried at the base of the Bone Tree. Her hands scraped frantically at the dirt, digging and digging until she had freed the object from its burial plot. She held the object in her hands; it was surprisingly heavy. Slowly, Angie brushed off the excess dirt from the top of the object, causing debris to fall to the ground below. The object appeared to be an ornate jewelry box with Victorian filigree work and the initials BEK inscribed on top in an elegant cursive monogram. Excitement coursed through Angie's body as she observed the jewelry box.

Who would bury such a beautiful treasure? Angie thought.

As Angie pulled on the clasp to unlock the box, a voice rang out from behind her. Startled, she jumped at the sound.

"We mustn't touch things that do not belong to us," the voice said in a cool tone.

Angie turned around quickly with a frightened look in her eyes. It quickly faded when she saw her cousin.

"Bernard ... You startled me," said Angie as her heart raced in her chest.

Bernard smiled a slight grin at his young cousin, though his powerful gaze did not leave the box. He seemed mesmerized by the object; obsessed. Suddenly, Tiffany and Misty-Lee raced by Angie and Bernard, earning a vile glare from their older cousin.

"You girls shouldn't play here. It's dangerous," Bernard warned coolly.

"Oh, be quiet, Bernard! My mother said to ignore you and your ridiculous stories!" shouted Tiffany with attitude rampant in her voice.

"Our daddy said that we aren't allowed to talk to you," said Misty-Lee with fear visible on her round face. Her voice shook as she spoke.

Angie looked at Bernard intuitively as he spoke. Bernard slowly turned to Angie's sisters.

With wide eyes he said to the girls in a malevolent voice, "Don't think for a second that I care about what your coward father or naive mother thinks of me!"

Tiffany and Misty-Lee stood stark still as they looked at the anger in Bernard Kendricks's face. He stared down at them, angry and threatening.

"Now go!" Bernard demanded, "Don't come back to this place!"

Bernard didn't have to tell them twice. Tiffany and Misty-Lee barreled up the path that led to Caribou Road as terror rose from their cores. When Tiffany reached the top of the path, she swung around on her heels and she was horrified to see that Angie was still standing with Bernard. Angie held the box firmly in her hands. She stood her ground, unafraid. Unlike her relatives, she wasn't frightened by her cousin, Bernard. Quite the opposite, actually. She was amused by his eccentricities.

"Angie! C'mon!" yelled Tiffany with panic in her voice.

"Angie! What are you doing?" yelled Misty-Lee as tears streamed down her round face. She couldn't understand why her sister wanted to remain in Bernard Kendricks's presence. Misty-Lee and Tiffany were terrified by Bernard's presence. Tiffany glared at Angie with anger and confusion.

"Forget her. She's crazy! Let's go!" yelled Tiffany as she and Misty-Lee vanished from sight.

Bernard looked at Angie sadly and remarked, "They just don't like me because I'm different."

Angie replied, "Different isn't such a bad thing."

Bernard smiled. "That all depends on your definition of different, I suppose."

Angie peered at Bernard with her pensive blue eyes. A sea of questions churned in her gaze.

"My father says that you're dangerous," Angie said cautiously as she waited to see a reaction form on Bernard's face.

"He says that I shouldn't go near you," Angie continued.

Bernard shrugged his shoulders. "He's probably right," Bernard admitted with an unfazed expression on his face.

"Why doesn't my father let you visit?"

"Because he doesn't trust me."

"Trust you with what?"

Bernard smiled a sly, sneaky smile. Just when Angie thought she was about to get some answers, Bernard simply shrugged instead. Without a beat, Angie continued her interrogation of her strange cousin. She was determined to get some answers.

"Why shouldn't we play back here?" Angie asked as she looked at Bernard observantly.

"The tree ... It's very dangerous," said Bernard in an eerie tone of voice.

"Seriously, Bernard? It's just a tree," said Angie quite reasonably.

Bernard laughed and replied, "It's not called the Bone Tree for no reason."

A perplexed look took over Angie's face. *The Bone Tree*, Angie thought. She had heard the stories before. Bernard paused for a moment, deciding upon how much information he should tell his young cousin. Finally, he decided to go forth.

"Rumor has it that everything that touches the Bone Tree dies," said Bernard creepily.

"That's a silly child's tale, Bernard. I climbed that tree yesterday. I'm not dead," replied Angie, refusing to believe Bernard's tall tales.

Bernard pointed at Angie's scraped knees.

"Maybe not, but look at your legs. It looks like the tree let you off with just a warning."

Angie rolled her eyes.

"Why did you bury a jewelry box by the tree?"

"It's not a jewelry box," replied Bernard. He was starting to get annoyed.

"What do you keep in it?" Angie asked as her persistence wore on Bernard's patience.

Bernard replied in a chilling voice, "Whatever I deem necessary."

Angie didn't say a word. She simply watched Bernard with an intent expression. There was something bewitching about him. He was a mystery waiting to be unraveled. Bernard stood quietly under the canopy of the Bone Tree. A sparrow landed gently on his shoulder. He peeked at the bird and smiled sweetly at Angie.

"So, do you want to see what I use this box for?" Bernard asked with an alluring voice.

Angie nodded.

"Okay, but only if you don't tell anyone. Can you keep a secret?" asked Bernard as his face came closer to Angie's.

"No one's ever told me a secret before," Angie admitted.

"Just because you haven't heard one before, doesn't mean they don't exist. Everyone has a secret. Even you."

"I don't have any secrets," insisted Angie.

"Keep telling yourself that. Everyone has secrets, and all secrets must come to light."

"No, really ... I don't have any secrets yet," said Angie convincingly.

Bernard's gaze darkened as he stared into his young cousin's face.

"Give it time. You will."

Suddenly, the sparrow flew off Bernard's shoulder and darted across the forest. It flitted from side to side, until finally it propelled its tiny body into the dark cavity of the Bone Tree.

"Hey! Where'd it go?" asked Angie with a start.

Bernard smiled. "You wanted to know what I use my box for ... Open it."

Bewildered, Angie did as she was told. She pulled the clasp on the ornate box and watched the lid gently rise. Inside of the box lay a small piece of red satin. Intrigued, Angie gently pulled the satin out of the box and what lay beneath caused her stomach to lurch. Cradled in the box was a sparrow that lay unmoving—dead. There were no signs of life, but also no evidence of decomposition, either. In a moment of sheer panic, Angie dropped the box to the ground and ran up the path that led out of the forest. A scream flooded the air as Bernard laughed with pleasure. Bernard cackled loudly as he watched Angie O'Mara run frantically up the path. The sparrow that had entered the cavity of the Bone Tree just a moment earlier emerged from inside the hollow tree and landed gracefully on Bernard's shoulder.

"I've always loved that trick," Bernard said evilly. He smiled in twisted delight as he stepped over the dead sparrow that lay on the ground with the live one still perched on his shoulder. Slowly, he meandered down the path that led deeper into the Forest of York as a song whistled from his lips.

Everybody in Elkhart has a secret, and if they say they don't, they're lying. I got out of there as quick as I could, and I never looked back. Longing to escape a past that kept me awake at night, I packed my beat-up hornet green Volkswagen with anything I couldn't live without and left without a goodbye or a trace. My mother would never forgive me for my hasty departure, but I didn't have a choice. I had to escape the evil that resided there. My life depended on it. With tears welling in my eyes, the VW met the open road. Its tires burned against the asphalt and I had no plans to ever show my face in Elkhart again.

As the landscape of the heartland raced past my window, I only had eyes for the road before me, with the exception of an occasional glance in the rearview mirror. I drove 2,700 miles to the coast. Not the Atlantic, which would have made more sense to some people, but the Pacific. The only thought that entered my mind was that I had to get as far away from Elkhart as I possibly could. And I did just that. I drove west from the mountains of Pennsylvania to the lush coast of the Pacific Northwest. I stopped only out of necessity; to rest, to eat, and to fill up the VW's tank. Finally, after five long days of driving, I had reached my destination: Seattle. A place where no one knew my name or the past that I was running from. It would be a brand new start. But the past has a way of catching up with you. Never in a million years did I think that I would be right back where I started twenty years ago, looking into the face of the one person I had spent my life running from.

PART ONE

The Long Way Home

I heard you whisper,
In the dark of night.
Your voice was clear,
But you eluded my sight.
A ghostly encounter,
A phantom's flight.
Quickened my heart,
Mind frozen with fright.
The rustling of leaves,
Sending shivers up my spine.
Shadows of memories,
Stepping out of line.
I looked for you,
But no friend I could find.
Alone in the dark,
Your face clear in my mind.

~Excerpt from Phantom Flight by Addison Kline

CHAPTER 1

June 15, 2000
2324 Mariner Avenue
Apartment 3B
Seattle, WA
6:00 A.M.

"GOOD MORNING, SEATTLE! This is Jill Mayweather and it's going to be a great day! Today is June fifteenth and we have all the headlines, but first let's check the weather. You'd better bring an umbrella with you, because, you guessed it! It's raining again! We're expecting heavy rain all morning and we can expect a light shower this afternoon. It is expected to clear up by the evening commute. Tonight will be mostly cloudy with a high of fifty-nine ..."

Angela O'Mara-Macklon's alarm clock spewed out the morning news as she lay discontented under her covers. With just two hours of sleep, she contemplated whether or not she should even bother trudging to work to face her boss Felix and his grand inquisition. Angie was supposed to log in from home last night so that she could finish preparing the Thire deposition. Thanks to Jeremy's series of dramatics, she never even got the chance to turn her computer on, let alone finish the necessary preparation needed for the upcoming court date. Jeremy, Angie's husband of four years, decided to throw a full-fledged, level-five, atomic hissy fit when Angie arrived home late for dinner last night. A whole three hours and fifteen minutes late. Jeremy had spent the entire afternoon preparing a special dinner for them. It was a last ditch effort to invigorate some long-lost spark between them. By the time she strolled into their apartment at ten before eight, the candles were doused, the tilapia was cold, and Jeremy was sitting in the dark of the dining room seething.

The last words that Jeremy spewed at Angie like battery acid before he left her life forever were, "I feel like I don't even know you anymore. What happened to you? Who the hell are you, and what have you done with my wife?"

The words still stung as the clock reflected the much dreaded hour of 6 a.m. Angie's head pounded as she ripped the covers off of her body, revealing her bed clothes—a wrinkled gray pant suit that she had worn the previous day. Sleepily, she grazed her hand over the empty space in the bed, his space, and sighed heavily as the weight of last night came crashing down upon her. Sucking up her pride, she forced herself to crawl out of bed. Angie's long blonde hair fell over her tired face. She glanced in the mirror and immediately regretted doing so. She shuddered at her appearance, noting that she always looked so much older when she didn't get a full night's sleep.

Angie forced herself to walk to her closet as her bare feet scraped along the rough carpet. Quickly, she flicked through her wardrobe that was overflowing with dull pant suits, dresses and other corporate wear. It was a veritable sea of black, blue and gray. Finally, she pulled out a navy blue pencil skirt, a white blouse and a pair of black mules—an outfit that was almost as boring as what she presently had on. Angie carelessly tossed her garments on the unmade bed as she forced herself to face the day. Angie decided that it would be better to stay busy than wallow in her misery. Angie was already expecting an ear lashing from Felix, prolonging it would only intensify his wrath. The last thing Angie needed was to be on Felix's bad side. Little did Angie know, her day was about to get a whole lot worse.

"Macklon!"

Felix DeSanto's bellowing scream called out over the sea of gray cubicles. His outburst had effectively silenced the hum of chatter that was emitting from the legal accounting division at Heath, Conrad, and Langston, LLC. Angie eyed the ajar door of Felix's office speculatively. She was intimidated by the heightened level of agitation in Felix's voice. As Angie walked grimly to her moody boss's office, fifty-two pairs of eyes followed her movements. They were all curious what Felix's star legal assistant had done to deserve such chilly treatment. Angie pushed open the door to Felix's office and allowed it to click behind her. Nervously, she glanced up at her irate boss, Felix DeSanto.

Felix DeSanto was a high-powered corporate defense attorney with a large client list of Fortune 500 companies and an even bigger anger management problem. He wasn't well liked, but thanks to his outstanding reputation as a criminal and corporate defense attorney, he was well-respected. As a result, his frequent outbursts were overlooked, as was his reputation as a relentless womanizer. Felix was not the type of boss you wanted to get on the wrong side of. Unfortunately for Angie, she had strayed from her long-maintained role as the boss's princess.

"Good morning. How are you today?" asked Angie in a friendly tone.

In response, Felix scrunched up his face and presented her with his usual take-no-shit attitude.

"Cut the crap, Macklon. Where's the file?"

"I can explain ..." Angie began but was rudely cut off by Felix.

"It's eight twenty. You were supposed to be here at eight fifteen," said Felix stingily as he glanced at his Rolex.

"I was booting up my computer," Angie explained.

"Seriously? This file better be immaculate."

Angie sighed.

"I have the file, but it's not finished."

Angie looked at her boss's face with worry. Felix's face had now turned a dangerous shade of purple. He literally looked like he was about to have a heart attack.

Good job, Angie. You've outdone yourself this time.

"You have got to be kidding me!"

"Sorry, I wanted to finish it last night, but Jeremy ..." Angie began but she was cut off immediately by Felix, who was waving her off disrespectfully.

"I don't have time for your personal melodrama! I need my goddamn deposition!" Felix barked.

"I can do it this morning ..." Angie explained.

"I told you before you left yesterday that it had to be in by eight fifteen today, and that was firm. So I'm going to give it to Swanson. At least I know that it will get done."

"Felix, I break my back for this job, for *you*. I was just trying to explain to you that my husband ..."

"Macklon, I'm going to be frank with you. I don't give a damn about your husband. He doesn't like me, and I don't like him. I don't want to hear it. You said the deposition would be done and now it's not."

Angie was taken aback by Felix's brutal admission.

"Look, DeSanto! You're way out of line! You gave me two hours to get the deposition together, so I took it home thinking I could finish it at home. I didn't have to though."

"The fact remains that it didn't get done!"

"It's not done because it's not humanly possible. You need to decide if you want it done right, or if you want it done quickly."

"Macklon! You know damn well I need both!"

"I was trying to do you a favor. I wasn't on the clock," Angie reminded Felix curtly.

"You would have gotten paid!" exclaimed Felix in a petulant voice.

"Would I? You still owe me overtime from last month," reminded Angie. She was nobody's fool.

Before Felix could answer her, there was a knock on the door.

"Now you're just being petty! Open the door. It's probably Swanson."

Timothy Swanson was fresh out of college and eager to build a name for himself. He did whatever Felix asked of him. Felix could ask him to go detail the advertisement on the highway and Swanson would be out on Route 99 with a bucket and rag, shining it up. Swanson was like a puppy dog, albeit a really hyper and well-caffeinated one.

"Yeah, boss?" said Swanson, poking his head into the door. He had clearly already guzzled down his Espresso Grande and was ready to tackle whatever Felix wanted to throw at him.

"Ah, Timothy, you're looking well-rested today!" said Felix in his most charming voice. Angie rolled her eyes.

"Thank you, sir. What can I do to help?" Swanson said in a chipper voice. Angie glared at him venomously.

"I'm going to assign you the Thire deposition. This is a very high-priority project, and it is for the San Francisco–based biotech company, Thire Biotechnical Products. It's coming off of Macklon's desk, along with all of her other assignments. Swanson, welcome to my elite team. Macklon, you're out."

Both Macklon and Swanson had to catch their breath.

"I'm sorry. What?" Angie asked, unsure if she caught Felix's drift.

"You're out. Pack up your desk. I'm terminating your contract."

"Because I'm late with one project?"

"Among other reasons. It was an important project. This will teach you that I mean business. You have to prioritize."

Angie could feel her anger rising inside of her. She just couldn't control herself any longer.

"I put you before my husband for three years and now he's gone! Shove this job! You are the most inconsiderate and undermining employer I've ever had in my life."

"Maybe you didn't hear me the first time. I don't have time for your melodrama. Pack up your desk because I've terminated your contract. Swanson, be sure that you get the Thire deposition from Macklon before she leaves. Security will be up in fifteen minutes to escort her out."

"Bastard!" Angie exclaimed vehemently.

"I've been called worse," said Felix, unfazed.

Angie stormed out of the office knocking over Felix's "World's Best Boss" trophy that sat on his desk. A crowd of employees had gathered outside of Felix's office. They were all eager to hear what was going on inside. Angie gave them all a heated glare.

"Don't you all have deadlines?"

At the sound of her agitated voice, the crowd dispersed, all acting as if they weren't really trying to hear the conversation inside the office. Anger took over Angie's body as she made a beeline for her desk. Swanson had disappeared and that suited Angie just fine because she found him to be an insufferable pest. She wanted to get her belongings, but she didn't plan on going down quietly. From behind her, Swanson reappeared with a set of brown legal boxes in his hands.

"Here are some boxes if you need them," said Swanson with a friendly but smarmy voice.

"Oh, shove off. Kiss-ass," Angie replied nastily.

Howard Cosgrove, an elderly accounting clerk who sat in the adjacent cubicle raised his bushy eyebrow at his saucy office mate before turning his eyes back to his work.

As Howard pecked at his keyboard, he said, "I told you he would get back at you for rejecting his offer for a date."

"I'm married. He should know better."

"What are you going to do now?" Howard asked sensibly.

Angie pondered his question. She stood perfectly still as a devilish smile grew across her pretty face.

"I'm going to expose him for the sorry sucker that he is," said Angie matter-of-factly.

"Are you going to make a scene?" asked Howard warily.

"I most certainly am ... I need your paper shredder," said Angie with her exit strategy already mapped out in her head.

"I knew I could count on you for some early morning entertainment. You know where it is."

Angie rolled out Howard's gigantic paper shredder from behind his cubicle and plugged it into the wall socket at her desk. While the beast of a machine warmed up, Angie began loading up her file boxes with all her belongings. She packed up pictures of Jeremy, a snapshot of their beloved cat, Nan, a picture of her sisters as children, her radio, and several pairs of shoes from her desk. Finally, both boxes were full, and Felix had just strolled out of his office to check on her progress. Felix primped in the glass window, adjusting his silk tie and flattening it against his maroon shirt. Finally, he turned to face his workforce as he put both hands on his hips.

"Almost ready?" Felix said to Angie as she sat rifling through papers on her desk.

"Just about. I'm grabbing the deposition."

"Security will be here in about two minutes," Felix warned.

"Duly noted," Angie said nonchalantly as she continued to flick through papers at her desk. She was calm on the outside, but a maelstrom was brewing just under the surface. Suddenly, Swanson returned with a smug smile cemented on his face.

"What are you smiling about?" Angie demanded to know. She was highly irritated at his gloating.

"Oh, just excited to get started. I just called Mother to tell her I am lead on an important case. The parents are going to take me to dinner tonight at Le Roux. Mother wants to have the mussels."

Under Angie's breath she commented, "I hope you and your mummy choke on your mussels."

Howard nearly choked on his croissant after hearing Angie's comment.

"That was not nice ..." Howard said to Angie.

"No. I guess it wasn't. He loves crawling under my skin!"

"So Macklon ... Did you find that deposition yet? I'm eager to get started," said Swanson excitedly.

Angie rolled her eyes as she continued looking through the paperwork.

"Just one minute, sir. Right away, sir. Seriously, dude? Weren't you someone's intern last year? Get off your high horse!"

Finally, Angie opened up her messenger bag and retrieved the Thire deposition from a manila file folder.

"Ah, here it is!" said Angie holding up the document for Swanson to see. He tried reaching out for the document, but Angie snatched it back.

"Not so fast, Swanson! This is a very important document. We wouldn't want something to happen to it, would we?"

Swanson shook his head from left to right as he eyed the document nervously.

"The thing that you have to understand about this particular client is that they are a Fortune 500 company. They are very high-profile and they make beaucoup bucks every year. If something were to happen to this document, Felix would probably jump out of his office window."

"Why would something happen to the document? It's safe in your hands. So pass it over and nothing will happen."

"Oh, I don't think so."

"What's going on out here?"

"I was simply explaining to young Swanson here the importance of this document. If something were to ever happen to this document, you would probably throw yourself out of your office window in despair."

"Don't play games, Macklon."

"You know, Felix, I knew you'd pull something like this when I turned you down for drinks the other night. I wonder what your wife would think about that."

"Macklon! I'm dead serious!"

Angie picked up her cell phone and grinned deviously. In her other hand she held the Thire deposition by the upper right corner with just her thumb and index finger.

"So, Swanson, it is very important to be careful with vital documents. Especially around paper shredders. We wouldn't want something to happen ... Oops!"

Angie dropped the deposition into the paper shredder. The ancient machine gobbled up the all-important document, breaking it down into little bits of confetti. She knew that there would be legal consequences for her actions, after all, a deposition is an official document. Angie didn't care. The only thing she cared about was getting back at Felix.

"What are you doing?" Felix screamed. His eyes were beginning to bulge out of his head.

Angie held her cell phone high in the air. The green screen was lit up, as if she was already on a call.

"You wanted to get back at me for not going for drinks with you. That's clear. So now I will get back at you for terminating my contract."

Felix stared at Angie with a lot of different emotions displaying on his face; anger and irritation were there, sure. But there was something else, too. He actually cared about her, but his jealousy got in the way. He was angry because she wouldn't choose him over her husband.

"Nothing to say, Felix? Okay. Say hi to your wife for me."

Angie dropped the cell phone into Felix's hand. When he saw the display, Felix screamed like a man who was being murdered at knife point.

Monica DeSanto

978-555-4189

Security had finally arrived and was rushing down the hall towards Felix's office. Angie grabbed her bag and her boxes. She gave Howard a warm hug and waved goodbye to her colleagues. Two security guards, one a burly man and another a tiny elderly woman, tried to secure Angie's arms to escort her out of the building. Angie pushed them off of her as she walked to the elevator bay and out of the main entrance for the last time.

Angie walked out of Seattle Commerce One and straight into the pouring rain. She didn't bother putting up her umbrella. After the day she was having, what was a little rain? After a short cab ride, she arrived at her apartment building. She knew she should check the paper to see who was hiring, but she just didn't have it in her today. Angie dug in her bag for her keys and as she approached her apartment door, she noticed that there was a piece of paper taped to the surface. Her pace quickened as she rushed down the hallway to snatch the paper off of the door. Angie frantically unfolded the paper and read Jeremy's messy scrawl:

Angela,

I hope this note finds you well. I have come to the conclusion that we are two very different people moving down two very different paths. I understand that your job is highly demanding, but being married is, too. I just think you will be happier alone. You can focus on your career. I'm sorry I stormed out, but I am tired of sitting here alone every night. Even when you're with me, your mind is off somewhere else. I plan to take my belongings, which, I might add, includes our cat Nan. I considered leaving her, but I got some news that may affect your standing at the apartment. I also don't want her to have to wait until eight, nine or ten o'clock at night to eat due to your lunatic boss.

I informed the landlord that I am leaving. We have not had a lease in a year, so that ends our contract with this building. You can try talking to Rich and see if he will allow you to stay. I don't think you can afford it on your own. I also called your mother to let her know our situation. She wants you to go home. To Pennsylvania. Your dad is even offering to buy you a plane ticket. I'll always be your friend, but loving you is just too hard on my heart.

Sorry, Jer

The look on Angie's face did not change or show the slightest hint of sadness as she read the letter. Her only emotion was anger. Swiftly, she stomped her foot on the rug as she screamed.

He took my cat!

How dare he call my mother!

I'm not going back there! Is he insane?

Angie tried to slow her breathing down but it just didn't help. Today was the day from hell. After a final deep breath, she turned the doorknob and walked into a disheveled apartment. It appeared Jeremy had already started clearing some of his stuff out. Angie walked across the living room, ignoring the empty spaces where the furniture used to be. She picked up the phone that hung on the wall in the kitchen.

"Mom. It's Angela."

"Are you coming home?"

Angie knew she was all out of luck.

"Yes."

It appears I have no other choice.

CHAPTER 2

June 15, 2000
Elkhart, PA
Dawn

"THIS IS NOT WHAT I SIGNED UP FOR," complained Officer Liam Morrow to his brother/partner Adam as a yawn escaped from his mouth. The sun was rising over the mountains and squad car E5 was parked just outside Healer's Park. Officers Morrow and Morrow were keeping a close watch on the park and surrounding houses on Caribou Road in Elkhart.

"Crime is at an all-time low. This is a good thing," Adam reminded his brother as he slurped the last of his soda through a straw.

Suddenly, breaking up the monotony, the obnoxious tones and petulant voice of the emergency response dispatcher squawked loudly causing Liam to sit up straight and listen intently. After weeks of no real action, with the exception of breaking up a schoolyard fight at PS132, Liam was hungry for a real call.

"Robbery in progress. Car E5 to 41 Mountain Road."

"Harrow's ..." remarked Adam as he flicked the button that controlled the patrol car's siren and lights.

"Who the hell would steal from those old crows?" exclaimed Liam in shock.

"I guess we're about to find out. Hold on."

Clouds of dirt kicked up as Adam pulled the car out of the parking space, leaving the quiet of Caribou Road behind them.

Squad car E5 rolled up Mountain Road and stopped outside Harrow's General Store. Edna Harrow and Peggy Dresher were waiting angrily in their housecoats with pink and purple rollers in their hair. Adam and Liam caught sight of their appearance and while Adam tried to keep a straight face, Liam couldn't contain himself.

"Jesus Christ. What did I ever do to deserve this?" Liam complained.

Adam smirked as he exited the patrol car. He tried to disregard his brother's reaction and put on a serious face.

"Edna ... Peggy ... What seems to be the problem?" asked Adam in a professional tone.

Edna was crying hysterically. She sobbed messily into her ratty yellow housecoat while her friend Peggy fanned her face dramatically, as if extra air was exactly what she needed.

"Oh, thank God you're here! Someone broke in! I can hear them in there!" exclaimed Peggy as she continued to fan her face.

"Are they still in there? Liam ... Go check around back. I'll keep an eye out front while I ask Peggy and Edna some questions."

Liam complied with his brother's request and ran around to the back of the property to check for any signs of a break-in. Liam expected to see an open gate, a broken window, or some other sign indicating that someone broke in to the old General Store. As Liam approached the chain link fence in the rear of the property, he was puzzled by what he found. The chain link fence was still secured with a padlock. Liam climbed the height of the fence, landing hard on the dirt ground of Harrow's yard. The yard didn't appear to be disturbed at all. Continuing to be perplexed, Liam slowly made his way to the back door of Harrow's General Store. Liam fully expected to find signs of forced entry or an unlocked door at the very least. Much to his surprise, Officer Liam Morrow found neither.

With great force, Liam kicked in the back door and he heard noises coming from inside—strange noises. He heard something scratching against a wooden surface fast and furiously. Liam pulled his gun out of its holster and stalked the room, listening for the source of the sound. Step by step, he was getting closer to the noise, but he still couldn't see the perpetrator. Finally, Liam identified that the sounds were coming from behind the front counter. Liam leaned over the wooden counter stealthily to get a better glimpse of the source of the noise. Officer Morrow couldn't believe his eyes.

"You've got to be kidding me!" Liam yelled in fury.

With both arms, he reached down and yanked up two fat and snarling black and gray raccoons. They hissed and tried to bite him as he yanked them away from their morning breakfast—a bag of half-eaten trail mix and a can of lightly salted peanuts. Liam held them away from his body as he charged to the front door. Adam saw Liam coming towards him with something in his hands.

"It looks like Officer Morrow may have found something ..." said Adam as he tried to make out what Liam was carrying.

"What did he find?" asked Peggy neurotically.

Liam had an amused look on his face as he crossed the threshold of Harrow's General Store.

"Just a couple of masked bandits."

Liam held the pair of angry raccoons up by their scruffs for all to see. Adam had to hide his amusement while Peggy and Edna squinted to see what Liam was bringing forward. As Liam came into the early morning light that was shining on the porch, Edna and Peggy got their first glimpse of their "burglars." Edna's eyes grew wide and horrified. Peggy, meanwhile, had run away down Mountain Road. Her curlers were falling out of her hair and her bedroom slippers had gotten muddy from a puddle that she ran clear through. Edna followed hurriedly behind her, petrified of the critters in Liam's grip.

"I've never seen two old bats run so fast in my life!" remarked Adam as he watched the pair run farther up Mountain Road.

"Where the hell are they going? They live right upstairs!" Liam exclaimed, unable to control his laughter anymore.

Suddenly, the raccoons began swiping at Liam's arms in an attempt to free themselves.

"Hey, get me one of those milk crates over there," Liam asked Adam as he pointed to a pile of orange milk crates that were stacked on the porch of Harrow's General Store.

"Ow! Hurry up they're clawing at me!" Liam protested.

Adam stared at his brother with an amused look on his face.

"Hurry! Don't you care if my skin gets scratched off?" yelled Liam in agitation.

Adam jogged to the porch and grabbed two milk crates and ran back to where his brother was standing.

"Finally! Okay, now when I drop him," Liam said, raising the raccoon in his right hand for Adam to see, "trap him."

"All right, Mr. Critter Control. Whenever you're ready."

"Very funny."

Liam dropped the raccoon to the ground and Adam forced the crate over its body, slamming it down tight. The raccoon hissed at Adam and reached its paw out through a hole in the crate. It swiped at Adam's leg but missed. Fortunately for Adam, he had the crate secured in place with his foot. Finally, both animals were secured, and they only had to wait for animal control to arrive.

Liam looked at his brother with a perturbed look on his face. "I went through all this. You call animal control," demanded Liam.

"Me? Oh, fine! Hold on. I hate dealing with these idiots."

Adam pulled a silver cell phone out of his back pocket, pressed a couple buttons and put it up to his ear.

"Hi, this is Officer Morrow ... Badge 7247 in Elkhart. We have a situation with a couple of raccoons. Can you send someone out to Harrow's General Store on Mountain Road in Elkhart? 41 Mountain Road."

Liam watched his brother as his aggravation intensified. Calling the geniuses over at animal control always managed to grate on Adam's nerves.

"What do you mean you're short staffed? I'm a police officer, not a zookeeper!" Adam declared loudly.

A moment later, Adam snapped his cell phone shut as he shook his head in disgust.

"What did they say?" asked Liam.

"Regina at Animal Control says to take the raccoons to a wooded area and set them free."

"After all that?"

"Come on."

Adam pushed open the heavy oak door of Morrow Manor with a groan as the fragrant aroma of seasoned meat caught his attention. Adam sniffed the air to make sure that he was not mistaken. Suddenly, the smell reached Liam's nose and the pair looked at each other in confusion. They both checked the address on the front door to make sure they had the right house. As if Morrow Manor could be mistaken for any other house. They followed the scent into the dining room where they were greeted by a most unhappy mood. Bridgette sat at the far end of the dining room table with a miserable scowl on her pretty face.

Liam, who was still enamored by the pleasant smell, blurted out, "Whoever is cooking, it smells amazing!"

As the words escaped his mouth, Liam froze in shock; he just realized that his aunt was in the room. Bridgette shot an evil glare at Liam and then at Adam, who was considered guilty by association. Bridgette was slicing up a watermelon at the dining room table. This was clearly someone's idea of letting Bridgette help with dinner since she could not be trusted with a frying pan or an operable oven. She proved that last month when she tried to make bacon and eggs for breakfast, and accidentally set the stove on fire. The blaze destroyed the kitchen. Angus paid for a total kitchen remodel with the stipulation that his daughter is no longer allowed to touch the stove.

Bridgette's agitation intensified by the minute. Each chop of her knife was more forceful than the last, causing watermelon juice to fly everywhere.

"Uncle Frank and Tristan are making dinner tonight. They've locked me out of the kitchen and told me to cup up the melon! My cooking is not that bad!"

Adam thought, *Oh, but it is! It really, really is!*

Adam and Liam stared at their aunt, wide-eyed and stark still. They tried not to laugh as the memory of the charred kitchen came to the forefront of their minds. They knew that if a single smirk crossed their faces, their aunt would send the entire bowl of butchered watermelon flying across the dining room. It took every ounce of strength they had not to laugh at her. It did no good, as she sent chunks of fruit flying across the dining room table when Adam smiled ever so slightly.

"Oh, shut up! Get out of my dining room!" Bridgette yelled at her nephews as she started to laugh.

"Uh ... Where is everyone?" Liam asked in a perplexed tone. Morrow Manor was never empty.

"They are all out back. Frank decided to throw an impromptu barbecue. Apparently, someone has some big news to share."

Adam and Liam looked at each other suspiciously.

"News?"

Bridgette shrugged her shoulders as she went back to mutilating the watermelon and the guys took that as their cue to go outside. Liam and Adam walked out the back door and found that a crowd had gathered in the yard. Joe Piedmonte was about to toss a horseshoe across the lawn as Jack, Shane and Blake cheered him on. In a huddled corner, Jenna DiNolfo, Cole, and Natalie were eyeing them speculatively as they worked out their game plan. Just before Joe was about to release the horseshoe from his grip, he spotted Liam and Adam and gave them a raucous welcome.

"Hey! Look who it is! Heroes of the day. I heard a rumor that you two foiled a robbery this morning."

"I wouldn't go that far," said Liam with a chuckle.

"I heard you caught the guys red-handed. Don't be so modest," urged Joe.

Jack overheard the exchange and laughed loudly.

"Oh, Liam is never modest!"

Liam grinned broadly flashing a hundred watt smile. Jack wasn't kidding. Adam finally decided to join the conversation.

"Oh, we got 'em all right. Regular masked bandits," Adam said in an amused tone of voice.

DiNolfo eyed her officers as her eyes lit up, illuminating her typically serious face. She knew all too well what her officers were up to. She also knew what had gone down inside Harrow's General Store this morning. It was her job to know. She had no problem keeping everybody guessing, though, at least for a little while. Suddenly, Jenna couldn't stifle her laughter anymore. Joe and Jack stared at Jenna with suspicious glances from across the yard. Joe had one eyebrow raised just a bit, giving him a somewhat menacing look.

"What?" Joe asked DiNolfo in response to her outburst of laughter.

DiNolfo looked at Joe and then at her officers.

"Oh, just tell them. I can't take it anymore," DiNolfo pleaded. Liam's face lit up with a smile.

"Okay, so ... The robbers at Harrow's turned out to be a pair of raccoons. The funniest part was watching Edna and Peggy run away down Mountain Road in their housecoats and hair rollers!" divulged Liam with a huge grin on his face.

Adam added, "They didn't even have their dentures in!"

Everybody laughed except for Jack who simply put his head in his hands and shook his head in disbelief.

"Thanks son, for the mental image that I could have lived without," said Jack, his voice wrought with sarcasm.

Moira, who has known Edna and Peggy since high school, laughed and said,

"I'm not so sure they own dentures. They never wear them."

"Hey, Jenna. Whose idea was it to make these two jokers partners? Isn't that against the rule book?"

"It was my idea. They work well together. As far as rules go, if I approve of the partnership, the captain's fine with it. So far, so good."

From behind Jack, the screen door swung open. Tristan had her hands full with a large tray of freshly prepared food. Frank followed behind her with another huge platter. The pair placed the food on the long picnic table that was waiting for them in the meadow. The smell of food lured the family to the table. Tristan and Frank had prepared fried chicken, roasted potatoes, corn bread, Jersey corn, baked macaroni, cole slaw, baby back ribs, baked beans, and a tall pitcher of freshly made lemonade. The table looked like it was about to crack under the weight of all the food.

Joe and Jenna approached the table first, gawking at the delicious spread. The Morrows always had a hearty spread of food whenever they came over. It just so happened that the food was usually cooked in Joe's own kitchen at his family's restaurant—Monte's Café. Not this time, though. Someone in the Morrow house had clearly taken some cooking lessons. Joe gave Frank a curious look.

"Is this the work of Bridgette?" asked Joe. Frank rolled his eyes and shook his head from side to side.

"God no. Bridgette can't boil water."

Jack nodded in agreement. Though she had many talents, Bridgette was downright frightful in the kitchen. The conversation ended as Bridgette came out of the house, slamming the screen door behind her. She was carrying her giant bowl of watermelon and Adam noticed that she had traded in her scowl for a pleasant smile. She never stayed mad long.

"Hey, Jack ... Where's Tommy?" asked Joe.

Jack could do nothing but roll his eyes. A rumbling noise sounded over the horizon, a loud growl of a motorcycle. Coming up the long dirt road to Morrow Manor, Tommy rode on the back of his brand new Harley. Casually, he jumped down from his bike and stared at the crowd with a grin on his face.

"What did I miss?" Tommy asked slyly as he took off his helmet.

Tommy laughed as a series of complaints regarding his motorcycle and his lateness began to flow from his well-meaning family members.

"Who the hell bought you a hog?" asked Jenna in shock. She cast a wary glance at Jack.

"Don't look at me!" said Jack. "I told him that thing is a one-way ticket to the emergency room, but as usual, he doesn't listen to me."

"He bought it himself. With money he had been saving up from odd jobs. He's an adult. But I'll tell you this, if he acts out, I'm locking the damn thing in the barn," explained Bridgette.

As a nurse who worked in the emergency room of Grier Mountain, Bridgette knew all too well the dangers that motorcycles presented. She had lectured Tommy at great length after she found out that he had purchased one. But as usual, Tommy only listens to one person and one person only in the Morrow household: Tristan.

"He's careful, guys. Lay off of him," Tristan urged. She always had Tommy's back.

Jack grumbled at Tristan, "Oh yeah, sure. Tommy is the poster child for motorcycle safety. I'll believe it when I see it."

"He wears a helmet, doesn't he?"

Jack had to admit, Tristan had a point.

"So what was this big announcement?" Angus demanded to know as he sat down at the picnic table with a crabby look on his face. He had just woken up from his afternoon nap, and he was not happy. No one seemed to notice though, because his query was drowned out by a cacophony of chattering as his family talked happily to each other. They were all excited for proms and graduations, college announcements and vacations. Angus, on the other hand, would be perfectly happy when this mandatory social event was over so that he could go back to his bedroom and watch TV. Angus continued to stare at his excitable family under a furrowed brow. The wrinkles on his forehead were becoming more pronounced by the second. At the opposite end of the table, Jack was talking in hushed tones to Joe, who kept making sneaky glances back at his girlfriend, Jenna. Something Joe said had Jack laughing and patting his good friend on the back. To Jack's right, Frank was rubbing his bald head in an attempt to ease the headache that was forming from listening to his wife's high-pitched laughter. Bridgette and Jenna were in deep conversation with Tristan and Natalie over their choice of prom dresses.

Tristan explained, "It only took seven hours to choose one, because Dad and Uncle Frank insisted upon coming with us. They couldn't agree what the right one was for me. Little did they know, Aunt Bridgette and I had already selected the perfect one last week and it was in the upstairs closet."

Tristan couldn't help but laugh at her uncle's face.

Frank, who was still rubbing his head, said, "You two think you're *so* clever! Seven hours at the bloody mall with Jack is *not* my idea of a good time!"

Bridgette and Tristan laughed at Frank.

"If you think that's bad you should try going shopping with Gus!" Bridgette blurted out to Tristan as she gave her father a look. Angus glared at Bridgette with an irate expression.

Next to Tristan, Cole was talking to Shane across the table loudly as they tormented Blake. They were dying to know who he planned to take to prom next week. Blake claimed to have a date, but he was keeping the identity of the special girl a secret. Meanwhile, Moira, who had claimed the empty seat next to Angus, was in the process of trying to break her husband out of his horrible mood. It wasn't that Angus was an unhappy man—he was quite happy. It just didn't show outwardly. He was easily annoyed, and when you add in his aging, wrinkled face, you have the appearance of an eternal sour puss. Angus loved his family, but he loved the quiet of his bedroom just as much.

"Can't you just smile?" begged Moira as she looked at her perpetually disgruntled husband.

Angus scowled at his wife with his bushy eyebrows furrowed over his piercing green eyes.

"I am smiling."

Moira rolled her eyes.

"Clearly."

Moira next focused her attention on her grandson, Tommy. She proceeded to lecture him on motorcycle safety, and even began to tell him about motorcycle accident rates.

Tommy groaned in protest, "I wear a helmet. It's perfectly safe and besides it helps me with my job!"

Jack gave Tommy an incredulous look.

"If Mr. O'Mara calls me one more time about that goddamn motorcycle, you're going to be riding a 10-speed around town!" shouted Jack across the table to Tommy.

Tommy couldn't help but laugh. Roger O'Mara was the father of Courtney O'Mara—Tommy's on again/off again girlfriend. It was well known throughout the Morrow house that Roger O'Mara hated Tommy's guts, and his motorcycle only added to his venomous fury. The worst thing that Roger O'Mara could have done was show Tommy how much his motorcycle annoyed him. Now Tommy revs his engine at 6 a.m. every morning down Caribou Road when he delivers the morning paper. The sound alone caused Mr. O'Mara's blood pressure to shoot sky high.

"That's my morning wakeup call! More effective than the noisiest of alarm clocks!" joked Joe as he laughed.

Frank and Jack couldn't help but laugh at Joe, who had lived next to Roger O'Mara for most of his life.

"See, Dad, not everyone on Caribou Road is so uptight!"

Frank stood up still laughing at Joe and Tommy as he called for everyone's attention. Frank didn't need to whistle or yell. When a man who goes by the name "Bulldog" stands up, you listen.

"All right, folks. Listen up," began Frank, earning everyone's attention including the persistently disgruntled Angus. Frank continued, his voice booming over the crowd like a megaphone, "I wanted to get everyone together. As you know, I don't really like big parties, but we definitely have some celebratin' to do this month."

The adults nodded in agreement while the kids sat with excited grins on their faces. Everyone was interested to hear what Frank had to say.

"I like to keep things casual. So we're celebrating the kids graduating from high school in a week, we've got prom next week, and some college announcements to get through. Today this is our celebration. Nothin' fancy ... Just good family, good friends and good times. Am I right?"

Everyone at the table cheered in agreement except for Angus who gave a half-hearted clap.

Liam blurted out, "And good food!" earning him a heated glare from his Aunt Bridgette.

Frank continued, "Okay, everyone. Dig in. Tristan and I have been working all afternoon on this beggar's feast for you all . And while you stuff your gobs, I'm going to read off some announcements!" Frank said excitedly.

Everyone at the table shifted uneasily. This was the moment they were all waiting for. The kids had decided that it would be fun to keep their college decisions a secret until just before graduation. Only one person in the Morrow house knew where all the kids at the table were attending school next year: Frank Kilpatrick. If there was anyone in the Morrow house that you could trust with a secret, it was him. Only two people didn't find this idea amusing. Cole was quite frankly on edge because he didn't know if he'd see his girlfriend next year, depending upon her college choice. Jack, meanwhile, was uneasy because he wasn't ready to let Tristan out of his sight just yet. Although three years had passed since Tristan's English teacher had kidnapped her and tried to claim her as his own, Jack was still on edge. Every time Tristan left his line of sight, Jack could feel anxiety rising in his chest. Frank, on the other hand, had known the results of the college acceptances since early March and kept assuring Jack and Cole that everything would be just fine.

Frank grabbed a folded-up piece of paper from his shirt pocket and cleared his voice. He squinted at the tiny print on the page and grabbed his reading glasses off of the picnic table. He had brought them for the occasion. Everyone laughed at him because Frank actually looked quite studious with his Ben Franklin-esque frames.

"Okay. First up ... Cole Piedmonte. Stand up, kid."

Cole did as he was asked, but not without an embarrassed expression forming across his handsome face.

"Cole Piedmonte is graduating from Steeplechase Academy with a GPA of 3.4."

Everyone at the table clapped for Cole with the most boisterous applause coming from Joe and Tristan.

"Yes, very nice indeed," said Frank. He continued, "He was accepted to Skole County Community College, Widener University, Albright College, Temple University, Bloomsburg University, and Lock Haven University. He plans to major in Business and help make us all filthy rich," Frank declared, earning big chuckles from Jack and Joe.

They were both very proud of Cole's plan.

"So kid," Frank continued, "Which one did you choose?"

Cole looked over the crowd and his eyes lingered on Tristan, who looked only a tiny bit nervous.

Cole happily declared, "Bloomsburg."

Joe jumped in his seat and shouted, "You're staying local?" Joe was thrilled with his son's decision.

Cole laughed, "Yeah, Dad. It's only a twenty minute drive from Elkhart."

Joe breathed a sigh of relief as Frank regained control of the conversation.

"Nice job, kid. Okay. Next up on the list is Tommy. Stand up."

Tommy did as he was told and gave everyone his proudest smile. Jack couldn't help but grin with pride. His troublemaker was finally graduating from high school. It only took him three years of senior classes to do it.

"Tommy is graduating from Steeplechase with ... Good God! Do you really want me to read this?" Frank exclaimed glaring at Tommy with a shocked look on his face. Tommy shook his head up and down giving his uncle the go ahead to announce his deplorable grade point average.

"All right. If you're sure ... Thomas Morrow is graduating with a 1.97 grade point average. By the skin of his bloody teeth, I might add!"

Jack let out a triumphant shout, "Finally! I don't care, as long as he gets that diploma."

Tommy laughed. "Third time's a charm."

Frank shook his head and raised an eyebrow at his nephew.

He continued, "All right then. Tommy was accepted at Skole County Community College and the Kremmings Technical School."

Loud applause erupted from the table, most notably from Jack, who didn't think Tommy would get accepted anywhere.

"So, laddie ... What did you pick?" asked Frank calmly.

"Erm ... Kremmings ..." Tommy said sheepishly. Tommy felt a bit embarrassed admitting that he was going to a trade school to learn how to be a mechanic. Regardless of how Tommy felt, Jack was prouder than ever just knowing that his son was applying himself somewhere other than just goofing off.

"And what program?" demanded Frank as he stared down at his nephew over the frame of his glasses.

"Auto mechanic," replied Tommy.

"All right, Tommy!" cried out Jenna. "You mean I'll have someone affordable to fix my fleet of broken down police cruisers other than Traffords?"

Liam and Adam laughed at her.

"Yeah, please. Before we have to peddle around town on a bicycle for two," Liam encouraged.

"I'd actually like to see that," admitted Joe with an amused look on his face.

"That's great, Tommy. It's only a twelve-month program. You'll be done before you know it," said Bridgette supportively.

Frank checked his paper again to see who was next on his list.

"Next on my list is Blake," said Frank, moving right along.

"Blake is graduating from Steeplechase with a 3.5 grade point average. Blake has been accepted to Lock Haven University, Widener University, Albright College, Skole County Community College and Bloomsburg University."

Jack listened in awe. He knew his youngest son was smart, but the long list of acceptances surprised him. Blake certainly had his mother Catherine's intelligence.

"So, Blake," Frank said, "What will it be?"

Blake smirked shyly around the table before admitting, "Bloomsburg."

Cole reached over the table and gave his buddy a high five, while Shane gave Blake a hard pat on the back. Jack smiled. He was beyond thrilled that all of his sons would be staying close to home.

Frank continued, "And what will you be majoring in?"

"Education. I want to teach history."

This surprised everyone at the table. Sure, Blake had always had an interest in history, but he had many other interests, too. No one at the table was more pleased than Moira was. A former Language Arts teacher, Moira rose from her chair and approached her grandson. She squeezed him tight from behind as she smothered his face with kisses.

"A boy after my own heart!"

Her mauve lipstick left stains on Blake's cheek.

"Grandma stop!"

"I can't! I'm just so proud!"

Blake couldn't help but laugh as his grandmother smothered him with affection.

"All right, Mom! Let him breathe!" yelled Jack from the other end of the table.

Frank lowered his eyes to his list again. When he spotted the next name on the list, Frank's stomach turned with worry.

"Next up. Shane Angus Kilpatrick. My baby boy."

Shane stood up and smiled broadly. He shook hands and gave high fives to other members of his family as if he had just won an Oscar. Frank stared at him with an amused look.

Frank continued, "Shane is graduating from Steeplechase Academy with a 2.3 grade point average, which, might I add, is the bare minimum that was needed to stay on the football team at Steeplechase." Frank gave his son an agitated glare.

Shane bellowed, "Go Mustangs!" which earned him mild laughter from his family. Frank simply shook his head at his son. The apple hadn't fallen far from the tree.

"Shane was accepted at Skole County Community College, Kremmings Technical School, and *what the hell* ..." Frank stopped abruptly, perplexed by one of the school names on the paper.

"Miss Betty's Beauty School?"

No one laughed louder than Shane. He knew his father would be the one reading the names of the schools off of the list. Shane couldn't resist the opportunity to play a prank on his father.

Shane yelled loudly, "Gotcha!"

Frank gave Shane a glare that was reminiscent of Angus.

"Thank you for nearly giving me heart failure. What school did you choose?" asked Frank.

"I'm going to Skole Community. I'm going to take some photo-journalism classes," said Shane in a more rational tone.

Frank's heart rate slowed as he processed this thought. Shane was actually quite skilled with a camera. Bridgette smiled with delight. She loved when the kids embraced their passion. She loved it even more when it was something that they were good at. Not like her cooking. She was pleased with the announcements so far. Cole had an excellent mind for business and both Monte's and the Morrow farm could use a good business manager. Tommy had a passion for cars and motorcycles, so he had made a wise choice as well. Shane, meanwhile, could be found taking pictures of everyone and everything. It was another great choice. Now Bridgette was eager to hear what her niece had decided.

Frank looked nervously to Tristan, who was patiently waiting with a sly smile on her face.

"I could still kill you for not telling me," said Jack to Frank in a hushed voice.

"Stop panicking. Everything is going to be fine," Frank reassured his nervous friend and brother-in-law.

"Okay, girl," Frank said to Tristan. "You're up."

Tristan stood up smiling as she peered at everyone's faces. She was surprised how nervous everyone looked.

"Tristan is graduating from Steeplechase Academy with a grade point average of 3.9," declared Frank.

The adults at the table gasped in shock. Everyone seemed to voice their opinions at once:

"Wow, Tristan ... That is outstanding!" exclaimed Jenna.

"Holy crow," added Joe.

"You nerd!" cried Shane.

"I taught her *everything* she knows," insisted Blake.

Jack leaned in to Joe and proudly boasted, "That's my girl."

Meanwhile, Bridgette and Moira were brought to tears by Tristan's accomplishment. It was a remarkable feat. Especially after all that she endured. Tristan brushed off her accomplishment as if it was nothing at all.

Frank continued, "Tristan was granted a scholarship from Vice Principal Irwin for sixteen straight marking periods on the honor roll in the amount of $10,000. She has been asked to act as the class valedictorian at the graduation ceremonies next week."

Jack's jaw dropped. Words would not come to his mouth. His pride could not be measured in simple words and expressions.

Frank continued, "Tristan has been accepted to the following schools ... Bear with me, this list is long. Okay, here we go. Tristan has been accepted to Stanford University, Bloomsburg University, University of Pennsylvania, Temple University, Princeton University, Albright College, Skole County Community College, and lastly, the University of California, Berkley."

Frank had to catch his breath after reading the long list out loud. Jack felt as if he was on the verge of a heart attack.

University of California and Stanford?

Bridgette tried to keep her face under control, but internally she was freaking out. Cole's right leg started tapping nervously under the table. Meanwhile Blake, Liam, Adam, Shane and Tommy looked at Tristan in shock.

Frank, who was always the cool one under pressure, said aloud, "Oh, Jesus Christ ... Put them out of their misery. Which school did you choose?"

Tristan laughed at how stressed out everyone seemed to be.

"Well, it was a really tough choice. I love home so much, but I had to choose the school that was right for me," Tristan explained.

The more she spoke, the more Cole felt like he was going to throw up all over the picnic table.

"Like I said, it was a really hard choice for me. I hope you will all understand."

Jack felt dizzy, and he thought he was going to faint. Everyone stared at Tristan as they waited for her to spill the beans.

"Just tell us ..." Blake begged.

Tristan nodded with a smile on her face.

"I hope you will understand that I will be attending Bloomsburg University for the next four years, and I'll be around here bugging you all ..."

Tristan couldn't resist herself. She laughed loudly as everyone celebrated. There were tears in Cole's eyes. Jack stood up, red-faced and excited. He went to her, and hugged her. Jack lifted Tristan's body off the ground and swung her around.

"Dad! Stop!"

"I'm sorry! I'm just so happy!" exclaimed Jack.

Bridgette breathed a sigh of relief. Frank interrupted everyone once again.

"Wow, you really had them going for a second! Okay, so what is your major?"

"Health physics."

Everyone gave Tristan an odd look except for her Aunt Bridgette who smiled from ear to ear. Angus, who had fallen asleep during all the excitement, woke up at the sound of the two words.

"Did you just say health physics?" Angus demanded to know.

Tristan laughed, "Yes. I did."

"You're going into medicine?" Angus yelled loudly.

Tristan wasn't sure if he was happy or angry. Sometimes it was so hard to tell.

"Yes. I plan to follow up my education at Bloomsburg with a med program at Penn," explained Tristan confidently.

Jack gasped and clutched his chest. Jenna put her arm around her friend.

"Don't die on us now ... Are you all right?" Jenna asked, only half joking.

Jack choked up a laugh, but there were tears in his eyes. Bridgette and Moira had tears flooding down their faces.

"She's something else ... Isn't she?" Jack said to Jenna, who smiled in return.

"Your girl did real good," Jenna agreed.

Suddenly, something that hadn't happened in a very long time occurred.

"Oh, my God!" Frank bellowed as he looked at Angus's face.

Everyone's eyes focused on Angus's face as his lips turned up into a brilliant smile. He flashed his movie star smile at everyone at the table, but no one received the courtesy more than Tristan. No one had ever witnessed Angus look so happy before.

"What kind of medicine are you going into?" Angus asked his only granddaughter.

Tristan replied with a confident smile, "Veterinary."

Angus, who was already happy, nearly fell out of his chair with excitement.

"You mean we will have a real vet in the family and I won't have to be the on-call doctor for the barn?"

Tristan shook her head happily. Angus had never been so happy in all his life.

CHAPTER 3

June 16, 2000
Seattle International Airport
Gate 24A – Flight 1304
7 A.M.

ANGIE MACKLON SAT IN SEAT 13B as her leg tapped nervously up and down against the plane floor. She reached into her carry-on bag and pulled out another stick of gum. As she stared out her window at the runway, she chewed her gum quickly as panic gripped her mind. Angie could feel her anxiety increase with each passing moment. After talking on the phone last night, Angie's parents, Roger and Gwen, quickly booked Angie on the 7 a.m. flight from Seattle International Airport to Philadelphia. Angie wasn't keen on the idea of flying. She felt so out of control being nearly forty thousand feet above the ground. She also wasn't too thrilled with the idea of going back to Elkhart. The very place she had spent her life running from. But it appeared at this late hour, she had no other choices. She had little money, no apartment, no husband and no one else to turn to.

Suddenly, the speaker over Angie's head squawked to life as a most annoying voice addressed the passengers of flight 1304. Angie jumped at the noise and cast an evil glare towards the speaker while she listened to the announcement.

"Good morning passengers and welcome to Pacific Northwest Airlines! The time is now 7:07 a.m. and we are expecting bright and sunny skies once we depart the Seattle area. Our flight time is approximately five hours and twelve minutes. It's a beautiful day to be flying Pacific Northwest! We will be taking off momentarily. Thank you for your patience and enjoy your flight!"

As the plane began to move, Angie's knuckles blanched from panic.

Angie is not what you would call an ideal flyer. She didn't even have what most would consider as flying anxiety. Angie's fear was astronomical. For five hours straight a seemingly endless train of irrational thoughts entered Angie's mind and tortured her as she clung to her arm rest.

What if we crash?
Or the wings fall off?
Is the pilot drunk?
I wonder if I ask, if I could see the pilot's credentials?
I should have taken the train.
What if the engines stop?
What if the engines fall off?
And turbulence ... What if we hit turbulence?
What if the turbulence is so bad that we crash?
Oh, my God. I'm going to die on this flying tin can!

By the time the plane had reached maximum altitude, Angie was in the midst of a full-fledged panic attack on the plane. Her face was red, her eyes were watering and her knuckles were white from holding on too tight. The seating arrangement didn't help matters much, either. A young mother and her screaming son had taken the seats next to Angie. The boy had been screaming since they left the airport and Angie thought she was going to start screaming, too.

Somebody shut this kid up!

"Miss ... Are you okay?" asked June, an elderly but bubbly stewardess with a Texan accent.

Angie looked at the stewardess with a forlorn expression on her face.

"I need alcohol."

"Well, here's our menu, honey."

"Rum and Coke. Keep them coming."

The plane came to a jarring halt on the runway at Philadelphia International Airport. Angie felt like she was about to lose her lunch, which consisted of a few packs of finely salted peanuts and a half dozen alcoholic beverages. It took forcible measures to remove her still white-knuckled hands from the arms of her seat. Although the plane had landed, Angie didn't feel much in terms of relief. She knew what lay before her. A three-hour drive to Elkhart with her sisters Misty-Lee and Courtney. She often wondered if all their years of using peroxide to bleach their hair blonde had finally deteriorated their brains. Angie needed to pop an Excedrin to prepare herself for the ordeal.

Angie grabbed her carry-on bag and walked down the center aisle. As she exited the plane, she expected to feel some sense of relief. After all, she wasn't thirty thousand feet in the air anymore. Strangely enough, she was even more stressed out after disembarking the plane. If anything, Angie felt more nervous now that she was closer to home. Closer to the demons of her past.

The airport was packed with travelers and Angie felt disoriented thanks to her cocktails and a minor case of jet lag. She looked up at the sign that hung from the ceiling as she weaved through the maze of an airport in search of her luggage. Angie walked for what felt like miles through the crowded airport. Finally, she found the baggage claim area, and she waited patiently for her luggage to come shooting down the conveyor belt. As Angie bent down to grab her suitcase, she heard them.

"Like! Oh, my God, Misty! Is that her?" shouted Courtney in her rage-inducing *Valley Girl* accent.

"No. That can't be her. She looks so old!" insisted Misty-Lee.

"Umm ... No ... I think it is her! She's what, like forty now?"

"Thirty-seven, I think."

Angie rolled her eyes as she listened to her dim-witted sisters argue over her identity. If Angie thought their voices were embarrassing, it was nothing compared to the way they were dressed. Misty-Lee's peroxide-dyed blonde hair was crimped and fried by years of damage and mistreatment. Her fluorescent orange mesh shirt hung off of her right shoulder exposing her tan lines. She completed her ensemble with a pair of too-tight, too-short jean shorts and a pair of pink and orange sneakers. Meanwhile, Courtney was wearing a pair of skin-tight flare jeans with a black tank top and noisy sandals. Her stick straight blonde hair was cut at an angle, but instead of looking stylish, she just looked slightly lopsided. Angie decided to put them out of their misery and wave.

"Over here, girls," Angie called, waving her hand at her sisters.

Angie watched as Misty-Lee stage whispered to Courtney, "Oh, my God, Court! It is her!"

Suddenly the pair let out screams of excitement as they sashayed across the linoleum floor. It was like watching a tornado comprised of bright colors, bad hair and fake nails racing towards you. Angie stared at them with wide eyes, mortified to be seen in public with them. Angie tried to look happy to see them, but the end result was that she looked horrified.

"Oh, my God, Angie! Look at you!" cried Misty-Lee.

"You look ..." Courtney started.

"Old?" Angie suggested, recalling their previously made comments.

"No! You look so mature!"

Angie rolled her eyes but couldn't help but laugh at her excitable younger sisters. It was hard to believe that they were from the same gene pool. Clearly, the water in the gene pool became tainted after Angie was born.

Angie hugged both of her sisters, but sneezed from the overabundance of fruity body spray they were wearing.

"Oh! Are you sick?" asked Misty-Lee with a disgusted look on her face. She jumped back to save herself from Angie's germs. Angie held her tongue.

"No, I think I might be allergic to your perfume."

Misty-Lee disregarded Angie's complaint and just nodded in return.

Your perfume is killing me. Thank you for concern. Three hours from now, I could be dead from an allergic reaction.

"Oh well ... C'mon! Our car is outside!" exclaimed Courtney, ready to hit the road.

Angie followed her sisters out to their car and had to laugh when she saw it. Misty-Lee and Courtney drove a purple Camry with a license plate that read "Vixens" in bright pink letters.

My mother needed better prenatal care.

Against her better wishes, Angie got into the backseat of their car as she prepared herself for three hours of vapid, shallow, and intelligence-depleting conversation, courtesy of Courtney and Misty-Lee.

Courtney drove seventy miles per hour down I-95 as Misty-Lee puffed a cigarette in the passenger seat. The smoke caused Angie to gag in the backseat.

"So, Ang! We have so much to catch up on!" said Misty-Lee in between puffs.

"Oh, I know ..." said Angie, playing along. As far as she was concerned, she'd rather not catch up. No good could come of it. She had to make the best of a bad situation, though.

"So, what's been going on back at home?" Angie asked, just trying to make conversation.

"Eh, same old. Dad's mad at Mom because she has a QVC shopping addiction. Cory threw Dad's keys down the toilet this morning and he was late for work. Old man is so uptight these days!" Misty-Lee complained.

"I would be pretty uptight if my wife spent all my money and my grandson flushed my keys down the toilet, too," admitted Angie.

Misty-Lee rolled her eyes.

"Ugh! You're just like him!"

"How's Allison and Beatrix?" Angie asked ignoring Misty-Lee's statement.

"Oh, you mean Trixie and Ally?" asked Courtney.

Angie curled her lip up at the nicknames.

Have they all turned into bimbos?

"Trixie's great. She's the captain of the cheer squad and she's about to graduate from high school. Mom is throwing a huge party tomorrow night. Ally is in the middle of some pre-teen angst phase. Biggest attitude *ever!*" said Courtney with ample attitude herself.

"Attitude, huh?"

"Oh, my God. The worst! She's a complete know-it-all, too! Yesterday she kept trying to tell me that the capital of Pennsylvania is Harrisburg, when we all know it is Pittsburgh!"

Angie stared at the back of Misty-Lee's head in shock.

Is she really that stupid?

"Ah ..." said Angie not even bothering to question it.

There is no use arguing with an idiot.

"How's Mom doing?" asked Angie.

"Full of hell! She stole my cigarettes the other day and said she was so disappointed in me for smoking. She had a Pall Mall hanging off her lip as she said it! Hypocrite."

"She was a total bitch this morning! Woke us up at 6 a.m. and screamed at us to get up before we were late."

I can so feel the love in this car. Now I remember why I stayed away for so long.

"What about Bernard? Is he still hanging around?" asked Angie inquisitively.

Courtney and Misty-Lee glanced at each other with troubled looks on their faces. It was as if their shallow façade dropped completely, and all that was left were two scared little girls.

"Um ... You didn't hear?" asked Misty-Lee warily.

"Hear what?" asked Angie as a chill ran up her spine.

"Dude ... He's dead," said Courtney bluntly.

Angie's eyes went wide.

"Dead? How?" Angie asked in astonishment as if the thought alone was purely preposterous.

"I can't believe no one told you," said Misty-Lee in amazement.

"Tell me what? What happened?"

"He was shot. Mr. Morrow shot him in the head."

Angie took the thought and mulled it over in her head. She was missing something.

"What's the whole story?" asked Angie, desperate for the truth.

"Apparently Bernard kidnapped Mr. Morrow's daughter. Tristan, her name is. Courtney goes out with her brother. The girl escaped back to her house, but Kendricks followed her there. Mr. Morrow caught him in his house and shot him dead. Turns out Bernard was also responsible for four other deaths, including Mrs. Morrow."

Angie appeared to be stunned. She never thought that anyone would have the power to stop Bernard Kendricks. Angie knew the depths of his depravity. She knew it all too well. No wonder no one had told her after all that she had been through with Tiffany. *Poor Tiffany.* The thought that she had been in close proximity of Kendricks only heightened the fear that she had carried all these years. It could have been her. The thought shook Angie to the core of her soul.

"I'm shocked," Angie admitted.

"Are you? We always knew that he was a nut job."

"I, for one, am not surprised at all," said Misty-Lee bluntly.

"You know what I think ..." said Courtney.

Misty-Lee gave her a sharp look.

"Can we not discuss Tiffany right now?" asked Misty-Lee casting a wary glance at Angie.

"I'm just saying ... I swear that he was the one responsible for Tiffany's death. I'd bet my life on it."

"Don't say stuff like that. You were too young to remember any of this," scolded Misty-Lee.

The topic of conversation caused Angie's nerves to go on edge. She remembered vividly how her sister had died. It still kept her awake at night. She wouldn't put it past someone like Kendricks to do something that vicious, especially if he was responsible for four other deaths. As the car barreled down the highway, Angie felt the demons of her past breathing down her neck.

Gwen O'Mara sat at her Gateway computer browsing the sales on QVC's website when she heard a car pull into the gravel driveway.

"Roger! She's here!" yelled Gwen out to the kitchen where Roger was reading the *Wall Street Journal*.

Gwen jumped up from her cushy computer chair which spun around on a plastic mat that protected the rug. She barged out the storm door to greet her daughter who she hadn't seen in years. Her clog sandals scraped perilously across the gravel driveway. Then she saw her. Angela looked so much older than Gwen remembered, but she also looked much better than she expected. Break ups, job terminations and eviction do terrible things to people; especially when they all happen on the same day.

Angie dropped her suitcase in the driveway as she braced herself for her mother's hug. Gwen ran to her and swept Angie into a hug. She was thrilled beyond belief to finally have her back home. Angie thought that Gwen was about to squeeze the life out of her when Roger appeared at the door. Roger, who was Angie's father, smiled down at her and winked.

"All right, Gwen. Give the girl some room to breathe," said Roger with a laugh.

Angie gave her father an appreciative glance as she broke free of her mother's embrace. Angie ran towards her father and gave him a big hug. Angie didn't have a very close relationship with her mother, but Roger and Angie very much saw eye to eye. It didn't matter how much time had passed. They would always have each other's backs. As Angie walked into the O'Mara house for the first time in two decades, she felt the slow burn of anxiety begin to rise in her chest.

The O'Mara family gathered in the cramped kitchen of 27 Caribou Road for dinner. Gwen prepared spaghetti and meatballs and called everyone down to the dinner table. Courtney and Misty-Lee protested that they had other things to do, but were quieted when they met Roger's stern glare. Ally, Angie's youngest sister, stormed into the kitchen with a miserable scowl on her face.

"He won't get out of my room!" yelled Ally as a chubby toddler chased behind her with a messy face.

"Cory! No!" yelled Roger as his face turned a shade of vibrant red.

Cory, who is Misty-Lee's son, had a major case of the terrible twos. Roger was beginning to wonder if it was really the child's personality as opposed to just a phase. Cory chased behind Ally with a black magic marker, threatening to draw all over her brand new jeans.

"Misty! Can you control your son?" yelled Roger across the dinner table.

With a huff, Misty got up from the table and picked up the precocious toddler. She took the magic marker from his hand as he screamed in protest. Without a word, Misty-Lee put him in his highchair as he kicked and slammed on the tray in anger.

"Cute kid," Angie said to Roger facetiously. Roger shook his head in annoyance.

Suddenly, the front door swung open again and a teenage girl wearing at least five pounds of makeup and a too-short black dress walked into the living room cursing loudly into her cell phone.

Roger yelled, "Who let Trixie out of the house looking like that?"

Roger was infuriated, and rightly so, that his daughter Trixie continued to ignore his rules about wearing age-appropriate clothing.

"What, Rog? It's the style," insisted Gwen.

"What style? She looks like a prostitute!"

Gwen turned around quickly and gave her husband a stern glare.

"Shush! You'll hurt her feelings!"

"Good! No daughter of mine—" Roger started but was cut off by another of Cory's temper tantrums.

I need a vacation away from my family, thought Roger.

"So, Angela," said Gwen as she dished spaghetti out of a steaming pot onto a plate that sat in front of her. "Tell us what your plans are."

Angie looked at her mother and sighed. She had no idea what her next move would be. While she would love nothing more than to loaf around and wallow in her misery for a while, she decided that it went against everything she stood for.

"I suppose I will be looking for work. I'll start in the morning. I'll check over in Danville and Sunbury. I'll need a ride though."

Roger nodded in approval.

"Smart girl. Keep busy and get right back up on the horse."

"Take the station wagon. Nobody's using it tomorrow," suggested Gwen.

"All right. I will."

"And tomorrow night, we're having Trixie's graduation party here at the house." Angie shook her head in understanding.

"And everyone and their grandmother is coming," mentioned Roger.

"Dad!" Trixie complained, "I only graduate high school once. Go big or go home. Right?"

"I am home," said Roger gruffly as he cast a perturbed look towards Trixie.

"Oh, Rog ... Lighten up," begged Gwen as she plopped a spoonful of spaghetti on his plate.

After dinner, Roger and Gwen showed Angie up to her old bedroom. They climbed to the third floor that led to two empty bedrooms. Angie recognized them immediately. The first bedroom had a sign on the door that read, "Tiffany's Room— Keep Out!" Angie eyed the door precariously as they continued to make their way down the hallway towards the other bedroom. Roger pushed open the door to the front bedroom. Angie's name tag was still hanging from the door. As the old door creaked open, Angie was horrified to see that it still looked the same and relatively untouched. The only things that were missing from the room were the items Angie took with her when she left twenty years ago.

"We didn't have the heart to touch it," Roger explained.

"It was a very difficult time for us. We just left the third floor alone. No one comes up here," lamented Gwen as a memory came to the forefront of her mind.

The third floor was a tomb. The memories of their two lost daughters: one who lay six feet under, and the other who fled cross-country. Angie's stomach curled into tight knots just thinking about it. Another thought occurred to her. Not all haunted houses are the same. While Morrow Manor fits the bill, the modern O'Mara house had more secrets than the whole of Elkhart combined.

Angie laid her suitcase on the bright purple bed spread that had faded dramatically since she last saw it. She plopped down on the bed as the bedsprings groaned under the weight of her body. Roger closed the door. Of course they would want to talk to her. Gwen would want to lecture her for being gone for so long. Gwen sat on the bed next to Angie and grabbed her left hand. Angie could feel her dinner rising in her throat.

"So, I know that Courtney and Misty-Lee told you about your cousin," said Gwen calmly, trying to broach the subject as painlessly as possible.

"They did," replied Angie wearily. She did *not* want to discuss it. She was still trying to process the news, but knowing Gwen, she would push the issue.

"I want to make sure that you are okay. I know that you were close with him when you were younger."

Angie laughed darkly. "I was petrified of him."

"Yes, but you also seemed to be intrigued by him, too."

"Mother, I have no idea what you're talking about," Angie said with a bite. She had tried to block it all out.

"Gwen ..." warned Roger from the doorway with a piercing glare.

"Just hold on, Roger ..." snapped Gwen. She continued, "The reason I bring him up is because when I was going through his estate, I found something that was addressed to you."

Angie looked alarmed and surprised.

"To me?" she asked doubtfully.

"Yes. It is a cardboard box that is addressed directly to your address to Seattle. It was never shipped though. I wasn't sure what was inside of it, so I didn't want to send it myself. It is over there on the desk."

Angie glanced over at her old desk. Sitting on top was a medium-sized shipping box. Somehow, Angie thought she knew what was going to be inside of it. The thought alone sent her mind reeling.

"Thank you. I'll open it later."

Roger looked at his daughter with a speculative glance, as if he had something he wanted to say, but the moment passed and Roger held in whatever it was that he needed to say.

"We'll let you get unpacked," said Roger as he motioned for Gwen to follow him.

As Angie sat alone in her bedroom, the lure of the box became too much for her to bear. Slowly, she approached the box, like a predator sneaking up on its prey. Gently, she lifted the box as she stared at Bernard Kendricks's neat scrawl on the shipping label. How did he know where she lived? The shipping label indicated that he had intended to ship the package to Angie on October 7, 1997.

Didn't Courtney say that was around the time he died?

Angie sat on the bed with the package on her lap for quite some time. She tried to build up the courage to open it. Angie took in deep breaths, exhaling laboriously. Finally, she plucked up the nerve to tear at the tape that secured the box shut. She dug her nail under the clear packing tape and ripped the adhesive straight off the surface of the box. Angie moved her hands quickly in fear that she would lose what little courage she had. She opened the box flaps only to find that there was yet another box inside. This time she was looking at a handsome black gift box. She lifted the box out of the shipping package and noted how heavy it was. A feeling of dread weighed on Angie as she allowed the shipping box to fall to the floor. She held the black box in her left palm and gently lifted its lid with her right hand. Inside, there was a sheet of dark red tissue paper that concealed what lay within.

With just two fingers, Angie lifted the delicate tissue paper and found what she knew she would. The box that she found buried at the base of the Bone Tree all those years ago. Angie gulped as she took the heavy, ornate box out of its holder. Her finger rested on its release, determining whether or not she should even open it. Finally, she plucked up the courage, and its contents caused her to drop the box to the floor with a bang.

Inside the box lay a photograph of Angie and Tiffany with a note that read, "You're next."

CHAPTER 4

July 25, 1974
27 Caribou Road
Elkhart, PA
9:42 P.M.

"NO, GWEN, ABSOLUTELY NOT!" yelled Roger O'Mara, red-faced and furious at his wife, from across the living room. Gwen set the black rotary phone down gently on its cradle as she gave her husband a looking of warning.

"Roger, he has nowhere else to go."

"I don't care. I don't trust him."

"But I'm not sure why."

"You're not? Just look at him ... He always looks like he's up to something."

Gwen sighed in disgust.

"Roger, you're being stubborn. Aunt Dorothy said Bernard and Ernie have been at each other's throats. She's desperate."

Roger looked at his young wife as a serious look crossed his face. He felt bad for Dorothy Kendricks. She was Gwen's aunt and a lovely person. It's just too bad that her son was so damn creepy.

"I have my reasons for not trusting him, and we have a house full of little girls."

"He's their cousin."

"Look, Gwen, I have my reasons. I will allow him to stay in the basement just this once, but he has to be gone by the morning."

"Thanks, Rog. I'll call and let Aunt Dorothy know."

"It sounds like someone just came in the front door," remarked Misty-Lee who was supposed to be in bed asleep. Instead, she was sitting on Tiffany's bed pulling her sister's strawberry blonde hair into a French braid.

"It's late. Who would be showing up at this hour?" asked Tiffany, who sat perfectly still atop her mattress as her sister braided her hair.

"Can you two go to sleep!" yelled Angie from the next bed over. "Shut the light off!"

"You're never going to get a boyfriend with an attitude like that," remarked Tiffany snootily.

Suddenly the sound of raised voices came from the living room. Misty-Lee noticed that it sounded as if her father was scolding someone.

"Let's go see who it is," said Tiffany as Misty-Lee fastened her French braid with a barrette.

Misty-Lee followed her sister out into the hallway as their nightgowns swayed at their feet. The sisters stood at the stair banister while they listened to the conversation below.

Roger spoke in a stern voice, "You are to be gone by dawn. Do *not* wander through the house, either. You are here to sleep. Am I clear?"

Bernard Kendricks replied in a cool voice, "Like crystal."

"Good. Now follow Gwen down to the basement. There is a bed down there."

Misty-Lee's eyes went wide as she looked at her sister.

"Was that Bernard?" Misty-Lee quipped with fear visible in her eyes.

"Why is *he* here?" exclaimed Tiffany. "Have they lost their minds?"

The sound of an adult climbing the steps startled the girls, who stood perfectly still in the dark of the hallway.

"Girls ..." Roger called from the top of the steps. "You are supposed to be in bed."

"Daddy, who was that?" Tiffany asked curiously. Roger sighed loudly.

"That was Bernard. He is staying in the basement for tonight only."

"Why?"

"He has nowhere else to go."

Tiffany and Misty-Lee stared at their father with confused faces.

"Come on. Let's go to bed."

Roger ushered his daughters off to bed and closed the door quietly behind him. He kissed each of his daughters on the forehead, including Angie. He hovered for a moment by her bedside.

"Here is the key to your room. Keep the door locked tonight."

Angie looked at her father with a horrified look on her face as she took the key and tucked it under her pillow. She didn't sleep a wink that night.

CHAPTER 5

June 16, 2000
Monte's Café
Elkhart, PA
Late Afternoon

"ORDER'S UP!" YELLED JOE PIEDMONTE from the kitchen of Monte's Café as he slammed his hand hard on the bell that sat on the counter. Tristan, who had just finished wiping off an empty table, came rushing up to the front counter to grab the freshly prepared tray of food. She checked the order slip and carried the tray over to Jesse Trafford's table where he sat alone. For a young man, Tristan noted that Jesse had very dark circles and a forlorn look about him. His greasy blonde hair fell to his shoulders, his teeth were stained an unhealthy shade of yellow, and his beady eyes gave Jesse the image that he had seen far more terrible things than any of us would ever lay witness to. Life hadn't been easy on Jesse. He had lost his mother to lung cancer when he was only seven, and he hadn't had the best upbringing due to his father being in and out of the penitentiary for various offenses. Tristan didn't feel too bad for him though, because he hadn't made the best choices in his twenty-one years of life. It is easy to see why Jesse strayed. The Traffords weren't known to be model, law-abiding citizens. His father, Harry, had served seven years for attempted robbery. Coming from that family, it was a miracle that Jesse Trafford wasn't either dead or locked up. Jesse came in to Monte's Café every evening at five for dinner and he always sat alone.

Tristan thought, *What a lonely existence that must be.*

Although the Traffords were a large family, and his father and five brothers were all alive, they were not the kind of family you want to come home to every evening.

As was routine, Tristan brought Jesse his dinner. She placed his order of meatloaf and mashed potatoes on the table in front of him, followed by a tall glass of iced tea. Tristan rested her hand on the table as she made sure Jesse had everything that he needed.

"Can I get you anything else?" asked Tristan courteously.

"No, but thank you, Miss Morrow," said Jesse with a slight twang to his voice.

"You can call me Tristan, Jesse," said Tristan in a friendly tone.

"Thank you, Miss—" Jesse began but he stopped himself. "Thank you, Tristan."

Tristan smiled. Jesse Trafford did have manners when he wanted to use them.

"Okay, Jesse. You take care of yourself," Tristan said nicely.

As Tristan turned to walk away, Jesse grabbed her hand tightly with his rough, calloused fingers and squeezed tight.

Tristan's stomach jolted. He was making her uncomfortable.

"Jesse, let go of my hand," said Tristan firmly.

"I'm sorry, Ms. Tristan. I mean no disrespect, but I was wonderin' if I could ask you a question," said Jesse in a quick, nervous voice.

Tristan stared at him sharply. Her initial reaction was to tell him no and get the hell off of her, but she was determined to keep her cool.

She replied, this time in a more firm tone, "Yes, but please let go of my hand."

Jesse reluctantly removed his fingers from Tristan's hand as he stared at her through deep set eyes.

"That boyfriend of yours ..."

He said boyfriend as if it was the name of a particularly disgusting bug or reptile. Tristan pursed her lips. She knew what was coming. Jesse Trafford had never liked Cole for reasons unbeknownst to her, and Cole despised the ground Trafford walked on for the way he treated the waitresses in the restaurant. The only one Jesse seemed to be polite to was Tristan.

"My boyfriend has a name," Tristan said curtly.

"Yeah, Cole ..." said Jesse, as his voice became coarse and rough with attitude.

Tristan stared at him with a wary look on her face.

"Tell him I'm taking you out tomorrow night," Jesse said coolly as he grabbed Tristan's hand again.

Here we go again.

"Jesse," Tristan said softly as she removed her hand from Jesse's grasp. "Cole is a good guy whether you admit it or not. And I have no intentions upon seeing anyone else."

Suddenly, the bell that hung over the front door of Monte's Café rang loudly, and Cole jogged in from the scorching June heat. He stood at the front register as he sorted through the mail that had arrived earlier that day. After a moment he looked up, and his thoughts turned to rage as he took in the sight of Jesse Trafford with his hand squeezed tightly around Tristan's wrist. Tristan appeared to be backing away from Jesse as he stared at her. Apparently their conversation had taken a turn for the worst. Jesse appeared to be asking a question, and Tristan was reluctant to answer. Cole had warned Jesse to leave all the waitresses alone—especially Tristan. Cole sighed in disgust as he observed them, trying not to jump to conclusions. He had no problem whatsoever laying Jesse Trafford out, flat on his back, but he knew Tristan could not stand it when men tried to do her fighting for her. Reluctantly, Cole kept his distance. For now.

"Let's just pretend this never happened, Jesse," said Tristan sternly, now more angry than irritated.

"Tristan," Jesse said as he squeezed her wrist tighter.

"It's Miss Morrow to you!" spat Tristan venomously as she ripped her wrist from his grip.

She turned on her heel and made a beeline for the kitchen. Cole watched as Jesse reached for Tristan's shoulder in an attempt to turn her around, and Cole saw red. As Tristan raced towards the kitchen she whipped right past Cole and stormed out the back door.

Before Cole could take charge, Joe had barreled out of the kitchen. He slammed his hands down on Jesse's table causing Jesse to jump back towards the window.

"What did I tell you about bothering the girls in here? Time to go!"

Joe lifted Jesse by his shirt collar and pushed him out the front door, causing him to land face first in the dirt.

"You'll be sorry, Monte! Mark my words!" yelled Trafford as he scrambled off down Mountain Road.

Cole pushed open the back door of Monte's with a loud squeak. He found Tristan sitting red-faced and seething on the bench that sat against the back wall of the property. She kicked at the gravel with her white sneaker as she stared down at the ground, deep in thought. Cole was trying to keep his cool. One of the things that Tristan loved most about Cole was his ability to keep a level head when things got heated. He wasn't a hot head like Tommy, Adam, or her father, Jack. He worked well under pressure and he rarely lost his cool.

"What did he say?" asked Cole calmly.

Tristan simply shook her head. She wasn't in the mood to talk about it. Though he didn't like to, Cole pressed the matter. He had to know if he needed to kick Trafford into next month. Lord knows he could have the Morrow boys assembled on Mountain Road in less than an hour, if need be.

"Tristan ..." Cole urged, trying to get a conversation out of her.

"I don't want to talk about it," Tristan said abruptly.

"Tristan, you can tell me," said Cole. His patience was hanging on by a fragile thread. Tristan looked up at Cole with watery eyes.

What did that bastard say?

Tristan wasn't exactly known for turning on the water works. Trafford must have really said something vicious.

"Let's just drop it," pleaded Tristan firmly.

Cole wasn't having it.

"Tristan," he said more firmly than before. "You need to tell me!"

"Please!" she barked at Cole.

Tristan hated having to be so firm with Cole. The fact of the matter was that she couldn't bring herself to repeat the words that came out of Jesse Trafford's mouth just five minutes ago. All sympathy that Tristan once harbored for Jesse was gone and was now replaced with the sentiment that he was nothing more than a trouble-making chauvinistic pig.

"I'm not leaving until you tell me what he said."

"Oh, fine!" said Tristan getting annoyed.

She didn't want Cole or her brothers getting into fights over something petty. Tristan did not understand that something that she conveyed as petty, was actually taken quite seriously by Cole and her brothers. Tristan whispered into Cole's ear and told him exactly what Trafford said. His impatient look turned into an expression of supreme fury. Though he had much that he wanted to say, Cole bit his tongue.

"Look, I have to finish my shift. It's just Trafford being a pig. No need to get yourself arrested, or my brothers, for that matter," said Tristan as she rose from the bench.

"When you're done with your shift, come for a walk with me," Cole suggested. He didn't like seeing her upset, but there was no use fighting with her. Tristan could handle herself, he knew, but he also felt like it was his job to protect her from idiots like Jesse Trafford.

Tristan smiled as she agreed, "Okay, like a half hour ... And thanks."

Cole pulled Tristan into a hug while the gears in his head spun. As he watched his girlfriend go back inside, Cole pulled a black cell phone from his jean pocket.

"Yo, Tommy," Cole said into the phone with a dangerous tone to his voice.

"What's up?" blurted Tommy from the other end of the line.

"Meet me behind Monte's in ten minutes," Cole demanded.

"On my way."

Joe was in the kitchen when Tristan returned. Nonchalantly, he glanced at Tristan as if nothing had happened. He focused his attention on slicing a tomato on a cutting board, trying not to make her feel uncomfortable.

"You good?" he asked.

"Yeah, I'm good," said Tristan reassuringly.

"We have a few more tables to collect orders for, and then you can go for the day."

"You got it."

A group of women in their late thirties had converged in the dining room and were now seated in the same booth where Jesse Trafford had sat earlier. Their presence immediately lightened Tristan's mood. The ladies were part of a group called the Corrigan Street Literary Collective, which was a book club comprised of five friends who all happened to grow up on Corrigan Street. The members of the group included Audrey Henning, April Dearing, Jackie Prince, Claudia Black and Shauna Peck. Only four of the ladies had arrived, so Tristan decided to give them a few minutes before she would take their order. The ladies showed up every Thursday night to gossip, catch up and discuss their book of the week.

From behind Tristan, the front door of Monte's swung open again as the final member of the book club arrived. A petite, dark-haired woman with a pixie cut walked in and loudly greeted her companions as she traipsed across the restaurant without a care in the world.

"Oh! Look who decided to join us!" said April Dearing, a fair-skinned woman with a crew cut.

As Audrey Henning took her seat at the table, she smiled at everyone and continued to chatter loudly, clearly ignoring April's comment.

"You will *never* guess who I just saw!" declared Audrey in an excited voice.

Collectively, the women replied, "Who?"

Audrey paused for dramatic effect, and then blurted out, "Angie O'Mara!"

"Get the hell outta here!" yelled Shauna, a blonde woman who wore entirely too much hairspray.

"You serious?" said Jackie with a shocked look upon her face.

"Dead serious!" replied Audrey.

"Who?" asked Claudia, their absent-minded friend.

"You don't remember? Oh, my God, Claud ..." blurted out April.

"Tiffany's sister," said Audrey.

"The weird girl that followed Tiff everywhere?" exclaimed Claudia.

"Yeah!" the group said in monotone.

"I thought she left."

"She did! Years ago. Right after Tiffany was found murdered. It was too much for her, I guess," Shauna lamented.

"Oh, my God. That was horrible! How did Angie look?" asked April with muted concern.

"Not as good as us, that's for sure!" said Jackie. "Right, Aud?"

Audrey did not disagree.

"She was looking pretty run down."

Tristan tried not to laugh as she listened to the conversation. Finally, she approached the table, since it was almost time for her to clock out. Tristan was greeted warmly by the ladies.

"Our favorite waitress!" proclaimed Audrey loudly. Tristan smiled warmly in response.

"How's your aunt doing?" asked Jackie. "Tell her I said hi!"

"I will. She's doing good."

"Oh good, you're here. I'm starving," said April rudely.

Tristan took their order and passed it off to Joe before clocking out. She was happy to put the chaotic work day behind her.

"He said what?" Tommy barked at Cole as he got off his motorcycle.

"Trafford said he wanted to get to know Tristan on an up-close and personal basis, and not me or you would be able to stop him."

"Like hell he will."

"He tried to tell her that I was controlling her and that he could show her what it meant to have a good time."

"And you didn't deck him right there on the spot?"

"Joe got in the way."

"Probably a good thing. You don't want to do jail time."

"Yeah ... Handle that for me."

"Not a problem, dude. He's got it coming."

As Tristan stepped out the back door of Monte's, she heard the faint roar of a motorcycle skidding off into the distance.

"Was Tommy here?" Tristan asked in a surprised voice.

"Yeah. He stopped by for a minute," said Cole casually.

Tristan shrugged. This was nothing unusual. Cole and Tommy had become very close over the years, especially since Kendricks kidnapped Tristan just three years ago.

"So where are we going?" Tristan asked.

Cole shrugged his shoulders casually as he smiled.

"Wherever our feet take us."

Tommy Morrow had a dangerous look in his eyes as his motorcycle came to a screeching halt outside of Trafford's Auto Body. He was in a foul mood after talking to Cole and he wasn't about to back down from the likes of Jesse Trafford. Tommy's jaw clenched as he dismounted his bike. Attitude poured from Tommy like venom, infecting everything it touched. He marched across the gravel parking lot with vengeance in his step.

Jesse Trafford had better say his prayers.

Tommy pushed the front door to Trafford's Auto Body open with a bang. His loud footsteps echoed through the shop breaking up the silence like a howl in the night.

"Trafford!" Tommy yelled loudly.

Harry Trafford appeared behind the register with a nasty look on his face. He wiped grease across his yellowing shirt that barely covered his bulging beer belly. As he spoke, Tommy caught a whiff of his putrid breath.

"Morrow ... What the hell do you want?" griped Harry, clearly not in the mood for any lip.

"Where's your boy?" asked Tommy brazenly. He tried not to gag at the smell of Harry's horrible breath—a by-product of poor hygiene and neglect.

Before Trafford could respond, Tommy heard what sounded like someone running fast across the gravel parking lot. Tommy whipped around and cursed loudly.

"Son of a bitch!"

Tommy stormed out the door and ran for his bike. The engine of his Harley revved to life as Tommy chased after Jesse down Elk Road. Jesse was fast, but he was no match for Tommy's juiced up engine. No matter how fast Jesse ran, he was a sitting duck. Tommy's engine roared up Elk Road and when he had Jesse right where he wanted him, he made a sharp turn. The wheels of the motorcycle screeched in protest. A cloud of dirt kicked up around Jesse and he couldn't see a thing. When the dust cleared, Jesse knew he was done for. Tommy had Jesse pinned between his bike and the back wall of Quiver's Ammunition and Hunting Shop. There was nowhere to run.

"Why you runnin', Trafford?" Tommy yelled with anger in his voice.

Jesse didn't say anything as he stared at Tommy with a clenched jaw.

"I just want to talk to you. Why you runnin'?" Tommy asked again, only this time a tad bit calmer.

"There ain't nothin' to talk about!" insisted Jesse.

"Oh, but you see, there is," said Tommy coolly as he climbed down off his bike.

Jesse stayed silent as he tracked Tommy's movements with his deep-set eyes.

"First, you bother my girl at her house. Then, I find out that you're bothering my little sister," said Tommy, just barely holding on to his self-control. "And I'm supposed to be calm?"

Jesse laughed.

"Trust me, dude. I don't want nothin' to do with your girl," Jesse said seriously, but a sly smile soon grew across his face revealing his decaying teeth. "But I wouldn't mind gettin' to know your sister better!"

It took less than a second for Tommy to get in Jesse's face. He pushed him against the brick wall of Quiver's with brute force. Holding his arm across his neck, Tommy snarled at Jesse.

Through gritted teeth, Tommy seethed, "You touch either one of them and you're a dead man."

CHAPTER 6

June 17, 2000
27 Caribou Road
Elkhart, PA
Before Dawn

ANGIE WOKE UP with a dull, familiar ache searing in her chest. She felt like the walls were closing in around her. There is nothing quite as sobering as returning to the place where your nightmares played out before your very eyes. Then, with the unwanted inheritance from Bernard, it was no wonder Angie couldn't sleep. The pressure weighed on her like an iron anvil.

"Shit," Angie muttered as she threw her blankets off of her.

The clock radio only said 5:45 a.m., but Angie's mind wouldn't let her fall back asleep. She swung her legs out of bed and onto the floor. She jammed her foot into something hard and she yelped in pain.

"Yow!"

Angie looked down at the floor to see the source of her pain as her thoughts turned violent.

"Goddamn box! Curse you to the depths of hell, Bernard!"

Angie scooped up the box and tossed it in the trash bin that sat next to her desk as the photograph that rested inside fluttered to the floor.

Roger O'Mara was already sitting at the kitchen table when Angie went downstairs.

He was pouring over the *Elkhart Bugle* with a warm cup of coffee in his hand.

Without looking up, Roger said, "Early bird Angie."

Angie replied with a slight smile, "You know me."

Angie was always the lightest of sleepers in the O'Mara household and always the first one awake with Roger when she was a child. She was the first to wake up on Christmas morning, the first to beg for breakfast, and always the first out the door to see what adventures waited for her beyond the confines of 27 Caribou Road.

"There are donuts on the counter," Roger offered, pointing to the white box that was overflowing with chocolate and powdered sweets.

"I'll pass. I'm just going to grab breakfast while I'm out."

"Getting an early start?" Roger asked.

"Yeah. I have a lot of ground to cover."

"Hold on," said Roger, holding up a finger, "let me get you the keys."

Roger got up from the table and pushed out his chair loudly against the cracking linoleum floor. He was already dressed for work in a smart gray suit with a navy blue striped tie, and white dress shirt. Angie followed Roger into the living room as the grandfather clock in the dining room boomed six times. Roger opened the vestibule door and retrieved a set of keys from a hook on the wall. He dropped the keys into Angie's open hand.

"Don't forget to fill it up when you're done and please don't be late for the party. Your mother will have your head," Roger said only half-joking.

Before Angie could reply, a loud screech from outside interrupted her train of thought. Roger O'Mara's calm demeanor was now replaced with an irate and agitated mood. He raced to the front door and onto the porch. Angie followed him, close on his heels. As Tommy Morrow's motorcycle roared up Caribou Road, Mr. O'Mara's thoughts turned belligerent.

"Goddamn menace! Morrow!" Roger yelled up the road. Angie looked at her father wide-eyed.

"Who was that?" Angie demanded to know.

"Tommy Morrow. Your sister's idiot boyfriend!"

As Tommy's motorcycle turned off Caribou Road, he yelled back, "Love you too, Mr. O!"

Angie spent the day driving around Dansville, Sunbury, and Shepard's Grove looking for work. By the time three p.m. rolled around, she had a manila folder filled with job applications, and pangs of hunger began ravaging her stomach. She hadn't eaten anything since her greasy egg sandwich this morning and she needed to fill her stomach. Trixie's graduation party didn't start until seven p.m. and she wasn't sure that she could wait that long to eat. Angie walked into a packed house at Monte's

Café and there wasn't an empty table in sight. She waited by the front counter for someone to assist her.

Joe Piedmonte greeted Angie warmly, "Hey! Look who's back in town!"

Angie smiled broadly at Joe. He was always so friendly. The memories of living next door to the Piedmontes for all those years brought back pleasant memories for Angie.

"Jenna ... You remember Angie, right?" Joe asked.

Jenna DiNolfo turned around on her barstool to face Angie and Joe. She was dressed in jeans and a t-shirt and was clearly enjoying her afternoon off as she picked at her cheese steak and fries that Joe had just served up.

"Oh, of course I do!" Jenna exclaimed happily. "We went to high school together. It's been a long time, Ang," said Jenna politely.

Jenna wiped her hand on a napkin before reaching to shake her hand. Angie was surprised to see Jenna. She never thought that Jenna would stick around these parts for long. Angie always thought Jenna was the type of girl that was on to bigger and better things, beyond the borders of tiny little Elkhart. Regardless of her story, she looked great and she seemed to be really happy. Unlike Angie.

"Hi Jenna! Good to see you!" gushed Angie, happy to see a familiar face.

"What are you up to these days?" asked Jenna curiously.

"I actually just came back. I'm looking for work. How about you?" asked Angie.

No need to tell them your life story, Angie.

"I came back a few years ago. I was in Pittsburgh for years."

"Oh, what do you do?" asked Angie curiously.

Jenna raised an eyebrow as Joe took over the conversation. He loved telling people he was dating the town police sergeant.

"She's the sergeant," said Joe proudly.

Angie was taken aback and she smiled in surprise. That was the last thing Angie expected to hear Joe say. She assumed Joe would say sales clerk or secretary. But sergeant? No way.

"Damn, Jen! I never expected that ... Good for you," Angie said in a sugary sweet tone as she eyed the dining room to see if any seats had opened.

"Well, it was good seeing you," said Jenna as she turned back around to her dinner.

"You, too," replied Angie.

"I'm not too sure how long the wait is," said Joe apologetically.

"It's okay. I'll wait."

Suddenly, Angie noticed that someone was waving at her from the back of the restaurant. She squinted her eyes as she tried to make out who it was. A man stood up beside the last booth on the right and Angie couldn't believe her eyes. Standing at six feet two inches with tan skin and tattoos from his neck down was none other than Hunter McCord. Hunter was Angie's high school boyfriend and the only guy who hadn't broken her heart. Angie approached him with a big smile on her face.

"C'mere, beautiful," said Hunter in a raspy voice.

Angie kissed Hunter on the cheek as he pulled her into a tight hug.

"What the hell are you doin' here? I thought I'd never see you again," said

Hunter excitedly.

"Me either! Going through a divorce, so I'm home now," said Angie.

"Good for you. Good for me, too. Hey, join me," Hunter said pointing to his booth. It was more a demand than a request.

For the first time since arriving in Elkhart, Angie felt like she was exactly where she was supposed to be.

Hunter and Angie talked for a long time in the back of Monte's café. He immediately ordered Angie a platter of chicken parmesan and he watched as she slowly ate, savoring each bite. Hell-bent upon catching up, Hunter and Angie revealed what events had transpired since they last saw each other.

Angie learned that Hunter had done five years for a drug-related crime, but he claimed that he was now completely rehabilitated. He worked at the gas station on I-80 and did some inspirational speaking gigs at the local high schools about the dangers of drug use. Hunter listened intently as Angie told him about the circumstances surrounding her separation.

"You know, I'd never treat you like that," Hunter assured her.

"I know, Hunter. You've always been good to me."

"Give me a chance."

"Let's see how things go. The separation is still very fresh to me."

She hadn't even signed the divorce paperwork yet, but already her heart was wandering elsewhere.

"Hey, do you have plans tonight?" Angie asked as Hunter's face lit up.

"Not any that can't be broken," Hunter said slyly.

"Come to my parents' house. We're having a party for Trixie," Angie suggested.

"I'll be there."

Angie said goodbye to Hunter and thanked him for dinner. It was nearly five o'clock and she had to get back home to help set up for the party. She pulled the car out of the parking lot and turned onto Mountain Road. She was about to speed off when suddenly, she had to slam on the breaks. Someone had run out in front of her car! Angie hadn't fastened her seat belt yet, and the sheer force of the stop caused her head to crash hard into the steering wheel. The impact caused Angie to see spots. She lifted her head as the warm flow of blood rushed down her face. Jesse Trafford had run out in the middle of the road just inches from Angie's front bumper. The car came to a screeching halt as gravel and dirt kicked up around them. Jesse stared at Angie through her windshield with an ill-tempered look on his face. Angie was alarmed at the hatred that she saw in his gaze. Angie let out a deep sigh of relief. She thought for sure that she had hit him. Suddenly, Jesse brought both of his fists down hard onto the hood of Angie's car.

"Watch where y'er goin', ya old bitch!"

Now Angie was far from old, but she couldn't quite disown the bitch comment. A deep scowl grew across her pretty face. Angie laid on the horn, causing Jesse to go scrambling across the road, quick and afraid, like a rat running through a maze.

Pathetic weasel.

Angie shook her head as she thought, *Home sweet home.* Everyone had aged, and the new generation seemed to be as ill-favored as the last. As Angie prepared to hit the gas pedal, the slow, warm ooze of blood dripped down onto her dress shirt.

DiNolfo knocked on her driver side window with a worried look on her face. "Are you okay?"

Angie didn't hear her at first. There was a loud ringing in her ears and her vision was spotty.

"Angie, I'm taking you to the hospital," said DiNolfo with an official tone to her voice.

Angie nodded as she moved over to allow room for Jenna in the front seat. Jenna wiped off the steering wheel with a napkin, and drove Angie to Grier Mountain Medical Center where she could be checked out. Jenna thought that she might have a concussion from the impact. After waiting for a half hour, a triage nurse brought Angie back to the emergency room where she waited for a full evaluation. Angie was still a bit dizzy, but overall, she felt better than she had when she walked in. Jenna sat in a chair beside her gurney as she flicked through a magazine. Nurse Bridgette Kilpatrick strolled through the door with an air of authority about her. She grabbed a blood pressure cuff and proceeded to take Angie's blood pressure.

"Are you still feeling dizzy?" Bridgette asked as she marked notes into Angie's file.

"A little, but I'm okay."

"We need to be sure. It could be a concussion. So we are going to send you for a CT scan to ensure that there is no internal bleeding."

"I'm fine. This place just makes me nuts. I've been waiting forever!" said Angie angrily. Her arms waved around as she spoke, expressing her level of agitation. "That kid just barged out in front of me! Is he insane?" Angie complained in an irate tone.

Bridgette raised an eyebrow at Angie as she watched her animated expressions and listened to her complaints. Bridgette wrote something else on her clipboard. She watched Angie's reaction; the flying arms, the shaking hands and legs, the intensely irate look in her eye.

In a messy scrawl, Bridgette notated the chart:

Recommend Psych Evaluation

As quick as Bridgette entered, she left, assuring Angie that she wouldn't have to wait long for her tests.

Angie left Grier Mountain Medical Center with an even bigger headache than she walked in with. She couldn't believe that nurse recommended a psychiatric evaluation. Angie adamantly refused it and walked out, vowing never to return to that hospital again. As Angie pulled her car onto Caribou Road, a dull familiar ache returned to her chest.

CHAPTER 7

June 17, 2000
Morrow Manor
Fox Hollow, PA
6:30 P.M.

TOMMY MORROW WALKED ACROSS the threshold of Morrow Manor with intense purpose in his stride. He was dressed nicely in a light blue button-down shirt and black slacks. Tommy's heavy footsteps echoed through the foyer as he glanced around with a perplexed look painted upon his face.

Where the hell is everyone?

Tommy walked into the kitchen, but no one was there. The living room was vacant too. For once, the dining room table was completely unoccupied, and even the back porch was empty.

Maybe they left for the party already. The party is in a half hour, after all.

Suddenly, Tommy heard a banging noise emit through the ceiling. It came from the second floor and it was followed by a loud series of grunts and profanities. Irritated, Tommy stomped up the steps to see what was going on. He walked into his old bedroom which had since been converted into a rec room. Shane and Blake were lounging on the floor playing a video game. Tristan was lounged out on the sofa reading a novel with her legs propped up on Jack's lap. Jack, meanwhile, was sound asleep and snoring at an offensively loud octave.

"Why aren't any of you dressed yet?" Tommy demanded with an agitated tone in his voice.

Tristan looked up from her novel and gave her brother an annoyed glance.

"Tristan," said Shane as he continued playing his video game, "what on earth is he complaining about *now*. I'm busy trying to defend *Middle Earth*."

Shane continued to assault his video game controller with his thumbs.

"What are we supposed to be ready for?" asked Tristan.

"And why are you so dressed up?" asked Blake.

"You guys are the worst with keeping dates straight. Trixie's graduation party is tonight and Courtney's mom asked us all to attend," reminded Tommy impatiently.

Tommy thought he could hear the gears grinding in Tristan's head from across the room.

"It would mean a lot if you all came," persisted Tommy.

Tristan saw the nervousness in her brother's eyes and she simply didn't have the heart to tell him no.

"Give us an hour," Tristan said reluctantly.

❧

"Explain to me again why we are going to Trixie O'Mara's graduation party," begged Blake with an annoyed look on his face.

Tristan laughed as she rolled the statement around in her brain for the millionth time.

"Because it will hurt Tommy's feelings if we don't."

"Feelings ... This is the same guy who dropped a bucket of mud on your head from on top of the barn and put two chickens in the back of my car because he thought it would be funny. And we're concerned about his feelings?" asked Blake incredulously.

Tristan smiled at Blake as he cast a most disgruntled glare at her.

"You betcha, sunshine. Now go get dressed before he has a total meltdown."

Tristan inspected herself in the mirror as Tommy stormed back into the room.

"*That* is what you're wearing?" asked Tommy in a stunned voice. He clearly did not approve of Tristan's cute but casual attire.

Tristan looked down at her outfit. She was wearing a red top with a cute polka dot pattern, a pair of boot cut jeans, and black sandals. She had just put a pair of silver hoop earrings in, and she tousled her curly hair in wild ringlets down her back.

"Sure is. Love it or leave it," said Tristan matter-of-factly.

Tommy left the room in a huff and chose to put out bigger fires than arguing with his fashion-inept sister.

❧

"Shane ...Blake ... You guys better hurry up! Tommy's on the war path. I'm going downstairs to see if Cole is here yet," Tristan urged, trying to spare them from

Tommy's wrath.

Tristan walked down the long hallway past her old bedroom which was now being used as a closet for all of Jack and Frank's tools. She poked her head into her aunt's bedroom. Bridgette was sprawled out on her bed reading a book. Tristan had to stifle her laughter when she noticed the book title. The spine of the book read, "101 Easy Meals for the Unskilled Culinary Enthusiast." The second that Bridgette noticed Tristan standing in the doorway, she flung the book behind her in fear that Tristan would see it. Tristan pretended not to notice.

"Cute outfit, Tris. Are you going out?" asked Bridgette with a smile.

"Yeah, we don't have much choice in the matter, apparently," Tristan said grouchily.

She really did not want to go to this party. Tristan and Trixie were polar opposites and could barely hold a conversation with each other. But since she was Tommy's girlfriend's sister, she was required to attend.

"Someone needs to tell that boy to simmer down," said Bridgette with a healthy dose of attitude.

"You should. He might actually listen."

"It'll be in one ear and out the other. But I'll try. I get that he's excited, but he has the whole house in an uproar."

Suddenly Tommy rushed by Bridgette's bedroom and she had the perfect opportunity to put her fiery attitude to good use.

"Oh, Thomas!" Bridgette called in a sing song voice. Tommy poked his head in his aunt's doorway and looked at her as if she was insane.

"Uh ... Yeah?" he asked with a question on his face.

"Care to tell me why you're stomping and yelling like a lunatic all throughout the house?" It was a perfectly legitimate question.

"They aren't cooperating," Tommy whined like a child.

"Well," began Bridgette. "I'd like your full cooperation for a moment," she said sweetly.

Tommy looked at her like she had a million heads, and sheepishly replied, "Ok ..."

All sense of Bridgette's former sweetness was removed as she berated Tommy from across the bedroom.

"Simmer down! You're bossing everybody around, you've given your father a major migraine, and your uncle is threatening to hang you by your boots until you start acting right!"

Tommy stared at his aunt with wide eyes.

"Now," continued Bridgette in a much nicer tone. "If you can promise to act like a decent and civilized human being, I'll let you go to the party. If not, I'm locking that death machine in the barn. Do I make myself clear?"

Tommy shook his head in agreement.

Damn, she's scary when she's pissed.

Tristan walked down the stairs as she laughed at her brother's reaction to her aunt's outburst. Her amusement wouldn't last long though, because with each step she took she was moving from one family drama to another. Frank was standing at the bottom of the stairs, red-faced and hunched over. At first Tristan thought that her uncle might be choking on something, but then he let out a bellowing laugh. Tristan looked at Frank with a surprised look.

"What's so funny?" Tristan asked.

Frank held up a finger as he tried to get a hold of himself. He just couldn't stop laughing. His attempts did him no good, so after a moment he pointed to the dining room as he continued laughing. Wondering if her uncle had gone clinically insane, Tristan looked towards the dining room. The smile faded from Tristan's face as she reached the dining room door. She could hear her father loudly lecturing someone in the kitchen.

Oh, dear God. What now?

Tristan walked quietly over the ancient wooden floor boards as she tried to figure out what the situation was. She hoped that the groaning floorboards would not give away her surprise entrance. She stood just outside of the door of the dining room where she could hear multiple male voices chattering. Suddenly, she heard someone say her name. Tristan gritted her teeth in response. She opened the dining room door just slightly so that she could get a better look. Jack and Joe had Cole cornered at the dining room table. While the two men looked concerned, Cole looked utterly mortified.

"You see, Cole ... It is important that we discuss your intentions with my daughter on prom night," Jack explained.

Tristan groaned loudly in the doorway, "Ugh! Dad!"

Jack whipped around and glared at his daughter.

"Tristan, it's my job to ask. You're my daughter."

"Your eighteen year-old daughter who is going to prom with her boyfriend of three years," reminded Tristan. Cole gave Tristan a look of supreme gratitude. Tristan could still hear Frank laughing in the foyer.

"And if you must know, we planned on going bowling after prom. So, his intentions are to take me dancing and take me bowling. We may get something to eat, too. That's that. Interrogation's over."

"Thanks, Tristan!" yelled Cole with a smile on his face.

"This ain't over yet," said Joe with a suspicious look on his face.

Tristan took a seat at the table to offer her boyfriend support while the men shot questions at him.

Poor Cole. Dad seriously needs to learn to trust him.

"Are we ready to go yet?" yelled Tristan from the foyer.

A rumbling noise echoed from upstairs.

"All right, Dad! We're leaving!"

Tommy, Blake and Shane ran down the stairs, nearly knocking Tristan out of the way.

"We're taking Cole's Jeep," reminded Tristan.

"Okay," Jack shouted from the dining room. "Keep your brothers out of trouble. Don't forget curfew!"

"Midnight, right?"

"11 p.m., young lady. Sharp!"

Caribou Road was mobbed with cars when Cole turned his Jeep on the gravel road.

"Jesus Christ, did they invite the entire neighborhood?" asked Shane in surprise.

"Gwen knows *a lot* of people," mentioned Tommy.

"Yeah, every time they have a party the cops show up," mentioned Cole.

"Are there going to be any cheerleaders here?" asked Blake hopefully.

"Oh, God. I hope not!" said Tristan in annoyance.

27 Caribou Road was jam packed with people when they arrived. Tommy led the way and weaved through the crowd as he waved to random people he recognized. Roger O'Mara spotted him coming his way and furrowed his brow in irritation.

"Mr. O!" Tommy yelled across the living room. He loved to grate his nerves. Finally, he found Courtney in the sea of people and gave her a peck on the cheek while his brother and cousin made fun of him.

"Hey Court, where's your sister?" asked Tristan.

"Hey, Tristan. Um, like ... Which one? I have like a hundred," said Courtney dumbly.

Tristan could feel her IQ dropping by the second.

"Trixie ... We have a card for her," explained Tristan.

"Oh ... She's probably in the yard with her friends."

"Okay, thanks."

She didn't know how her brother put up with that airhead. Tristan desperately wanted to take a pin and jab it in her forehead to see if her head would pop. Cole and Tristan made their way outside while Blake and Shane mingled with the other party guests. Blake saw Natalie by the radio and started to dance really badly with her; she seemed embarrassed by his total lack of rhythm. Shane, meanwhile, tried his luck chatting up two cheerleaders who were standing near the back door. When they outright rejected him, he shrugged his shoulders nonchalantly, and joined his cousin on the makeshift dance floor.

Angie stood outside by the tiki bar her father had installed as the party raged on. With a beer in one hand, she smoothed down her black dress with the other. Angie decided that she would need to make the best of the situation and try to have a good time. She had even worn makeup for the occasion, which was exceedingly rare these days. Hunter took her in from the far corner of the yard. She looked beautiful and completely at peace. Angie O'Mara had definitely come a long way since their high school days. Angie watched Hunter approach her. He was dressed smartly in a pair of khakis and a white button-down shirt that was rolled up at the sleeves. She could just make out her name on his arm.

"Look who decided to join us!" said Angie excitedly.

"I told you I'd be here," Hunter said with a cocky half-smile.

"Can I get you a drink?" Angie asked.

"Shot of whiskey. Straight."

Angie passed a shot glass to Hunter. The amber liquid in the glass swirled gracefully and permeated the air with a bitter smell.

"Bottom's up!"

Tristan and Cole found Trixie in the yard. She was surrounded by her legions of friends. This included girls from the cheer squad, guys from the football and track teams, neighborhood kids and some faces that even Cole didn't recognize. They weren't able to squeeze through the sea of people, so Tristan left Trixie's card on the kitchen counter where other gifts had gathered. Cole glanced over at Tristan warily. He could tell that she didn't want to be here. Frankly, neither did he.

"Let's get out of here," Cole said as Tristan let a smile creep across her face.

Cole started the engine of his Jeep as Tristan climbed in the seat next to him. He grabbed her hand and suggested, "How about a drive to Wilhamette Creek?"

She smiled.

"Okay, we just have to be back by curfew to pick up the guys."

Cole's Jeep wound the steep curves of the Wilhamette backwoods as they climbed farther away from Elkhart. The Wilhamette Creek was located about twenty minutes from Elkhart and there was plenty to see and do there. Nature trails wound through the deep woods and you never knew what you might find hidden amidst the waterfalls and cliff-side scenery. Cole turned the Jeep off of the asphalt road and rumbled down a dirt path. The way down was winding and steep and you could find yourself wrapped around a tree if you didn't have your wits about you. Tristan enjoyed the sights outside of her window as the Jeep sped down the hill, going deeper and deeper into the Wilhamette woods. Finally, they reached level ground and Tristan's heart raced from excitement. She and Cole loved coming back here because it was so quiet and peaceful. The Jeep rambled down the road until it came to an abrupt stop. Cole had slammed his foot on the break. Tristan looked alarmed as she looked over at Cole.

"What's wrong?" she asked with wide eyes.

Cole pointed out his window.

"Look. Someone broke into the old mine shaft," Cole said with worry in his voice.

Tristan peered out the driver's side window. The wooden gate that was intended to prevent entry to the dangerous mine was demolished. It looked like someone had crashed right through it with their car.

"Who would break in there? It's so dangerous!" Tristan exclaimed.

"My best guess is that somebody is either hiding something in there or smuggling something."

"Smuggling?"

"Yeah. This mine is long and runs all the way to Elkhart. An old map my father has shows that the other entrance to the mine is in the basement of Harrow's."

"There are a lot of entrances. There's one at the old lighthouse, too."

"Yeah, but apparently they've all been boarded up for over fifty years."

With a dark tone to her voice, Tristan quipped, "Not all of them."

Cole gave Tristan a knowing look as he grabbed a flashlight out of the glove box and flashed it down the mine. Something had definitely ripped through the tunnel. There were chips of black paint scuffed on the wood. Suddenly, a pair of headlights appeared on the road behind them, and they were approaching fast. Cole scrambled into action. He threw the flashlight into the Jeep, jumped into the driver's seat and slammed on the gas.

"Let's get outta here."

⁂

"Where the hell did Tristan and Cole go?" lamented Shane as a beer bottle flew over his head and crashed against the wall behind him.

"I don't know but we need to get out of here," remarked Blake as he eyed the rowdy crowd warily.

"And what about him?" asked Shane as he pointed to Tommy who was rolling up his sleeves and preparing to go toe-to-toe with Hunter McCord.

"Dude's lost his mind. Let's go wait it out in Cole's yard," suggested Blake smartly.

⁂

The scene at 27 Caribou Road had changed dramatically in the short time since Cole and Tristan left. A group of people huddled in the yard as a fist fight broke out.

"That better not be Tommy!" yelled Tristan as she ran from the Jeep towards the fight.

"Shit ..." said Cole as he chased after her.

He jumped the fence into the yard and fought his way to the center of the huddle. Tommy was engaging Hunter McCord, an ex-con, in a fist fight. Cole had heard of beer muscles before, but this was just ridiculous. He didn't see Blake or Shane anywhere. So it would be up to him to take down the raging bull.

"I walk away for two seconds and you creep up on my girl," yelled Tommy.

"I just offered her a drink, man. I was being friendly," explained Hunter reasonably.

"I know all about you, McCord. Drug runner ..." accused Tommy with a silver tongue.

Tommy had hit a nerve. Courtney grabbed Tommy's hand and said, "C'mon, it's not worth it!"

Tommy yanked his hand from her grasp and prepared for whatever Hunter was about to dish out. Hunter punched Tommy not once, not twice, but three times. Blood gushed from Tommy's nose and mouth and ran down onto his shirt. Tommy kicked Hunter in retaliation, sending him flying back into the crowd. Cole had finally reached the center of the circle.

"C'mon Tommy, time to go!" yelled Cole as he grabbed hold of Tommy's shirt collar.

&

"I don't know how you do it, Jack," said Joe Piedmonte as he got out of Jack's truck. "I can barely handle two kids, let alone six."

"You used to have your step-kids to take care of."

"Maria's eldest kids visit every now and then. After she passed, they went to live with Maria's mother. They are grown now though."

"How old are they now?"

"Joanna is twenty-three now ... She's living in New York with her boyfriend. Joey is twenty-two, he's in law school up in Boston."

Joe, Jr. who was actually named after his birth father, Joseph Boone, not Joe Piedmonte, was now twenty-two and entering law school in Boston. Joe married Maria in 1980, and had taken on shared responsibility of her children, since their father was not alive. When Maria passed in '81, the kids decided to live with Maria's mother instead of with Joe, because their grandmother gave them greater comfort after the loss of their mother.

"You've had your share of bumps with your family, too. You don't need six kids to be stressed out at home."

Joe shrugged. "I guess so ... But I will say two is much easier than six."

Jack shrugged. "I've definitely earned my gray hair, that's for sure."

Jack and Joe looked up. It became immediately apparent that the party had turned ugly. Beer cans and bottles were strewn everywhere. A crowd of rowdy people gathered in the yard as they hooted and hollered. Trash littered the entire front yard. Joe gritted his teeth at the scene.

"I'm so glad that I don't have neighbors!" remarked Jack.

That would be the last joke that Jack would tell that night as he recognized one of the men that was fighting in the back yard. Tommy and Hunter McCord were circling each other with their fists bared, ready to fight.

"I'll kill him. What is wrong with that boy?" Jack said explosively.

"What is he thinking going up against McCord?" yelled Joe.

Jack rampaged across the road and jumped the fence in much the same fashion as Cole had just done. He pushed people out of his way as he gripped Tommy by the back of his shirt. Hunter looked as if he was going to pummel Jack instead. Jack looked Hunter dead in his eyes.

"I fucking dare you."

Jack stared Hunter down until he backed away, with his face beet red and a vein bulging out of his forehead. Hunter gave Jack a fearful glare as he grabbed another beer from the cooler. Even at the age of forty-nine, Jack was not a guy that you wanted to cross.

Angie watched the whole scene with disgust as she gulped down the last of her beer.

"Rehabilitated, huh? Yeah right!"

She chucked her beer can into the trash can as she made a beeline for the backdoor. She climbed the stairs to the second floor and slammed her bedroom door behind her. With an agitated click, the door locked as Angie sunk her weary bones onto her bed.

Jack was in a fit of rage as he pushed Tommy to Cole's Jeep. Tristan, Blake and Shane were waiting inside. They turned wide-eyed with alarm when they saw Tommy's face. There was blood everywhere. Jack pushed Tommy down into the back of the Jeep.

"You and I have a major problem," spat Jack, his face scrunched into an ugly snarl.

"So I'm not supposed to stick up for myself?"

"Not here. We will discuss this *at length* later," yelled Jack. It was more a threat than a promise.

Tommy was becoming increasingly irate in the back seat of the Jeep. He pulled at his seatbelt and tried to get out. Cole slammed Tommy in the chest and secured him in the back seat.

"Chill out, man! Do you want to get arrested or worse? That dude is known for shanking bigger guys than you in bar fights. Are you stupid?" yelled Cole, losing his temper for the first time in years.

Finally, Tommy simmered down and stared out his window in anger. As Cole skidded off Caribou Road, Tristan could hear the faint wail of a police siren approaching in the distance.

Frank pulled his truck up Caribou Road and approached the Harley that was parked in the driveway of 27 Caribou Road. There were beer cans strewn about and one crunched under Frank's heavy step, the weight of his boot crushing the can flat.

"Guess the party turned sour," Frank said aloud as he grabbed the bike and wheeled it to his truck. Tommy would not be riding it for a long time.

Jack slammed his foot on the gas as he ripped out of his parking spot on Caribou Road. The wheels screeched as the truck bolted from the scene. Two officers were leading Hunter McCord to their cruiser while DiNolfo scolded the O'Maras for allowing underage drinking on their property. Roger O'Mara was three sheets to the wind drunk, while Gwen had a glassy look to her eye. DiNolfo dismissed them with a curt wave when they gave their finest excuses. She wasn't in the mood to hear it tonight.

Jack's glare was lethal as he stared at the road ahead trying to catch up with Cole's Jeep. Gravel kicked up and the cab rumbled as Jack's fury catapulted the truck towards the onramp of Cavegat Pass. Finally, he saw them. Cole was driving at a reasonable speed, no doubt he'd be able to cut him off. Tommy wasn't escaping this conversation tonight. Just ten feet behind them, Jack sped up, honking his horn as he blocked the entrance through the covered bridge.

Cole came to an abrupt stop, his heart racing as he watched just how heated Jack was. For an older guy, he was a force to be reckoned with. All that ran through Cole's head was, *I sure as hell wouldn't mess with that.*

Jack stepped up to the passenger door, and gave his second youngest son a glare.

"Get out."

"What?"

"Get out!"

"Why?"

"Because you and me are having a conversation and I'm not going to have Cole drive an hour out of his way. You don't get the courtesy of running from my fury.

You messed up, Tommy!"

"Oh, for Christ's sake!" Tommy complained.

Jack slapped Tommy in the back of the head lightly. "Don't you take this out on the Lord. This is your problem. Let's go."

As everyone shuffled out of the car, Tristan gave Cole a kiss goodbye.

"Call me when you get in," Cole called from the Jeep.

"Have you lost your ever loving mind?" Bridgette yelled as she stormed out the front door of Morrow Manor at Tommy who was being led by Jack who had a fist full of his stained t-shirt in his grasp.

"No. I haven't! Haven't you ever stood up for anything?" Tommy asked letting his temper get the best of him. He knew damn well his aunt had.

"As a matter of fact, I have. I didn't pick a fight with a violent drug dealer, though! Get in. Your uncle is grabbing your motorcycle and it's being locked in the barn."

Tommy looked his aunt square in the eyes as a few choice words sat on his tongue just waiting to roll off. He knew better, though. She had raised him. Bridgette treated Tommy no different than her own son. Tommy turned on his heel to face his father.

"Is this your call?" Tommy demanded to know.

Jack glared at his son seriously. "Don't look at me. It's not just me that you hurt with your actions. Now listen to your aunt and go inside."

Bridgette could feel the heat radiating off of Tommy as he pushed his way past her and went into the house. Bridgette gave Jack a look that showed just how annoyed she was.

"I'll make damn sure he apologizes," Jack assured his sister with a serious look written across his features.

"I don't care about an apology. He has got to get his act together, Jack, before he winds up in prison or worse! He's going to piss off the wrong person one of these days!"

Jack gave his sister a knowing look.

"Trust me, you don't have to remind me," Jack said in a whisper as Tristan, Blake and Shane passed by.

"Straight upstairs. Go," Bridgette said to the trio that looked more than a little upset.

"Don't be mad at them. They at least stayed out of trouble," Jack reminded Bridgette.

"I'm not. I'm just concerned."

"C'mon. We have a rebel to sort out," Jack said as he put his arm around his sister and led her into the house.

⟋⟍⟋

"Damn it!" screamed Tommy as he pummeled a fist into the wall above his bed. Several of Blake's chess figures fell down onto the floor. The knight spun on its axis crashing into the queen while the bishop slid along the hardwood floor landing just inches from the door.

"Dude, what did you expect to happen? You put yourself in danger."

"You weren't there," said Tommy darkly to his cousin as he dropped his head into his hands.

"You're right. I had enough sense to get out of there and wait for Cole and Tristan to come back.

Blake and Tristan walked in and while Blake shook his head at his brother, Tristan skidded on the bishop chess piece and slammed into Shane's bed stand. Growling at the situation, she reached down and picked up the rogue chess piece and placed it on the nightstand.

"You know what I don't get, Tom?" Blake said as he glared at his brother, his eyes narrowing as he spoke.

"No, but I'm sure you're going to tell me," Tommy said with an attitude.

"Just two days ago, you were ready to break up with her. Now you're going toe to toe with Hunter McCord for her."

"She's still my girl."

"You're all over the place, man!" Blake said, the rage clear on his reddened face.

"I don't need this right now!" Tommy said standing up from the bed.

Tristan had retreated into her bedroom to escape the argument that was boiling to a head. She could still hear their voices which had risen to shouting level. She understood why everyone was mad. Tristan was most in shock that Tommy would put himself in danger, when there wasn't a real threat. Kicking off her shoes, she reached for her phone to let Cole know she was home safe. After only a few rings, he picked up the phone.

"It's about time," Cole said sounded nervous.

"Fog set in trying to get up the mountain, and you know how Jack drives when he's annoyed."

"Ah ... like a lunatic."

"Yelled at Tommy the whole way home."

"He brought it on himself."

Even his best friend saw his actions as irrational.

"Enough about him. Are we still on for tomorrow?"

"Yeah, movies and mini-golf, right?"

"Pick you up at noon."

"Have a good night, honey."

Suddenly the voices in the next room had grown to a deafening level.

"What the hell are they fighting about?" Cole asked.

"Whether Tommy is off his rocker or not."

"I can answer that one," Cole said with a laugh.

Trying to control the chuckle that was building, Tristan quickly said goodbye and hung up the phone. Hearing that the argument was quickly coming to a head, Tristan jumped up from the bed and swung open the door.

"You!" She grabbed Blake's shirt and pushed him on his bed. "And you!" She grabbed Tommy's arm and pushed him inside her room. "Sleep in here tonight. I need rest. I cannot deal with any more drama tonight!"

Tommy gawked at his sister, his eyes wide and stunned, that is, until she slammed the door, giving him the quiet he so desperately needed.

CHAPTER 8

June 18, 2000
Elkhart, PA
Dawn

THE RAIN FELL HEAVILY from the stormy sky over Elkhart. It pelted loudly against the window panes and rooftops, and drowned the newly planted flowers in the Piedmontes' garden. At 25 Caribou Road, Joe Piedmonte was just dragging himself out of bed. Reluctantly, Joe threw the covers off of him and slid his feet into a pair of moccasins. Jenna, who was in bed next to him, was still fast asleep. With great effort, Joe pulled himself out of bed. It was the last thing on earth he wanted to do, get up, but a restaurant doesn't run itself. Twenty minutes later, Joe was showered and dressed but didn't feel much more motivated to tackle the day. Loudly, his hiking boots tromped down the hallway towards the staircase causing Natalie's fat tabby cat Scamp to retreat into her bedroom with a hiss.

"Devil Cat!" Joe yelled at the cat as it nearly scared him out of his skin.

Joe was a pretty laid back guy. He didn't have a lot of rules for living in his house. Just five:

1. Stick to your curfew

2. Keep the house clean

3. No drugs, booze or cigarettes

4. Don't do anything you don't want me to find out about.

5. Don't talk to me before I've had my morning coffee.

Scamp had broken Joe's number five rule. Joe peeked into Cole's bedroom first—an old habit of his. Cole was knocked out cold with his cordless phone still in his grip. He must have fallen asleep talking to Tristan again. Joe took the phone from

Cole's grasp and put it gently back on the charger where it belonged. Joe closed his door quietly and continued walking down the hall. Next he checked on Natalie, who was snuggled in bed with her cat. As soon as the cat caught sight of Joe, it lifted its fat head and hissed at him again. Joe grabbed a pink spray bottle off of Natalie's vanity that was filled with water and sprayed it in the cat's general vicinity.

"Bad cat!"

He had gotten a droplet of water in the cat's eye. The cat twitched a little then lay down in submission. Joe shook his head.

That's right. I'm the boss. Not you.

Joe trudged down the stairs, one by one, and made his way to the kitchen to brew his coffee. Joe loved his coffee. Like a moth to the flame, Joe was positive that he couldn't survive without his morning coffee. It wasn't just any old coffee though. Joe's choice of coffee blend is a topic of heated debate in the Piedmonte household. He drinks only the Ethiopian Yirgacheffe blend that Mr. Agape sells at the farmers market over in Chiefsdale. He drove an hour, once a month, to Chiefsdale just to buy this imported blend of coffee. Joe could vividly recall the reaction he got when Jenna had taken a swig for the first time.

"Got any coffee?" asked Jenna as a yawn escaped from her mouth.

Joe smiled broadly, clearly excited to share his special coffee with someone else.

"Do I? I've only got *the best* coffee ever ..."

Natalie rolled her eyes at her father's boisterous declaration.

Jenna looked nervously at Joe, skeptical as to whether she should believe him or not.

"Okay ..." Jenna replied.

Joe began pouring Jenna a cup of his special blend of coffee. She noted how it looked remarkably like mud, and the smell wasn't that far off either. Cole and Natalie were sitting at their father's kitchen table giving DiNolfo looks of warning.

"Don't do it," Cole warned with a laugh as he ate his cereal.

"Be quiet!" Joe scolded Cole as he handed Jenna a mug that read "World's Best Chef."

"You can't say we didn't try to warn you," remarked Natalie as her eyes scanned the fashion magazine in front of her.

"How bad could it possibly be?" DiNolfo asked as she prepared to take a sip.

Joe watched Jenna's face as she took a sip of his coffee and immediately regretted standing so close to her. After just one sip, coffee came spewing out of her mouth and showered down over Joe's face, hair and shirt.

Jenna yelled, "What the hell is this shit?"

Joe, who had closed his eyes at just the right moment, was now wiping coffee off of his forehead, nose and chin. He grabbed a napkin and dried his mustache which was dripping of his beloved Ethiopian Yirgacheffe coffee.

"Clearly some people don't recognize culture when they see it! I pay twenty-two dollars a pound for that glorious roast!" insisted Joe.

"I'd say you got ripped off, my friend!" said Jenna as she, Cole and Natalie laughed until they were red in the face.

Joe still laughed every time he opened the pantry and saw the coffee can with the smiling camel on it.

More for me!

Joe took one last delightful sip of his coffee before throwing the hood of his coat over his head and stepping out into the miserable weather. Joe always took the same route to work. He walked straight out his front door and made a left on Caribou Road. At the end of the road, he took a shortcut through the Forest of York, past the Bone Tree, and down a narrow path that led straight to the back of Monte's Café. It was an overgrown area of the forest, but it was the easiest way to get to work. He opened the back door of Monte's with a swift twist of his key. Time to turn the lights on; his kitchen and wait staff would be arriving soon. He went through the same motions every single morning, and after thirty-plus years of opening the restaurant, his movements were second nature. He flicked the lights on, powered up the cash register, checked the answering machine for any messages, and preheated the oven to prepare for the morning rush. He walked with purpose through the dining room to make sure all the tables were clean and the floors were swept the night prior. He wanted his guests to have an enjoyable experience. Next, he had to take on the task of pulling up all the shades on the windows. All eight windows.

I really need to figure out a way to make this process automatic.

Finally, when he came to the last window, he pulled the shade like the others, but this time something caused his breath to shorten. As he peered out onto Mountain Road, it wasn't the rain that caught his attention, or the gaudy lawn ornaments that Edna and Peggy had displayed outside of Harrow's General Store. It was the erratic tire tracks that swerved through the mud, and the red puddle that lay in the middle of Mountain Road. Amidst the bleak scene were discarded clothes, a gun, and other debris. But nothing troubled Joe Piedmonte quite as much as seeing the undeniably dead body of a young woman lying face down in the mud.

Jenna woke up to the unrelenting squeal of the telephone that sat on Joe's bedside table. She woke with a start, reaching for the phone.

Something has to be wrong, she thought. Joe had always let her sleep in before. Jenna looked at the alarm clock.

6:17 A.M.

Jesus Christ.

"Hullo?" Jenna said groggily into the receiver.

"Better get your boys down on Mountain Road. There's been a murder."

Jesse Trafford left the Elkhart Police Station with an ill-favored look upon his face. He threw the hood of his sweatshirt over his head as he trudged out into the rain. Skulking down Mountain Road, he was swallowed by the darkness as a feeling of discontent grew in his chest.

CHAPTER 9

June 18, 2000
Elkhart, PA
Dawn

THE SUN ROSE RED AND FIERY over Mountain Road when officers Adam and Liam Morrow arrived on the scene. They had no idea what waited for them outside Monte's Café. DiNolfo spat into the phone, "Get to Monte's. NOW!" before she hung up abruptly.

Liam pulled a roll of police tape from the trunk of the police cruiser as he began blocking off the road to oncoming traffic. Adam approached the crime scene with caution as he tried to disturb as little as possible. It took him a moment to process the scene before him. They were in the fickle hour when the sky was just waking but the road before them was still dark. Adam took a flashlight out of his pocket and flicked it on. The bright light cut the early morning darkness and provided glimpses of what nightmare lay in front of them. Puzzle pieces cloaked by darkness. Adam's mind processed the evidence piece by piece:

A pool of red pulsed under the weight of the heavy rain.
An abandoned gun was carelessly tossed into a puddle.
A ripped t-shirt was soaked and muddy from the rain.
The print of a hiking boot lay stranded in the mud.
A wallet left in plain sight with a driver's license sticking out.

Adam slowly scanned the road for more signs of evidence. He had thoroughly checked the road ahead. If there was blood, surely there had to be a body somewhere. Suddenly, a thought occurred to him. He pointed the flashlight towards his feet. It took a moment for Adam's brain to process what he saw. A dead woman, no older than twenty years of age, lay dead at his feet. She was a blonde woman with a thin figure and a small "T" tattoo on her right shoulder. Lying face down on top of a green tarp in the mud, she was scantily dressed with just a bra and a pair of ripped jeans on her body.

She wasn't killed here.

Adam kneeled at the victim's side to get a closer look. He hoped he would be able to identify the victim. The torrential rain reduced visibility as it pounded atop his hat and trickled down his shoulders. Crouching down, he was able to get a better view of the victim's profile. Identification was still difficult because the victim's face was bloody and bruised. With gloves on, he moved the victim's head out of the mud, hoping to be able to ID her. Rain poured from the early morning sky, slowly revealing the victim's identity. The mud washed away from her face in gentle streaks. Her face was badly bruised and her nose was clearly broken. Adam lamented at the victim's beauty; a life that was taken before it's prime. Finally, the rain washed away the mud from around the victim's eyes. Adam became frozen in his shock. A pair of eyes of the deepest blue stared back at Adam. The eyes held a certain depth and sorrow that he had never witnessed when the victim was alive. Adam's hands trembled and his stomach churned. It took forcible measure to turn his eyes away from Courtney O'Mara's gripping stare.

How on earth am I going to tell Tommy?

Liam secured the perimeter of the crime scene and recommended that Monte's and Harrow's close up shop for the day. They closed off Mountain Road to traffic so that they could thoroughly investigate. Edna and Peggy locked themselves inside their apartment above Harrow's, too petrified to even look outside. Meanwhile, Joe Piedmonte closed up shop to the public but offered to keep the kitchen open for the officers who were processing the crime scene. It was the least that he could do. He felt absolutely horrible for the O'Maras.

DiNolfo arrived on the scene at twenty of seven with a look of deep concern on her face. She lifted the crime scene tape and quickly ducked underneath. She made a beeline over to Adam who was taking photographs of the crime scene. He began to fill her in on what he had discovered so far.

"The victim is Courtney O'Mara, age twenty. I'm trying to bag as much evidence as I can before the rain destroys it," Adam began as a frustrated sigh escaped his mouth.

DiNolfo was impressed. Processing a murder scene in the pouring down rain was like watching a bomb tick off its final seconds. If you're not quick enough, some crucial evidence could be washed away.

"The evidence I've bagged so far is locked in Joe's office, so you can check it out there."

DiNolfo nodded as she looked down at the victim.

"What are these marks all over her?" DiNolfo asked.

"She sustained multiple injuries. The cause of death was clearly the gunshot wound to the back of her head. There was obviously a struggle. Her nose is broken, her face is bruised and her neck is broken, but I think those injuries came later."

DiNolfo listened intently as Adam Morrow pieced together the crime scene. She had trained him well.

This kid knows what he's talking about.

"But these marks," Adam said as he pointed to the black broad marks that ran across her legs and torso, "are tire tracks."

"Good work, Morrow."

"That's not all though ..."

"Oh?"

"No, not by a long shot ..."

Adam crouched down next to Courtney's battered body.

"Look here," said Adam as he pointed to the green tarp that lay underneath Courtney's body.

"A tarp."

"She wasn't killed here. This is a dump site. I think she was pushed out of a moving vehicle and that is when her neck and nose broke. Post-mortem."

"Decent hypothesis. But what about the tire tracks?"

"They probably ran back over her to add insult to injury."

The thought was chilling but DiNolfo thought Adam was right on the mark.

"Solid work. Keep going. I'm going to review the evidence inside. Continue bagging as much evidence as you can. The weather is working against us."

Joe walked into his office and closed the door shut behind him. He tried his best not to look at the evidence on his desk as he grabbed his cell phone out of the top drawer. In a quiet voice, Joe talked in to the receiver.

"Hello?" asked Jack in a grouchy tone of voice.

"It's Joe."

"Hey, what's up?"

"It's Courtney ..."

Jack paused.

"What about her?"

"She's dead. Murdered by the looks of it. We found her out on Mountain Road. Keep your boy under lock and key. This doesn't look good at all."

Adam had finally finished bagging up the evidence when the van from the medical examiner's office arrived. A burly officer and a short female officer dressed in white covered the body with a sheet and lifted it into the back of the wagon. The medical examiner would need to perform a full autopsy to provide an official cause of death.

DiNolfo scanned the evidence that was labeled and bagged on Joe's desk. This was definitely not a cut and dry case. Adam had collected a leather wallet with a ten dollar bill and a driver's license belonging to Jesse Trafford. There was a photograph of a single black hiking boot track caked in the mud. There was also a semi-automatic handgun, a tattered shirt, and a single piece of black thread which was retrieved from the victim's hair. The unskilled mind would have all officers beating down Jesse Trafford's door. Fortunately, DiNolfo had some inside information. Jesse Trafford had an iron-clad alibi from seven p.m. on June sixteenth to approximately five a.m. on June seventeenth. DiNolfo had arrested Jesse herself for disorderly conduct in Shooter's Pool Hall. She left him sitting in a holding cell overnight until he decided to calm down. His brother posted his bail and he was now a free man. The trouble was where was he between the hours of five and seven a.m.?

DiNolfo came out of Monte's with a serious look on her face.

"Liam, start canvassing the area and ask if anyone saw or heard anything. Adam and I need to pay the O'Maras a visit."

Lightning illuminated the stormy sky as Adam and Jenna approached 27 Caribou Road. Adam knocked on the wood door twice as he waited for someone to answer. Gwen O'Mara opened the door with a quickness. She was still dressed for bed in her yellow robe and slippers, and she had a tired and worried expression upon her otherwise pretty face.

"Hi, Mrs. O'Mara. I'm Officer Morrow. This is Sergeant DiNolfo. May we come in?"

Gwen let the officers in and quickly closed the door behind them. Roger O'Mara was still wearing the same outfit he wore the night before. He looked disheveled and stressed. He stood up as the officers approached him.

"Please sit. You too, Mrs. O'Mara," said DiNolfo firmly.

"Is everything okay?" asked Roger nervously.

"I am afraid that I am the bearer of bad news. This sort of thing is never easy to say, so I'm just going to come right out with it."

DiNolfo was trying to be firm but sensitive. It was not an easy balance for her. Angie came into the living room with a concerned look on her face. She wrapped her arm around her father's shoulder as she listened.

Jenna spoke in a tone that was all business, "Your daughter, Courtney, was found dead on Mountain Road this morning."

It took a moment for the O'Maras to process what the Sergeant had just said. It was Angie who spoke up first.

"Dead? How?" she said as a horrified look crossed her face.

"Courtney was murdered. She was killed by a gunshot wound to the back of her head."

As Adam spoke the words, he could see the O'Maras begin to break. Gwen's face was frozen in a state of ultimate shock and grief. After a moment, her lips started to quiver as a terrible scream cried from her lungs.

"Not again! Not Courtney!"

Roger O'Mara had to steady his wife as she fell to her knees.

"Please know that we are doing everything we can to find the person responsible," said Adam, trying to sound reassuring.

"We are deeply sorry for your loss," said DiNolfo somberly. She patted Gwen on the arm.

"We will be in touch very soon. You take care."

Adam shook Mr. O'Mara's hand and wished him well. A look of deep sorrow radiated from Roger O'Mara as he took Adam's hand. After Jenna was done consoling Gwen, she approached Angie and she was surprised by the look on her face. Whereas Gwen and Roger had shown their complete devastation and despair, the only emotion on Angie's face was anger. Pure unfiltered, unwavering rage poured from Angie's eyes as she heaved deep breaths from her chest. In that moment,

Jenna was catapulted back twenty years to a memory that she forgot she even possessed.

CHAPTER 10

June 4, 1980
27 Caribou Road
Elkhart, PA
9:15 P.M.

IT ALL STARTED WITH THREE GIRLS and a dance. PS 132's prom was just around the corner and no one was more excited to attend than Tiffany O'Mara. As captain of the cheerleading squad and the president of the year book committee, there wasn't a person in school who did not know Tiffany O'Mara. Unfortunately for her, popularity has its costs.

"Oh, Tiff, you're definitely going to be prom queen with that dress!" gushed Jenna DiNolfo as she approved of her friend's purple off-the-shoulder prom dress.

"Do you think so?" said Tiffany trying to sound self-conscious when in reality she was as vain as they come. She flounced her floor-length gown with a sassy simper.

Jenna looked at her friend with an incredulous look on her face. "Well, it sure as hell isn't gonna be me!" laughed Jenna.

Tiffany rolled her eyes. "Well maybe if you wore something other than black and gray, you'd be able to find a date!"

Jenna looked down at her own prom dress—a black tea length dress that was elegant and classic. Jenna lips curled up into a toothy smile.

"Actually, I already do have a date."

Tiffany whipped her body around and looked at her friend in shock.

"Who?" Tiffany demanded to know. Jenna gave her friend a sly wink.

"Joey Piedmonte asked if he could take me."

Tiffany looked shocked.

"My next door neighbor Joey?"

"Yeah, I saw him at his dad's restaurant and he asked if I needed a date."

"You know he's like twenty-one, right?"

Jenna smiled and shrugged her shoulders.

"I don't care, he's cute."

Tiffany rolled her eyes at her carefree friend.

"Oh, I know ... No one could ever compare to *your* Ethan," Jenna said facetiously.

"What's wrong with Ethan?" asked Tiffany in a high pitched voice.

"Oh, nothing other than the fact that he's a total bore and he has the IQ of a rock."

"I like him. He's sweet and he buys me pretty things."

Suddenly Tiffany's bedroom door swung open and Angie was standing in the doorway.

"Pretty gown, Tiff," Angie said, complimenting her sister with a smile.

Tiffany smiled a fake smile then said in a sugary sweet voice, "Thanks."

"Hey Jenna, are you going to prom?" asked Angie curiously. Tiffany rolled her eyes.

"Obviously! Now can you please leave us alone?" yelled Tiffany as her fake sweetness melted away, revealing her true nature. Jenna looked at her friend with a nasty look.

"Why are you so mean to your sister?" said Jenna irately, sticking up for Angie.

"She's *so* annoying!" Tiffany complained.

"So are you! Now be nice or I'm leaving!" threatened Jenna.

"Fine, whatever," said Tiffany as she walked towards her window.

"Are you going to prom, too, Angie?" asked Jenna, trying to school Tiffany on how to have a civilized conversation.

"Yeah, Hunter is taking me," explained Angie with a smile.

"Oh, you guys should ride with us!" said Jenna in an excited voice.

Tiffany gave Jenna an evil stare as Angie's face lit up.

"Okay!" said Angie, excited for the offer.

"My dad rented a limo. You and Hunter can join us."

"Oh, my God, I can't wait!" squealed Angie, truly excited to feel like she was becoming a part of her sister's inner circle for once.

As Angie and Jenna continued to chat happily, Tiffany sulked by the window. She stared out into the darkness until something peculiar caught her eye. A silhouette of a man caught her attention. He was standing just outside their house. His figure was illuminated by the street light, but his face was cloaked by the shadow of his hat. He appeared to be looking right at Tiffany.

"Who is that?" asked Tiffany with a sense of alarm present in her voice.

Jenna and Angie both looked at Tiffany with concern.

"What?" asked Jenna.

"There. In the road. There is a man ..." Tiffany continued.

Jenna and Tiffany crowded the window trying to get a better glimpse of the man. Angie pushed her way through and she took a hard look at the man. He appeared to be nothing more than a shadow, but when a sparrow landed on the man's shoulder, Angie knew exactly who he was. As the man tried to come closer, a scream escaped from Tiffany's lungs. While Jenna comforted her, Angie watched the man race up Caribou Road and veer onto the path that led through the Forest of York.

June 19, 1980
27 Caribou Road
Elkhart, PA
6 P.M.

A white limousine pulled up outside 27 Caribou Road as two young men stepped out. Hunter McCord, dressed in a powder blue tuxedo, straightened his tie before knocking on the O'Maras' front door. Ethan Quiver followed behind Hunter, dressed sharply in an all white suit. Suddenly, the front door at 25 Caribou Road sprang open and Joey Piedmonte came down the front steps as Rose Piedmonte snapped pictures of him.

"So handsome, my Joey!" squealed Rose Piedmonte.

"Mom! C'mon, it's not even my prom!" complained Joe.

"So what? Besides, I like this one, Joe. Jenna is a sweetheart!"

Joe smiled sheepishly as he banged on the front door of the O'Mara residence while the flash of his mother's camera illuminated the front yard. Moments later the door opened again and Mrs. Piedmonte and her house full of guests had crowded back into the front yard. Joey helped Jenna down the stairs. She was wearing a classic black tea length dress with black pumps and tan stockings. Joey had given her a red rose corsage that beautifully offset her dark hair and dress.

"Help her down, Joey! Oh, doesn't she look gorgeous!" yelled Mrs. Piedmonte as her son blushed.

"Ma! C'mon!"

Jenna couldn't help but laugh.

"Thank you, Mrs. Piedmonte."

"Okay, now smile!" yelled Rose.

The cameras threatened to blind Jenna and Joe as the bulbs went off, capturing the moment forever. Next, Angie came out of the house with Hunter. His powder blue suit perfectly matched her blue taffeta gown. Her blonde hair was pulled up into an elegant French twist, which showed off her toned arms and shoulders.

Mrs. Piedmonte snapped another picture and said loudly, "You look so pretty, Angie!"

Angie smiled and let Hunter lead her to the limo. Lastly, Tiffany came out of the house with Ethan and suddenly the crowd began to disperse.

Rose whispered to her sister Rita, "I never did like that girl."

The prom was a total hit and everyone was having a really good time until it was time to announce the prom king and prom queen. Tiffany waited anxiously as she watched Principal Gottlieb take the stage.

"Ladies and gentlemen ... It's the moment we've all been waiting for. Time to announce our prom queen and king! Mrs. Coolidge ... The envelope if you please!"

An elderly woman with a rear end that was equal in mass to a mid-size Honda waddled up to the stage and handed Principal Gottlieb a silver envelope.

"Drum roll, please"

As the crowd cheered, Gottlieb's voice boomed through the auditorium's sound system.

"The 1980 prom king and queen are ... Tiffany O'Mara and Hunter McCord!"

The look in Angie's eyes said it all. Her cheeks had flushed and her eyes began to water. Of all the guys in their class, why Hunter? Hunter looked at her sadly. He knew how much she loathed her sister.

"Chin up ... I promise I won't enjoy it at all," Hunter said with a laugh.

"Yeah, but *she* will!" Angie said coldly.

Angie watched as Tiffany smugly took the dance floor with Hunter. He was simply trying to be polite, but Tiffany was laying it on awfully thick. She loved to be the center of attention, and it didn't matter who she stepped on to get there. Jenna thought that Tiffany was acting as if she had just won the *Miss America* pageant. Tiffany smiled alluringly at Hunter as the music began to play. Angie felt as if her skin was on fire. The more Hunter swung Tiffany around the floor, the deeper her rage became. Finally, when Tiffany kissed Hunter on the cheek, she felt as if she might combust on the spot. Jenna looked over at Angie and saw the rage written all over her face.

"Take a breath ..." suggested Jenna, but before Angie could take her advice, she was gone.

Prom ended at midnight and as the students and chaperones flooded into the parking lot, Angie sat on a picnic bench holding hands with Hunter.

"You okay?" he asked.

"I'm fine," said Angie in an overly sweet voice, pretending that she didn't want to rip her sister's up-do off of her perfectly shaped head.

"My curfew's in ten minutes, so I gotta go."

"Okay, I'll see you tomorrow," Angie said with a smile. She leaned in to kiss him goodnight.

Joey and Jenna waved to them from the parking lot as they wandered back to his house so he could drive her home. Joe had his arm wrapped around her shoulder and was listening intently as she talked. Suddenly, Tiffany and Ethan burst out of the auditorium doors. Tiffany looked irate.

"Fine, be that way, Ethan! But that's the end of it!" yelled Tiffany as some of her hair escaped her up do.

Ethan laughed as he waved goodbye, "See ya!"

"No you won't!" Tiffany threatened.

Angie smiled darkly. Karma really was a vindictive bitch.

Angie and Tiffany only lived two blocks from the school so they decided to walk home. The road was dark and due to the late hour, there was barely any traffic on the road. A car full of students whizzed past them, causing Tiffany to jump.

She screamed in protest, "I'm the prom queen! Why should I have to walk?"

Angie rolled her eyes.

"Oh, shut up, princess! Get over yourself! Let me know when your pumpkin carriage arrives!"

"Humph," groaned Tiffany as she crossed her arms over her flat chest.

The road became eerily quiet. Angie got a strange feeling; a feeling that they weren't alone. They had to get home. The only sounds she could hear were her sister's sighs and their heels click-clacking against the hard asphalt road. Angie glanced over her shoulder nervously. She just couldn't shake the feeling that they were being followed. Angie nearly fainted when she saw a man's silhouette in the road just twenty feet behind her. Panic rose from the pit of Angie's belly. She was frozen still for a moment. Finally, quick thinking prevailed. She ran forward and grabbed Tiffany's hand.

"C'mon!"

"Why are we running? Ow!" complained Tiffany.

"We're being followed!" said Angie urgently.

"Followed?" spat out Tiffany hysterically, "Is it that creepy guy from the other night? I don't see anyone, Ang!"

"Just c'mon!"

Angie and Tiffany crossed the tree line into the Forest of York. They were just minutes from home. If their speed continued, they could outrun him. Angie ran ahead of Tiffany. She was always the faster of the two sisters. She could hear someone approaching in the background. Angie whipped around to get a better look. The figure ducked behind a tree so that their identity remained hidden. Tiffany ran as fast as she could. Angie gasped as she watched the scene unfold before her. Tiffany got her foot caught in the brush and she went down vanishing from sight. As she went down, Angie swore she could make out the faint outline of a man standing over her sister.

Wide-eyed and nervous, Angie screamed, "Tiffany!"

CHAPTER 11

June 18, 2000
Morrow Manor
Fox Hollow, PA
7 A.M.

JACK SLAMMED THE PHONE into its cradle with such force that a framed photograph of Shane and Blake fell off the wall and smashed to the floor. Frank, who was already awake and eating a bowl of cereal, gave Jack a worried look. The milk from Frank's cereal dribbled down his chin. He brushed it off quickly with a flick of his wrist.

"You're not gonna believe this ..." said Jack as a look of disbelief grew across his face.

"What?" asked Frank with a mouth full of cereal. He chewed loudly as he waited for Jack to continue.

"Hell just broke loose on Mountain Road," Jack said with a serious tone of voice.

Frank pushed away his cereal bowl as a look of anger began to emerge. Jack clearly had his full attention. Jack took a deep breath before speaking, as tension rolled off his shoulders.

"Courtney O'Mara was found dead outside of Monte's. A bullet to the back of the head."

Frank's chair skidded loudly against the hardwood floor as he shot up out of his seat. The muscles in Frank's jaw, arms, and chest flexed as tension coursed through his body. He rubbed his massive hands over his face as he tried to gain some composure.

"Shot?" Frank yelled, still trying to come to grips with the news.

Jack nodded somberly.

"Jesus Christ, is nowhere safe? What the hell are you gonna tell Tommy?" Frank exclaimed, clearly upset about the news.

Jack considered Frank's question for a moment. He couldn't just come right out with it. Tommy obviously had some feelings for the girl. How deep remained to be seen.

Jack replied, "The truth, but I'm going to need your help keeping him calm."

"No kiddin'. Kid's got a nastier temper than his ol' man!" Frank joked trying to lighten the mood.

Jack replied, "Oh, shut up. At least we had a reason to be ticked off."

Frank chuckled as his mind roamed back to yesteryear.

"Consider where we were in the summer of '77 ..." Frank said with a raised eyebrow.

Jack gave Frank an agitated glare.

"I hate when you do that," Jack said to Frank referring to his little trip down memory lane. Even Jack had to admit that Frank had a point. At Tommy's age, Jack was married with a family. He and Frank were going to war with Kendricks for harassing Catherine. They were also engaged in a separate war against the Traffords when Harry Trafford stole Angus's car right outside of Monte's café. The families had not seen eye to eye for a very, very long time.

"If you recall," Frank added, "We had our fair share of drama, too. Besides, Tommy has every right to be pissed off."

"Yeah ..."

"Did you know that Jesse Trafford was harassing Tristan at work?"

"What?" Jack yelled, furious that he was just now finding out about this occurrence.

"She didn't tell you?"

"No! She did not!" said Jack, enraged.

"Well, guess what? Trafford was also bothering Courtney at her house last week. Tommy handled Trafford yesterday. Cornered him behind Quiver's."

"My aching nerves. Then there is the whole Hunter McCord issue."

"McCord has a rap sheet as long as a roll of toilet paper."

Jack sighed. It was true that Hunter McCord was one of the low-lifes that gave Elkhart residents a bad name, and as far as the Traffords went, they made some of the criminals at Pennington Prison look tame.

"Shit," said Jack as he stormed out of the kitchen with Frank on his heels. The same thought rolled around in both men's minds.

What if Tristan was next?

Jack shuddered at the thought.

The two men climbed to the third floor, causing the old wooden stairs to creak loudly under the pressure of their weight. They crept into the boys' bedroom where they found three teenagers sound asleep. Jack bypassed Blake and Shane's beds where they were snoring loudly, and approached Tommy's bed. The blankets rose and fell peacefully. Tommy was so high strung lately, it seemed a shame to wake him; especially with such horrible news. Jack knew he must be the one to tell him, though.

Jack shook the mattress first, hoping to wake Tommy. When he didn't stir, Jack tried nudging Tommy in the shoulder. Suddenly, the blankets rumpled off the bed and fell to the floor. Jack quickly realized that he did not find the person he intended. Tristan shot up in bed with a highly disgruntled look on her face. Her curly hair stood on end and her scarlet Steeplechase Mustangs t-shirt was wrinkled badly from only a few hours of restless sleep. Angry from being woken up so early, Tristan yelled at Jack in a hoarse voice.

"Dad!"

Jack had a perplexed look on his face.

"Why are you out here? And where the hell is Tommy?" Jack asked in an annoyed voice.

Tristan rolled her eyes as she got out of bed.

"Have some consideration for other people's need for sleep! Just because you're up at four a.m. every day, doesn't mean that I want to be, too!"

Jack looked taken aback by his daughter's grouchy demeanor.

"Err ... Sorry, but I need to find Tommy," Jack said in a sheepish voice.

"Oh, please! He was in my room on my phone arguing for half the night with Courtney. I got him to hang up for two seconds so that I could call Cole. Then I came out here so I could get some sleep. He was yelling 'til at least three in the morning!" Tristan complained in an agitated voice.

Frank shook his head in agreement and said, "I had to come up here three times to tell him to simmer down. I could hear his voice through the damn ceiling."

Jack's face grimaced in frustration. Tommy's actions in recent days could portray him in a very negative light. He needed to understand that his actions and reactions carried a heavy weight; especially in light of what happened to Courtney O'Mara. Jack reached to open Tristan's bedroom door, but was met with resistance.

Jack growled, "Locked! I hate locked doors in my own house! Tristan, where is the key?"

Sleepily, Tristan replied, "It's in my room hanging on the wall. I never use it. Does anybody want to tell me what is going on and why I'm awake at seven a.m. on a Saturday?"

Jack ignored her question and instead issued an order of his own. He barked, "Go wake everybody up and get them in the living room in ten minutes."

"But—" Tristan protested.

"Please stop asking me questions. I'll explain downstairs," Jack pleaded.

Jack was growing more agitated. Just as he was ready to kick the bedroom door in, Frank grabbed a large set of keys from his belt loop. He flicked through each key slowly as he looked for the correct one that would open Tristan's locked bedroom door.

"Oh, where is the bloody key ...basement ... storm cellar ... shed ... barn ... work shop ... guest house ... boy's bedroom ... office ... Ah, here it is. Tristan's room," Frank rambled. Jack looked at his oldest friend impatiently as his scowl deepened.

Frank shook his head as he handed the key to Jack. "Always ready to jump to conclusions. I see where the boy gets it from. Here ya go," Frank said as passed the key to Jack.

"If he's not in there, we've got a real problem on our hands," said Jack with a worried look in his eyes.

"He's in there. I locked his motorcycle in the barn last night."

Jack let out a sigh of relief as he inserted the key into the lock and twisted hard. The door swung open slowly, revealing Tristan's neat and tidy bedroom. The bed was still made, the desk was uninhabited and there were no signs of Tommy anywhere in the room. Frank and Jack raced into the room with frantic looks on their faces. They scrambled around the room looking for any trace of Tommy. Suddenly, the bathroom door swung open and Tommy was standing in the doorway with a miserable look on his face.

"There you are," said Frank, relieved.

Tommy looked as if he hadn't slept at all. Jack clutched his chest in relief, but it wouldn't last long. Jack had some terrible news to share. He addressed Tommy in a firm voice, "I need you to come down to the living room."

"Now? It's only seven o'clock!" protested Tommy.

"Yes. Right now," Jack said firmly.

When Tommy failed to move, Frank barked, "C'mon. Move yer feet!"

Cole was woken up out of a deep sleep by the obnoxious ringing of the telephone. Sleepily, he climbed out of bed and wiped his eyes with his hands. Glaring at his alarm clock, his eyes bugged open at the early wake up call.

"Ten to one, he's calling me in to work," Cole guessed.

Sure enough it was Joe who was calling at this early hour.

"Hello?" said Cole groggily.

"It's Dad. I need you to listen to me very carefully," said Joe in a slow, calm voice. Cole was alarmed by his father's voice. Something was wrong.

"I'm listening. Is everything okay?" Cole asked in a worried voice.

"I'm fine. Jenna's fine. Tristan's fine."

"Okay," said Cole, his mind reeling from the silence on the other end of the line.

"I need you and your sister to go to Jack's house right now. Stay there and don't go back to the house. Jenna and I will be up tonight."

Cole remained silent for a moment as he processed his father's request.

"What are you talking about? What is going on, Dad? I'm nineteen years old. I'm not a little boy," Cole complained.

More silence took over the phone line as Cole waited for a response. Finally, Joe spoke, "Courtney O'Mara was found dead outside the restaurant this morning. Jenna, Adam, Liam and a few other officers are investigating. I need you to go to Jack's house and keep your sister away from all this. Jack is going to tell everyone the news. Go now. He's expecting you."

Joe hung up the phone abruptly, leaving Cole momentarily speechless. After a moment, he sprang into action. Quickly, he pulled on a pair of jean shorts, a gray Philadelphia Flyer's t-shirt, and a pair of white sneakers. He raced into his sister Natalie's bedroom in a huff.

"Nat ... Get up!" said Cole loudly.

"Ugh! Leave me alone! I'm sleeping!" complained Natalie as her brown hair fell over her face.

"Dad said to get up. We have to go to the Morrow's ..."

"Why?" Natalie asked sleepily.

"Something bad has happened."

"Oh, my God! Is Dad okay? Is Jenna? What about Nonna?" asked Natalie in hysterics. As neurotic as Natalie could be, Cole should have known to use a gentler tactic in getting her out of bed.

"They are fine. Jack is going to fill us in when we get there ..."

"Do I need a bag? Oh, my God! I wonder what's happened."

Cole raised an eyebrow at his excitable sister.

"Please just get dressed. Tristan has stuff you can borrow if we have to stay."

Within five minutes, Cole had Natalie in his Jeep.

"Strap in," Cole said with an edge to his voice.

As soon as he heard Natalie's seat belt click into the harness, Cole hit the gas pedal sending the Jeep veering onto Caribou Road and racing towards Cavegat Pass.

Cole and Natalie arrived at Morrow Manor around eight a.m. The Morrow family had already converged in the living room. Sleepy bodies filled up the couch, loveseat and arm chairs that were scattered around the entertainment system in the living room. When Tristan saw Cole and Natalie walk in, she confronted her father head on.

"Dad, tell us what is going on! You're freaking me out!" said Tristan in an irate voice. "Are Liam and Adam okay? Joe and Jenna?"

Tommy and Blake concurred as they grunted groggily at their father. Shane raised his hand as he swallowed a mouthful of his waffle, and Angus loudly slurped his coffee as he eyed his son in irritation.

Moira peered down over her glasses at her youngest son and asked, "We're all awake and assembled as you requested. What's this all about?"

"Okay, everyone settle down," yelled Jack, but no one seemed to hear him because they were all chatting loudly amongst themselves.

Everyone was speculating as to what was so important. Frank pressed two fingers between his teeth as an ear piercing whistle sounded through the room. Suddenly, all eyes were on Jack. Jack grabbed the remote control and flicked on the big screen TV that sat on the entertainment stand against the wall. It infuriated Jack that Channel 4 was airing live news coverage of the murder investigation. Three years ago he couldn't get a single paper or news station to report that Tristan was missing. Suddenly, the TV that hung on the wall came to life. A blonde-haired reporter wearing a bright yellow rain jacket was live on the scene at the corner of Mountain Road and Mayfair Lane. The rain poured down upon her as she delivered her news report just feet from the police perimeter that Liam had set up an hour earlier.

In a solemn voice, the reporter spoke, "This is Rebecca Hargrave, field reporter for KMRT Danville, reporting live from the scene in Elkhart, Pennsylvania. Elkhart is a sleepy little town that is located just an hour from Danville. Police are investigating the murder of an as of yet unidentified female."

The camera panned off of the reporter's face and zoomed in on the crime scene. The cameraman could not get a very clear shot, since Liam's perimeter had pushed them back nearly one-hundred yards from Monte's Café. The torrential downpour wasn't helping matters, either.

The reporter continued, "As you can see, police are still processing the crime scene. The victim is covered under a black tarp, and police are continuing to search the area for evidence."

Suddenly, Liam approached the police perimeter to secure one end that had loosened thanks to the fierce winds that accompanied the rain. The reporter took advantage of Liam's close proximity.

"Excuse me, officer?"

Liam looked at the woman with a serious expression. She shot question after question at Liam with precise aim and calculation.

"Do you know who the victim is?"

"How did the victim die?"

"Are there any suspects?"

"Officer?"

Liam sighed as he responded, "At this time, we ask that anyone that has any information in relation to the crime to contact the Elkhart Police Department at 717-555-9624. Thank you."

Liam walked away, ignoring the reporter's follow-up questions.

The TV faded to black as Jack set the remote down on the coffee table. Jack let out a deep sigh and everyone looked at him with questions in their eyes.

"Tommy, I'm afraid I have some horrible news to share," Jack said in a soft voice.

Tommy looked at his father wide-eyed as he felt his control begin to quiver out of balance.

Jack continued, "They found Courtney outside of Monte's this morning. Someone shot her, son."

Tommy's jaw dropped just slightly. Tristan's eyes darted to her father's face with a hard glare. Natalie leaned against her brother and gasped loudly after hearing about her next-door neighbor's fate. After the initial shock, all eyes shifted to Tommy's face. It took him a moment to process what had just been revealed to him.

It was Tristan who moved first, wrapping her arms around her brother. As she gripped him tightly and brushed her fingers through his hair, Tommy lost his resolve. Tristan felt Tommy's body shake under the pressure of her hold. He grabbed her shoulder and squeezed tightly as emotion began to fill up his eyes. He didn't cry. No one expected him to. What happened was far more heart-wrenching than that. Bridgette watched her nephew's eyes as his sanity threatened to flicker out of sight; like a burning candle's flame in the wake of terrible storm.

"Steady, Tom ..." Tristan warned, talking in a calm, soothing voice.

She wasn't letting go. She couldn't. There were very few people that Tommy trusted on this earth, and Tristan happened to be one of the people he confided in most.

"Say something," Jack begged as tears formed in his eyes from watching his son endure so much pain.

He had been there himself at one point. Someone had taken his Catherine away. He knew what a blow to the gut it was. He also knew that no matter how much time passed, the pain didn't subside. Tommy allowed his head to fall into Tristan's lap. He balled his left hand into a tight fist and squeezed until it turned white. He slammed his fist into his thigh again and again. Finally, he raised his head. His brown eyes were distant, nearly vacant. Tommy tried to speak, but when his lips moved, nothing came out. Everything that Jack had said was racing through his brain. His thoughts battled with the memory of last night. Tommy's final words to Courtney were, "I'll see you around." They had ended on bad terms with Tommy calling off their relationship around three in the morning after Courtney had told him that her father didn't want her to have anything to do with him anymore. A sense of guilt rose in Tommy so great that it threatened to turn his stomach inside out. He looked up at the wall over the entertainment stand where various pictures hung. He found the picture of him and Courtney that was taken just a few weeks prior at Blake's birthday party. Tommy's eyes traced the curve of Courtney's smile, the shape of her eyes and the straight edge of her hair. He couldn't take it anymore. He allowed his anger to take free reign. Tommy's head dropped back into Tristan's lap as a horrible, bone rattling wail cried from his lungs. It bounced off every square inch of the manor house and threatened to seep into the wood. The sound fractured Jack's heart as Catherine's face came to the forefront of his mind. He knew exactly what his son was going through.

Moira did what she did best whenever there was a family crisis: Cook. Moira had served up a massive breakfast feast to try to help shift the dark mood that had set within Morrow Manor. The family had settled at the dining room table as they devoured their breakfast which consisted of eggs, French toast, home fries, and bacon. Everyone except Tristan and Tommy sat at the table stuffing their bellies with food.

After Tommy's breakdown, Tristan yelled at her father to clear the room. "You have the emotional depth of a boulder! That is not something you tell him in front of everyone! Clear the room. NOW!" Tristan screamed in fury.

Tristan was highly upset with Jack that he didn't have the emotional sense to pull Tommy aside and break the news gently. Jack cleared the room as his daughter commanded, leaving her and Tommy alone in the living room. If anyone could talk some sense into Tommy, it was definitely Tristan; especially after everything that she went through just three years earlier.

Jack looked up from his breakfast in surprise as Tristan walked into the dining room with Tommy in tow. His face appeared calmer and more somber instead of the wild, angry and out of control expression he wore in the living room. Whatever Tristan had said to him had certainly backed Tommy away from the ledge.

In a blasé tone of voice, Tristan yelled out, "You heathens had better saved us some breakfast!"

Tommy sat down next to Jack without saying a word and dug into his breakfast without making eye contact with anyone.

Tristan whispered in her father's ear, "Give him space."

"He can have all the space he needs, but he's not leaving the house except to go to school," said Jack warily.

"He has no intension to. He's going to be using my bedroom for a while."

"That's fine, but I'm taking the key."

"Do you have any idea who did this?" Cole asked Tommy with a worried edge to his voice. Cole had the same worry that Jack and Frank had. *What if whatever man did this, comes after Tristan next?*

"I have two main suspects," said Tommy in an exhausted voice. It was the first he had spoken in the dining room, and suddenly all eyes were on him.

"Who do you think did it?" asked Cole knowing damn well what two names would fly out of his best friend's mouth.

Tommy's eyes went dark.

"That slimy bastard Hunter McCord and the rodent that is Jesse Trafford."

Jack shook his head at Tommy.

"It probably wasn't Trafford. Joe and I were in Shooter's Pool Hall last night when he got taken out in cuffs. DiNolfo arrested him herself after he was spoutin' off terroristic threats to one of the bikers in the pool hall. He wasn't such a fan of you either. He dropped your name a few times. He was like a caged animal. I don't know who pissed him off, but I never saw him look that out of control. I guess it all depends on what time he got released this morning."

Tommy rolled his eyes. He didn't want to mention that it was him who pissed off Trafford, because then he'd have to explain why he had confronted him in the first place. Jack was breathing down Tristan's neck enough as it is.

"One of those two greasy rats had something to do with this," insisted Tommy.

"Maybe he put someone up to it, then," suggested Cole as he caught a glare from Jack. "After all, he was bothering Courtney at her house last week."

"It definitely wasn't McCord. Liam and Adam took him out of the party last night in cuffs. Cole got you out of there just in time," Jack warned with a nervous glare.

"Like Cole said ... Maybe it was one of them and they are working with someone," said Tommy.

"Or maybe it was none of them. An outsider that nobody expects," thought Tristan.

"Or maybe we should leave the investigating up to the professionals," suggested Jack. Jack's comment caused Frank to do a double-take.

"Now there's a change of tune that I never thought I'd hear! Jack Morrow cooperating with the local police," Frank quipped loudly with a tone of surprise.

Jack couldn't help but laugh.

"Well, yeah ... Considering the police squad isn't comprised of a bunch of corrupt weasels anymore. I'm more than happy to let them do their job."

Frank eyed Tommy. "Are we in agreement that with the exception of school, you are to stay put until this is all squared away?"

Though Tommy wanted to hit the streets and pound in the face of whoever was responsible, he had heeded Tristan's words very carefully.

"I'm not going anywhere. Especially since you're holding my ride hostage."

"Better believe it," added Frank with a serious tone of voice.

"With that being said," Jack mentioned cryptically as he stared at Tristan. Tristan's stomach dropped. "I want you to stay put, too."

"This is not about me, Dad."

"An innocent young woman was murdered outside of your work. I want you here."

"I have school and I have work. I'm saving up for a car."

"Well then, you are going to be escorted to and from."

Tristan rolled her eyes.

"When are you going to realize that I am more than capable of handling myself?"

"When I'm dead."

PART TWO

A Thickening Plot

Footsteps approaching,
A hallow heart soaring.
I wasn't alone,
As the day was dawning.
Cool breath on my neck,
Your veil was falling.
The sunlight revealed,
Your nightly calling.
You presented yourself,
In a glow of white.
What horror struck me,
For such a heavenly sight.
Your eyes took me in,
Wild and bright.
And as you reached for my soul,
I screamed with all my might.

~Excerpt from Phantom Flight by Addison Kline

CHAPTER 12

June 18, 2000
Trafford's Auto Body
Elkhart, PA
3 P.M.

"WHERE HAVE YOU BEEN, BOY?" yelled Harry Trafford at his youngest son Jesse, who had just walked through the front door of Trafford's Auto Body.

Jesse was soaked to the bone from the rain. Jesse ignored his father's question that was overloaded with innuendo. He brushed by his father bumping hard into Harry's burgeoning stomach. This only caused Old Man Trafford's mood to worsen. Before Jesse could get away from his father's wrath, Harry gripped Jesse by his hair. Jesse screamed as he felt Harry's dirty, long fingernails dig into his scalp. Pieces of hair ripped from Jesse's scalp as Harry yanked his son just a mere inch from his face.

"You better not have had anything to do with the murder of that girl!" Harry yelled as his putrid breath reached Jesse's nose. Jesse scrunched up his face in protest.

"Damn! Your halitosis is enough to kill me," said Jesse ignorantly.

This only caused Harry's temper to flare. Harry gripped Jesse's hair even tighter as he came nose to nose with his son.

In a threatening voice Harry grilled Jesse, "Piece of shit. If I find out that you had anything to do with this, the cops will be the least of your worries! Trust that! What would your mother think?"

"What girl? I don't even know what the hell you're talking about! And don't even bring Mom into this! What would she think about you doing time for theft and leaving me with Mick and Jerry?"

Suddenly, the bell over the front door rang as Sergeant Jenna DiNolfo walked through the front door with an impatient scowl on her face.

"Afternoon, Trafford. I need to have a word with your boy," Jenna said pointing in Jesse's direction.

Harry quickly loosened his grip on Jesse's hair as blonde wisps of hair fell to the floor. Jesse rubbed his red scalp where his hair once was.

"Me? Why you gotta talk to me?"

"I'm going to need you to come back down to the station and answer some questions I have."

Jesse stared at DiNolfo with deer in headlight eyes. Jenna knew what would happen next.

"I suggest you don't run away. If you make me chase you, it's just going to make things a whole lot worse for you. I know you can't stand me when I'm pissed off," Jenna reminded with a hard edge to her voice as she recalled how Jesse had called her a "bulldozin' bitch" when she had to tackle Jesse in the back of Shooter's Pool Hall last night.

Jesse contemplated DiNolfo's warning, but as usual, he threw caution to the wind. He barreled out the back door of Trafford's Auto Body, ran across the dirt yard, climbed up the wet chain link fence and landed hard on the other side as he fell into a puddle of mud. A figure stood over Jesse and shook his head.

"You'll never learn, will you?" yelled Adam Morrow as he lifted Trafford to his feet.

"We just want to ask you some questions, but when you run, that makes you look awful suspicious."

"Questions ... Questions about what?" Jesse asked in an agitated voice.

"About the murder of Courtney O'Mara. Now let's go," said Adam as he pushed Jesse into the back of his patrol car.

Police Officer Liam Morrow walked into Quiver's Ammunition and Hunting Shop with a manila envelope in his hand. His boots tread loudly over the linoleum floor alerting Ethan Quiver that someone had come into the store. Ethan turned around on his stool, casting a wary look towards the officer. He knew they'd be showing up eventually.

"Ethan ... Is your old man in? I have a couple questions for him," asked Liam cordially.

Ethan breathed a small sigh of relief. Liam took note and lifted his left eyebrow.

"He's actually on leave from the store. He had to get surgery on his back. Is there anything I could help you with?" Ethan reluctantly offered.

"Yeah. First, I want to ask where you were this morning between the hours of five a.m. to seven a.m.?"

"I was at my other job."

"What other job?"

"I work at the bottling factory at night."

"Can anyone vouch for your whereabouts?"

"Sure. The overnight supervisor."

"Can I have his information?"

"It's a her ... Donna Giampetro."

Ethan wrote down the overnight supervisor's phone number and passed it to Liam. Liam was verifying the whereabouts of all the men in Elkhart. They had to be sure they weren't missing anything. Liam eyed him speculatively, unsure of whether or not he could rely on Ethan's assistance. He hadn't been the most reliable source of information in the past. Since Ed was out on medical leave, it appeared he didn't have much choice in the matter.

"Is there something else I can help you with?" asked Ethan with a puzzled expression.

"All right, maybe you can help me with something else then," said Liam as he opened the envelope. He pulled a Polaroid photograph out of the envelope and passed it to Ethan. Ethan could tell that it was the print of some sort of hiking boot that was captured in the mud.

"I need to know if you can identify this print. It appears to be a hiking boot. I need to know if you sell something here that would make this print."

"Hard to say right off the bat, but there is an easy way to tell," said Ethan as he hopped down from his stool.

Liam followed Ethan to the far wall where all of Quiver's boots were displayed. Ethan began picking up each boot and comparing its sole to the photograph. After about thirteen pairs of boots, Ethan had finally come up with a match.

"This is the Expedition style 2032 hiking boot. It's an exact match."

"Any idea who might have purchased this shoe?"

"Not offhand because it's not a very popular style this time of year," explained Ethan.

"How do you know they bought it recently?"

"The track ... The design is not worn down at all."

"Can you check your records? It's a size eleven," Liam pressed, becoming impatient with the shop clerk.

"Yeah, I can do that ... Hold on."

Ethan went to the back of the store and returned with a binder that contained a book of barcodes.

"Hmm ... Let me see ... This is the Expedition style 2032 ..." mumbled Ethan as he referenced a page in his binder. He typed in a series of numbers into his register, as Liam waited patiently.

"Only three people purchased this particular boot in the last three months. It's really only popular during hunting season," Ethan explained.

"I need those names, Ethan," Liam pressed as he glanced impatiently as his watch.

Ethan scrawled the names of the three customers on a white notepad. As Ethan passed the paper to Liam, he mentioned, "Hey, your kid brother bought a pair, too."

Liam controlled his face as he took the paper. Ethan had scrawled messily on the paper:

Hunter McCord

Thomas J. Morrow

Jesse H. Trafford

Liam took the paper and stormed out of the store with the envelope in his hand as his temper threatened to get the best of him.

"So Trafford ... Long time no see," said Jenna with a lethal hilt to her stare.

Trafford stared at Jenna with an angry glare.

"It's not a normal day in Elkhart, when we don't meet. I'm starting to feel like we're really getting to know each other," joked Jenna darkly.

"I don't wanna get to know you."

"Well whether you wanna or not, you're gonna spill what you know to me."

"I don't know nothing."

"Beautiful English, there ..."

"Are you testing me on my grammar or my knowledge of the crime?"

Jenna snapped at Jesse. "Where were you between the hours of five and seven a.m. this morning? And don't bullshit me, Trafford!" Jenna yelled, knowing full well that he would have some ridiculous story.

"You should know!"

"My records show that Officer Graeves released you at five a.m."

"That's bullshit!"

"Really? Then what time were you released? I don't see a watch on your wrist."

"The clock on the wall said 7:56 a.m.!" Trafford yelled.

"You mean the clock out there?" Jenna pointed through the glass window in the interrogation room towards a clock on the wall that still said 7:56 a.m. It had been stuck on that time for the past two years because Adam keeps forgetting to replace the battery.

"You all tricked me!" yelled Trafford dramatically.

Jenna raised her eyebrow.

"Seriously? We tricked you?" Jenna shook her head as she started scrawling notes in her notebook.

"Are you ready to answer seriously?" asked DiNolfo with a bite.

"I did. I thought it was 7:56 a.m.," griped Jesse.

"Fine. Let's pretend that's the truth," Jenna said as she continued to write down notes into her book. She continued, "What did you do after you got out?"

"I got breakfast."

"Where?"

"Monte's. Where else?"

"Wrong. Try again."

"I'm telling you the truth."

"You're a bullshittin' liar! Monte's is closed because there is a dead girl outside his front door! Now tell me the goddamn truth!" Jenna screamed in an agitated voice.

Jesse stared at the police sergeant with a look of defiance.

"You better speak," warned DiNolfo, her anger starting to rage out of control.

"I went straight home," said Jesse, trying to sound as convincing as possible.

"Wrong. Care to try again?"

"Since you know so much, why don't you tell me where I was?" suggested Jesse as his temper boiled over.

"Fine. I will. Edna Harrow reported that she saw you walking down Mountain Road around 5:30 this morning and she reported that at the time, there was no body in the middle of the road."

Newsy old bat, Trafford thought.

"So, you got me."

"Is that a confession?"

"No!"

"Be clear, Trafford! I don't have time for these games!"

"Yeah, I was on Mountain Road around five-thirty but I ain't no murderer!"

DiNolfo raised an eyebrow in contempt.

"I have a source that tells me that you had bothered the victim a week prior at her house. You wouldn't leave, and her boyfriend chased you away."

"I didn't want nothin' to do with her!"

"Then, I heard you were bothering Tristan Morrow at the diner. What's that all about?"

"I like Tristan. I couldn't give two shits about Courtney O'Mara."

DiNolfo scribbled furiously.

"You didn't care about Courtney O'Mara? Enough that you would dump her body on the side of the road?"

"No! I told you I ain't no murderer! I was actually stopping by to talk to her father because his car was at the shop, but Courtney took it the wrong way. Morrow is such a hot head he got the wrong idea!"

"But you *were* at the restaurant bothering his sister, weren't you? And the other waitresses the month before."

"Just Tristan and Natalie."

"Why?"

"They are nice girls. Not like the rest of the trailer park girls 'round here."

"So why bother them?"

"Not tryin' to bother them."

"Well apparently you made them uncomfortable. So tell me ... Why do you feel the need to lie to me? You know I'll get the truth out of you," DiNolfo said bluntly. She wasn't bluffing. She could spot a liar a mile away.

"I don't wanna get in no trouble."

"I'd say you've gotten yourself in enough by running and lying to a police sergeant. Don't leave town."

Jesse watched as DiNolfo's chair skidded out from the table as she opened the interrogation room door.

"You're free to go ... for now."

Hunter McCord trudged up the driveway to the Easy Goin' Trailer Park with a venomous glare in his eye. He had just been released from his holding cell after Angie O'Mara had scrounged up enough money to post his bail. She didn't stay, though, not even long enough to say hello. She had entirely too much going on at home and she wanted to be there to comfort her mother. Hunter was grateful that she was able to come to his rescue. Hunter knew that something had happened in town due to the hustle and bustle in the police station, but he didn't know the extent of what had occurred. He had no idea that Angie's sister was found dead on Mountain Road.

Hunter trudged up the muddy path towards his double-wide trailer. He walked up the steps of his splintering wood deck with his legs feeling like dead weight underneath of him. He fished for his keys from his jean pocket but suddenly noticed that his pockets were empty. He didn't need them, though. His front door was hanging wide open. Inside the trailer, Hunter's Pit Bull, Ox, was waiting with a pained expression. The dog was starving and thirsty from being without nourishment for nearly twenty-four hours. Hunter would get to that once he determined that everything was in its proper place. You never could tell with the kind of neighbors he had; common thieves, drug addicts, prostitutes, and all the people who lived with them. The Easy Goin' Trailer Park was comprised of the lowest of the low in Elkhart. It just didn't get much worse off than that. Hunter knew he had locked the door behind him before he went to that party last night. He began to inspect the trailer to make sure nothing was missing. His fireproof cash safe was left untouched in his broken oven. The coin jar remained half full in plain view on the coffee table. Even his vintage leather jacket was still hanging on the back of the door. Hunter began to relax as he realized that if anyone had come into his trailer, they would have likely taken the things of value in plain sight first. He wandered into the bedroom and peeled his soaking wet shirt from his tired body. He tossed the shirt onto the floor at his feet. He grabbed a beer from his mini-fridge and cracked it open. It wasn't until he took his first chug that a red flag was triggered in his mind. His gun cabinet was open, and two signature pieces of his gun collection were missing. His twin Ruger 9mm's were gone. Hunter's anxiety skyrocketed because not only did he have a large number of people who wanted him dead, it also meant that it was someone that knew him well. He kept his gun cabinet locked at all times. He kept the key hidden, taped to the underside of the toilet tank lid. For that person to have gotten past Ox, it had to be someone Hunter knew well. The only people that had been in his trailer in the past week were his mother, Shirley, and his buddy Ethan Quiver. Someone definitely had some explaining to do. Hunter locked all the doors and windows of his trailer and pulled up the stairs that led to his deck. He was in no mood for visitors of any kind. He pulled out a TV dinner and popped it in the microwave. Salisbury steak would have to do for tonight's dinner. Hunter was entirely too uneasy to go out. He'd definitely wind up back in the slammer for getting into an argument with some loser, or worse. Hunter flopped down into his old recliner and turned on the TV. Part of him was relieved to be home, but another part of him felt safer in the jail cell.

Suddenly, a news reporter came onto the screen with a late breaking news report:

"This is Rebecca Hargraves with the Danville Evening News. This just in. The woman who was found dead on Mountain Road in Elkhart, PA has been identified as twenty-one-year-old Courtney O'Mara. Police have confirmed that she was killed at close range by a Ruger 9m handgun and subsequently dumped on Mountain Road. Anyone with more information is being asked to contact the Elkhart Police Department."

"Son of a bitch!" yelled Hunter as he threw his beer bottle across the room.

Someone was trying to frame him. The question was, who?

"Officer Morrow speaking," said Liam Morrow as he picked up the phone on his desk.

"Oh, really? That was fast. Yes, I'm ready."

Liam started scribbling on the back of a receipt on his desk.

"Thanks again."

Abruptly, Liam hung up the phone and ran from his desk to the parking lot where Sergeant DiNolfo was just pulling up.

"Just heard back from Harrisburg. That gun is registered to Hunter McCord."

Jenna's jaw tightened as she put the car in reverse. Liam watched as her patrol car pulled back out onto Mountain Road and screeched towards the Easy Goin' Trailer Park.

CHAPTER 13

June 18, 2000
Easy Goin' Trailer Park
17 Spotted Skunk Trail
Elkhart, PA
5 P.M.

DINOLFO FELT THE SENSATION that she was being watched as she pulled her police cruiser up the dirt road that ran through the center of the Easy Goin' trailer park. Blinds parted as eyes peered out, dogs barked loudly, doors slammed shut, and mothers hurried their children inside as the sergeant weaved through the trailer park.

Man. These people really know how to make a girl feel welcome.

DiNolfo parked her patrol car outside Hunter McCord's double-wide trailer and walked towards his deck as gravel crunched under her feet. She banged on the trailer three times with her night stick. She knew she didn't have to worry about McCord running. He was more the type that would shoot first and run later. DiNolfo kept one hand on her holster as she waited for Hunter to appear at the door. With a bang, the screen door swung open and Hunter emerged on the deck with a sneaky smile on his face.

"Afternoon, Sergeant," said Hunter in a pleasant tone of voice.

Jenna raised her right eyebrow. She was used to McCord's games. She's known him for over twenty-five years. Not much could surprise her.

"What can I do for you on this *lovely* day?" asked Hunter warmly.

DiNolfo chuckled. Lovely is not a word she would use to describe today. While the rain had stopped for now, the sky was still a threatening shade of gray and the ground was wet underfoot.

"Can I come in?" asked DiNolfo, getting straight to the point. She didn't have time for games.

I am resistant to your charms, McCord. Cut the bullshit and let's get this show on the road.

Hunter smiled and invited Jenna into his trailer. "Welcome to my humble abode."

Jenna followed him through the door and was immediately greeted by the snarling growl of a Pit Bull. Ox bared his teeth at Jenna as he growled, but she didn't flinch or back away. She grabbed a bone off of the floor and threw it to the back of the trailer. Ox chased it and began gnawing on it.

"He's *cute*," said Jenna facetiously, knowing that cute was certainly not a word that Hunter McCord would want to describe his dog.

"Cute? He's supposed to be a vicious guard dog."

"Oh, really? What's he guarding?" asked Jenna slyly. She didn't miss a beat.

Hunter broke eye contact and he mumbled, "Nothing."

Jenna eyed a faint white residue on Hunter's kitchen counter. She ran a finger along the surface and brought her white-tipped finger just a half inch from her nose. She smelled it, careful not to inhale, then quickly rinsed her finger off in the sink. She turned around with a scathing expression on her face.

"If I find out that you're running this shit through my town, or supplying dealers, I will not hesitate to send your ass back to Pennington."

"It's sugar."

"McCord ... You've known me for over twenty-five years now. When have you ever known me to be stupid or naïve?"

Hunter sheepishly responded, "Never."

"So don't even try to bullshit me!"

Hunter's smile quickly faded as he looked to the ground. He jumped as the phone rang. DiNolfo could tell he was on edge. Hunter had no intention to pick up the phone and instead he let the answering machine pick up the call. Suddenly, Angie's voice filled the living room.

"Hey, it's Angie. I posted your bail, so you should be out by now. Give me a call. Something horrible has happened."

So it was Angie who bailed out Hunter. Interesting.

"Okay, Hunter," said DiNolfo seriously, "let's get down to business."

Hunter sat down as he waited to hear what DiNolfo had to say.

"I was wondering if you could explain to me why a gun that is registered to you was found at the scene of a murder?"

"I was in jail all night. You saw me there yourself."

"Indeed. But still, a Ruger 9m registered to a Mr. Hunter Harrison McCord was found just feet from the body with just one round discharged. Do you know where that round was discharged?"

Hunter shook his head in denial, but he had a good idea thanks to the news report.

"In the back of Courtney O'Mara's head!"

Hunter went on the offensive. "Look, somebody broke in here while I was locked up. They stole two of my guns ... Two Rugers."

The story sounded farfetched. Who on earth would break into an ex-convict and known drug dealer's trailer when they knew he was heavily armed? But as DiNolfo watched Hunter's face, she knew he was telling the truth.

"How do I know that you didn't give your two Rugers to one of your trailer park idiots that do your bidding for you?"

"Do I look stupid?" asked McCord with an exasperated look on his face.

"Do you really want me to answer that?" asked DiNolfo with a smirk.

"Why would I give my guns that are registered to me to some loser who would get me caught?"

DiNolfo had to admit that McCord had a point.

"All right, lead the way."

Hunter showed DiNolfo his gun cabinet and told her how he found the trailer earlier that day. DiNolfo offered to file a police report. As she was writing the report on a white slip, Hunter looked at her with a worried expression.

"Someone is setting me up."

Without looking up, DiNolfo responded, "Certainly appears that way."

"But who?"

"I don't know, Hunter. It could be anyone. You've burned a lot of bridges and made a lot of enemies in this town."

Hunter rubbed his hand over his face as stress pulsed through his body. Jenna gave him a stern look.

"Lay low, but don't leave town."

Angie's leg tapped nervously as she sat in a wicker chair by her bedroom window. She was trying to get her mind off of her sisters, Courtney and Tiffany, but she was not having much in terms of luck. Although twenty years had passed since Tiffany's death, it felt like no time at all. The same dark eerie mood that existed then still roamed free and unchecked. The sickness loomed over Elkhart and threatened to pollute Angie's mind. She wanted to rest but every time she closed her eyes, she saw Courtney's face. Angie continued to stare out the window as her memories consumed her thoughts.

Natalie Piedmonte opened the front door of 25 Caribou Road as she eyed the rain with irritation. She pulled her hood over her head as she waited for her brother on the porch. Natalie couldn't seem to shake the unsettling feeling that she was being watched. She stared down Caribou Road, but it was eerily quiet. She could hear nothing but the sound of the rain pounding hard on the roof. The front door opened behind Natalie as Cole emerged from the house with a tired look on his face. He locked the front door with a swift turn of his key.

"Ready to go?" asked Cole.

Natalie nodded as she continued to stare nervously around her. Natalie followed her brother to his Jeep. As Cole unlocked the vehicle something caught Natalie's attention. There was a silhouette in the second-floor window of the O'Mara house. Angie, who was looking out her bedroom window with a nervous expression on her face, appeared to be staring right at Natalie. Cole noticed his sister staring up at the window.

"What's wrong?" he asked with a perplexed look on his face.

"That woman gives me the creeps."

Cole looked up at the window as Angie backed out of sight.

"Everyone is on edge, Nat. Her sister was killed. How would you feel if that happened to me?" Cole asked, patting his sister on the shoulder.

"I'd be a wreck, too."

"Right. C'mon. Let's go," urged Cole as Natalie broke her focus on the window.

Angie continued to stare into the distance as the flood of memories came to a sudden stop. Something had distracted her. A girl was staring at her. Natalie Piedmonte from next door was staring at her strangely from outside. The girl stared with a hard gaze as she stood in the pouring rain. A chill ran down Angie's back.

"What a strange, strange girl," Angie commented as she backed away from the window.

A knock at the front door broke Angie from her thoughts. She immediately recognized the voice, but she wasn't in the mood to talk. Especially after everything that had occurred. Then there was the issue of that godforsaken jewelry box. It was a frightening reminder of her dead cousin, and the message he left still induced shivers down her spine. It was a chilling reminder that the insane and the obsessed do not forget who wronged them, no matter how much time has passed.

Roger O'Mara opened the front door for Jenna and led her to the living room where Gwen was still stifling back tears.

"She hasn't moved from that spot. I think she's in shock," said Roger with worry in his voice.

"Of course I am, Roger! Another of our daughters has been murdered!" Gwen screamed through her tears.

Jenna looked at Mrs. O'Mara somberly, truly feeling awful for her. Roger nodded for Jenna to follow him. He led her out to the patio and motioned for her to take a seat.

"Do you have any leads yet?" asked Roger with a glimmer of hope in his voice.

"Some. Mostly dead ends, but we're following all leads. How are you holding up?"

"As well as can be expected," Roger choked.

DiNolfo nodded in understanding.

"Do you have any idea who would have done this to your daughter?"

"I have my suspicions," Roger said as he cleared his throat. "Part of me thinks maybe the same person responsible for Tiffany's death also killed Courtney. But another part of me suspects that boyfriend of hers. Tommy Morrow. That boy has a temper."

"Who do you think is responsible for Tiffany's death?"

"Oh, Bernard Kendricks. Without a doubt. But he's dead now, so he couldn't be involved this time around."

Hearing Bernard's name made Jenna's skin crawl.

"How did you know Bernard?"

"I'm surprised you don't know. Bernard was my wife's cousin. Angie and Bernard were very tightly knit for a while, but then something happened. She became afraid of him. She was absolutely terrified. I couldn't stand the creep."

"I had no idea that Angie even knew Bernard. She never mentioned him before," said Jenna suspiciously.

"She can be very guarded. It's hard to get information from her, sometimes."

"Don't worry. I always get the information I need, one way or another. Thanks for your time, Roger."

Angie shot an agitated look in the mirror as someone knocked loudly on her bedroom door.

"Go away! Please," Angie pleaded.

"Angie, it's Sergeant DiNolfo. Open up."

Oh, it's Sergeant, is it? She must feel so important. Trying to act like you've known me for the last twenty years!

Against her greatest wishes, Angie opened the door. Jenna noticed that Angie hadn't masked her disdain at her presence outside her door.

"Hi again," said Angie in a bored tone. "Can you please respect my privacy? My sister just died."

"Hi there, Angie. I had some follow-up questions I wanted to ask you."

"Come in. I have some of my own."

This surprised DiNolfo.

"Oh?"

"Something important of mine has gone missing."

"Okay, what is the item?"

"It's an antique jewelry box."

"Did it have anything of value inside?"

"No, but the box itself has value."

"Does the box have any special markings or designs?"

"It's an antique. It is a metal jewelry box with Victorian filigree work on top of the box. There are initials inscribed on the lid. BEK."

BEK. Bernard Ellis Kendricks, perhaps?

Jenna took note with how pained Angie's description of the box sounded. She must *really* want it back. It sounded as if it was an item of great importance.

"Okay, we'll file a police report. Do you know who might have taken it?"

"No, but it could have been anyone at that party."

DiNolfo scrawled in her notebook as Angie talked.

"Let's talk about Courtney for a moment," said DiNolfo. She watched as Angie's eyes grew heavier.

"Who do you think would have had reason to kill your sister?"

"I don't know. She was a sweet girl. I mean, don't get me wrong, Tiffany had her moments and she had made enemies, but Courtney was a sweet girl and she seemed to have a lot of friends. I don't know of anyone that disliked Courtney, whereas ninety percent of our senior class was jealous of Tiffany."

Jenna sat quietly for a moment as the gears in her head turned round and round. No, Tiffany wasn't a sweet girl, but she also didn't deserve to die. Neither did Courtney. Jenna got the impression that Angie knew more than she was leading on to.

"Can I ask you a question?" Angie asked with a strange look in her eyes.

"Of course," said Jenna as she looked up at Angie.

"How sure are you that Bernard Kendricks is dead?" asked Angie in a worried voice.

Her question made Jenna chuckle a little bit. Not out of humor but out of surprise.

"Interesting question. I'm positive that Bernard Kendricks is dead."

"One hundred percent positive?" asked Angie nervously.

"Considering that I was one of the people that helped scrub his brain matter off the wall? I'd say yes."

Angie winced at the mental picture.

"Why do you ask?"

"Because I'm pretty sure that he killed Tiffany, and Courtney's death is too similar to be an accident. The box, the one that is missing. My mother found it in Kendricks's home after he died. It was addressed to me at my home in Seattle, and this was inside."

Angie passed the photograph of her and Tiffany to Jenna.

"Turn it over."

Jenna's eyebrows rose as she read Kendricks's neatly scrawled threat on the back.

"The package was postmarked October 7, 1997, but it was never mailed."

"May I have this?" asked Jenna as she held up the photograph. Her curiosity was piqued.

Angie nodded in agreement.

"Thank you. I'll be in touch. Stick around."

DiNolfo stormed through the front door of the Elkhart Police Station with a determined look on her face. She walked fast across the linoleum floor, earning nervous glances from Liam and Officer Rutledge. She quickly ran down the stairs to the file room. The door unlocked loudly and before it could bang shut, Sergeant DiNolfo had re-emerged with Tiffany O'Mara's thick case file. She ran up the steps, two-by-two, and approached Liam's desk. Without warning, she slammed the case file onto Liam's desk as he looked at her for further instruction.

"Scour this file. Our answers are inside."

CHAPTER 14

June 19, 2000
O'Mara Residence
9:52 PM

GWEN O'MARA SAT ON THE COUCH surrounded by her daughters with a photo album on her lap. Roger sat adjacent from her with his hands folded across his lap, peering down over his glasses with a serious set of downcast eyes. Angie sat beside her mother, resting her hand on her back as Gwen narrated the story of their lives. Trixie sat at her mother's feet listening to the stories but not daring to look up in fear that her father would see the tears streaming down her face. Ally sat on the opposite side of Gwen, her fingers clutching Gwen's nightgown. Misty-Lee stared darkly out the front window with her son Cory in her clutches. She had taken the news worst of all.

Gwen had stopped her sobbing. She was dealing with the death of Courtney the only way she knew how. She took solace in their time together. With the photo album on her lap, she pointed to each picture that stirred a memory within her.

"Oh, Angie, do you remember this one?" Gwen asked, pointing to a photograph of her that was taken in the summer of 1974. A pale green sundress fell over her scraped knees.

Ally laughed at the photograph. "Angie, you look like a perfect lady until you see your knees and your grubby finger nails."

Roger smiled. "Angela was of the adventurous variety. Always digging in the dirt or climbing a tree. Tiffany was the princess; as girly as they come."

Gwen smiled at the memory.

"Oh, look," she continued, "here is Angela, Tiffany and Misty-Lee together playing jump rope in the garden." Misty-Lee was weaving her legs through the ropes as Angie and Tiffany taught her how to play Double Dutch.

Gwen's manicured nails continued turning page after page, telling the younger girls of the memories that surfaced, reminding her elder daughters of the life they used to lead. Angie could feel the mounting pain with each turn of the page. Finally, Gwen turned the page to a photograph that made her hand shake. The photograph showed Angie holding baby Courtney just a few hours after being born. Gwen touched the photograph, tracing the line of Courtney's white baby blanket as a single tear dropped onto the page. With a heavy gasp, Gwen fell back against the couch cushion as her emotions overwhelmed her.

"Come on, guys. Let's give Mom some space," said Angie as she took the book from Gwen's grasp and returned it to the bookshelf in the corner. Leaving Gwen with Roger, Angie slowly climbed the steps as her own emotions came unhinged. She was able to control her heaving sobs until she was safely behind her bedroom door.

A nightmare stirred Angie from a deep sleep. She had cried herself to sleep, the emotions from their trek down memory lane too much for her in the wake of her sister's death, and now Bernard Kendricks's face had awoken her. Angie opened her eyes with a deep-seated fear shining out from her irises. Her skin was clammy, her nerves shot and her anxiety had reached an all-time high. Sitting up in her bed, she looked at the time. 12:52 a.m. Her hands shook as she walked to the bathroom to splash cool water against her face. Angie couldn't help but wonder, would she be next?

"I need fresh air," Angie said as she pulled on a t-shirt and a pair of jeans. She knew a killer was on the loose, but she felt as if she were suffocating in the dense fog of the house. Bolting down the front steps, she grabbed the car keys and stepped out into the night.

Hunter couldn't sleep. He was on edge, unsure of who to trust. He wasn't sure who had been in his trailer earlier that day, but whoever it was, they were clearly trying to set him up. It was shortly after one in the morning and sleep was evading him. He lay sprawled on his couch as he listened intently, trying to hear if anyone was stalking outside the trailer. The crunch of gravel caused Hunter to sit up. He grabbed his baseball bat that sat next to the sliding glass door and he hid waiting to see who it was. Whoever it was, was brave enough to step right up on his porch and knock on the glass window. Knock. Clearly this was no intruder.

"Hunter?" Angie called from the other side. "Please open up."

Hunter let out a breath and dropped the bat, hurrying to unlock the door and let her in.

"What the hell are you doing out? That son of a bitch is still out there!" Hunter said, pulling Angie in quickly.

"I can't sleep. The air in that house. The grief. I feel like it is swallowing me whole. I needed to see you."

"Well, come in. I heard what happened."

"It's like 1980 all over again."

CHAPTER 15

June 19, 2000
Steeplechase Academy
Elkhart, PA
9:30 A.M.

BLAKE MORROW SLUMPED OVER HIS DESK in Chemistry 201 as he felt a swift kick to his leg.

"Ow! What was that for?"

He looked to his left and caught a nasty glare from his sister, Tristan.

"Pay attention! Finals start tomorrow!" Tristan whispered loudly.

"I got this, Tris. Relax!" assured Blake.

"I got this, too," said Shane with a sly smile. "I've got my chemistry buddy to rely on." Shane motioned towards Tristan.

"Oh, no. I'll sit in the hallway."

"Then I'll have to follow you, since Jack said I have to keep an eye on you at all times," said Cole playfully.

"What are you, his Golden Retriever? Tristan ran off, better bring her back? Someone might steal her? I'm fine!" Tristan insisted.

"He's just worried. Frankly, I am, too," Cole mentioned.

Tristan rolled her eyes.

These men worry too stinking much.

"Are you going to follow me to the bathroom, too?" asked Tristan as she tried not to laugh.

Cole's face turned a vibrant shade of red.

Jack was taking this entirely too far in Tristan's opinion. She was perfectly capable of getting to work, school and maneuvering through the hallways to her next class without a male chaperone.

"Cheer up. At least he trusts Cole now. He trusts him more than he trusts any of us. He didn't bother asking any of us to follow you around."

"That's because you *already* follow me everywhere I go."

Shane shook his head up and down. "That is true."

"You keep us out of trouble," quipped Blake.

Tristan rolled her eyes as she thought about it. Jack wasn't thrilled that Tommy and Tristan were even going to school, but when Tristan reminded him that they needed to pass finals to graduate, Jack relented. He was so worried that whoever had come after Courtney would get Tristan next. Jack had all the kids ride in Cole's Jeep, and told him that if there was any trouble to call him.

The man is becoming more overbearing with each passing day. Maybe I should've selected a west coast school, Tristan thought.

Suddenly, the school bell rang and everyone put their books in their bags. When they got into the hall, Shane complained, "Is it lunch time yet?"

"No. We have that ridiculous assembly now," explained Tristan.

"Not the 'Don't do drugs' one?" complained Blake.

"Yup."

Cole groaned in response. No one looked forward to this assembly.

"Apparently there is a guest speaker this year."

The group approached the auditorium where a poster-sized picture of Hunter McCord was displayed on a tri-fold stand. Hunter was smiling broadly with his arms spread wide. Under the picture, the words "Hugs Not Drugs" were written in big bold letters, causing Tommy to grit his teeth. Many of the students at Steeplechase knew that McCord was an active drug dealer and not someone you wanted to mess around with. Somehow, he had fooled the faculty at Steeplechase, though. As part of his community service requirement, McCord gave inspirational anti-drug speeches to local high schools about the dangers of drug use. Tommy refrained from knocking over the poster as they took their seats in the back of the auditorium.

"I find it really hard to believe that they don't know that he's still dealing," Tommy complained.

"Apparently, Jenna's had her eye on him, she just hasn't been able to pin anything on him yet," Cole admitted.

"So, he can just go about doing this until he's caught?"

"I guess."

"This baffles me. Vice Principal Irwin seriously does have rocks in her head," complained Tristan.

"Does this really surprise you? This school hired a complete psycho for an English teacher, and *this* surprises you?" exclaimed Shane in utter disgust.

"True."

Joe opened the doors of Monte's Café after two days of being closed due to the investigation. DiNolfo had cleared it as a crime scene and gave Joe the go-ahead to re-open to the public. Joe woke up early and plugged in his power washer to clean the red stain from his cement walkway. He then brought out a bouquet of daisies and placed them where he found Courtney's body, just two days ago. A small memorial for a life that was cut short.

Joe put his roadside sign out in clear view of the road letting patrons know that all entrees were fifty percent off today in an effort to ramp up business. Only time would tell if this terrible tragedy would silence the life of Monte's, too.

The audience clapped as Hunter McCord walked proudly up the center aisle. He was dressed sharply in a black suit with silk royal blue lapels. He spoke loudly into his microphone as the crowd came alive. Music played from the speakers and everyone rose to their feet. Everyone except Cole, Tristan, Tommy, Blake and Shane. Tommy and Shane booed loudly from the back, but stopped when Tristan elbowed them both.

"Good mornin', everybody! My name is Hunter McCord and I've got a message for you! Hugs not Drugs!"

Tommy nearly jumped from his chair in anger. Cole stretched his long arm across his friend to prevent him from getting in even more trouble.

Hunter continued, "Everybody do me a favor! Face the person next to you and give them a hug!"

Cole and Tristan played along, and hugged each other happily. Shane went to give Tommy a bear hug, but was met with a look that said, "Go ahead. I dare you."

Tommy bluntly said, "Touch me and I'll give you a brain duster."

Shane shrugged his shoulders and instead hugged Blake, lifting his scrawny cousin off of his feet.

"Hugs not drugs," said Cole. "What are we, five?"

"It's better than last year's theme, I guess. Don't you remember 'Drugs Are For Thugs'? When Vice Principal Irwin dressed up as a gang member? That was *way* worse."

"At least that was funny. This is just insulting."

Tristan took her eyes from her boyfriend and glanced nervously at Tommy. As the presentation continued, he glared at Hunter through his seething rage. Like a ticking time bomb, Tommy was going to go off. It was just a matter of time.

Joe flipped the sign in the front door of Monte's Café from closed to open. He didn't know if his regulars would come and he felt bad even worrying about it. Roger and Gwen O'Mara had lost a daughter, and he was worrying about sales. He had to shrug it off, though. He had a business to run. Around ten a.m., many of Joe's regulars started to crowd the dining room.

"Morning, Joe!" called Reverend Briggs from the front door as a waitress showed him to his usual seat.

"Good morning, Reverend," replied Joe. He was surprised how, despite what had just occurred over the weekend, his regular customers were still packing into the dining room. Committing to take his mind off of his worries, Joe got to work in the kitchen and promised to keep Courtney O'Mara off his mind. No matter how busy he was though, he couldn't help but worry about Natalie and Tristan's safety.

Should I tell them to stay away until this is all settled? Joe thought.

Joe wanted nothing more than for Tristan and Natalie to go to school and go straight back to Jack, away from the dark cloud that now hung over Mountain Road. He would feel better once the creep responsible was behind bars. But until then, what could he do? Joe's thoughts continued throughout the day, unrelenting and nagging. At least at the restaurant, the girls were under his close, watchful eye. But what about when they left? That is when Joe remembered that Jack was having Tristan and Natalie escorted just about everywhere. Though most people thought Jack's actions were overbearing, he was cautious for good reason. He had lost Tristan once. Both Jack and Joe knew what it was like to lose someone due to another's careless actions. They would never forgive themselves if it happened again.

Hunter managed to calm the crowd down and he now paced the front of the auditorium with a serious look on his face. The sleeves of his dress shirt were rolled up, and he held his microphone just a few inches from his face.

"Let's get serious for a moment. I went down a dark and dangerous path. I nearly didn't return. That is why I wanted to talk to you all and to warn you. Don't take the path I took. Drugs will lead you to the devil's door. They take your soul and leave you an empty shell that will do anything and everything to get your fix. Don't do what I did. All my family and friends turned against me. I was lying, stealing, dealing, and eventually flatlining. I nearly died. I sometimes think that the only reason I'm still alive is because God gave me another chance to warn all of you."

Cole leaned to Tristan who was eyeing Hunter with a look of total disbelief. "Is this guy for real? I feel like I'm watching a televangelist."

Hunter continued, "I now live a straight-edge life. No drinking, no smoking, and no drugs. Do you know why? Because I'm worth it. I deserve a chance to be the best I can be, and you do too!"

Suddenly, a voice rang out over all the rest.

"You're full of shit, McCord!"

Tristan's eyes went wide as she looked over at Tommy who had stood up from his seat. His face was red and he was casting a vicious glare at Hunter McCord. Cole and Shane were trying to hold him in place. All eyes were on Tommy.

"You've always been a scum bag and you always will be!" Tommy shouted over the crowd at Hunter.

"Let him go," Tristan urged.

As soon as Shane and Cole let go of Tommy's arms, he bolted. At first Cole thought he was going to go rip McCord off the stage, but instead he barged out the auditorium side door. He sat on the back steps of the school, waiting for the ridiculous spectacle to end. It took every ounce of strength in his body not to attack McCord right on the stage in front of everyone. The only thing stopping him was the fear of being expelled just days before graduation.

Tristan joined Tommy on the steps, warning the others to stay. Cole, Shane and Blake remained in the auditorium as Tristan requested. Cole refrained from accompanying her this time. He knew the one person who could calm down Tommy was Tristan, and he didn't want to irritate him further.

Hunter continued, "As that guy just showed, drugs can give you a bad reputation and can cause you to burn a lot of bridges. Don't lose friends like me. Make the right choices with a clean, straight-edged life."

"If he's straight-edge, I'm the damn Pope," declared Shane to Blake and Cole.

"Pope Kilpatrick. I like it," said Blake with a laugh.

"You are four days from graduation. Seriously?" complained Tristan as her brother gave her a testy glare.

"I'm sorry, I cannot stomach that!"

"Neither can I."

"Then why didn't you say anything?"

"Because he's a violent drug dealer, and I don't want him coming after me!" exclaimed Tristan reasonably.

"Let him try to come after me. Especially after what he did to Courtney."

"You don't know that."

"I have a good hunch."

Roger O'Mara walked through the entrance of Monte's Café with a strained look on his face. He needed to get out of the house, even if it was just for an hour. Gwen had been sobbing on the couch all night long, Ally and Trixie hadn't left their rooms, saying it was all just too much for them. He had let them stay home so that they did not have to face questions or prying eyes at school. Misty-Lee had slept at her boyfriend's house last night. She wailed to Roger saying, "It's just like before, Dad! I can't do this again!" Roger just needed a break from the stale depressive state that had taken over his house. Joe saw Roger as he walked in and his guilt immediately kicked in. Joe felt so bad for the guy but his guilt was immediately stifled when Roger gave him a faint smile.

"I'm glad to see that you're back open," said Roger as he extended his hand to Joe. Joe shook it and returned the smile.

"Please let me know what I can do to help," offered Joe.

"Actually, you could post one of these for me," said Roger as he handed a poster to Joe.

"I'm offering a two-thousand-dollar reward for anyone that has information that leads to the apprehension of the person responsible."

"Of course. I'll post it. Leave a stack on the counter too, and I'll make sure the customers see it."

CHAPTER 16

June 19, 2000
Morrow Manor
Fox Hollow, PA
3:10 P.M.

FRANK SAT AT THE KITCHEN TABLE reading the *Elkhart Bugle* when he began to growl from behind the pages. Jack looked up at his brother-in-law with a glare.

"What now?"

"You haven't read the paper today, have you?"

"No, I'm trying to avoid it."

"You're gonna want to read it today," Frank said as he tossed the paper to Jack.

On the front page, in big bold letters, the title of the article read, "Three Suspects Revealed in Elkhart Murder."

In the center of the page, Tommy Morrow, Jesse Trafford and Hunter McCord's photographs took precedence.

"Goddamn it!"

Sergeant DiNolfo waited for Tommy outside of Steeplechase Academy's main gates when the 3:09 p.m. bell rang. His stomach dropped when he saw her standing just outside the wrought-iron gate with her patrol car in the background. He couldn't read the look on her face, but he knew what this was about. It was his turn to tell her what he knew about Courtney's murder. Without struggle, Tommy climbed into the back of DiNolfo's patrol car as Tristan and Cole watched with deep-rooted worry.

DiNolfo charged into the interrogation room as she slammed the door behind her. Tommy had never seen her so angry before. Avoiding eye contact, she grabbed a metal folding chair and sat less than a foot away from Tommy as she shook her head from side to side in disgust. Finally, she looked Tommy dead in his eyes and he immediately wished that she hadn't. Her dark eyes were an abyss, bereft of emotion. Her usual calm was removed. There was no story behind her eyes, no sense of familiarity. DiNolfo was all business and Tommy would not find a friend in her today.

He shuddered as he thought, *Holy crap.*

"Tommy, this is serious shit!" DiNolfo yelled as the atmosphere in the room became bleaker by the second.

"I didn't do it," Tommy insisted, defending himself.

"This doesn't look good *at all*! Your clothes were found at the scene of the crime. A size eleven footprint that matches a pair of boots that you own were found in the mud next to the body. Not to mention reports of domestic disputes just hours before the murder," protested DiNolfo as her tone became increasingly belligerent.

"I didn't do it and you know it!" insisted Tommy.

"At this point, all I know is that much of the evidence we've bagged up points to you," said DiNolfo very matter-of-factly.

"I didn't kill my girlfriend!" yelled Tommy, his patience reaching the breaking point.

DiNolfo picked her chair up, swiftly turned it around and squatted down, aggressively getting as close to Tommy Morrow as she possibly could.

In a cool voice, DiNolfo continued, "Where were you between the hours of five and seven a.m. on June the seventeenth?"

"Asleep," Tommy quickly replied.

"Where?" DiNolfo demanded.

"In my sister's room. In my father's house. You know. Morrow Manor."

"Can anyone confirm your whereabouts between the hours of two a.m. and eight a.m. on June seventeenth?"

"Sure. Everyone can confirm because they heard me arguing on the phone with Courtney until about three a.m., and then they all saw me at breakfast."

"Who is everyone?"

"Uncle Frank cursed me out around ten of two in the morning because I was on the phone in Tristan's room arguing with Courtney."

"What did he say?"

"Get the eff off of the bloody telephone and get yer arse out of your sister's room so she can sleep. The whole feckin' house can hear you! Some of us have work in the mornin'!"

"Nice impersonation," said DiNolfo as she wrote down his comment word for word.

"Thanks."

"Who else saw you?"

"Tristan. She kicked me off the phone at one point because she had to call Cole to tell him something she forgot. Then I got back on the phone with Courtney. Then Tristan saw me around seven a.m. at breakfast. Uhh ..." Tommy said, trying to think of who else saw him at the house. He continued, "Blake and Shane saw me come into the bedroom last night."

"Why were you arguing with Courtney?"

"It's stupid, really ... When you look back."

"I have to know."

Tommy let out a heavy sigh. In retrospect, he would have handled their relationship much differently if he would have known what was going to happen to her.

"I saw her flirting at the bar with Hunter McCord at her sister's graduation party. He had his hand on her waist and she was laughing. I told her I wanted to break up. She didn't want to hear it."

"So you were jealous?"

"Of course. What guy wouldn't be?"

DiNolfo continued to scribble into her notebook as a charged look took over her face.

"So jealous that you'd want her dead?" asked DiNolfo with a bite to her voice.

"No!" Tommy yelled, getting angrier by the second. "And you're way out of line! I have five people who can account for my whereabouts. You can't move in that house without running into someone! They can all vouch for me."

DiNolfo nodded. *Well played, Tommy.* She hated having to do this to him but it was part of her job. While she had doubts all along about the role Tommy played, she had to rule him out completely.

"Did you love her?" asked DiNolfo, hoping to get a reaction from Tommy.

She watched and waited as emotion took over Tommy's face. He felt horrible for what he was about to say.

"Come on, Tommy. Cat got your tongue? Did you love Courtney O'Mara or not?" DiNolfo demanded to know.

Tommy sighed as tears pooled in his eyes.

"No. I didn't love her!" Tommy said as he tried to read DiNolfo's reaction. When he couldn't discern her reaction, he continued talking frantically. "But I didn't hate her either! I liked her a lot. She could be a lot of fun, when she wasn't complaining or flirting with other guys. But no, it wasn't love."

"Fair enough," DiNolfo said as her demeanor seemed to calm. "I've already confirmed your whereabouts with your family. I was out at Morrow Manor this morning. Your story checks out. What I need to determine is how the hell your clothes wound up in the middle of Mountain Road and how a footprint that matches your boot found itself at the scene of a murder crime!" explained DiNolfo heatedly.

"First off," said Tommy, becoming irate, "those boots are sold over at Quiver's. It could've been anyone."

DiNolfo raised an eyebrow. Tommy Morrow wasn't an easy kid to trick. Jack definitely didn't raise any fools.

"We actually looked into that. We could determine by the print that the shoes were fairly new. Apparently, Quiver's sold three pairs of size eleven Expedition-style hiking boots in the past sixty days. One pair belonged to you; the others belong to Jesse Trafford and Hunter McCord. All three of you are suspected of murder."

Tommy was outraged. "What? I didn't do anything wrong!"

DiNolfo eyed Tommy speculatively, her resolve not waning an ounce. "Then, Tommy, how'd your clothes and boot prints end up on Mountain Road just feet from your girlfriend's dead body?" DiNolfo demanded to know.

"Those weren't even the clothes that I was wearing last night! Ask Cole. Mr. Piedmonte saw me, too! I was wearing a blue button-down shirt, black slacks, and a pair of nice lace-up shoes."

DiNolfo was scribbling fast and furiously into her notebook.

"The clothes you found. I had taken them off after work at Courtney's house. Obviously, I couldn't go to her sister's party wearing dirty work clothes. I got changed at Courtney's house and set the clothes on her windowsill; the boots were on the floor. Anybody who was in the house that night could have taken them."

DiNolfo looked utterly perplexed. She knew a liar when she saw one, and while the story was outlandish, she knew right then and there, Tommy Morrow was telling the truth.

"Describe the clothes you left at Courtney's house."

"A black Steelers hoodie, a pair of old jeans, a brown belt, a black t-shirt and a pair of boots."

"What size were those boots?"

"Size eleven."

"Who could have accessed Courtney's room?"

"Anyone that lived there, I guess. But they also had a bunch of people going in and out that night, too."

DiNolfo continued writing in her leather notebook. Finally she stopped and put her pen down. She looked at Tommy and he could tell that her mood was calming.

"Do you have any idea who would have wanted to hurt Courtney?"

Tommy slowed as his eyes burned with tears.

"It sure as hell wasn't me. I think it was McCord."

Suddenly, Tommy could hear raised voices from the next room—beyond the two-way mirror. It continued. He could almost swear it was Adam. The commotion was followed by an urgent knock on the interrogation room door. Adam poked his head in; his face was bright red and he looked like he had been running.

"We need you."

"I'm just about to wrap this up."

"No, now ... On scene at Healer's Park. There's been another murder," said

Adam urgently.

The look on DiNolfo's face morphed from anger to murderous rage. She brought her fist down hard on the table, causing Tommy to jump.

"Dammit!" she screamed. "Who is it?"

Adam waited with controlled patience at the door as she regained her composure.

Adam continued, "Liam and I found her in Healer's Park. The body has been positively ID'd as April Dearing."

DiNolfo snapped her notebook shut as she rose from her chair.

She eyed Tommy seriously and said, "Tommy, you have what I like to call an iron-clad alibi. Thomas Morrow, you are hereby released as a suspect in the murder investigation of Courtney O'Mara. You're free to go. Stay out of trouble!" she said with urgency and warning laced in her voice.

A moment later, DiNolfo was gone, following Adam out to his patrol car.

When Adam returned to the murder scene in Healer's Park, he felt an awful sense of déjà vu creep over him. If he didn't know better, he'd think he was looking at the same crime scene that he encountered outside of Monte's Café just days prior. The tire tracks. The bullet wound to the head. The tarp. Only this time, instead of random objects being strewn about, there were business cards thrown on the victim's body. The first belonged to Trafford's Auto Body. The next belonged to Hunter McCord – Public Speaker. The third belonged to Morrow's Horse Farm.

Someone seemed intent upon framing the suspects. But the question was, who?

"Tommy! Tommy! Why'd you do it?" yelled J.J. Penn, news reporter for the *Elkhart Bugle*, as Tommy exited the double doors of the Elkhart Police Department. Danville News was at it again, too. They had the pathway blocked with cameras and news vans lined the curb. Frank grabbed Tommy by his shoulder and led him through the crowd.

"Don't say a word, boy," warned Frank.

Even though Tommy was released as a witness, the media would use everything he said against him and with someone with as hot of a temper as Tommy, it was better just to stay quiet. Frank opened the passenger-side door to his pick-up truck, ducked Tommy's head inside and slammed the door behind him. As Frank left his side, reporters drew closer to his window, continuing to ask questions. Frank jumped in and hit the gas, causing smoke to kick up and gag the reporters. As the aggressive reporters coughed and heaved from the dust, Frank barreled up Mountain Road with Tommy in tow.

CHAPTER 17

June 19, 2000
Lake House
Morrow Manor
Fox Hollow, PA
7:00 P.M.

LIAM MORROW STORMED INTO THE LAKE HOUSE at Morrow Manor as anger radiated from his pores. It was bad enough that they had one young woman dead, but now they have another who had died in a nearly identical fashion. The lake house, which was once inhabited by Angus and Moira, now served as Adam and Liam's bachelor pad. In light of recent events, the tiny house that overlooked Croft Lake also acted as home base for all things related to the murders of Courtney O'Mara and April Dearing, and bringing those responsible to justice. Liam dropped Tiffany O'Mara's case file down on the kitchen table as he hurried to get out of his uniform. He needed a night off in the worst possible way. They hadn't had a proper night of sleep since Friday night, but he knew he had to get through the case file to get some answers. Two women had already been brutally murdered. They had to hurry before any more innocent blood was shed. Adam Morrow trudged up the front steps and slammed the door behind them.

"This is a fine, deranged mess we're in!" yelled Adam across the living room.

Liam nodded in agreement as he pulled a gray t-shirt over his head.

"If you ever say that you're bored again, I'll throw you in the lake," quipped Adam as he gave his brother a heated glare.

It was only four days since Liam had uttered those words, but it felt like an eternity to them. Liam settled onto the couch as he opened the file labeled Tiffany O'Mara. He didn't know what he would find inside, but DiNolfo was pretty sure that they would find some answers. Liam opened the file with a steady hand as he prepared himself for what he might find. On top of the large file lay a crime scene report that detailed when and where Tiffany was found, how she was suspected to have died, and what objects were present at the scene of the murder. Attached to the report with a rusty paperclip was a graphic photo of the deceased. Tiffany's strawberry blonde hair was matted and crimson from the gunshot wound to the side of her head. Gory chunks of blood, brain matter, wounded flesh and tissue were exposed and already decomposing due to the warm summer heat. Her green eyes peered out with a lost stare and her neck was savagely bruised and broken. Liam passed the photograph to Adam, who had just joined him on the couch. A chill coursed through Adam's veins as he looked at the tragic photograph. The similarities of the two sisters and the way they died did not escape him.

"Now I see why DiNolfo pulled the file. What does the dossier say?"

Tiffany O'Mara, age eighteen, was found dead on June 20, 1980 at 7:22 in the morning in the Forest of York. The body was discovered by her sister, Angela O'Mara, who said that the body was laid on a tarp at the base of what locals call, "The Bone Tree." Upon examination, the victim suffered a gunshot wound to the side of the head which obliterated a portion of the girl's face. The victim's neck showed evidence that she was strangled as well. Because the victim was on a tarp, it is not believed that she was killed in the Forest of York, but in a different location. Evidence found at the scene includes a size eleven hiking boot, two daggers with wooden hilts, an assortment of bird feathers and an antique box with the initials BEK inscribed into the metal. Deputies Amos Cope and Earl Buckley surveyed the area, but incidentally, no one heard or saw anything of concern. Officers will follow-up with the family this afternoon.

"You've got to be kidding me!" yelled Adam as soon as he heard the names Cope and Buckley. "If they were involved, you know nothing was done to find the culprit."

Liam sighed heavily. There was only one thing to be done.

"Get dressed."

"Where are we going?"

"To Pennington."

It was around ten thirty when Liam and Adam reached the Philadelphia city limits. The long brick exterior of Pennington Prison was foreboding in the dim glow of the street lights. As the pair walked through the front door, the building looked like it was about to swallow them whole.

Adam nearly didn't recognize Amos Cope as he walked towards him from the other side of the booth. Though he still had a face only a mother could love, his scrawny body had bulked up a bit from hitting the weights. Amos smiled at Adam as if he was his long lost best friend.

"Adam! What brings you here?" exclaimed Amos, looking truly excited to see a familiar face. Adam was perplexed.

"Why do you look so happy to see me?"

"You're my pal!"

"You covered up my mother's death. We are not friends," said Adam glaringly.

Liam pushed Adam aside.

"You're gonna ruin any chance we have in getting any information from him. Shut up!" barked Liam with his hand covering the phone.

Liam sat down on the stool in front of the phone and put on his most charming smile.

"Amos!" he said in a cool voice.

"Liam, it's great to see you!" said Amos excitedly.

Either he is really bored in prison or the inmates are really awful. Either way, it serves him right, thought Liam.

"Buddy, listen. I was wondering if you could help me out with something."

"Oh, anything you want kid. What do you need?" asked Amos in a casual voice as if Liam was simply asking for a cup of coffee.

"Do you remember Tiffany O'Mara?" Liam asked as a look of seriousness glinted from his eye.

Liam noticed that the warmth had vanished in Amos's eyes. He let out a deep breath.

"Boy, do I ever. That case was a nightmare."

"Please tell me this isn't one of the cases you flubbed."

"No, this is actually the case where we got an idea of just how sick Kendricks was."

Liam lifted his chin and tightened his jaw at the sound of the name.

"Tell me what I need to know."

Amos nodded as he prepared to speak.

"Fifteen minutes!" a prison guard yelled behind them.

"I'll try to hurry ..."

Liam nodded, becoming impatient.

"Earl and I answered a call at the O'Mara residence on Caribou Road. Gwen O'Mara was frantic with worry because her daughter Tiffany hadn't come home the night before," Amos said as a serious look overtook his face.

"While we were talking to Gwen and her husband, their one kid came running in ... Angie. She was a hysterical mess, crying, falling all over the place. She said she found Tiffany dead in the Forest. She said it had to be him! It had to be him!" continued Amos.

"Roger and I tried to get more information out of Angie, while Earl went to search the forest for a body. Let me tell you, Angie was as white as a ghost. She looked like she had ran into the devil himself. Her eyes were all wild and crazy-like. I ain't ever seen anybody look so scared in my life."

Liam could tell that the worst was still to come, because Amos had a deeply troubled look on his face.

"Then, all of a sudden, she just got quiet. She looked at me with an expression that was more dead than alive, and said, 'It was Bernard. And he's coming after me next.' Suddenly, the girl passed out on the floor. I didn't know what to make of it."

Liam and Adam continued to watch Amos as he spoke. He wasn't making this up. He couldn't have. This was beyond his repertoire.

"So we continued investigating. We interviewed Tiffany's boyfriend, Ethan Quiver, but he had no information whatsoever. We tried banging on Kendricks's door, but no one was home. We even tried his mother's house, but she wasn't even answering. Then that night, Angie disappeared."

"Disappeared?" asked Liam quizzically.

"Yeah. Her mother was so afraid that what happened to Tiffany would happen to Angie, too."

"So what happened?" Liam pressed.

"Turns out Angie just left. Apparently she was so distraught over Tiffany that she couldn't bear to be in Elkhart anymore."

"No one thought it was suspicious that she would flee town on the day her sister turned up dead?"

"No. You should've saw this girl. She was shaking like a leaf. I've never seen anybody so scared in my entire life."

"What about Kendricks? What happened?"

"It turned out that Kendricks was out of town that week with his mother. They were vacationing in Maine. He showed me the itinerary and everything. There should be a copy of it in the case file."

Adam sifted through the paperwork in the file and sure enough, there it was: A trip for six days and five nights in Maine at the Bar Harbor Lobsterman's Inn.

"He was livid when he found out what the girl accused him of. He called her a liar and a snake. Roger O'Mara came after Kendricks accusing him of chasing off his daughter."

"Crazy."

"He was nuts. What do you expect?"

"Is there anything else I should know?"

"Let's see ... Yeah. The suspects."

"Kendricks wasn't the only one?"

"Oh, no ... Ethan Quiver was suspected ... Hunter McCord, too. But at the end of the day, we were never able to pin her death on anyone. There simply wasn't enough evidence."

"Time's up!" yelled the guard. "All prisoners line up against the wall!"

"Thanks for talking to us, Amos," said Liam honestly.

As a guard slapped a set of cuffs around his wrists, Amos yelled out skeptically, "The secret lives under the city!"

As the pair walked out of Pennington Prison and into the warm night air, Liam asked the obvious question, "So who do you think did it?"

Adam didn't reply. He was too deep in thought.

Liam continued, "I think McCord has something to do with this. He wanted it to look like it was Kendricks. But I think he is the only suspect capable of committing this sort of violence. Trafford's got a record, but he's a chicken. What do you think?" Liam asked again.

"I think it's someone completely off our radar. Someone who knows how to cover their tracks very well."

"So we heard Amos's side of the story. But the question is, do we believe him?"

CHAPTER 18

June 19, 2000
Pennington Prison
Cellblock D
11:45 P.M.

AMOS COPE STARED AT THE CEILING from his top bunk as he scraped his pencil along the chipping paint to mark yet another day holed up in Pennington for his previous misdeeds. His mind kept replaying the conversation he had with Officer Morrow. He had told him what he needed to know, but no more. Should he have told him the entire story? How this story still haunted his dreams at night? How this is the case that broke him and made him afraid to go to work in the morning?

He didn't want to scare Liam, but he did want to make him aware of just how twisted that case was. There was a copycat that went to great lengths to make it look like Bernard Kendricks was to blame, when in reality he was an eight-hour drive away. They checked on the Kendricks household and no one was answering the door. Amos told the truth. They did investigate this case to the best of their ability, but they simply weren't able to track down the killer. Amos wandered deep into the back of his mind, retrieving a memory that he had long tried to store away.

June 21, 1980
27 Caribou Road
Elkhart, PA

"Mrs. O'Mara, please try to calm down," Amos insisted as she sobbed into her hands.

"We are doing everything we can to try to find her."

"What if she winds up dead like her sister?" yelled Gwen O'Mara, now in hysterics.

"Please try to calm down. We are going to continue searching for Angie and the person responsible for this."

"How old is your daughter?" asked Deputy Earl Buckley as he scribbled notes on a steno pad.

"Eighteen. Today is her birthday!" said Gwen as she began to cry again.

&

"Earl!" cried Amos from the base of the Bone Tree. "I found something."

Earl ran towards him down the long path that led deeper into the forest. The sun had already set and they were about to call off the search for the night when Amos saw something of interest. Something that would change the course of the entire investigation.

Amos shone his flash light in the knobby hole of the Bone Tree.

"Get a load of this ..."

Earl gave Amos a perplexed look, but did as he was told. He poked his head into the hole and about sixty feet down there was a light.

"How the hell?"

"It's a hollow tree."

"What's down there?"

"The old mine I reckon."

"What is that down there?"

"Looks like dried blood to me."

Suddenly, Amos and Earl heard a sound that echoed up through the tree and out into the forest. A horrible screeching that pierced their ears. Earl took another look through the hole, but suddenly the light was gone.

"What the–"

But before Earl could finish his sentence, a dark flock of crows flew up the tree and screeched towards them in a violent fury. The sound of ruffling feathers and screeching calls hurt their ears and caused them to flee.

&

Amos and Earl convened at the Bone Tree the next morning, ready to determine what it was that they saw below the tree. Earl knew of an entrance to the mine, just outside the city limits. He wasn't sure if they'd be able to get through since the mine had been shut down since the late '50s, but it was worth a shot. Amos brought the patrol car to a stop outside the Shepard's Grove Fire Department. The old fire department sat on a hill that overlooked the tiny town below. Amos and Earl walked around to the back of the property with a set of backpacks in tow. On the back of the hill, there was a wooden door with a yellow danger sign displayed. Ignoring the warning, Earl pulled on the door hard.

"Let's go."

Amos got out his flashlight and shone it into the dark tunnel. There were dozens of routes they could take. The mine weaved through the underbelly of Elkhart like a den of snakes. The rafters overhead were splintering and appeared to be cracking under the weight of the world above.

"Are you sure this is safe?" asked Amos with worry.

"No, but if you want to catch whoever's responsible, we're going through."

As Earl trudged ahead, Amos reluctantly followed.

After what felt like hours, Amos and Earl finally reached the end of the tunnel. A light shone just a few feet ahead.

We must be directly under the Bone Tree, Amos thought.

The light beamed down into the circular space. The other tunnels that they had encountered previously emptied out into the space like the arteries of a heart. Amos and Earl approached the natural light with care, their eyes open for any clues that waited for them. There in the shadowy mine, Earl and Amos heard someone talking from the ground above.

"I don't recommend crossing me," a male voice said sternly.

Amos looked at Earl and put a finger to his lips.

A female voice replied in a snakelike voice, "I will cross whoever crosses me."

"I taught you what you know. I can undo you," the male voice warned.

"I thought you'd already done that!" said the woman testily.

"You'd love that, wouldn't you?" said the man angrily.

"Not as much as you would," replied the woman with a bite.

"You're messing with things that are over your head!" barked the male voice.

"Thank you for your concern, but I'm fine," quipped the female.

"It wasn't concern," assured the male voice. "I would love nothing more than to see you fall, but you're not taking me with you."

"We'll see," said the female in a lulling voice.

"I'd love nothing more than more than to silence your rambling. Quiet you, like her ... But there are too many eyes on me," said the man warily.

"Scared?" asked the woman with a snarky edge to her voice.

"Please," said the man angrily.

"You are," the woman assured matter-of-factly.

"I take what I want, when I want and I don't need your permission to do it," the man growled.

"The fact that you are here talking to me about it, instead of doing it, proves you wrong."

Amos and Earl exchanged confused glances as they continued to listen. They could hear footsteps across the earth above them. When finally all was quiet again, a terrible scream broke the silence. The man leaned against the Bone Tree as a murderous scream flew above Elkhart. He appeared to be holding himself there, preventing himself from doing something that he would regret. As the last cry echoed from his mouth, he threw something into the cavity of the tree. Amos and Earl watched as the object fell from the light above to the dark, moist ground of the mine. Sitting in the dirt, abandoned and alone was the dark body of a Ruger 9MM.

"Well?" pressed Earl as Amos walked into the Elkhart Police Station.

"You're not going to believe this," insisted Amos as he carried the ballistics report in his hand.

"No match. There were no fingerprints on the gun."

Earl groaned in annoyance.

"I swear I recognize those voices. If only I could pinpoint from where."

"I was able to find out who the gun is registered to, though."

"Who?"

"Kendricks."

June 19, 2000
Angie's Bedroom
27 Caribou Road
Elkhart, PA

Angie remained face down on her bed, not wanting to move, but desperately needing to escape the dark cloud that had taken over the family. Her head was pounding, and her mind kept wandering back to 1980. The memories of Tiffany and Bernard were fighting for control, and desperately begging for her attention.

"Tiffany!" Angie yelled as her blue gown got caught on a bush. She listened as it ripped a good four inches of material from her skirt. She had to keep moving though.

It was so strange, one minute Tiffany was there and the next she was gone. It was like she vanished out of thin air. The man was no longer chasing them. He, too, seemed to have vanished. Suddenly, a scream polluted the night air. It wasn't coming from the bushes where she last saw Tiffany. It seemed to be coming from underneath her.

"Tiffany?" Angie screamed, bewildered and afraid.

Tiffany's screams were inaudible at first. Then suddenly she found the word she was looking for.

"Help!" she cried at an octave higher than Angie's own scream.

"Where is she?" Angie said to herself in complete bewilderment.

Angie looked all around the forest floor but couldn't find her sister anywhere. Suddenly, it occurred to her. They were in the Forest of York. Angie ran to the Bone Tree and looked inside. Sure enough, Tiffany had fallen into the cavity of the tree. She was pacing the mine floor at the bottom, some sixty feet below.

"Tiffany!"

Tiffany's calls for help got louder.

"Hold on, I'm coming for you!"

CHAPTER 19

June 19, 2000
25 Caribou Road
Elkhart, PA
11:15 P.M.

JOE PIEDMONTE'S EYES WEIGHED HEAVILY as he waited for Jenna to finally come home. She had left the house around five this morning and she still had not returned. She was up to her neck in paperwork thanks to the investigation of not just one murdered woman, but two. He wanted to wait for her because they were going to be sleeping up at Morrow Manor for the night, away from the tension and drama of Elkhart. Jenna walked through the door at 11:35 p.m. with a serious look on her face. It was a long time since she witnessed a crime scene that grisly, and she wasn't in the mood to talk about it. Fortunately, Joe wasn't the type to press for details about her day at work. He was much happier not knowing.

Joe's eyes had closed despite his attempts to stay awake. Jenna smiled slightly when she saw him. She took off her uniform and slipped on her favorite sweats. Watching him sleep so peacefully, Jenna didn't want to disturb Joe, but she couldn't resist curling up next to him, at least for a moment. Jenna flopped down on the couch and laid her head against Joe's chest. He was her little bit of stability in her hectic life as police sergeant. After a moment he stirred and smiled, happy to see that she was finally home.

"What time is it?" Joe asked sleepily.

"Late," Jenna replied sounding utterly exhausted.

"We have to head up to Jack's."

"Yeah, that's probably a good idea."

Jenna didn't like the idea of sleeping next door to a murder victim's family during an investigation. In a small town like this, everyone knew where she lived. It put her, Joe and the kids at risk. That is something that she simply would not stand for.

Jenna and Joe arrived at Morrow Manor around 12:30 p.m. Jack was still awake talking to Frank on the front porch when Joe's car pulled up. Both men nodded as the car approached, although they appeared to be deep in conversation.

Jenna noticed and mentioned to Joe, "Is it me, or do they look like they are discussing battle plans?"

"Would that surprise you at all?" Joe asked with a wink.

Jenna groaned. "No, not one bit."

Joe and Jenna got out of the car and were greeted warmly by Jack and Frank.

"Pull up a chair," Jack suggested, pointing to two rocking chairs that rested on the opposite side of the porch.

"I will in a second, I'm going to go put these bags upstairs," mentioned Joe.

"Are you moving in?" exclaimed Jack when he looked at their bags.

"We might!" Jenna winked. "You've got plenty of space."

"Jeez. First Tristan wants me to build her a small house back by the orchard, now you two are moving in. This is becoming a compound," Jack pretended to complain. Jenna and Joe knew he'd love to have them stay.

"In case you haven't noticed," quipped Frank with a devilish grin, "this *is* a bloody compound."

"I'm going to go check on the kids and run these bags upstairs," said Joe as Jenna followed on his heels. "We'll be back down."

They walked into the foyer and were surprised to see that everyone was still awake. Tristan, Cole and Tommy were sitting in the living room watching a movie. Shane and Blake were in the throes of a heated game of Battleship in the dining room, while Bridgette, Moira and Natalie sat at the table reading. Moira kept looking up over her glasses at the pair whenever their noise level rose above what she deemed to be their inside voices. Joe ran the bags upstairs, while Jenna grabbed something to drink from the kitchen. Suddenly, the front door banged open loudly. Jenna could hear the complaining voices of Adam and Liam coming closer. She glanced at them speculatively.

"Why are you two still in uniform?"

"Because we had to make a trip to Philly."

"Philly?"

"Pennington."

"Are you kidding?"

"I wish we were."

"Amos and Earl were the ones that handled Tiffany's case. Earl declined to speak with us, but Amos sure had a lot to say."

"Too bad he didn't give us the whole story."

"What makes you say that?"

"He gave us random facts about the case, but he didn't elaborate. By the time he was getting to the meat of the story, the guards cut him off."

"I guess you should be glad you got anything. Are you sure it's the truth?"

"Much of what he said matches up against the case file."

"Wow. Maybe he's turning a new leaf."

Liam gave DiNolfo a look that said, "Get real."

After Joe took their bags up to the guest room on the second floor he went downstairs to check on the kids. He kissed Natalie on her forehead as she read her latest romance novella that she picked up at the pharmacy. Joe gave a simple nod to Cole, who was fixated on the TV. He was glad to see that the kids were settled in and not focusing on what was going on in town too much.

Jenna and Joe settled out on the porch with Jack and Frank. They eased their weary bones onto the rocking chairs as they allowed the serene calm of the manor to wash over them. A cool breeze rustled through the trees and brushed against their skin. It was exactly what they needed after a long day like today. Liam and Adam joined them on the porch with tired faces.

"So, how goes it, boys?" asked Frank, breaking the comfortable silence on the porch.

"It's going," said Adam honestly.

"Had to pay Amos a visit tonight," admitted Liam.

"I'm sure that went well," Jack said sarcastically.

"I don't know what to believe out of that guy's mouth."

"At least he was willing to assist," added Jenna.

"True."

"Out of curiosity, what do you know about this case?" Liam asked Jenna with a serious look on his face.

Jenna sighed as she gave Joe a weary look. They didn't like digging up old memories as much as Angie and Amos.

"I was friends with both Angie and Tiffany, so I guess I'd be the best person to tell you this. Tiffany had pissed *a lot* of people off. Tiffany was popular, and flirted with all the guys in school. She even tried to flirt with Joe once, and I told her off. Even though she was popular, she didn't have a lot of good friends. She had stepped on too many toes."

Joe grew serious at the memory.

"There were a lot of people who Tiffany had walked on to get her popularity and social status. Angie, her sister, was one of them. Tiffany was *really* nasty to her. Tiffany was also fairly mean to her boyfriend at the time, Ethan Quiver."

"Old man Quiver's son," added Jack.

"I remember she tortured Angie by flirting with Angie's boyfriend at the time, Hunter McCord."

"McCord?" Liam asked with a question in his voice.

"Oh, yeah. Apparently, they are back together."

"Interesting."

"Wouldn't it look bad to date a suspect in your sister's murder investigation?"

"Yeah, but look at his record, too. Violence ... Drug dealing ... She doesn't seem to mind that."

"What's her deal?" asked Adam.

"I've known Angie for a really long time. She has always been a bit aloof. From what I remember she was really tightly wound. When Tiffany died, she was distraught. On the night after Tiffany was murdered, Angie left and didn't come back until last week. We thought she was missing, but it turns out she just ran off."

Jenna looked at Adam as a thought entered her head. Twenty years. Angie left after her sister was murdered, and just two days after she returned another sister is murdered. That girl either had some serious bad luck or some major skeletons in her closet.

"Let me look over the case file tonight," DiNolfo suggested.

"We'll look it over with you. We're not going to sleep."

"The murders aren't the work of a woman," said Liam.

"No, but what if it's someone connected to her?" suggested Adam.

"What makes you think it's not the work of a woman?" DiNolfo probed.

"All the evidence points to a man," said Adam and Liam in unison.

"The shoes, the shirt, the brute force needed to throw a dead body from a moving vehicle ..."

"Then there's Trafford."

"He lied about his whereabouts after leaving the precinct that morning and he was spotted on Mountain Road at 5:30 a.m." Jenna said.

"Tommy said he had an intense interest in Courtney," Liam remarked with piqued curiosity.

"Trafford claims he stopped at the house because Roger's car was in the shop," added Jenna.

"He's obviously trying to cover his ass," said Adam brusquely.

"What about McCord. He seems to be the most likely candidate," Liam remarked.

"He's got an alibi. He was in jail at the time of the first murder," Jenna said, dismissing Liam's comment.

"It wasn't Tommy. You've got five people inside that can vouch for his whereabouts."

"That's obvious, "admitted Jenna.

"What if it's someone else? Someone not on our radar?" suggested Adam.

"That's always a possibility. Let's keep digging," Jenna said as they continued to read through the contents of the file.

DiNolfo went to sleep around four a.m. after combing through Tiffany O'Mara's case file for hours on end with Adam and Liam. They weren't any closer to finding the culprit, but they did know that whoever was responsible was likely the same person who committed the murders of Courtney O'Mara and April Dearing. Jenna was nearly able to rule out Jesse Trafford as a suspect. The only thing keeping her from doing so was that no one could vouch for his whereabouts from six a.m. to seven a.m. on the morning of June the seventeenth.

At 6:04 a.m., DiNolfo's cell phone rang loudly. Joe was in the shower at the time, and wasn't able to reach the phone in time to silence it. He wanted her to sleep at least until eight a.m. so that she could function. Two hours of sleep simply would not cut it. Jenna woke up with a start as she reached for her phone. She didn't recognize the number that was blinking on her screen.

"Who is calling me at this hour?" Jenna answered her phone, "Hello?"

"Hi, is this Jenna DiNolfo?"

"This is she. Who is calling?"

"My name is nurse Mary Wells. I am a nurse at Pittsburgh Medical Center. I am calling because your father, Charles, is a patient here."

"A patient? What is wrong with him?"

"Mr. DiNolfo suffered a heart attack last night. Your mother asked that I call and inform you."

"Thank you. I will be there soon," said Jenna as she hung up the phone.

"Who was that?" Joe asked as he stepped out of the bathroom.

"A nurse from Pittsburgh Medical Center. My dad had a heart attack."

Joe didn't wait for Jenna to say anything further. He put on his shoes, grabbed his wallet and his keys, and he was ready to go. Jenna breathed a sigh of relief knowing that she didn't even have to ask Joe to come along for moral support. He gave it automatically. Jenna pulled on a pair of jeans and a black t-shirt, slid on a pair of sneakers, pulled a brush through her hair and they were off. Joe had staff that could hold down the restaurant for the day. Natalie had a set of master keys to lock everything up, and Cole had offered to pick her and Tristan up when they were done with their shift. Joe wanted to be there for Jenna, just as she had been there for his family for the past three years.

Cole loaded everyone into his Jeep as he drove to school. Finals started today, and no one was looking forward to the task at hand. Even Tristan was nervous.

"What if they don't sit me near you?" Shane asked Tristan worriedly from the backseat.

"You didn't study at all?"

"No. That's your job."

Tristan rolled her eyes.

"What if I fail?" spazzed Natalie.

Now it was Cole's turn to roll his eyes.

"You're a junior. It's not that serious."

"Dad will kill me," Natalie insisted.

"No he won't," Cole reassured.

"For the love of God, would you all chill out?" yelled Tommy.

Tristan smiled.

That is a nice change; Tommy telling everyone else to calm down.

Edna Harrow stood on her front porch with a nervous look on her face. Her eyes shifted from side to side and she clenched her housecoat as if she was afraid that someone might steal it from her. In reality, no one on earth would want to steal Edna's ratty housecoat. Adam Morrow stepped onto Mountain Road from behind Monte's Café and his eyes locked on Edna. He stared at her for a moment as he tried to refrain from laughing at the woman. Edna saw him and waved him down.

"Officer Morrow!"

Oh dear, God.

"Oh, Officer Morrow!"

What now?

"Good Morning, Edna," said Adam politely.

"Could you help me with something?" Edna begged with an uncomfortable look on her face.

"Uh, sure. It has to be quick though. I'm in the middle of an investigation."

"It will be *so* quick."

Adam followed Edna inside, still wondering what it was that he was supposed to be helping her with.

"More raccoons have gotten into the store, but now there are birds too. I just don't understand!" Edna squealed dramatically.

"Has anyone checked the basement for holes?"

"No."

"Well, there's your problem."

Adam walked down the rickety wooden staircase that led to the basement of Harrow's General Store. The stairs creaked and moaned as Adam descended the staircase. When he reached the bottom, he was shocked at what he saw. There were animals *everywhere*.

"Jesus Christ!" he yelled. "Edna! You have an infestation of animals in your basement!"

"An infestation? There aren't mice, are there?"

"No, not that I can tell, but you do have a basement full of pigeons and raccoons. There's a couple dead birds on the floor. It looks like the raccoons got to them."

In one corner of the basement, several raccoons had crowded and were hissing and swiping at the birds. Meanwhile a large flock of pigeons had gathered in the opposite end of the basement and were skittering about nervously. Adam tried to be careful where he stepped, but there were animals and their leavings everywhere. A raccoon swiped at his foot as he tried to get by. He noticed that there was a board at the end of the basement nearest the gaze of raccoons that appeared to be covering a hole.

"Well here's your problem, Edna!" Adam yelled up to her through the floor boards.

"This board is loose and all the animals are getting in through here."

"Can you fix it?"

"Probably not today, but I can bring some plywood down tomorrow or Friday."

Adam pulled at the damaged wood panel and immediately noticed that there was a sizable hole in it. On the opposite side of the board appeared to be a tunnel of sorts. Adam grabbed some steel wool that was sitting on a storage rack on the adjacent wall and stuffed some in the hole so that no more critters could climb through. Adam turned to leave the basement but the pigeons had followed behind him, blocking his path.

"Git!" Adam yelled as the pigeons scuttled away neurotically again.

Edna looked almost as crazed as the animals when Adam emerged from the basement.

"Just keep the basement door locked for now. You might want to call animal control to come out. Today. Don't wait. I'll come back and fix that hole. I stuffed some steel wool in the space for now."

"Oh, thank you, Adam!"

"No trouble. I must be going now."

Adam couldn't get away fast enough.

How the hell does one basement manage to get so many animals trapped inside?

Adam was thrilled to be out of Harrow's when suddenly he looked at his foot. One of the pigeons left him a present.

"Ugh! Bird shit!" He reached down to clean it off with a napkin as a look of disgust formed on his face.

Joe drove eighty miles per hour down I-80 West, trying to get to Pittsburgh as quick as possible. Jenna looked nervous beside him and he really couldn't blame her. Heart attacks were nothing to play around with. He had only spoken with Chuck DiNolfo a few times on the phone, but he had always thought he was such a nice guy. Joe hoped he would be all right.

"Okay students, papers down," said Mr. Keppler as he eyed his students precariously.

Shane groaned in protest.

"Five more minutes?"

"Pencils down," Mr. Keppler repeated.

Tristan, who Mr. Keppler had sat on the opposite side of the room, had finished up the final exam twenty minutes earlier. She eyed her cousin warily. Hopefully he at least got a D so that he could still graduate. She glanced back at Tommy who was still scribbling on his test paper. He filled in the final answer as Mr. Keppler snatched the paper from him.

"Good luck, ladies and gentlemen. I'll have the grades for you tomorrow."

Joe and Jenna arrived at Pittsburgh Medical Center just after one p.m. They made a beeline for the front desk which had a line of people waiting. Within five minutes, they had reached the front of the line where a woman with short red hair and gentle brown eyes was waiting to assist them.

"Hi there. Are you visiting a patient?" the woman asked Joe and Jenna.

"I am," replied Jenna nervously.

"What is the patient's name?"

"Charles DiNolfo."

"Can you spell that for me?"

Jenna proceeded to spell her last name for the clerk.

"Hmm ..."

"Yes?" said Jenna with a worried look on her face.

"We don't seem to have a patient here by that name."

Joe's stomach lurched. Jenna pressed the matter at hand.

"I received a call from a nurse here. Her name is Mary Wells."

"I'm sorry, but there are no nurses here by that name. Are you sure you have the right hospital?"

"I'm positive."

Suddenly, it struck her. What if someone just wanted to get her out of town? What if they saw that Jenna was getting close to figuring them out, and they just wanted to get her out of their hair? What if there was another murder about to go down? The hair on Jenna's arm stood on end. Joe noticed the alarmed expression on her face.

"Hun, what's wrong?"

"I have to check their house. I have to make sure they are okay."

"Okay, let's go."

DiNolfo jumped in the driver seat, waited for Joe to get in and slammed on the gas. She weaved in and out of some of Pittsburgh's tiniest streets until she finally came to a halt outside of 351 Evergreen Court.

"Are you sure you're okay?" Joe asked in concern, but Jenna waved him off.

Jenna grabbed her keys from the ignition and searched for the key that would open her parents' one-floor rancher. Within a moment she was in her parents' living room. She called upstairs, but no one answered.

"It doesn't look like anyone is home," said Jenna to Joe, growing increasingly alarmed.

Joe walked around the living room to see if he could find any note left behind or any clue as to where they might be. He didn't find anything in the living room so he wandered into the kitchen.

"Hey, hun," Joe called from the kitchen.

"Yeah?"

"There's some hotel reservation for Atlantic City out here on the table."

"What?"

Jenna stormed into the kitchen to see what Joe was talking about. Sure enough. A one-week stay at the Sands Casino. Jenna raced to the telephone and dialed her mother's cell phone number. It rang six times before she picked up.

"Hello?" Anita DiNolfo yelled loudly into the receiver.

"Mom ... It's Jenna."

"Oh, Jenna! Hi honey!" said Anita in a high-pitched voice.

"Where are you?" asked Jenna with a perplexed look on her face. This did not sound like a woman with a sick husband.

"Uh ... I'm on the beach in AC. Where are you?"

You've got to be kidding me.

"I'm at your house!" Jenna said in an exasperated voice.

"Why on earth are you there?" said Anita, her voice getting louder and louder.

"Is Dad all right? I got a call saying ..." Jenna stopped herself. She didn't want to make her mother more paranoid than what she already was.

"Is Dad okay?" Jenna asked calmly. She thought she knew the answer.

"He's fine. He's right next to me getting a tan. We're going to do some shopping and gambling later!"

"Oh, thank God."

"What, honey? I can't hear you. You're breaking up!" Anita yelled into the phone. She knew two octaves, loud and louder. Anita was now at her loudest and her voice hurt Jenna's ear drum.

"Nothing, Mom. I'm glad you're having a good time. Enjoy your vacation!"

Jenna hung up the phone as relief and dread both flooded her system. She was relieved beyond measure to know that her father was well and not in the hospital. Unfortunately, her relief was short lived because there was the very real problem of someone calling her out of town. It was someone who knew her father's name, where her parents lived, and it was someone who wanted to get her out of town.

"Is he okay?" asked Joe nervously.

"Yeah! They are on the beach in AC!"

"What the hell was that call about this morning then?" said Joe with a serious tone of voice. Jenna didn't blink. She knew without a doubt that someone had tried to purposely get her out of town.

"We need to get back to Elkhart. ASAP."

CHAPTER 20

June 20, 2000
Morrow Manor
Fox Hollow, PA
11 A.M.

STORM CLOUDS CHURNED IN THE GRAY SKY above Morrow Manor as Frank and Bridgette Kilpatrick rode on horseback through the orchard. The heavy hooves of Frank's thoroughbred clopped against the dirt as it sped ahead. The horse seemed spooked.

"Easy girl," Frank said as he stroked his calloused hand against the horse's neck. The horse seemed to calm in response to his touch.

Tumultuous clouds warning of an impending storm blocked out the sunlight, leaving Bridgette and Frank standing in a strange late morning dim. The wind kicked up and whipped Bridgette's long red hair across her face. Frank's brow furrowed as his eyes teemed to the sky above.

"A storm is brewing," said Frank with a weary expression. He spoke on more levels than one.

Frank and Bridgette continued to survey the apple crop that had flourished remarkably well this year. They would have plenty to bring to the farmer's market next week.

"I think we're about done back here," mentioned Bridgette to Frank. "I think Jack will be pleased with the result."

Bridgette continued speaking but Frank did not respond.

"Frank?"

Frank was staring up at the manor house with a grave look on his face.

"Were we expecting company?" Frank asked in a strange tone of voice.

"No. Unless its Joe and Jenna back already."

"It's definitely not Joe or Jenna."

"What are you talking about?" asked Bridgette with a perplexed tone of voice as her horse galloped to where Frank's horse was standing.

"I'm trying to figure out who the hell that is, and why they are standing on our porch," Frank said in an angry voice as he pointed to the figure that stood on the porch of the Morrow Manor. The figure was dressed plainly in a pair of jeans, a black t-shirt and a black hat and it appeared to be staring right at Frank and Bridgette. Bridgette's blood ran cold.

"Giddyup, girl. C'mon!" yelled Frank as he nudged his horse into a full gallop towards the house. Bridgette followed behind but she couldn't keep up with Frank's horse.

As fast as the figure appeared, it was gone again. Whoever it was slid off of the side of the porch and ran into the tree line that bordered the manor house. Frank sped after the intruder, hell bent upon determining their identity. Bridgette watched as Frank barreled through the tree line on his horse with his gun drawn. Suddenly, Bridgette noticed something odd sitting on the porch. A simple brown box with no markings or address was waiting for her. Her stomach lurched as she took in the sight of it. Bridgette dismounted her horse and tied his reins to the wooden railing of the porch as she continued to eye the box. Slowly, she climbed the steps of the manor house. Whoever was just on the porch must have left it. It certainly wasn't delivered by regular post. Ted, the mailman, usually didn't arrive until about one p.m.

Bridgette carefully approached the box. The flaps were open and unsecured. Bridgette reached into the box to see what lay inside. She retrieved another cardboard box, this one was firmly sealed. Bridgette tore the packing tape from the box in one fell swoop. The lid sprung open with tissue paper popping out. Bridgette swallowed as her nerves frayed. She pulled out the tissue paper one by one, until she discovered an ornate box. The box was incredibly old, with Victorian filigree work and a beautifully inscribed monogram on the lid. Bridgette was perplexed.

"Who would leave this here? This doesn't belong to us," Bridgette said aloud.

Bridgette continued to admire the external beauty of the box for a moment. She just couldn't believe someone would discard this all the way up here. They were an hour from Elkhart. It just didn't make sense. Bridgette tried to figure out how to open the box and found a clasp on the front. She released the clasp as the lid slowly rose. A strange scent escaped from the box. Bridgette thought it smelled as if it was used for purposes other than storing jewelry or trinkets. Bridgette peered down into the box and noticed that a stack of photographs lay inside. She put the jewelry box on the floor of the porch as she flicked through. The first photograph in the stack was of Tiffany O'Mara. She was dressed in a pretty green frock in the Forest of York. Bridgette flipped the photograph over, but the only notation was a date: June 20, 1980. Bridgette flipped to the next photograph; a recent photo of Courtney O'Mara. The picture showed Courtney standing in the middle of Mountain Road dressed in a striped shirt. She wore a pensive look on her face. On the back of the photograph, there was another date: June 17, 2000.

Bridgette got a funny taste in her mouth as her brain started piecing the puzzle together. Bridgette flipped to the third picture in the stack. It was an old yearbook picture of April Dearing. Marked in pen over her picture was the date June 19, 2000. A heavy sigh released from Bridgette's lungs. She knew what the dates meant. The date on the back of the photograph was the date that each of the women had died at the hands of another. A brutal murderer, who seemed to have it out for the women in Elkhart, had left the Morrows a box of clues ... Or were they warnings? Without pause, Bridgette flipped to the next photograph. Angie O'Mara's photograph stared up at Bridgette. She wore a nude-colored dress and appeared to be at the Farmer's Market in Shepard's Grove. On the back of the photograph, Bridgette read the date June 20, 2000. *Today.*

Bridgette released a breath as she glanced at the next photograph. Tears began to water from her eyes as she looked down at a recent picture of Natalie Piedmonte. She was smiling and dressed nicely in a red tea-length dress. Bridgette's hand shook as she turned over the photograph. A neat scrawl on the back read June 20, 2000. Bridgette had to catch her breath. After a beat she flipped to the next photograph, placing Natalie's picture gently at the back of the pile. A young Jenna DiNolfo peered up at Bridgette with a sassy smirk from the photograph. She was dressed in an all black prom gown with Joe on her arm. Someone had circled her face with a black magic marker. On the back of the picture, the date June 20, 2000 was marked. Anger rose in the pit of Bridgette's stomach. There was only one picture left. Somehow, she knew who would be on it. As she flipped Jenna's photograph to the back of the pile, she felt as if she was going to faint on the spot. Tristan and Bridgette smiled broadly in the photograph. It was the photo that was published in the *Elkhart Bugle* last month for the Mother/Daughter luncheon that Steeplechase held. Bridgette remembers how thrilled she was that Tristan had asked her to attend. Now Bridgette felt empty. Her heart beat rapidly in her chest. Finally, she did the only thing she could think of in that moment to do. She called the one person who would know how to handle this calmly and rationally.

"Frank!" Bridgette cried loudly as the photographs fluttered to the porch floor, one by one.

Jesse Trafford had a sneaky look on his face when he emerged from the back door of Trafford's Auto Body. He saw someone standing by the chain link fence that surrounded the property. With a sly grin, he emerged from the back gate with tightened fists.

"You got what I need?" he asked as he approached the gate.

"Shut up! There's snitches all over the place back here."

"You're paranoid, bro."

Hunter McCord hid under the shadow of his black hoodie as he took something from Jesse Trafford's hand. He reached into his pocket and pounded something into

Trafford's hand.

"Pleasure doin' business with you," Trafford began to say but was stopped when he saw that another person had approached the gate.

"Down on the ground, McCord!" Officer Liam Morrow yelled.

He had witnessed the entire exchange. He saw Hunter approach the back gate from his patrol car, and he just waited for his moment to pounce. Jesse backed towards the middle of the yard but he had nowhere to go as Officer Adam Morrow climbed the chain link fence.

"Empty your pockets, Trafford!" Adam yelled as he approached him.

"Shit!"

"Don't try to run. There's nowhere to go," Adam said as he cornered him in the lot. Aware that he had run out of choices, Jesse reached into his jean pockets and pulled out a bag of white powder.

"Cuff 'em," demanded Adam.

Frank's horse raced down the winding path through Cavegat Forest but he couldn't see the intruder anywhere. He set off a warning shot towards the sky to make sure they were good and gone. As he turned the reins on his horse to leave the woods, a desperate scream flooded the air.

Adam and Liam secured Trafford and McCord in separate holding cells at the Elkhart Police Department where they would await DiNolfo's wrath. As the officers headed down the hall back to their desks, Adam's cell phone rang.

Francis Kilpatrick – 717-555-8014

"Hello?"

"Get up here. NOW."

"What's happened?" asked Adam in an urgent voice.

"There was someone on the property and they left something that you're going to want to see."

"Can you fill me in a little?"

"It's a box that has pictures of all the deceased women with dates of their murders on the back, but four others who are still alive. The date on the back of their photos is today's date. The killer is going to try to take them."

"We'll be there in twenty minutes."

CHAPTER 21

June 20, 2000
Somewhere on I-80
Grove City, PA
4 P.M.

JENNA DINOLFO SLAMMED HARD on her horn in anger and she shot a vicious stare at the car in front of her. Jenna and Joe were stuck in bumper to bumper traffic that accumulated thanks to a three-car pileup on I-80.

"Why is it that when I need to get somewhere fast, stuff like this happens?" Jenna demanded to know.

Joe nodded his head in agreement as he cast a disgusted look out his window.

"I'd really like to know who set you up," Joe said angrily.

"I'm just worried about getting back. I really hope nothing has happened. I know Adam and Liam have the investigation under control, but I still worry."

"I know what you mean, and I can't even get a signal out here on this phone."

Joe tossed his cell phone in the glove box in annoyance and slammed it shut. His eyes continued to glare out the car window.

"What does that sign say up there?" asked Jenna as she squinted out the windshield. There was a roadside sign with flashing lights situated about one hundred yards away.

"Construction. Expect delays."

"If it's not one thing, it's another."

"You're going to need to get off. There is an exit coming up. We can take the streets."

"Please don't get us lost."

"It'll be quicker."

The crawl towards the exit seemed to take forever with traffic moving at a snail's pace down I-80. Jenna was becoming more on edge with each passing mile marker.

Joe had become quiet and he looked like he had something on his mind. He scratched his head in a perplexed manner.

"What's wrong?" asked Jenna as she peered over at Joe. Joe, who was always so jovial and light-spirited, looked as if he had a heavy weight on his shoulders.

"Something just occurred to me," Joe began with a troubled look on his face.

With the car stalled in traffic, Jenna looked over at Joe with a concerned look.

"What is it? Tell me," Jenna urged.

"Explain to me how Angie knew Kendricks."

Jenna swallowed. Joe gave her the impression that he had something big that he wanted to share. He did live next door to the O'Maras since he was a kid, after all.

"Well, I just found out from Roger O'Mara that Bernard is Gwen's cousin. So that would make Angie and Bernard cousins, too."

"No, that can't be," remarked Joe with a dark look in his eye. He looked utterly confused.

"Why do you ask?"

"I remember seeing him at a lot of parties when we were younger. That's actually where I first met him. But Jenn, there is no way in hell that they could be cousins."

Jenna looked at Joe with an inquisitive look on her face.

"I can't believe I didn't think to tell you this before ..." said Joe as his memory went crashing back to the spring of 1980.

May 2, 1980
Elkhart, PA
3 P.M.

"Pop ... I'm leaving!" yelled Joey Piedmonte as he exited the back door of Monte's Café. He had just finished up a six hour shift and was eager to get home and get ready for his date with Jenna. Joe slung a trash bag into the dumpster and meandered down the dirt path that leads through the Forest of York. Though the forest was muggy and overrun with mosquitoes, Joe found it to be the quickest way to get home. As he stepped onto the dirt path he realized that he wasn't alone in the forest. He could hear voices just ahead of him. This surprised Joe because he never ran into anyone in the secluded forest. Bernard Kendricks stood just a few feet away talking to Angie O'Mara at the base of the Bone Tree. Bernard held her hand and looked at her as if she was a possession of great value. Angie smiled back at Bernard broadly until she saw Joe and her smile quickly faded. Angie nodded in Joe's direction as Bernard turned around quickly with a violent look on his face.

"What do you want, Piedmonte," Kendricks called with deep disdain in his voice.

Joe raised an eyebrow at Bernard and gave him a testy look.

"I'm minding my own business. What are you doing?" asked Joe angrily.

"Laying low."

"You know Jack is looking for you, right?"

"Let him look."

"He's pretty pissed."

Bernard shrugged his shoulders. Jack was always angry when Bernard showed up at Morrow Manor unannounced.

"Hey Angie, Hunter was looking for you earlier. Does he know you're here?"

"I'm not his possession," said Angie firmly.

Bernard smiled strangely at Angie's comment and he whispered something in Angie's ear.

He could swear that he heard Bernard say, "No, but you're mine."

Angie laughed as she grabbed her necklace, relishing the attention that Bernard was lavishing upon her. Joe stared at the odd couple, wondering what he was missing. Joe knew for a fact that Bernard was one hundred and fifty percent obsessed with Jack's wife, Catherine. Meanwhile, Angie was in a relationship with Hunter. They both had their hearts elsewhere, but yet, here they were in each other's arms looking utterly inseparable. Joe felt awkward. There was something very strange going on. For one, Joe never condoned infidelity, in marriage or dating. *If you want to stray, break it off,* Joe thought. The other thing that bothered Joe was that Angie and Bernard just seemed off. He was entirely too old for her. It was as if they were hiding something dark and twisted behind their sly smiles. Bernard was a strange guy to begin with, and Angie hadn't exactly endeared to the Piedmontes with her aloof manner.

Awkwardly, Joe said, "I have to go."

Joe walked away from the pair, much quicker than he had approached them, with a strange feeling in his heart.

As Joe departed, Angie asked in a worried voice, "Do you think he'll tell?"

Bernard replied in a slick voice, "Let him."

Joe approached his parents' house and jumped over the white picket fence with a hop. Tiffany O'Mara was in the front yard sitting on her mother's porch swing when Joe saw her.

"Joey!" Tiffany called with a sweet smile. She was holding a baby on her lap.

"Hey Tiff. How's it going?"

"Okay. Have you seen my sister?"

"Angie?"

"Yeah. Mom's been looking for her."

"I actually just saw her with Bernard in the woods."

"Bernard?" Tiffany said his name like it was a disease.

Tiffany stood up with baby Courtney in her arms.

"Yeah, I didn't know they were going out," said Joe looking perplexed.

Tiffany stared back at Joe with a surprised and disgusted look. She didn't reply to Joe's comment, but instead ran in the house, calling after her father, with Courtney in tow.

"Dad!"

Joe thought nothing of the exchange and went inside to get ready for his date with Jenna. He was taking her to the roller rink in Shepard's Grove. That night when Joe returned to Caribou Road, he was alarmed to see that a police car stood outside the O'Mara house. Roger O'Mara was on the lawn screaming, but Joe couldn't quite tell who was on the other end of his tirade. Joe parked his car in his parents' driveway and tried to get a closer look at what was happening. A police officer was trying to detain Roger O'Mara from attacking Bernard Kendricks in his front yard.

"Mr. O'Mara, please!" Officer Rutledge begged but Roger was not backing down. He struggled to free his arms from the officer's grip.

Roger spat at Bernard with venomous fury, "Touch my daughter again, and you're dead! How dare you!"

Bernard glowered at Roger causing his anger to intensify. From behind Roger, Angie was crying.

"Daddy, please!"

"Go inside, now! Let me go, I'm going to get that son of a bitch!" Roger screamed.

Joe had never known Roger O'Mara to be a man with a temper. In fact, Joe had never heard him raise his voice before. Suddenly, Tiffany came to the door with a twisted smile on her face.

"Dad, Mom said to come inside."

"No! I should've never let that bastard in my house!"

"Tiffany, get a life!" Angie yelled from across the lawn.

"Pfft! That's funny!" said Tiffany as she cackled loudly.

"This is entirely your fault!" screamed Angie as she ran towards Tiffany with fury.

As Angie took Tiffany to the ground, Joe went inside his parents' house and slammed the door shut. *These people are nuts,* Joe thought. That night a yellow taxi cab came and took Angie away for two weeks and she didn't return until just before prom. Bernard Kendricks never stepped foot on Caribou Road again after Roger O'Mara threatened to kill him on the spot if he did. The O'Maras didn't tell anyone where Angie had gone, but Joe had a pretty good idea. Just a few days after Angie had left, Joe was in the front yard going through the mail. The mailman had given the Piedmontes a piece of Roger O'Mara's mail by accident. Joe thought nothing of it at first, until he read the envelope. It had come from the St. Mary Psychiatric Crisis Center for Women in Harrisburg, and it was addressed to Roger O'Mara in care of Angela O'Mara. When Angie returned, she refused to talk about Bernard Kendricks with anyone.

"How did I miss this?" asked Jenna who was actually friends with Angie at the time.

"Her father told me that she was sick at home."

"I guess to save face?"

"I don't understand why they would send her to a mental institution, though," said Joe, still confused.

"Angie had problems," admitted Jenna. "She probably still does."

Joe looked at Jenna as the gears in her head turned.

"Oh, my God," said Jenna as her hands dropped from the steering wheel. "It's been in front of me this entire time."

June 20, 2000
27 Caribou Road
Elkhart, PA
4 P.M.

Misty-Lee slammed the front door shut as she walked in the house with a tired look on her face. Life was hard without Courtney around. She missed her sister and friend, and it was hard moving on in life without her companion by her side. Though there was a fourteen year age difference between them, they were as close as twins. She didn't feel the same connection, the same closeness with Angie, Ally or Trixie. She felt a bit lost without her.

Misty-Lee climbed the stairs to her room so that she could get changed. She was still wearing her work clothes from her part-time job at the grocery store and she was desperate to change into something more comfortable.

Gwen O'Mara yelled up the stairs to Misty-Lee, "Misty-Lee, is that you?"

"Yeah, Mom!"

"Can you check on Angie? I haven't heard from her all day."

Misty-Lee climbed the steps to the third floor to check on her sister. She walked down the long hallway to her bedroom, but it was empty. Confused, Misty-Lee walked back down the hallway. As she passed Tiffany's bedroom she heard a noise. It was the sound of a music box playing from inside Tiffany's long unoccupied room. Goosebumps formed on Misty-Lee's skin as she listened closely to the sound. Misty-Lee pushed open the old door to Tiffany's room as the hinges squeaked loudly. Much to Misty-Lee's surprise, there was someone standing in the middle of Tiffany's room.

"What are you doing in here?" Misty-Lee asked Angie, sounding offended. Angie stood at Tiffany's bureau listening to her sister's long-forgotten music box. She watched the ballerina twirl round and round as *Swan Lake* played from the box. The sound was ghostly and unforgettable.

"It's so terrible, what is happening," said Angie in a chilling voice.

Misty-Lee watched her sister somberly. Misty thought that Angie really seemed to be upset over the tragedy that had struck their family once again. It almost seemed like a dark cloud was hanging over their family tree, or the water from which it gained its nutrients was tainted with disease.

"I know," Misty-Lee agreed, "I'm afraid to go outside."

Angie remained silent continuing to listen to the hauntingly beautiful melody that the music box was playing.

"We never come in here," commented Misty-Lee.

"How come?"

"Because losing her and you at the same time. It was very traumatic for everyone."

"I'm sorry. I didn't want to leave. I was scared."

"I probably would have done the same thing. I was still pretty young at the time."

Angie turned around to look at her sister. Misty-Lee did have some depth to her. She wondered if the shallow exterior was a façade to cover something else up. Angie thought it might be to hide her own pain and self-consciousness. Misty-Lee smiled a half smile at her sister as she tried to bury her pain.

"Come downstairs, Mom is asking for you. There is going to be a vigil tonight for Courtney, and she wants us all to attend."

CHAPTER 22

June 20, 2000
Elkhart, PA
4:00 P.M.

"I'LL BE BACK AT EIGHT to pick you up," Cole said to Tristan out of his driver's side window as she walked towards the entrance of Monte's Café.

"Okay, thanks. Have fun with your buddy," Tristan said as she winked at Cole with a sly smile on her face.

Cole would be biding his time this afternoon at Morrow Manor and Tristan knew Jack would be more than happy to put Cole to work. At least it was only four hours and not eight.

"Oh, yeah ... I can't wait to clean out stables and detail his car," Cole said facetiously as he pulled off and headed down Mountain Road towards Cavegat Pass.

"Yo, Tony! Is my pizza done yet?" Salvatore Piedmonte yelled over the counter of Monte's Café becoming irate.

"Hold yer horses!" Tony Piedmonte yelled from the kitchen.

Joe's father, Sal, was waiting impatiently at the counter for his eldest grandson to bring him his pizza that he had ordered only ten minutes ago.

"Y'know, in my day I had pizzas done in ten minutes flat!"

"Yeah, yeah, yeah ... In the snow, barefoot and you walked five miles to deliver it, too! Didn't ya?"

"Now that you mention it."

"Yer pizza's coming out now."

Tony, who was Joe's sister Candace's son, was helping out with the restaurant in Joe's absence. Tony was a high-energy guy who loved to be in the kitchen, but his personality could be felt all the way in the dining room. He was loud and boisterous and always had a joke for whoever was willing to listen. He could make a pretty mean pizza, too. Tristan was thrilled to see Tony. He was always so much fun to work with.

"Hey, cuz!" Tony yelled at Tristan. Tony insisted that Cole and Tristan would marry someday and he was adamant upon calling Tristan "cuz" prematurely.

"Hey, Tony! How's it going?" Tristan asked.

"It's going. Busy as hell in here today. Do me a favor. Take this pie over to table four. The grumpy old guy is hungry."

Tristan laughed. "Be nice to your grandpa."

Tristan took the pizza over to Cole's grandfather, who was sitting at table number four. Sal greeted her with a smile.

"Hey cutie! Join me for a slice."

"I wish I could, Monte. This place is packed today!"

"Tell my grandson to speed it up!"

Tristan laughed at Cole's spunky grandfather as she went to wait on the next table.

"What the hell is going on up here?" asked Liam as he and Adam barged through the front door of Morrow Manor.

Frank gave his nephews a death glare from the doorway of the dining room. The two officers walked straight past him into the dining room as they tried to understand what the issue was. Bridgette sat at the sprawling dining room table across from Jack who had a desperately worried look on his face. He was trying to convince her to stay home from work due to her traumatic experience this morning on the porch.

"No, Jack! I'd like to see anyone try to pull anything on me. They'll be dead before they could try."

"And what about Tristan and Natalie?" Jack asked in worry. Bridgette glared at Jack.

"Oh, here we go again! Tristan knows how to defend herself, for the umpteenth time!"

"That doesn't mean that Frank and I don't worry!" Jack explained.

"I'm worried too, Jack, but it doesn't mean that we jump to conclusions. I refuse to live scared. We prepare. We take precautions, but we go about our lives. You and Joe have poor Cole chauffeuring Tristan and Natalie everywhere. I will be at the hospital working. All I have to say is God help anyone who tries to go after DiNolfo. Seriously. Let them try. We're not damsels in distress."

"We know, wild woman!" said Frank with a perturbed look on his face. "But you need to listen and listen good!"

"I'm listening."

"Cole is picking Natalie up at eleven p.m. tonight. You get done at eleven. Wait in the lobby for him. Do not wait out on the corner."

"Oh, Francis."

"I'm dead serious, Bridgette!" Frank barked with a serious look on his face.

"Fine. I will wait for Cole in the lobby."

"Liam and Adam are here."

"Tell them to come in."

Cole walked into the dining room of Morrow Manor where he found Jack, Frank, Liam, Adam and Bridgette huddled together around the dining room table. Their conversation had heated up since Adam and Liam's arrival and now they were trying to figure out how to handle the latest turn of events.

"What's going on?" Cole asked as he laid his car keys down on the table.

Jack sighed deeply and said, "Take a seat."

Cole became nervous at Jack's request but did as he was told.

"This was left on the porch this morning," Jack said as he passed the box to Cole.

"Don't touch it," warned Liam as he lifted the jewelry box out of the cardboard box with a pair of rubber gloves sheathing his fingerprints from the surface. He displayed it on the table for Cole to see. Cole eyed the box precariously.

"Who sent it?"

"We don't know. But it was hand delivered. The intruder ran off before I could catch him," explained Frank.

A troubled look grew in Cole's eyes.

"Ready?" asked Liam as he pressed the release with his gloved index finger. Cole nodded. The lid of the jewelry box lifted gently and revealed a stack of photographs inside.

Liam pulled the photos out of the box and explained each photograph to Cole. He slowed as he got to the picture of Natalie.

"Now these photographs are a bit different. They all have today's date on the back of them, which leads us to believe that the killer is planning an attack."

Cole looked at the picture with a murderous glare.

"I'll kill 'em. Whoever it is, if they hurt my sister ..."

"Hold tight, kid ... It gets worse," warned Adam.

Liam showed Cole the picture of Jenna, and Cole's anger intensified even further.

Finally, in a gentle movement, Liam put the picture of Tristan and Bridgette on the table in front of Cole. His eyes took in the photo and he seemed fixated on Tristan's face. Jack watched Cole very carefully. The quiet, mild-mannered boy had quickly come into his own as a man. In Jack's opinion, there are few times when you could read the contents of a man's heart more easily than when his significant other was in danger. The contents of Cole's heart were splayed out for all to see. Cole's face seethed with anger. His eyes had a dangerous quality to them as all of the warmth quickly vanished.

Suddenly, Cole's fist came slamming down on the dining room table.

"Not a fucking chance."

For the first time in his life, Jack realized that there was one person on this earth that loved Tristan more than himself, and he was sitting right in front of him.

A crowd gathered at dusk outside of Monte's Café. Elkhart citizens carrying flowers, signs and stuffed animals arrived at the site where Courtney O'Mara was found dead. They laid their gifts next to Joe's bouquet of flowers. Soon, the simple memorial grew into a mountain. More people came, some carried candles, but all gathered around the place where Joe had found Courtney lying dead just days before. Tristan and Tony stepped out to listen to the vigil. Roger O'Mara stood next to the spot where his daughter was found. Tears pooled in his eyes as he spoke.

"Thank you all for your tremendous support and generosity during this very trying time. Gwen and I cannot thank you enough."

Roger pulled his wife closer to him. Her tears fell from her face onto her candle threatening to douse the flame, but the fire shot up angry and red instead.

"Courtney was a sweet girl who had many friends. I cannot for the life of me understand why anyone would want to hurt her. Please continue to keep Courtney and us in your prayers. Her sisters are suffering. Misty-Lee, Angie, Trixie and Ally all mourn the loss of their sister. Please remember Courtney as she was, not for how she was taken."

Tristan watched the crowd as Roger spoke. Angie and Misty-Lee held each other as tears streamed from their eyes. Ally stood sullen and stoic against her father. Even Trixie looked sad and shook up. Other members of the crowd cried for the memory of Courtney. Audrey Henning wiped tears from her eyes as she listened to Roger speak. When the crowd was done talking, praying and consoling each other, they moved in unison down Mountain Road. Their candles led the way to Healer's Park where they planned to say a similar blessing for April Dearing.

"We want everyone to finish their night out, and we will take it from there," explained Frank. "We do not live in fear."

"Natalie is upstairs, and Tristan is safe at work with Tony."

"Oh, Tony's on tonight?" asked Jack.

"Yes. He'll keep her safe 'til I return at eight. Then Natalie has to close up with Tony and I'll pick up Natalie and Bridgette at eleven."

"Does Jenna know yet?"

"I tried calling her but her cell phone is dead."

Tristan opened the back door of Monte's Café as she lugged a heavy bag of trash out to the dumpster. She lifted the bag but before she could toss it, something stopped her dead in her tracks. Someone was standing in the forest just twenty feet from her. Tristan could feel the intensity of the watcher's stare from under their hood. As the beams of the bright moon cast down upon the watcher's frame, Tristan could barely make out the person's face. But she definitely recognized them. Suddenly, the person turned quickly on their heel, discarded something in the cavity of the Bone Tree, and ran off into the woods.

The back door opened behind Tristan and Tony called out, "Tristan, leave the trash. I'll get it. I need you back inside."

Tristan did as she was told. Tony peered out the back door for a moment making sure that there was no one lingering out back. A moment later he slammed the back door shut and locked it tight as a strange feeling crept over him.

CHAPTER 23

June 20, 2000
Morrow Manor
Elkhart, PA
9 P.M.

LIAM AND ADAM MORROW SLUMPED DOWN at their father's dining room table feeling exhausted as the pressure of the investigation came crashing down upon them. It was a tremendous weight bearing down on their shoulders: A murderer was on the loose and another young woman was dead. Now there was a box with leads for the murderer's next victims. The thought alone caused Adam's stomach to twist and tighten into a pretzel.

Tristan had just returned from her evening shift at Monte's Café, and she was worn out. She hung her apron on a hook in the foyer, along with her keys, and moseyed down the long hallway towards the dining room. As she entered the room, she found her older brothers sitting at the massive cherry wood table which had scattered papers, photographs, official police records, and handwritten notes strewn all over the surface. When Liam saw his sister enter the room he grabbed a handful of the photographs that were on the table, and quickly turned them over. Tristan only saw a flash of red, before the image was removed from her sight. Adam and Liam appeared to be combing through every single piece of documentation they had in an effort to find anything of relevance that they might have missed, any possible connection, but alas, they had come up empty handed. It pained Tristan to see the effect that this investigation was having on her brothers. They both appeared significantly older; their usual charm was removed from their eyes and replaced with a cold seriousness. They both looked as if they could use a good meal and a long sleep. She waved at her brothers with a smile and they nodded in return. *They have to be starving*, Tristan thought as she walked into the kitchen and reached for a large pot that hung over the range. She filled the pot with water and placed it gently on the stovetop. As she turned on the front burner, Jack walked in. He sighed heavily as he approached her.

"Oh, good. You're home," Jack said sounding relieved.

"Yeah, Cole drove me. He's turning a movie on in the living room if you want to join us."

Jack nodded. "Okay, what movie?" Jack asked as a smile formed on his tired face.

"Knowing him, probably *Rocky* again," Tristan added.

"I could go for that," added Jack as he gave Tristan a smile.

Tristan stirred the spaghetti that was now swimming in the boiling water.

"What are you making?" asked Jack nosily as he peeked into the pot.

"Spaghetti. They look like they are starving. Didn't anyone make dinner?"

"Who would have eaten it? Frank took Tommy, Shane and Blake to the movies. Your aunt is at work. Gus and Moira went to see a show ... Adam and Liam said they weren't hungry and I sure as hell wasn't just cooking for me. I ate the last piece of cheesecake from last night."

"And you listened to them? Look at them," Tristan said, scolding her father.

Jack was surprised at the agitation in his daughter's voice. He peered back at his sons and could certainly understand Tristan's concern. Neither of them had shaved in what appeared to be days. Liam had dark circles under his light eyes. Adam had a dangerous look on his face. They were in over their heads and he knew it. Jack ran his hand over the back of his head, wondering what he would say to them. Tristan pulled down five plates, one for each of them and Cole, and began to dish out spaghetti on each. She doused the pasta with marinara sauce and ample amounts of grated parmesan cheese. Jack grabbed two of the plates and followed his daughter into the dining room. Tristan placed a plate in front of Adam and Liam and watched as they started to chow down on the still steaming food. Tristan glanced at Jack with a knowing look as they sat down at the table with them. Jack eyed his sons precariously and confronted the elephant in the room head on.

"So ... How's the investigation going?" asked Jack with an upbeat tone of voice.

Liam looked up from his plate, exhaustion weighing down his typically handsome face. He replied, "We've hit a wall."

"That's the understatement of the year," said Adam with a bite.

"Remember when we had three suspects?" asked Liam with a serious look on his face.

Jack wearily replied, "Yes."

"Oh, good, because now we have zero," said Liam bluntly.

"What? How did that happen?" asked Jack with a perplexed look.

"Every single one of them has a rock solid alibi at the time of the second murder," explained Adam.

"That doesn't necessarily mean that they are innocent the first time around," Jack reminded.

"They are linked. I know they are. I'd even go so far to say that it's the same guy that killed Tiffany O'Mara twenty years ago," said Liam going out on a limb.

"We have no proof of any of that yet," Adam reminded his brother.

"This case is going to be the death of me," complained Liam as he allowed his head to sink into his hands.

"Have you talked to DiNolfo yet?" asked Jack reasonably. She would be the best person to give them advice at this stage of the investigation. She'd been through it all before.

"Not yet," Adam replied.

"Don't you think that's a good idea?" asked Jack as the anxiety rose in his chest.

Adam shrugged. "We can't get a hold of her. Her cell phone is dead."

Jack rolled his eyes in disgust.

"Now is not the time to be stubborn or proud. Girls are turning up dead! The killer is still out there, and lord only knows who he is or where he is or what he plans to do next!" shouted Jack across the table, hoping to get his sons to wake up and spring into action. Jack gave his daughter a nervous look whenever he spoke about the murders. If he could he'd keep Tristan at home until all this was over, but he realized that that just wasn't rational, and she wasn't a child anymore.

Through gritted teeth, Liam replied, "Says the stubborn old mule."

Jack gave his sons a glaring look.

"What seems to be the problem, boys?" Jack demanded.

"We could get in real trouble for telling you this, so keep this under your hat," warned Liam.

Jack took his blue trucker hat off his head, revealing his graying black hair. He pretended to put something under his hat, before returning it to his head.

Adam, satisfied with his father's response, asked, "So you know how there have always been three suspects?"

"Yeah," Jack replied, his patience wearing thin.

"And how the whole town thinks it's Tommy who is responsible?" asked Liam.

"Even though he's not responsible. Yeah," replied Jack with a start.

"Well, all three were released as suspects. We have nothing."

Jack looked around at the table that was filled to the brim with paperwork.

"What do you mean you have nothing? How is this possible? Even Trafford had a rock solid alibi?" Jack yelled.

"Him especially. Tommy was in an interrogation room with DiNolfo when the call came out for the second murder. Add in his alibi on the night of Courtney's death and he's off the hook," explained Adam.

Jack closed his eyes as he released a heavy sigh.

Thank God.

"And the others?" asked Jack.

"Jesse Trafford was in a holding cell over in Sunbury. He got arrested after being involved in a bar fight. It couldn't have been him," explained Liam.

"And Hunter McCord was at Steeplechase giving an anti-drug presentation."

Jack was amazed. "No wonder Tommy was so pissed off the other day. What about the gun you found at the scene?"

"We actually checked into that and McCord couldn't have been the one involved in Courtney's murder. He was in jail at the time for fighting with Tommy."

"Unreal," Jack noted.

"What?" asked Adam.

"Someone is trying to set these guys up. Tommy's clothes found at the scene of the first murder. Hunter's gun found just yards away. Trafford's wallet found at the scene of the murder. Someone is trying to make it seem like they are all working together."

"But who?" asked Liam, knowing damn well that neither of them had the answer.

"And who would forget their clothes or wallet at the scene of a crime?" said Adam incredulously. "Whoever is doing this is trying too hard, and they are bound to slip up."

"The last thing we want is for the person responsible to have an opportunity to slip up," said Jack nervously as he glanced at Tristan.

"That's why we need to find out who the guy is that did this. He had to have left some sign, some trace of DNA at the scene," suggested Liam.

Tristan, who was quietly listening as the conversation developed, interrupted her brothers and her father, "Ummm, what makes you think it's a guy?"

Adam and Liam both gave their sister a pained expression.

"Tris, you didn't see the crime scene and I hope to God you never have to see anything like that in your life," said Liam.

"It was brutal. Blood everywhere. The brute force and strength needed to do that much damage ... It couldn't have been a female. It was grisly," explained Adam with a grimace on his face.

"Not to mention what we found at the Bone Tree."

"Besides, we found a men's size eleven footprint in the mud," added Liam.

Jack didn't like the direction the conversation was taking. He eyed his daughter carefully. She seemed to have something that she was desperately trying to say. Tristan looked at her brothers, unrelenting in her resolve. She knew from personal experience that a woman could do as much damage as a man—especially when motivated by anger.

Tristan continued, "You said the Bone Tree, right? In York Forest, right behind Monte's?"

Tristan's questions had piqued Jack's interest. "Baby, do you know something that you're not telling us?" Jack asked.

Tristan got up from her chair, and began gathering the empty dishes from the table. She had a worried expression upon her face, a look that caused Jack's stomach to jolt in fear.

With her eyes full of honesty, knowledge and depth, Tristan said, "I know who you are looking for."

Roger O'Mara stood by the fireplace in his living room as he prepared to lecture his family to an intense degree about increased safety measures taking place within the O'Mara residence. Gwen had gathered up the family per Roger's request. Trixie and Ally sat on the loveseat with disgruntled looks upon their faces. Misty-Lee and Angie sat on the couch with Cory, who was trying to kick free. Gwen sat down beside them with an exhausted look on her face. Misty-Lee asked Angie to hold Cory for a moment. She took him and held him like a sack of potatoes out from her body. She treated him like he was something vile and disgusting. Cory, in turn, kicked his legs and complained, "Put me down!"

"You're not very maternal are you?" Misty-Lee quipped as she looked at Angie's repulsed face.

"Children and I don't see eye to eye," said Angie, who never had any desire to have offspring of her own.

"What's this all about, Roger?" asked Gwen wearily.

Roger cleared his throat.

"I want to make sure I am very clear."

All eyes were on Roger as he prepared to deliver what he presumed would be unwelcomed news.

"Until this is cleared up ... I want no one leaving the house. No one is to use the cars unless you are going to work or school. Do I make myself clear?"

"Dad!" Trixie complained! "It's senior week!"

"Beatrix Ann O'Mara! I don't care if the President has invited you to supper! You're not going out unless it's for school."

Trixie sighed dramatically.

"Young lady! In case you haven't noticed, your sister was murdered! Another woman was just murdered, too! I'm not losing a third daughter! I refuse!"

Angie spoke up, "Dad's right, Trix ... It's dangerous out there."

PART THREE

The Long Way Down

My past has found me,
And I've found him.
Hiding in shadows, rotting within.
The mask is gone, the bed is made,
No intention of giving me
All that I gave.
Blinded by the day,
You escaped from view.
Cowering in corners,
Covering up clues.
The dawn erased him,
Swallowed by the blue
Waves crashed upon him,
Erased from my view.
Awoken from slumber,
Mind dizzy and askew.
Thoughts, I had many,
But words, very few.
And I'll never understand,
Why this is true,
But night time always,
Brings me back to you.

~Excerpt from Phantom Flight by Addison Kline

CHAPTER 24

June 20, 2000
Seattle, WA
7 P.M.

FELIX DESANTO STROLLED UP MARINER AVENUE with a bounce in his step and a bouquet of yellow roses in his left hand. He pushed the sleeve of his suit jacket up as he glanced at his gold Rolex. It was exactly seven o'clock. Felix had felt bad for how things had ended with Angie and he wanted to at least apologize. Although he could be a real jerk in the office, outside the confines of Seattle Commerce One, he was a somewhat decent human being. While he had eyes for lots of women, including Angie, he had never actually cheated on his high-maintenance wife, Monica. In fact, it was Monica who urged Felix to pay Angie a visit to apologize. Although Felix couldn't give Angie her job back, he wanted to stop by with a small token of his gratitude for all of her help through the years. Felix climbed the steps to 2324 Mariner Avenue and entered the old brownstone building that Angie called home. He hoped that she would be willing to see him.

The phone rang loudly on Officer Liam Morrow's desk as he sat combing through Tiffany O'Mara's case file. He and Adam had escaped the chatter of the Morrow Manor, and decided they could concentrate better at the office. Liam was busy making a comparative list between Tiffany O'Mara's case file and Courtney O'Mara's file. He broke his concentration for the first time in hours to answer the phone on his desk.

In an agitated tone, Liam said, "Elkhart Police Department. Officer Morrow speaking."

A deep and serious voice spoke from the other end of the line.

"Hi. This is Detective Mitch Croyden with Seattle PD. Is Sergeant DiNolfo in?"

"I'm afraid she's out of the office. Is there something that I can help you with?"

"I guess so ... I am investigating a murder here in Seattle and we believe that the suspect is now in the Elkhart, Pennsylvania vicinity."

"Could you fax me everything you have? We're dealing with a double homicide. We've got very few leads at this point."

"Of course. Please give me a courtesy call after apprehension. What's your fax number?"

Liam provided the detective with the Elkhart Police Department's fax number.

The detective continued, "I'm sending it now and please call if you have any questions."

Angie gently shut her bedroom door trying not disturb her still heavily grieving mother. Gwen had gone upstairs to rest after listening to Roger's intense lecture on family safety. Angie exchanged her uncomfortable trousers and blouse for a pair of sweats. As she lowered herself onto her chair at her vanity, her exhaustion was beginning to show. Angie looked at the mirror with a wary expression. The weight of her sister's murder, along with all the questions from the police, was certainly taking its toll on her too. She reached up and slowly pulled her hair pins from her neat bun that was secured atop her head. Piece by piece, her blonde hair fell down her back and over her shoulders. Angie's eyes looked heavy and dark with deep circles weighing underneath. She hoped the police would arrest their suspect soon. She didn't know how much more of this she could take.

Felix walked down the long hallway towards Angie's apartment when he saw something hanging on Angie's apartment door. Felix quickly approached the door and determined it was a letter. He plucked the letter off the door and unfolded it. He arched his thick eyebrows as he read Jeremy's goodbye letter to Angie.

Damn, Jer ... That was cold.

After he was done reading the letter, he stuck it back up on the door with the worn piece of scotch tape that was attached. Felix went to knock on the door, but as his knuckles met the wood surface, he realized the door was slightly ajar. With an eerie groan, the door opened and Felix stepped over the threshold of Angie's disheveled apartment.

"Ang, are you here? It's me, Felix."

Felix waited for a response but no one answered him. There was something definitely off. The apartment was in utter disarray. Felix wondered if the apartment had been broken into prior to his arrival. The TV was missing, the furniture was gone, but there were traces of evidence that someone once lived there. There were CDs scattered about and broken on the carpet. Empty prescription pill bottles lay strewn about on the kitchen floor; others lay on the countertop on their side. Felix picked up a few of the bottles, but the medication was a long, official sounding word that Felix could not pronounce. A colorful assortment of pills lay on the countertop, the floor and in the sink. There was no telling what bottle they belonged to. There were just too many. Dirty clothes littered the hallway that led to Angie's bedroom that she once shared with her husband, Jeremy. Felix could detect a strange smell in the apartment. It was a foul and peculiar odor, a combination of mildew, ammonia, and decay. The smell lingered down the hallway and seemed to be seeping from under Angie's bedroom door.

Liam Morrow's eyes widened with shock as Adam handed him the fax from Detective Croyden. The machine groaned loudly as page after page of information cranked through. As Liam's eyes lingered over the photograph of their suspect, his breath shortened.

"Oh, my God ... Tristan was right."

Angie's face was tired and taut as she brushed her hair. Suddenly, the lines of her smile curved upwards as a thought came to mind. Her blue eyes stared forward, revealing an expression of both incredible sadness and unbelievable depth. Much like Courtney's eyes, Angie's eyes looked like water. But while Courtney's eyes resembled a tranquil sea, Angie's were more like the ocean within the stronghold of a storm. Like the Pacific in a maelstrom, ready to swallow ships whole and chew up sailors for lunch. The devil only knew what monsters lay within. Angie's brows furrowed as her eyes cast a disturbing glance into the mirror. She spoke in a voice that was nothing more than a whisper.

"All secrets must come to the light."

"Angie ..." called Felix from the hallway as he slowly crept closer and closer to Angie's closed bedroom door. The smell was getting stronger, more pungent and offensive with every step that Felix took. The hair on Felix's neck stood on end as his hand reached for the doorknob.

"Angie ..." Felix said softly, haunted by the strange silence in the apartment.

Finally, Felix mustered the courage to open the door. He twisted the bronze knob with bated breath. When the door swung open, a wall of stagnant, putrid air hit him. It was like nothing he had ever smelled before. It was a combination of death and decay, ammonia and vinegar. It smelled like something had died, and someone tried to cover up the smell. They failed miserably. Felix's stomach tightened into a ball as he stepped into the room.

"Pick up the goddamn phone!" Liam yelled as he tried to get DiNolfo on her cell phone again. He had been trying to get a hold of her all day long, but once again, she wasn't picking up.

"Shit!" Liam complained as he slammed his desk phone down.

Liam re-read the contents of the fax again, stunned by what he was reading. Words stuck out on the page that served as an eerie reminder of just how twisted this case really was. The killer was a sociopath with a long disturbing history of severe mental disease and psychosis. They had killed Jeremy Macklon along with his feline friend, Nan, in a most brutal manner and left them to rot in an abandoned apartment. The very thought sent chills up Liam's spine. Suddenly the front door of the Elkhart Police Station slammed open as a haggard-looking Sergeant DiNolfo walked through.

"I know who it is. Let's go."

"Finally! You need to see this!"

"It's not important."

"It is, though! She killed her husband!"

"How did you find out?"

"Seattle faxed us over all the details."

"We need to go now."

As the watch on his wrist ticked the seconds off to midnight, Adam raced after Liam and Sergeant DiNolfo out to patrol car E5.

⌘

Angie's lips curled into a malicious smile as the first strand of hair fell to the floor. The buzz of the hair clipper masked her quiet laughter. Chunks of blonde hair fell to the floor but Angie's eyes did not move from her reflection. She was fixated on her likeness in the mirror as she transformed before her own eyes. Everyone told her what a beauty she was. Now her outside would mirror the contents of her heart. She knew the mirror would soon strip her of her outward beauty and show her for what she really was. A ravenous lion in sheep's clothing. A monster under the guise of a damsel in distress. A killer hiding as a victim. She was bad to her core, as sick and twisted as they come. Bernard Kendricks had taken a sick and confused little girl and turned her into a monster.

⌘

The hideous stench of Angie's bedroom caused Felix's eyes to burn. He closed his eyes tight, but opened them again once he had grown more accustomed to the smell.

Swarms of flies buzzed around his head. There had to be hundreds of them in the room. As the swarm cleared, Felix had to adjust his eyes. The queen-size bed was covered with documents, all scattered about in the messiest of ways. Medical records and doctors notes, court orders and court summons covered the bed from foot to head. It looked as if someone was looking for something of great importance, and then just gave up. Felix's eyes wandered to the floor where he saw the unmistakable trail of blood on the cream carpet. On the opposite side of the room beside Angie's queen-size bed, Felix could see a pale leg sticking out, bare and bloody.

"Angie!" Felix yelled as he tried to get to the body on the floor, but when he reached the body, it wasn't Angie.

Jeremy Macklon lie dead on the floor with multiple gunshot wounds to his head and chest. To his right, in a puddle of her own blood, Angie's cat, Nan, lay dead, savagely destroyed at close range by a barrage of bullets. Felix felt the blood rush to his head as he tried to get out as fast as he could.

"Oh my God," Felix whispered as his emotions got the best of him.

He repeated the phrase over and over again as he tried to make sense of what was happening. Jeremy Macklon was dead and Felix had a feeling he knew who was responsible. A train of thoughts entered Felix's mind:

Did she know that I would come?

My fingerprints are now all over the apartment. On the front door handle, on the bedroom door handle, on several of the prescription bottles in the kitchen ...

Had she known?

His breathing intensified as he hurtled himself towards the front door. Felix clambered over the laundry in the hall, skidded on an empty pill container, and finally as he made it to the front door of the apartment he bolted down the stairs and out the front door. As he crashed into the hard brownstone exterior of 2423 Mariner Avenue, rage poured from his body and tears burned from his eyes.

In a heavy voice full of emotion and infliction, Felix said aloud, "Oh, my God, Angie. What have you done?"

Angie was happy with what she saw. Her smile grew wide as her teeth bared at her reflection. She ran her bony hand over her bald head as a chill ran up her spine. It was time to finish what she had set out to do. She pulled on Tommy Morrow's black hoodie, laced his hiking boots tightly over her size nine feet and crossed the room with a fuming vengeance. As she threw the window open, she gave the room one last glance.

She didn't plan to ever see it again.

"I don't know why I do the things I do," said Angie from under her black hood.

Tommy Morrow's hiking books cloaked her tiny feet perfectly as she trudged loudly on the roof of Gwen and Roger O'Mara's kitchen. Angie's feet stood precariously close to the edge of the roof. It would only take one false step to send her falling to her death. A gentle breeze blew westward, gracing over Angie's body. She dropped her hood and let it flow over her closely shaved head. For a moment, Angie closed her eyes to try to find the calm she needed to prevent herself from causing further bloodshed. She breathed in and out, again and again. Her lungs rasped as the sickness within consumed her. When she opened her eyes again, there was only bitter contempt, hostile depravity, and evil disdain lingering in the pools of her eyes. The monster had taken over again.

As a strange smile curled from her lips, Angie whispered into the night, "I'm not sorry for what I've done. Remorse is a foreign emotion to me. Where was *his* emotion when he left me bereft of my innocence? I won't run this time. I won't stop. The animal that Bernard awoke in me has come to devour those who stand in my way. No one can stop me. Not even myself."

As the cool breeze came to a sudden halt, Angie jumped from the kitchen roof to the dirt below. As she ran down Caribou Road in the dark of night, Angie whispered, "It all ends tonight."

June 20, 1980
Kendricks Residence
9 Barn Owl Road
Shephard's Grove, PA
After Midnight

Bernard Kendricks sat in the dark dim of his bedroom which was illuminated by the light of a candle. The burning flame danced in the darkness and grew more wild and impassioned with each passing moment. The candle illuminated Bernard's face in a sickly glow as he poured himself over his "work." A photograph of a young Catherine Morrow sat in a bronze frame on his desk. Her dark hair cascaded over her bare shoulder and her beautiful smile was certainly meant for a man other than Bernard. Bernard liked to imagine that Catherine was staring at him as he wrote a letter to her—his one-hundredth letter this month. A bang from the opposite side of his bedroom door jarred Bernard's concentration. His eyes perked up as a dangerous mood overcame him. He didn't like interruptions when he was writing his letters to Catherine. It was their only time together.

"Bernard," called Bernard's aging mother, Dorothy. "You have a visitor."

"Mother, I thought I said no guests tonight?" snapped Bernard at his frail mother.

"Bernard, be nice!" she sweetly encouraged. "We had such a wonderful time on vacation, didn't we?"

"Yes, Mother. It was a nice escape."

"Such a shame we had to come home early. Now be nice to your guest," said Dorothy.

Mrs. Kendricks made way for Bernard's visitor and closed the door behind her as she went back down the hall to her bedroom. When Bernard turned around, he was not surprised to see his cousin, Angela, standing in the doorway. Angela hoped that he had finally returned home from Maine. She had something important to share with him.

"I've asked you countless times to leave me alone at home, Angela," Bernard said in a bored tone. His eyes changed suddenly when he saw Angie's appearance. Her prom dress was torn above her knees, she had scrapes on her face and legs, her hair was a disheveled mess and her eyes were in a wild frenzy.

"Has someone touched you?" Bernard yelled in fury. "If anyone has touched you, I'll kill them myself!"

Angie ignored Bernard's questions and rushed to him with a jubilant smile.

"I did it, Bernard! Just like you said to!" Angie exclaimed manically.

Bernard's eyes went wide.

"What did you do?" asked Bernard in a horrified voice.

"I did what you said. You said to remove the obstacles from my path and I did it! She's gone!"

Bernard's eyes raged with anger.

"Stupid girl!"

"What? Why are you angry?" Angie asked sweetly.

"I meant better yourself. Not kill your sister!"

"But you said—"

"I know what I said!"

"Bernard, it's over now."

"You must go," Bernard said sternly as he turned back to his desk to finish his letter.

"And you must come," said Angie alluringly.

But before Bernard could respond, Angie encroached upon his work space.

"What's this?" yelled Angie as she grabbed the letter. "Are you *still* obsessed with Mrs. Morrow?"

"Don't call her that!"

"Her name is *not* and will *never* be Catherine Kendricks!"

Angie ripped the letter into tiny pieces and threw them into the air. They fell to the floor like confetti. Bernard sped across the room as fury seeped from his skin. His hand gripped Angie's neck as a devious smile grew across her face. The tighter he squeezed, the wider she smiled. Her lips curled until nearly all of her teeth were bared back at Bernard. Bernard's face morphed from an expression of relentless anger to one of uncontrollable fear.

"She will be your undoing, Bernard," said Angie slyly as she slithered out of Bernard's hold.

Bernard grabbed Angie and pushed her to the floor as he pinned his knees on her arms. He lowered himself to within an inch of Angie's face and barked, "And I will be the one who unravels you to your wicked core."

An evil smile spread across Angie's face.

"Oh, Bernard, we all know how you like to unravel teenage girls," said Angie in nothing more than a whisper.

Bernard looked down at Angie with a contemptible glare. His eyes grazed over her bare shoulders, her slender neck, and the bird pendant that he had given her just months prior.

"What would Catherine think of a man who takes advantage of teenage girls?"

"Stop! I told you it was a one-time thing. It was a mistake!"

"It happened twenty-seven times!"

"It was a mistake!"

"I wonder what your mother would think. A twenty-eight-year-old man with his sixteen-year-old cousin. You are a sick, sick man, Bernard."

Tears began to flood Bernard's eyes as he held his head with both hands in an attempt to stop the mental anguish that was now ridiculing him.

He screamed, "Oh, my God! What a monster I've created!"

"Yes, created and out of your control. You don't like our little game now that you're not in control? *Pity.*"

"What is to stop me from calling the police right now?"

"Oh, Bernard. You've shown me all your secrets. Don't you remember? I can easily show the police the bone yard that you created down in the mine, just under the Bone Tree. I can even expose our biggest secret."

"You wouldn't," said Bernard in a fearful voice.

"Oh, but I would."

As Angie glared at Bernard with a vicious stare, Bernard swallowed the saliva that had pooled in his mouth.

"Speak a word of this, and I'll undo you before Catherine has the chance," threatened Angie as she stormed out of Bernard Kendricks's bedroom and life forever.

CHAPTER 25

June 20, 2000
Morrow Manor
Fox Hollow, PA
10:45 P.M.

TRISTAN WOKE TO THE SOUND OF STATIC. The harsh white noise was coming from the television and assaulting her ear drums with firm aggression. She rose from her pillow on the couch groggily, where she had fallen asleep while her father and boyfriend were watching *Rocky III*, a movie that she had watched more times than she would like to count. Tristan rubbed her eyes as her vision slowly returned after her cat nap. Jack and Cole lay sprawled out on their respective couches. The others had not returned yet. Aunt Bridgette was still at work. Uncle Frank was at the movies with Tommy, Blake and Shane. Liam and Adam had gone back to the precinct. Angus and Moira had left earlier that day for an evening in New York. Moira wanted to escape the heavy state of affairs in Elkhart and enjoy a nice dinner and a show with Angus. Meanwhile, Natalie was still at the diner. The house was eerily quiet and Tristan was the only one who was awake. She rose from the sofa and stretched her limbs which were sore from lying in one position for too long. It had gotten really dark and Tristan wondered what time it was. As she glanced at the wall clock, panic nearly struck her.

10:45 ... Cole should've left a half hour ago to pick up Aunt Bridgette and Natalie.

"Cole," Tristan called as she shook her boyfriend's foot. Cole groaned in protest and fell back asleep.

"Cole ... Wake up." Cole snored loudly as Tristan stared at him and rolled her eyes. She felt bad having to wake him up. After all, Jack and Joe were having him do a lot of pickups and drop-offs. It seemed unfair.

Surely I can manage a quick pick-up. Right? He probably won't even notice I'm gone. I can't just leave the girls stranded on Mountain Road. Not with a killer on the loose.

Jack would be furious when he found out that Tristan went to get Bridgette and Natalie on her own, but Tristan was sure that, with time, he would get over it. Tristan's thoughts raced a mile a minute as she went into Frank's gun cabinet and pulled out a revolver.

Just in case.

Tristan decided to bite the bullet and do what she felt was right. Poor Cole had been running all around, and Jack was exhausted himself. She was an adult now and she decided to make a last minute judgment call. As Tristan crossed the threshold of Morrow Manor, she glanced back at Cole and Jack's sleeping faces and smiled.

"Where the hell is he?" fumed Bridgette as she looked at her wrist watch. The time was 11:20 p.m. and Cole had not arrived yet. She was waiting in the lobby of Grier Mountain Medical Center with a worried look on her face. Cole was usually so dependable. Bridgette hoped that nothing was wrong.

Carla, a nurse from the Pediatric unit, said to Bridgette, "Hey, isn't that your brother's truck?"

Bridgette's eyes perked up to the parking lot and sure enough it was Jack's truck pulling up. She looked perplexed as she looked at the driver though, because it definitely wasn't Jack or Cole behind the wheel.

"All right, Carla. Have a good night. Be safe," Bridgette urged as she bid her colleague adieu.

Bridgette swung the passenger side door of Jack's truck open as she gave Tristan a look that was peppered with both bewilderment and amusement.

"How on earth did you get past your old man?" asked Bridgette.

"Both him and Cole fell asleep. Uncle Frank is still out with the boys. It was either I come or you spend the night here."

"I appreciate it. Let's go grab Natalie and get back before he notices."

"And let's get out of Elkhart before anyone gets any ideas," said Tristan darkly. She knew who was responsible, and she wasn't thrilled being in such close vicinity to where that person was living.

"Want me to drive?" asked Bridgette, detecting a hint of nervousness in her niece's usually steady voice.

"Yeah."

Bridgette slid over into the driver's seat as Tristan walked around the truck to climb into the passenger seat. As she was about to get into the truck she noticed that Natalie was walking up Mountain Road towards the hospital parking lot.

"Natalie's coming," said Tristan as she boosted herself into the passenger seat and strapped her seatbelt across her lap and chest.

Bridgette glared nervously out the windshield as she watched Natalie approach.

She was only about one hundred feet away; she'd be in the truck in a matter of minutes. Suddenly, something dark interrupted her view. A black van had pulled up right in front of where Natalie was walking. It had come to a complete stop. Tristan saw it first, and her blood ran cold. Bridgette rolled down the driver's side window.

"Yo! Leave that girl alone!"

When the driver did not respond, Bridgette slammed on the gas, veering dangerously across the parking lot at full throttle. At first Tristan thought her aunt was going to crash into the black van, but the vehicle came to a screeching stop with just an inch to spare.

"Gimme the gun," said Bridgette to Tristan.

Tristan complied and pulled the gun out of the waistband of her jeans and passed it to her aunt. Bridgette stormed from the truck towards the opposite side of the van where the sliding door was opening. She could hear the heavy rasp of breathing and a faint whimper.

"Let her go!" yelled Bridgette as she pointed the gun at the head of Natalie's captor.

Natalie sat shaking in the back of the van with a black pillow case over her head. The person who took her stood confidently at the door and didn't back down from Bridgette. They masked their identity under the dark shadow of their hooded sweatshirt. Though Bridgette couldn't see the person's face, she knew who it was. She could feel the person staring at her, and she stared back. After a moment, when she felt as if the hooded person's resolve was weakening, she made her move. Bridgette stepped quickly towards the open van and grabbed Natalie's leg and pulled her forward causing her to fall into the gravel below.

"Run, Natalie!" Bridgette screamed as she pushed the hooded perpetrator hard into the side of the van.

Bridgette held them down, hoping to give Natalie a chance to get away. Natalie did as she was told and ran fast down Mountain Road with the pillowcase still restricting her vision.

"You shouldn't have done that," the hooded person said as they fought back, hitting Bridgette in the mouth with a nasty uppercut.

Bridgette spit blood on the side of the van before returning a vicious elbow to the perpetrator's face.

"I don't have time for your bullshit! You wanna put me on your list? Well to hell with that!" Bridgette spat as she kicked the assailant hard in the gut, causing them to fly back into the cargo area of the van where they had stored Natalie.

Bridgette ran as fast as she could, hoping to get back to the truck so that she could catch up with Natalie before the person in the van did. Luck was not with her tonight though, because as she reached the driver's side door of Jack's truck, Bridgette heard the unmistakable click of a gun.

"911 Operator... What's your emergency?"

"There is a van on Mountain Road and Mercy Street. Someone is trying to kidnap my friend!"

"Please stay on the line with me while I contact the authorities. Do you have a direct line of sight with the perpetrator?"

"No, they are on the other side of the van. My aunt is trying to get the girl from her!"

"Can you tell me what kind of van it is?"

"It's a black cargo van. Like the type businesses use. I can make out the license plate number."

"What is it?"

"PAJ08256."

"Please stay in the car and on the phone with me until the authorities arrive. They are on their way."

"Oh, my God! Aunt Bridgette! Natalie!"

"Miss? Are you still there?"

But as the operator asked her question the line went dead.

Liam, Adam and Jenna returned to the Elkhart Police Department after coming up empty-handed from the O'Mara house. Angie was not at home for questioning. Jenna decided she would ride around the neighborhood to see if she could spot her. As a call came over the radio for a kidnapping in progress on Mountain Road, Liam and Adam bolted into action. Liam jumped up from his chair, nearly knocking over his desk as he scrambled to the back door of the Elkhart Police Department. Adam, who was right on his heels, grabbed the car keys for patrol car E5.

Natalie ran in what she hoped was a straight line up Mountain Road as she grasped at the rope that was tied around her neck. The assailant covered her eyes with a black pillow case and bound it with rope around her slender neck. Natalie couldn't see a thing. For a moment she wondered if she had gone blind. Natalie tried to allow her hearing to guide her. She heard the cracking sound of gun shots and screaming in the background. She heard the pounding beat of her heart, and her sneakers furiously pounding against the gravel. Then she heard it—the ominous sound of a vehicle approaching. Tires rolled heavily over the gravel road, coming closer and closer until Natalie couldn't run anymore. Natalie's panic raged out of control. Tears streamed down her face making it even harder for her to see. Suddenly, she felt her right foot get caught on something. She pulled and pulled, but she couldn't free it. Just as she pulled her foot from its temporary prison, she felt the firm grip of a hand grab the back of her shirt and throw her into the back of a van. From about fifty yards away, Natalie could hear Tristan Morrow's murderous cry.

"We're coming for you, Angie! You better count on that!"

"Are you all right?" asked Tristan frantically as she ran to her aunt, who was crouched down against the side of the truck with a gunshot wound to her arm.

"I'm fine! It's just a graze."

"You're bleeding!"

"I'm fine we have to get Natalie!"

Bridgette climbed into the passenger seat of the truck as she wrapped an old rag around her upper right arm, holding the material with her left hand and her teeth. She wrapped the rag taut around her wound as she tied a tight knot to secure it. Tristan pounded her foot on the gas as she sped after the van. Dust billowed into the night air leaving Mountain Road in a haze.

Jenna DiNolfo climbed out of her patrol car in the parking lot of the Elkhart Police Station. She had choice words on her mind, and she knew exactly who could answer her questions. With a vengeful look on her face, she stormed straight to the holding cells in the back room of the police station and came face to face with the one person she knew could answer her questions.

"So we meet again," Jenna said in a less than delightful voice.

"Surprise, surprise," said Hunter McCord as he peered at her through the bars of his jail cell.

"Tell me now and tell me straight. What the hell is Angie O'Mara up to?"

"Slam the gas! We're losing sight of them!" yelled Bridgette as she clutched her arm.

"I'm doing seventy-seven miles per hour!"

"Go faster! This bitch isn't hurting anyone else. Tonight or any other night!"

"Hold tight," Tristan said with a serious look in her eye.

The van barreled through the forest at breakneck speed. Tristan pressed the gas pedal and put Jack's truck into four wheel drive as they crossed from the gravel road onto the dirt ground of the forest.

"Where the hell is she taking her?" yelled Bridgette as she reached over to honk the horn several times.

"Pull over, psycho!" Bridgette screamed at the van, which was now just ten feet in front of them. Now barreling down a hill, Tristan knew exactly where she was.

"I know where she's taking her."

"I don't even know where the hell we are. I can't see a thing!"

"Wilhamette. She's going into the mine."

Bridgette's face was wiped clean of emotion.

"You've got to be kidding me?"

"I wish I was."

"That mine stretches for miles. It branches off into many different tunnels. She can hide really easily in there."

"Relax. I have a plan."

The black van wound tightly around the mountainside and Tristan followed close behind, mocking the van's every tilt and turn. Tristan smiled darkly as the van stormed through the barricade that covered the entrance of the mine at Wilhamette. She glanced over at her aunt and they exchanged a knowing look.

"Pull in that mirror and strap in," said Tristan with a dangerous edge to her voice.

Bridgette's eyes went wide as her niece hit the gas again. The truck barreled into the cavernous tunnel of the dark mine.

"We're catching ourselves a killer. Scared?" asked Tristan with a dark edge to her voice.

"Yeah, okay!" Bridgette said as she laughed. "Let's do this ..."

"Dad is going to love hearing about this ..." Tristan mentioned as the smile faded.

"Oh, God," groaned Bridgette as Jack came into her mind.

Tristan wound the tight curves of the mine, right on the bumper of the black van.

"Where is your sense of adventure, Aunt Bridgette?"

"Oh, my God. Your father is going to kill me."

Natalie struggled and squirmed in the back of the van. She still had the hood over her head, but now her kidnapper had bound her wrists and her feet, too. She wriggled her wrists as she tried to break free. Suddenly, the sound of a gunshot and shattering glass jarred Natalie's composure.

"Son of a bitch!" the voice of her kidnapper spoke.

That voice is so familiar!

"See if you can catch me now," said the voice as they veered the van down a narrow passageway that the truck would not fit down.

"McCord, don't feed me any bullshit. I'm not in the mood!"

"She's never in the mood!" yelled Trafford from his holding cell down the hall.

"Watch your mouth, Trafford!" DiNolfo yelled trying to stifle a laugh. "Now you, what's the deal?"

"I'm being honest with you. Someone stole my guns just before Courtney turned up murdered. No one had access to my trailer except for Ethan and my mom, and it definitely wasn't any of them. But then I remembered that I had put my keys down on the table right before that fight with Tommy Morrow. I'm willing to bet that she took my keys."

"Wouldn't that beast of a dog have mauled her?"

"Ox really liked her. She had spent the night a few times."

"Cute. Her sister's dead but she's cuddling up with you."

Hunter shrugged his shoulder nonchalantly.

"Have you ever known Angie to be a violent person?"

"Not with men. Only women. She would get jealous a lot. Especially of her sister."

"Are you sure about that?"

"I've never witnessed her show aggression towards any men."

"Hmm ..." said DiNolfo curiously, leaving Hunter guessing. He stared back at her with a nonplussed expression on his face.

"What? What am I missing?"

"Oh, nothing ... Except for the fact that her husband turned up dead two days ago. Murdered."

Hunter looked shocked. His eyes darted wildly in his head, and he rubbed the side of his head as his anxiety mounted.

"What else? Give me something I can use."

"All right ..." said Hunter warily, as he prepared to tell DiNolfo what he knew.

"Shit!" said Bridgette as she watched the black van squeeze into a tunnel that was too narrow for the truck to fit into.

"No ... It's perfect. I know where that empties out."

Bridgette did a double-take. Tristan certainly seemed to know an awful lot about the mine.

"How?"

"How do I know? This is where Bernard took me after we left the fishing shack, three years ago. There is a central place under Elkhart where all the tunnels merge. He called it the heart of the mine and it is located right under the Bone Tree."

Tristan slammed on the gas once more and took a tunnel that veered to the right as Bridgette looked at her niece in amazement.

"Hold on tight," warned Tristan with an edge to her voice as the truck plunged into the murky dark of the tunnel.

Natalie kicked the back door of the van over and over again, trying to make enough noise so that someone, anyone, would hear her. She had no idea where she was, other than the fact that she was in a moving vehicle against her will and she couldn't see a thing. She scooted on her butt as she tried to get to the back of the vehicle. When she finally found it, she kicked hard with both legs until she was out of breath.

"Keep it down back there!" yelled Angie from the front seat with an ugly expression on her face.

"Where do I know your voice from?" Natalie demanded to know.

"Shut up and sit down!" Angie yelled again.

Natalie had her father's stubborn pride and her mother's determined resilience. She absolutely refused to do what her captor said. If anything, she was adamant on doing the exact opposite of what she was told. A scream rallied in her body, starting from her toes and boiling through her stomach and out her lungs. Her terrible scream bounced off every square inch of the moving van, out Angie's open window, through the tunnel, out the airshaft and escaped from the gaping mouth of the Bone Tree.

"What is it that you're asking me?" asked Hunter with a perplexed look. His tattooed arms slunk out of the jail cell as he continued to talk to DiNolfo unenthusiastically.

"Did you and Angie ever work together?"

"God, no. Angie is a loner, and frankly, so am I. I prefer to work alone so that no one else's mistakes land me in here. That's why I avoid jokers like that one over there who make stupid mistakes," Hunter said as he pointed in Jesse Trafford's general vicinity.

"So your relationship was just platonic."

"Not exactly."

"Be straight with me."

"Fine," said Hunter as he released a deep sigh. "I took her on a run with me."

"A run?"

"A drug run. It was a quick one. This particular client of mine has access to the old mine from his basement, so he always asked that I deliver through there. Angie and I drove through the mine in my van. We dropped off the goods, and left. It was an easy way to keep a low profile. Then when we were done we went to the Chiefsdale Cineplex and watched a movie."

"So you broke into the mine. Trafficked drugs. Completed a drug deal. Then went on a date."

Hunter rolled his eyes.

"Yeah, I guess you could say that."

DiNolfo shook her head.

"Classy."

Hunter shrugged his shoulders.

"I have to ask. Who was your client?"

Hunter groaned. He wasn't a snitch, but he knew that there was a more serious issue going on here. Women were turning up dead. He had to do what was right. He might be a drug dealer, but he wasn't a murderer.

"Hank Dresher."

"Peggy's husband?"

"Yeah."

"There is an access point to the mine in Harrow's basement?"

"Yeah. There's just a piece of plywood there to keep the animals out."

Suddenly, DiNolfo's police radio squawked loudly and Liam's voice blared from the speaker.

"Officer in pursuit of black van, license plate number PAJ08256."

Hunter's face turned red and angry. "That's my van! Somebody stole my van!"

Liam continued shouting into his radio, "Silver SUV belonging to Jack Morrow is in pursuit of van. Shots fired on Mountain Road. Abduction of a white female, age seventeen, Natalie Piedmonte. It is believed that two females are in the truck. Tristan Morrow and Bridgette Kilpatrick. The van is headed towards the Wilhamette Mine! The perpetrator has been positively ID'd as Angela O'Mara. I repeat, the perp has been ID'd as Angela O'Mara."

DiNolfo rose from her folding chair with venomous fury. She bolted out the door of the Elkhart Police Department, bypassed her squad car, and instead ran as fast as her legs would carry her to 41 Mountain Road.

CHAPTER 26

June 20, 2000
Morrow Manor
Fox Hollow, PA
11:00 P.M.

COLE PIEDMONTE WOKE to the sound of the old oak door of Morrow Manor groaning open and slamming against the foyer wall. Sleepily, Cole rubbed his eyes as he looked to see who had come in the door.

"Cole ... Jack ..." called Joe Piedmonte from the foyer.

"Yeah?" said Cole confused, still half asleep.

Cole glanced around the living room. Jack was still asleep in his arm chair, but Tristan was no longer resting on him. The TV had been turned off.

Maybe she went to bed.

"Uh, son ... Where are your sister and Bridgette?" asked Joe warily. He prayed to God that they were upstairs sleeping.

Cole stood up in a panic. He glanced at the clock on the wall that read 11:16 p.m.

"Oh, my God. Oh, my God!" Cole said, his voice giving away his sheer panic.

"You never picked them up?" asked Joe heatedly.

"I slept right through it," said Cole sounding utterly horrified.

"Somebody must have gone to get them because Jack's truck is gone," said Joe as he looked out the front window.

Cole thought for a moment. Frank and the boys were still out at the movies. Jack was sound asleep. The only other person home was Tristan. Cole's heart raced as the thought came to mind.

"Tristan."

"Where is she?"

"She must have gone by herself."

Suddenly, Adam's police radio squawked loudly in the dining room. Joe listened closely to hear what was happening. Liam's voice rang out loud and clear over the radio, "Officer in pursuit of black van, license plate number PAJ08256. Silver SUV belonging to Jack Morrow is in pursuit of van. Shots fired on Mountain Road. Abduction of a white female, age seventeen, Natalie Piedmonte. It is believed that two females are in the truck. Tristan Morrow and Bridgette Kilpatrick. The van is headed towards the Wilhamette Mine! The perpetrator has been positively ID'd as Angela O'Mara. I repeat, the perp has been ID'd as Angela O'Mara."

Cole ran to his father's side and got there just in time to hold him up.

"Oh, my God. All three of them. Oh, my God," Joe said weakly as the color faded from his face. Cole held his father up. Joe looked like he was on the verge of a heart attack. His face turned beet red and his eyes carried a forlorn look.

"Sit down," Cole instructed as he ran back into the living room and slipped on his sneakers.

"Jack! Get up!" yelled Cole as he grabbed his keys off of the coffee table.

"What?" Jack said groggily as he jumped to his feet. His eyes were wide and alert. "What's happening? Where's Tristan?"

"Just get your shoes on and get in my Jeep. We will explain on the way."

"No, tell me now. Where is my daughter?" Jack demanded with wild eyes.

"We need to go get her. Something has happened down in Elkhart."

Jack's chest began to sear as his heart raced. He could feel his blood pressure rising by the second. Suddenly the radio squawked to life again as Adam's frantic voice boomed out of the speaker:

"Two more shots fired! Patrol car E5 in pursuit of black van in the mine. Silver SUV veered right, out of line of fire. Identities of the women in the SUV are confirmed as Tristan Morrow and Bridgette Kilpatrick. Natalie is still alive in the back of the van, we can hear her screaming. Officer discharge, badge #7274! Perpetrator took a shot on the police cruiser. Another shot! Officer down! Officer down! We need medics down here!"

Before Jack could say "Let's go," Cole was already in the Jeep with the keys in the ignition. Both Jack and Joe's minds were in a state of total shock. Cole seemed to be the only one thinking rationally.

"Not again ... Not again ..." Jack kept saying over and over again.

"Snap out of it, Jack!" yelled Cole as he demanded that Jack get in the back seat of the Jeep. Jack did as he was told, surprised at Cole's direct tone.

"You, too!" Cole yelled at his father.

Tears were filling up in Joe's eyes. He was absolutely beside himself.

Haven't the Morrow and the Piedmonte families suffered enough?

Joe didn't know what he would do if anything happened to any of them. His worry was not only focused on Natalie, but on Tristan and Bridgette as well. Then there was Liam, who had been shot. Joe prayed that the medics would get there in time.

"Strap in and hold on!" yelled Cole as he pounded his foot down on the gas pedal sending them catapulting down the mountain in the dark of night. Cole could do nothing but focus on the road in front of him. He could not worry that his sister was kidnapped. He could not worry that Tristan was in the mine fighting to get her back safe. He could not worry about his friends, Liam and Adam, who were in a firefight against the sick woman who was responsible for so much devastation. All that Cole could do was focus on getting there. If he let his heart take over his head, he'd break down on the spot. Cole, the typically mild-mannered and cool customer of the bunch, was proving just how cool under pressure he was. But as calm as he appeared, he would turn downright vicious if any of the girls were hurt.

"Hold on, Liam!" Adam said nervously as he took off his shirt and wrapped it across Liam's shoulder and under his arm.

Blood soaked Liam's uniform shirt where Angie's bullet had pierced the skin and muscle of his shoulder. It had just missed the bone by an inch. Liam thought the bullet might be lodged in his chest because the area over his heart hurt worse than his shoulder did.

"Hold tight, bud. We're gonna get her."

"I'm fine! Just go! Do not lose her!"

With determination and vengeance in his eyes, Adam sent the patrol car bolting into the darkness after the murderer.

Natalie pushed her fingernail through the tattered rope that bound her wrists as she tried to free herself from her binds. She kept at it, and slowly the rope began to fray. Strand by rough strand, she weakened the rope until finally she was free. Immediately her hands flew up to the rope around her neck, which she untied quickly and removed the black pillow case. Finally, she freed herself of the binds around her ankles. It took a moment for her eyes to adjust to the dark light in the van. She glanced at the floor of the van and was alarmed by what she saw. There were bags upon bags of cocaine and marijuana piled on top of one another in the back of the van. At her feet lay an ax that was bloody and rusted. Suddenly, Natalie had an idea. Natalie grabbed a bag of cocaine and she ripped into the bag with her sharp finger nail. She grabbed the ax with her free hand. Slowly and quietly, she crawled on the floor of the van until she was just behind the driver's seat. Angie was still shooting her gun out of her window back at the police car that was right on her tail. While Angie was distracted, Natalie capitalized. Natalie ripped the bag of cocaine open over Angie's head as white powder fell everywhere. Angie couldn't see anything as the cloud of white polluted her vision. Natalie rose over Angie with the ax and as her kidnapper hacked and coughed, she slammed the butt of the ax into Angie's bald head. As the van catapulted to the end of the tunnel, Angie's head slammed into the dashboard with a violent thud.

❧

"Are you sure you know where you're going?" asked Bridgette nervously as Tristan did ninety miles per hour through the dark mine.

The wooden beams above looked like they were ready to give way. The cavernous setting and close quarters were making Bridgette more nervous than the thought of an armed serial killer was.

Bridgette's face turned from perplexed to somber. It was so easy to forget that her intelligent, beautiful, and courageous niece had been through so much as such a young age. From that point on, Bridgette trusted Tristan more as a confidant than as a child.

❧

Cole's Jeep flew through the entrance of the mine as the men were catapulted into darkness. Immediately, they heard shots ringing out further up the tunnel. In the back seat of the Jeep, Jack cocked his gun. He then cocked a second and passed it to Cole.

"Time to end this."

Cole looked at Jack through the rearview mirror. Jack nodded firmly to Cole as they held eye contact. After all they had been through, Jack finally got it. If there was anyone he could trust Tristan with it was Cole, and he definitely wasn't going anywhere. Though he was young, Cole had already decided that he was in this family for the long haul. Angela Macklon-O'Mara picked the wrong family to mess with.

❧

"Does this tunnel never end?" yelled Bridgette becoming increasingly agitated.

"We're about halfway through. This empties out into the same open space as the other tunnel though. Kendricks called it the heart of the mine."

The sound of gun shots echoed through the long tunnels of the mine and ricocheted off the rock walls and the dirt floor. Dust scattered as the bullet cut through the dim light of the mine.

"I hope we make it in time," Bridgette said with worry.

"We will," said Tristan with fierce determination as she pushed down harder on the gas pedal causing the truck to go even faster through the mine.

Natalie dropped the ax to the floor as the white cloud caused her to choke. She tried not to inhale it, and pulled her shirt up over her mouth and her nose to guard her from the toxic drug. Angie had not lifted her head, but the van continued to speed through the darkness. Natalie knew that she had to get into the front seat and get control of the vehicle, somehow. The van was careening out of control as the sides of the van scraped along the mine wall. Sparks flew backwards into the windshield of the police cruiser at an alarming rate. Natalie climbed into the passenger seat. She watched Angie warily as she tried to determine if she was unconscious. After several seconds without movement, Natalie was fairly sure that Angie was knocked out cold. She reached over her kidnapper's body to grab hold of the steering wheel but before she had the chance, Angie's hand shot up and gripped Natalie's wrist—trapping it in a skeletal cage.

Adam held his shirt in place over his brother's wound as Liam winced with pain. Liam was trying to stay strong, but the pain was excruciating. Adam veered through the tunnel as sparks from the out of control van rained down over the windshield.

"She's losing control up there. I think Natalie is trying to fight back."

Liam sighed loudly as his pain intensified.

"Hang in there, bud."

"I'm fine! Let's pick up the pace!"

As Adam glanced over in worry at his brother, Liam rolled down his window.

"Grab my gun out of my holster."

"What?"

"Just do it!"

Adam did as his brother asked, while keeping his eyes on the road.

"Here," he said as he passed the gun to Liam.

Liam lifted his uninjured arm out of the car as he aimed the handgun at the swerving black van. Liam squeezed the trigger, determined to gain some leverage in the chase. The gun released a loud bang as the bullet catapulted through the mine and bounced off the van's rear bumper. Liam squeezed again, and a bullet crashed right through the van's back window, effectively smashing the glass to bits. Liam shot again, this time blowing a hole in the car's rear right tire, sending the car crashing into the light at the end of the tunnel.

"I see a light," said Bridgette, with hope in her voice.

"We're nearing the heart," said Tristan as she once again picked up speed. As the SUV shot out of the dark tunnel and into the light, Tristan jerked the steering wheel hard as she cut off the exit to the other tunnel.

"If she wants out she's going to have to go through me."

Within a split second, she saw the oncoming lights. Everything happened so fast. Just when Tristan thought she had met her end, once again, she felt her aunt pulling her into the back of the car, out of the driver's seat. As the lights swallowed Tristan's vision, she watched the van tear through the front of Jack's SUV. The seats where Tristan and Bridgette were sitting, were now replaced with the exterior of the van.

"C'mon!" yelled Bridgette as she pulled Tristan to the very back of the SUV. She pushed the back doors of Jack's truck open as she and Tristan ran on foot. Just ten feet ahead of them, Angie O'Mara was running for cover.

"Shit!" Adam screamed as he watched the van barrel through the front of their father's SUV.

"Where are Tristan and Aunt Bridgette?" yelled Liam.

"I don't know but O'Mara is getting away!"

Adam slammed on the breaks. There was nowhere for him to go. He couldn't turn around, and he couldn't get out of the tunnel because of the wreck that blocked the exit. All that they could do was wait for help. Adam flicked on a flashlight and looked at his brother with a look of disbelief. As they sat there in the darkness the ceiling of the mine began to fall down upon them. Rock and debris crashed down onto the hood and windshield of the police cruiser with a crash.

They were trapped in the mine.

❦

"No, Aunt Bridgette! You stay! Get to Liam, Adam and Natalie!"

"Tristan, you cannot go after her alone!"

"Adam and Liam could be hurt! You have to save them!"

Before Bridgette could stop her niece, Tristan bolted after Angie into the heart of the mine.

❦

Cole drove the Jeep at an alarming speed up the middle tunnel that Bridgette and Tristan had used. In the foreground they heard a horrible crash and raised voices of several women.

"What the hell was that?" Jack yelled from the backseat.

"We'll know in a minute, were almost to the light."

"My nerves! I'm getting too old for this shit!" yelled Jack.

"Please let them be okay," prayed Joe from the passenger seat.

As Cole's Jeep whipped out of the dark tunnel and passed the car wreck, he felt his heart stop for a second.

Tristan.

"Stop the car!" yelled Jack. "Let me out!"

Cole slammed on the brakes as both he and Jack ran out of the vehicle and they ran to the demolished truck. Cole fell to his knees as grief poured over him. Jack screamed as he gripped his hair, looking as if he was about to rip it out. Fortunately, their devastation was short-lived.

"Jack!" yelled Bridgette from the opposite side of the wreck.

"Bridgette?" replied Jack, stunned to hear his sister's voice.

Bridgette had climbed over the wreck in an attempt to get to Adam and Liam. Natalie was beside her helping move fallen debris out of the way. Rocks had fallen from above into the spaces between the demolished van and the police cruiser.

"Do you need help?"

"No! Go get Tristan! She ran up the mine after Angie!"

A look of pure horror washed over Jack's face. Before Jack was able to come to his senses, Cole had bolted, racing further down the mine. Chasing after a killer of women and the only girl he ever loved.

CHAPTER 27

June 21, 2000
Elkhart, PA
12:15 A.M.

"PLEASE EXPLAIN TO ME why I'm paying for a family plan on these cell phones, when nobody knows how to pick up the bloody phone?" yelled Frank Kilpatrick into his black cell phone. He was trying to track down Jack but he wasn't answering his cell phone. Frank and the boys had returned to Morrow Manor from the movies and found that the house was strangely empty.

"Something is wrong," said Blake. "I know it. Where *is* everyone?" he said nervously.

"We need to go find out what's going on," said Tommy rationally.

"Did you try calling Joe or Jenna?"

"They aren't answering either."

"What about Gus and Grandma?" Shane persisted.

"They are in New York," reminded Blake.

"All right, we need to go figure out what's what," said Frank as he put his truck back in gear.

"Liam! Can you hear me?" yelled Bridgette into the mine.

Adam yelled back, "It's Adam. I can hear you. Liam's trying to hold up. He just closed his eyes for a minute."

Adam's voice was muffled through the rubble.

"Tell him to open them immediately!" demanded Bridgette with concern rampant in her high-pitched voice.

Adam shook his brother's leg vigorously. "Wake up! Aunt Bridgette said that you have to wake up!"

Liam said, "Stop!"

"Liam!" cried Bridgette from the opposite side of the wreck. "Do you hear me? Wake up! Stay with us! Do not go to sleep!"

"I'm here! I'm just tired! My entire body hurts," Liam complained.

"Adam, where was he shot?"

"In the shoulder."

"Did you wrap it to control the bleeding?"

"Yeah, I wrapped my uniform shirt around his shoulder. It's soaked with blood now, though."

"Are you hurt at all?"

"No, I'm fine."

"I need you to try getting out of the car and pushing this debris towards me."

"The rocks have us trapped in. Even the windshield is blocked."

"Okay, hold tight! Joe and I are trying to get you guys out! Keep Liam awake, please!"

*   *   *

"Tristan!" Cole yelled down the dark tunnel where Tristan had just chased after Angie.

Cole couldn't see Tristan anywhere, but he heard two voices in the short distance ahead. From behind him, Cole heard the heavy tromp of a boot crushing against the dirt floor of the mine. Jack followed behind Cole, close on his heels. As the two men reached the end of the tunnel, they could hear a conversation break out between two female voices. Jack lifted his right index finger to his lips indicating the need for silence as he and Cole exchanged nervous glances. With bated breath, they listened to the heated exchange.

*   *   *

Moonlight shone brightly into the cavity of the Bone Tree and illuminated the spot where Angie and Tristan were standing. They stood just feet from one another, both in an aggressive stance, ready to take on the other should their emotions spill over into violence. The pale glow of the moon acted as a strange spotlight, casting Tristan and Angie in an eerie spectral glow. Angie glared at Tristan with a hostile but vacant expression on her face.

Tristan glared back. "You don't frighten me."

Angie shrugged her shoulders and quipped, "I don't care."

"You're not going to get away with this," Tristan assured her in a matter-of-fact tone.

"I don't care about that either," retorted Angie nonchalantly.

"So tell me, Angie, what the hell *do you* care about then?" asked Tristan, becoming irate.

Angie laughed darkly as she took in Tristan's face but she did not answer the question at hand.

"You only care about yourself. That is it. There is no other explanation for your actions."

Angie cast a venomous stare at Tristan as her once-pretty face morphed into something else. She was allowing her true self to come forth. Angie's rage was spilling over and taking reign of whatever acute amount of self-control she still possessed.

"Little girl, you just don't get it. Do you?" spat Angie in a hoarse voice.

"You're right. I don't. I don't get why you feel that it's okay to kill people that you're supposed to love," said Tristan bluntly.

Angie scoffed at Tristan. She could not control her envy or rage anymore.

"Love? What does love have to do with it? These people didn't love me!" screamed Angie in a most petulant voice.

"I guess when anger and hatred have polluted your soul so absolutely, it is hard to understand or see that people actually did care about you. Your parents gave you a second chance."

"Look, girl, the world wasn't just handed to me. I worked for everything I've had, and it was all stripped away from me. I wasn't raised with a silver spoon in my mouth."

"And I was?"

"By looks of it."

"Looks can be deceiving."

"Trust fund kid, right?"

"My father can barely afford to heat our house, thank you very much."

"Everything in my life has been stolen from me."

"Angie, you're not the only one who has had a rough life."

"Strolling all about town with no cares in the world with your little boyfriend. He'll hurt you one day, you know. They all do."

"You know nothing about him. Or me, for that matter."

"How hard of a life could you have possibly had? You live on an estate, you go to a prestigious private school and you probably never had to fight a single one of your own battles. I'm sure you never had to know the likes of what I went through."

"My life has been harder than most people care to know, and I fight all my battles. I have no problem going toe to toe with an asshole like you."

Angie was taken aback with Tristan's tone. Angie assumed that she would be the easiest target to take down because she knew she didn't have to take her, she could just lure her in by taking her friend. She never saw her as a real threat.

"My life hasn't been a walk in the park. How can you just walk around like a normal person, as if Bernard doesn't haunt your every waking moment?"

"Because he doesn't! I refuse to let him control my life or live rent-free in my head!" Tristan spat with anger.

"How can that be? He ruined me!" Angie demanded.

"You let him," quipped Tristan with an agitated look on her face.

"He turned me into what I am."

"That's no excuse to kill people," said Tristan matter-of-factly.

"What would you know of it?" Angie yelled as anger coursed through her body.

"I know that you loved Bernard Kendricks. I know what he did to you and I know you didn't fight back. That's the difference between you and me. You let him destroy you. I never gave him the chance. I fought back," said Tristan firmly.

Angie's lips twisted upward into a strange smile as she stalked circles around Tristan. The moonlight gleamed down upon Angie's thin frame, exposing her sickly face and dark circles.

"He made me into the person I am."

"You're proud of that?"

"I'm a victim."

"You're only a victim if you allow yourself to become one."

"You make it sound *so* easy."

"It's not easy, but it's a choice. You can choose to let his actions be what shapes and defines your future, or you can move past it, and put it to rest."

"Secrets cannot be buried."

"But they can be laid to rest once you've come to terms with what happened."

"There is no coming to terms with it!"

"It was no secret what Bernard did. I have nothing to hide. No secrets to bury. I fought for my life and I won."

"You didn't win. Not yet."

"What did I ever do to you, for you to hate me so much? I didn't even know you before you came to town."

Angie's anger intensified to a furious level.

She screamed, "You survived him!"

"What about your sisters? What about April Dearing? They didn't survive *you*. In this case, Bernard Kendricks is not the monster. *You are*."

"I'm not a monster! I'm a victim!" screamed Angie dramatically.

"You are off your rocker! Let me guess ... You went off your meds?" guessed Tristan.

"What would you know of that?"

"Bernard went off his medication just before he took me, you know. I figure you're a sociopath just like him."

"You have no idea what it's like!"

"You're right. I don't and I never want to know what it is like to feel that kind of hatred in my heart. What did your sisters ever do to you that was so horrible that you felt the need to murder them in cold blood?" yelled Tristan, who was now standing less than an inch from Angie's face.

"Tiffany was an insufferable snob and she stood in between me and my future," said Angie cryptically.

Tristan shook her head in disgust and asked, "And what about Courtney?"

"I have my reasons," said Angie with a charged expression on her face.

"You know, I don't buy your excuses. I think that you were jealous that they both, at some point, showed attention towards Hunter."

"Don't make me laugh! Hunter! He was a tool. He served a purpose."

"Or ... Maybe the real reason you killed Tiffany was because she knew one of your darkest secrets. And oh, my God, is it dark!"

"What would you know about it?" screamed Angie, becoming more paranoid by the minute.

"I know more than you think. After all, I spent three days listening to Bernard's incessant rambling."

"What did he say?"

"Everything. I know everything I could possibly need to know about you or him. Now what about April Dearing? Did she know your secret, too?"

Angie remained silent.

"You should know by now that all secrets eventually come to the surface. Now what did April Dearing do that was worthy of being executed in a park?"

Angie finally cracked.

"She knew too much!"

"Yeah, I guess she did. She suspected that you were the one responsible for Tiffany's death. Then when Courtney turned up dead, she told DiNolfo her suspicions."

"It was none of her business! What I choose to do is my business. Anyone who stands in my way is asking for trouble! Now what did he say? He promised not to tell!"

"There are consequences for your actions, Angie."

"What did he tell you?"

"He told me *everything*."

"He promised not to tell!"

Tristan rolled her eyes at Angie. Angie glared back angrily.

"Little Miss Morrow. Do you know why I put you on my list?"

Tristan rolled her eyes again.

"No, but I'm sure you're going to tell me."

"Because you walked away from his torment virtually unscathed. You survived."

Tristan looked Angie dead in her eyes. Tristan knew that Angie had gone completely mad. Her blue eyes scanned the room wildly, as if looking for her lost sanity somewhere in the chamber. Angie would not find it on this or any other night. Angela O'Mara's mind was tarnished and warped beyond repair.

"You survived him, too," said Tristan calmly.

"I didn't! I'm an empty shell!"

"You were obsessed with him. Your own cousin. And it boils you to this day that he chose a woman that didn't love him over you. Does it piss you off that I look just like her?"

"Yes!"

"Pathetic! The woman hated him!"

"Don't speak about Catherine to me!"

"Why? What did she ever do to you?"

"She existed! She was the cause of his unraveling."

"Ah, Angie ... That's where you're wrong."

"I'm not wrong! I'm never wrong."

"You are. You see, because it wasn't Catherine who brought Kendricks to his death. She was petrified of him. I was the one who had the courage and the nerve to deliver Kendricks to the devil's door."

"Jack Morrow."

"Yes. The devil in Bernard's eyes. He was dead in a matter of seconds. So if you want to be pissed at anyone, don't blame my mother, blame me."

"*You* ..." growled Angie in a sinister voice. She looked like she was about to pounce.

"Me," confirmed Tristan in a serious voice.

"I'll finish you."

"You won't get close," said Tristan in an annoyed voice as she pulled out her gun. She had heard enough. "I'm nobody's victim to claim. And neither is my aunt or my friends. Your sisters' lives were not yours to take, and neither was April Dearing's! But count on this ... By the time the sun rises, your life will be ours to take."

As the moonlight poured into the cavity and filled the heart of the mine, Tristan cocked her gun and pointed it at Angie's head. This time, she had made damn sure that the gun was loaded.

Frank's truck halted at the intersection at Mountain Road and Cross Street as he waited for the traffic light to turn green. The traffic light swung lazily over the intersection and time seemed to stand still. A cool breeze blew in from the southwest plain. The smell of fire laced the air as smoke billowed from the forest floor. The scent alone caused Frank to turn his head. Just as the light turned green, something else caught his attention; a raised voice that he would recognize anywhere cried into the night. Frank put the truck in park and stepped out onto the dirt road.

"Uncle Frank?" asked Blake with a perplexed tone of voice, clearly not understanding why he was getting out of the truck.

Frank ignored his nephew's question as he cast a serious look towards the Forest of York. Rather than asking questions, Tommy followed his uncle to the tree line. He trusted his uncle's judgment completely and he knew better than to ask questions when Frank was having a train of thought. Suddenly, Frank heard the sound again. Franks eyes darted to the ground. The noise was coming from beneath them.

"Go in my truck and get me my chainsaw, my flashlight and the long rope."

Without asking questions, Tommy went and quickly returned with the supplies that his uncle had asked for. Frank went over to the driver's side window and spoke to Blake and Shane in no uncertain terms.

"Do not leave this truck. Do not attempt to follow me. If there is any trouble, go straight to the police station. Nowhere else. Do you hear me?"

Blake and Shane nodded, wide-eyed and alarmed. Before they could ask any questions, Frank slammed the driver's side door shut and raced into the Forest of York with Tommy on his heels.

※ ※ ※

"Liam! Stay with us!" Bridgette yelled as she continued to move rock and debris with her good arm. Her right arm was still in excruciating pain from her own bullet wound.

"I am," said Liam groggily.

"Damn!" yelled Bridgette as the pain became too much for her to bear.

"What's wrong?" yelled Adam.

Joe replied, "Bridgette was shot too. The pain is getting to her."

"I can't get any reception down here. We called for a medic over an hour ago, but I don't think the call went through."

"Just hold tight. We're gonna get you out of there," assured Joe with a nervous look on his face.

※ ※ ※

Jack and Cole reached the heart of the mine where they found Tristan holding Angie O'Mara at gunpoint. She had the gun pressed to Angie's forehead firmly. Tristan could hear footsteps approaching. She craned her neck to see who was entering the mine. With Tristan distracted by the noise behind her, Angie capitalized. She twisted her body around, quick as a snake, and laced her hands around an old wooden lever that was installed in the floor of the mine. She pulled hard on the splintering handle and smiled grimly as a sharp metallic groaning emitted from the ground below.

Tristan didn't know what was happening. One minute she was standing on solid ground staring back at her father and Cole, and the next, she was plummeting down far below the earth's surface. Free falling into the dark depths of the mine, Tristan screamed at the top of her lungs. Her fear consumed her. In that dark, weightless moment, Tristan closed her eyes and prepared for the very worst.

What felt like an eternity falling through time and space was really only seconds and a matter of thirty feet. Tristan crashed into the hard dirt with a violent thud as pain coursed down her spine to her legs and feet. Dust billowed around her body as she tried to shake off the pain. As the air cleared, the trap door slammed shut. Tristan sat up as a muffled scream escaped from her lungs. She was in pain, but she was alive. In the distance, she could hear something shuffling along the mine floor.

"Can anyone hear me?" yelled Tristan in a cracking, desperate voice.

No one answered. The silence of the chamber was deafening. Tristan was absolutely, unequivocally alone.

Frank Kilpatrick's chainsaw roared to life, scaring away the wildlife that called the forest home. Squirrels and chipmunks scurried away from the noise as birds fled from their branches.

"Stand back!" yelled Frank to Tommy who was standing at the base of the Bone Tree.

"What the hell are you doing?"

"This is a hollow tree. We can get them out through here!"

"They are all down there?"

"Pretty sure. I heard Bridgette and Liam's voices. I just heard Joe's too."

"Which means the killer is down there."

"I would just about guarantee it," said Frank sharply.

"Get me down there now," said Tommy with a dark edge to his voice.

Frank nodded. Though he shouldn't encourage violence, Tommy had every right to be pissed off. As he revved his chainsaw one last time, Frank said, "You do what you gotta do."

Frank applied his blade to the white bark of the Bone Tree as the wood began to splinter. The tree groaned as if it was in pain as the grinding teeth of the chainsaw tore through its core.

"Get back!" yelled Frank, trying to see which way the tree was going to fall.

He prayed that it would not land on the roof of Monte's. Fortunately for Frank, it didn't. The monstrous tree fell with a great crash, bowling over the thicket and moss-strewn boulders that lay scattered about in the forest. Tommy was amazed by what he saw before him. There wasn't a tree stump, but an empty hole. It was as if the tree had just been placed there to cover up a manhole.

"This tree is dead. Completely hollow," explained Frank as he tied the rope to an adjacent tree.

Tommy grabbed the other end of the rope. Before Frank could give him instructions Tommy had barreled to the floor of the mine with the rope in his hand.

Angie laughed manically as Tristan fell to the depths of the mine. She kicked the old lever and slammed the hatch shut as she watched Cole and Jack's faces morph from concern to outrage. While Jack desperately tried to reopen the hatch, Cole stamped across the dirt, beating a war path across the mine. Just inches from Angie's face, Cole whipped out his gun and pushed it into Angie's right eye socket. The metal surface of the gun felt cold against Angie's eyelid, so she opened her eyes and looked straight down the barrel of Cole's gun.

With a smile she said, "Go ahead. Put me out of my misery."

"Nothing would give me greater satisfaction," spat Cole through gritted teeth.

"So do it."

"Open the hatch!"

"No."

"Open the goddamn hatch!"

"No."

"Don't make me do this!"

"I think I'll leave her down there. Let's see her escape this time."

"Cole, it's not opening!" yelled Jack as he tried to lift the hatch door with his bare hands.

Cole stared at Angie in her eyes with a look of pure hatred.

"Open the hatch."

"Or what?"

"I'll shoot you on the spot."

Angie laughed maliciously as she spread her arms wide.

"Do your worst."

Angie backed away slowly with a distant look on her face. She stumbled backwards and peered up at the moon that was shining down into the mine. She seemed transfixed. It was as if she was listening to someone talk to her from above, but there was no one there. While Angie's delusions kept her distracted, Cole reached for the lever. He pulled hard and the lever groaned loudly in protest. Just as he thought the hatch door would spring open, the wooden lever broke off in his hand. Standing just ten feet away, Angie laughed even louder. She glared at Cole intensely.

"I told you she wouldn't escape this time!"

As Cole whipped out his gun again, Angie bolted, chasing the darkness with furious vengeance.

The darkness was overwhelming as Tristan climbed to her feet. She felt as if the black abyss of the earth had swallowed her whole. She used her hands to learn her surroundings, scraping along the hard surfaces of the rock walls. Her leg bumped into what sounded like a piece of wooden furniture, then finally her hands found the surface of a wooden desk. She searched the desktop frantically hoping to find something that would give her light. There was something wet on the table and it gave Tristan an unsettling feeling in the pit of her stomach. A strange smell permeated the air. It was sickly, and like a cancer, it threatened to spread to Tristan, making her ill, too. Tristan continued her feverish search across the rough wood of the desk. Just as she was ready to abandon her efforts, she felt the cold metal surface of Bernard Kendricks's lighter under the weight of her touch. Tristan's teeth clenched when she recognized the object. Despite her rage, she picked up the heavy lighter and flicked the flame to life.

The flame shocked the darkness, illuminating the cavernous chamber in a ghostly glow. Tristan's eyes grew wide with alarm as her vision adjusted to the light. Tristan circled the room as she took in her surroundings. The chamber was nothing more and nothing less than a grotesque tomb. Bernard had lined the walls with photographs of Catherine; the love of his ever-so deranged life. Candid photos that Bernard took when he crept along the perimeter of Morrow Manor were scattered about the chamber as strange reminders of his obsession. Candles with half burnt wicks lined every surface. Tristan slowly circled the chamber as she lit the candles, one by one. Flickering light engulfed the strange room as Tristan peered around with unmuted horror.

Jack's old year book photo was cut out and left carelessly lying on the desk. Tristan recalled how much she always loved this particular photograph, but it was sullied for her now. Bernard had stabbed a rusted hunting knife through the photograph piercing Jack's eye. There was no telling how long it sat there like that. This room was a tomb for Bernard's obsession for Tristan's mother, and his abhorrent hatred for her father.

Tristan continued to survey the cavernous space taking in horror after horror. Spiders crept overhead weaving intricate webs just inches from where Tristan stood. Mice scuttled over and around Tristan's feet, causing her to dodge the critters at an alarming pace. She wanted to scream but her lungs would not rally a cry. The worst was yet to be, though. The deeper into the chamber that Tristan ventured, the more repulsed she became. Dead rodents littered the ground while live ones feasted on their flesh. A sparrow that was so darling in life, lay dead and decapitated on top of the desk. The sparrow was not lonely in its despair. There were dozens of birds lying dead in the chamber. Crows, blue birds, sparrows and one sole robin all lay dead and desecrated on the floor of the mine.

"What the hell is it with the birds?" Tristan commented aloud.

Then she remembered how Bernard thought that birds, especially ravens and crows, were guides to the afterlife. Had his desperation for Catherine consumed him so terribly that he even tried to contact her after he had taken her life?

No. Stop. He was a madman. Stop dissecting this. He was insane. You are stuck one hundred feet below the earth. Figure out a way to get out.

But Tristan's original thought was right on the mark. Bernard had thought that birds were messengers from the other side, from the beyond. He believed that they were secret keepers and that they had the power to relay messages from departed souls. Bernard Kendricks's depraved mind had many such delusions.

A raven perched on an old wooden shelf and stared at Tristan intently. It was alive and pecking at the wood which it stood upon. Tristan was intrigued by the bird, finding something distinctly familiar about it. The bird hopped along and Tristan followed it, curious as to how something so majestic could live in a place as despairing to the soul as this. The raven ruffled its feathers and spread its wings as it glided through the dim light of the chamber. Tristan followed the raven, intensely curious as to what it was trying to show her.

Tristan stalked further into the mine, tracing the raven's path. Her stomach tightened into painful knots with each step she took, each step moving towards the darkness. She lit another set of candles, illuminating more photographs of her mother. Tristan cautiously walked down a long and dark corridor to what she presumed was the end of the chamber. She lifted the lighter to see where the raven had gone, and she found that it was standing right at her feet, peering up at her. More photographs of Catherine lined the rock walls, only now, instead of being exalted, they were smeared with blood and dirt.

The raven led her to the back corner of the chamber, where the bird frantically cawed at something just out of Tristan's view. An intense heaviness weighed upon Tristan. She knew that she just had to follow the ebony bird to gain some twisted insight into what this chamber was used for. Tristan knew she just need to turn her head and she would know the truth. As her body shifted to face the corner where the bird continued to cry, the flame of the lighter lit up the dark space. Tristan gasped as she took in the grim scene. The dirt floor was stained red with blood. The rock walls were spattered with crimson and acted as a devastating reminder of the violence that occurred there. There were strange lines in the dirt; ten thin lines were imbedded in the stained dirt where someone had dragged their fingers in a desperate attempt to escape. Tristan's hands quaked as she stared at the tragic scene.

Tristan now knew exactly where the victims were killed. She just hoped that she wouldn't be next.

Angie was running out of breath as she bolted up another dark and cavernous tunnel away from the heart of the mine. Cole booked after her, pounding the floor of the mine with his feet, quickly closing the distance between himself and Angie. Angie veered down another winding tunnel that led her into desolate darkness. She choked on the smoke that was caused by the car wreck. She was surprised the truck hadn't blown up yet. Once she thought she had lost Cole in the dust, she stopped to catch her breath. There were just a few more feet to go. A few more feet until freedom. Angie could escape out of the access door to Harrow's and take her father's car wherever she needed to go. He wouldn't miss it that much, she was sure. Finally, she was at the wood panel. She would just need to move the wood and she was free as a bird. She couldn't decide where she would go now. She pulled and pried on the wood panel but it would not budge. She continued to apply pressure but the door simply would not slide. Her rage began to boil over. To get this far, and face this struggle. Certainly there had to be a way. She would shoot through it if she had to. Suddenly, the door swung open, but much to Angie's dismay she could not gain access to Harrow's basement. Sergeant Jenna DiNolfo was standing in the access door with her gun pointing directly at Angie's head.

"Get out of my way, Jenna!"

"No."

"Get out of my way, I don't want to hurt you!"

Jenna laughed. "You hurt me? I don't think so."

"Move!"

"No. You picked the wrong family to mess with." Jenna cocked her gun and pressed it firmly to Angie's temple.

"This has nothing to do with you!"

"It has everything to do with me. It's personal now."

Angie took a sharp look at Jenna's face. She was dead serious and not bluffing. Before Jenna could say anything more, Angie fled down the tunnel back towards the heart of the mine.

"I don't know where you think you're running. Those people out there want to kill you more than I do."

CHAPTER 28

June 21, 2000
The Mine at Wilhamette
12:30 A.M.

A SHADOW DARKENED THE TUNNEL blocking Angie O'Mara's escape. A man of tall stature and broad shoulders stood between Angie and the freedom she so desperately craved. Freedom from the demons that ruled her. Angie knew that once she reached the heart of the mine she could easily slither out another tunnel. While the tunnels would be treacherous for the search party, it would be a cake walk for Angie. She had been down here so many times with Hunter and with Bernard. She knew the arteries of the mine like the back of her hand. One wrong step and an inexperienced person could fall to their death down an unstable mine shaft miles below. The man, however, prevented Angie from her escape. She wasn't about to quit when she was so close to freedom.

DiNolfo followed behind Angie slowly, knowing that she had nowhere to run. Angie sped up the long, dark tunnel with her gun out, sending a bullet flying straight into DiNolfo's bulletproof vest. Angie could see the shadow of the man in the tunnel very clearly now, and her pace only quickened with hostility. She bolted forward preparing to tackle the man, but the man had no intentions upon giving up the ground he stood.

DiNolfo watched as the two shadows converged. It was hard to make out two separate forms as the pair fought in the dark of the tunnel. Angie struggled against the strong man, still unsure of his identity, but in reality, she didn't care. He stood in her way. She would fight her own father if he stood on that very ground. Angie raised her gun in the air, but the man batted it away sending it flying down the mine, just inches from DiNolfo's feet. The shadow of the man pushed Angie back and kicked her square in the chest sending her falling to the dirt ground below. As Angie went to get up, Tommy Morrow's foot met with her jaw, knocking her front teeth clear out of her mouth. DiNolfo bent down and picked up Angie's gun. It was identical to the Ruger 9mm that was registered to Hunter McCord and reported missing on the day of the first murder. DiNolfo grabbed her handcuffs off of her belt loop and approached Angie carefully. Though Angie had been delivered a swift and unyielding kick to the chest and the jaw, she remained conscious, seething on the mine floor.

"Don't make this harder on yourself than it has to be," warned DiNolfo.

This made Angie laugh. Not in amusement, but in bitter, unfiltered hatred. Before DiNolfo could cuff Angie, she climbed back to her feet as she braced herself to barge through the barrier that Tommy Morrow had created.

<hr />

"Bridgette! Tristan!" Frank's deep voice called down the gaping hole that lay where the Bone Tree used to stand. His booming voice echoed down into the heart of the mine and pulsed through the tunnels.

"Is anyone hurt down there?" Frank yelled again.

"Yes!" Jack yelled. "Bridgette and Liam have been shot and Liam and Adam are trapped in the mine! Tristan fell down a mine shaft and Angie locked her in! Oh, my God!" Jack screamed in a frantic voice that Frank had never heard before.

"She stabbed Tommy! Get down here! Bring that chainsaw!"

"I'm sending the boys for help!"

But before Jack could answer, a terrible rumbling sound echoed from the mine below.

"What the hell was that?" Frank demanded to know with wide eyes. He stared down the hole to the mine as he waited for a response, but one would not come.

After the sound faded, Jack ran in the opposite direction screaming as loud as he could, "Liam, Adam, no!"

<hr />

Patrol Car E5 was quiet and dark with the exception of Liam's labored breathing. He had lost a lot of blood and was becoming weaker by the minute. Adam shined his flashlight over the fractured windshield where fallen rocks were threatening to break through and crush them to death. The strength of the reinforced glass was failing. Suddenly, a terrible noise groaned overhead. More rocks were falling on top of the police cruiser, denting the roof of the car. It was only a matter of time before Adam and Liam would be crushed by the debris.

"You guys have to hurry!" cried Adam with hysteria clear in his voice. "We're being crushed alive in here!"

Bridgette's heart threatened to jump out of her chest at the sound. She dug even more furiously, despite her own injuries. She *had* to get them out.

"Keep digging, Joe!"

Frank ran back to his truck and alerted Blake and Shane to call 911 for an ambulance and police back-up. He ran from the truck back to the forest, grabbed the rope firmly, and barreled to the mine floor, determined to get his wife and his family out safely.

Jack raced to the sound of the noise with panic in his eyes.

"Get out of the way," he yelled at Joe and Bridgette as he barreled to the source of the sound.

"They are being crushed alive in there. We need to move these bigger rocks. Joe, help me. Bridgette, you need to go sit down next to Natalie, you are losing too much blood."

"Jack, they are my nephews in there. No!"

Realizing that Jack wasn't going to argue with her, she decided to go where she could be of assistance.

While Joe and Jack tried to shift the heavy boulders from the entrance to the tunnel where Adam and Liam were trapped, Bridgette ran, head on to where Tommy was fighting off Angie.

DiNolfo had her gun out and aimed at Angie's head, but she was unable to determine which silhouette belonged to her. The pair was engaged in a violent dance that lingered close to the edge. One would not come out of this fight alive.

"Get out of my way!" Angie screamed with bared teeth as she tried to claw her way past Tommy.

"Not a chance. You're not hurting anyone else!" said Tommy as he slammed Angie hard against the wall of the tunnel.

"You were supposed to be the fall guy!"

"I'm nobody's fall guy! This ends tonight!"

"You're damn right!" barked Angie as she took a hunting knife out of her back pocket and jammed it into Tommy's stomach and twisted vengefully. Tommy wretched with pain as he fell to the ground. Angie spat in Tommy's face and ran fast as a fox into the heart of the mine. Finally, DiNolfo had her shot and she took it, but missed. Angie wasn't going anywhere, though. Cole snuck up behind Angie and lifted his gun, aiming at Angie's head just ten feet behind her. DiNolfo saw that someone else was aiming towards the tunnel with a gun in their hand. Cole took an aggressive stance as he pointed his gun at the person who had caused so much heartache and bloodshed.

He pulled back on the trigger gently, as a bullet flew through the thick, dusty air of the mine. It cut through the dark like a knife through butter and slipped through Angie's skin, cracking through her skull, until finally it found a warm home in her delusional and disturbed brain. Cole Piedmonte delivered a swift death sentence with just a small twitch of his finger. DiNolfo watched as Angie's eyes went dead. The ethereal pools of blue were stained black as the life escaped from her eyes. Her chest still rose and fell, though. As Angie O'Mara's battered body fell to the ground, Jenna approached her and put another bullet in her chest for good measure.

"Game over," spat Cole as a cold glare emitted from his eyes.

Jenna stared at her boyfriend's son with a surprised expression and deep-seated respect.

"I didn't think you had it in ya, kid," said DiNolfo in shock.

Cole responded firmly, "No one messes with my family."

Despite the tension that still rampaged through the mine, Jenna and Bridgette couldn't help but breathe a sigh of relief. Cole would not feel any semblance of relief until Tristan was out of the mine shaft. The murderer was dead. Now, they had the seemingly impossible task of getting everyone out of the mine safely, including two officers who were trapped under hundreds of pounds of rubble and a young man with a knife wound to the stomach. DiNolfo tore off her shirt and handed it to Bridgette to help control Tommy's bleeding. She was glad that she remembered to wear a tank top under her uniform shirt.

"C'mon, Liam and Adam are in trouble," urged Bridgette as Jenna ran down the tunnel towards the wreck. Bridgette helped Tommy walk to where everyone else was, holding a firm compress over his wound.

Frank barreled to the bottom of the mine with the rope in one hand and his chainsaw in the other. He landed in the dirt with a loud thud as he ran to the spot where Cole was standing. He was trying to pry open the hatch to the mine shaft, but he wasn't having any luck.

"Watch out kid!" yelled Frank as he revved the chainsaw to life.

Cole jumped back as Frank pushed the blade of the chainsaw into the wood frame of the hatch.

Frank shouted into the shaft below, "Tristan! Look out!"

As the final piece of wood was splintered, the heavy metal door of the mine shaft fell to the floor of the chamber below with a loud bang.

"Tristan!" Frank and Cole yelled in unison.

Tristan coughed at the dust that had billowed in the chamber.

"I'm here!"

"Are you okay?" Frank asked loudly.

"In theory!"

"What?"

"She killed everyone down here! Get me out!"

Frank took another length of rope off his shoulder and tossed it down to Tristan. He passed the end of the rope to Cole, and he wrapped it around his hands. Frank grabbed hold of the rope and began to hoist Tristan out of the chamber. As her feet left the ground, the black raven flew out the mine shaft to freedom. After several moments of struggle, Tristan was lifted to the ground. As her feet reached the ground of the main level of the mine, tears flooded from her eyes. She tackled Cole and Frank, holding onto their necks tightly. She honestly didn't think that she would come out of the chamber alive.

"Oh, thank God," said Cole as he buried his face into her hair. The scent of vanilla and jasmine wafted from her hair and skin. The warmth of her embrace felt like home to him. Even down in the murky darkness of the mine, Tristan was his anchor. She squeezed him tightly as her fear left her body within his hold. The moment was sweet but fleeting, because Tristan soon remembered that the rest of their family was in trouble.

"We have to get to Adam and Liam."

Jack ran to the source of the noise with Cole, Frank and Tristan on his heels. "Jack!" Cole yelled with worry in his voice as he chased after Jack in the dark. Cole couldn't see him, but he could certainly hear him.

"Hurry up, I need you!" Jack yelled.

Cole's pace quickened at the sound of Jack's voice. Tristan ran to the wreck where Jack's demolished SUV was engulfed in flames. Smoke polluted the air and escaped up the passage where the Bone Tree used to stand. The flames were contained—for now.

Jack, Joe and Cole struggled to move the heavy rock from the entrance to the tunnel in a desperate attempt to rescue Adam and Liam.

"Careful! One wrong move and this whole this is caving in on us!" warned Cole.

Joe, Jack and Cole rolled a large piece of rock out of the way as a threatening sound emerged from the rubble. Rocks began to shift precariously towards them. From inside the rubble, the sound of Adam's voice startled Tristan.

"Hurry up! We're going to be crushed!" yelled Adam.

Dust and debris were beginning to fall into the police cruiser, choking Adam and Liam. The glass wouldn't hold much longer.

"Move!" Tristan yelled at her father as the rocks began to roll towards them.

Tristan climbed the mountain of rubble, careful not to disturb the unsettled rock below. If she wasn't cautious, the mine could quickly collapse on all of them. Tristan brushed some of the looser rocks to the ground from the rubble. She kept going, removing as much small rock and dirt as she could in a careful, but quick manner. She could not disturb the settlement of the larger rocks until she determined which ones would cause the least damage. It was a puzzle waiting to be solved—with dire consequences if the wrong piece was selected.

"Uncle Frank. Help Dad, Cole and Joe move this rock," said Tristan as she pointed to a large piece of concrete that stood in their way. "Be very careful and move quickly."

Jenna and Bridgette had just arrived back at the wreck with Tommy.

Jack looked at Tommy with wide eyes.

"Tommy!"

"She stabbed me," Tommy said weakly with little color left in his face.

"Is there anything we can do to help?" Jack said to Bridgette.

"Just hold tight. I'm keeping the bleeding under control."

Cole's hands were beginning to bleed from handling the large rocks, but with Frank's help, the large rock was much easier to move. Cole wiped his hands on his shorts before anyone could notice. Much to Tristan's relief, only a small bit of rubble fell from the pile. She continued removing small pieces of rock, dirt and debris from the wreck. She could move much quicker now that much of the larger, more perilous obstacles were out of her way. Finally, she saw it. The bright headlights of her brothers' police cruiser shining out of the tunnel. There was still a lot of rock to move, but they were making headway.

"We're coming for you guys! Just a little longer!" yelled Tristan.

"Hang in there! We're all trying to get you out!" Jack said.

Liam yelled from the passenger seat in an exhausted voice, "Please tell me someone has Angie in handcuffs."

Jenna laughed loudly. "O'Mara is taken care of."

Liam breathed a sigh of relief.

"What happened?" Adam demanded to know.

"Cole shot her in the head, and a shot to the heart courtesy of yours truly," said Jenna.

"Cole!" choked Adam in amusement. "You serious?"

"Oh, thank God. It's over," said Liam with a sigh of relief.

"Not quite, bud. We still have to get you guys out of there," said Tristan.

"Are you guys hanging in there okay?" yelled DiNolfo, trying to keep the worry out of her voice.

"Liam needs to get to the hospital."

"I'm fine! Just get us out of here in one piece."

"All right, hang in there, guys."

"Hey DiNolfo ..." Adam called.

"Yeah?"

"Did she confess to Tiffany's murder?"

DiNolfo looked to Tristan, who had heard her relentless monologue.

"She confessed to every single one of the murders. And I found the site of the murders."

Adam breathed a sigh of relief as his brother Liam smiled despite his pain.

"We'll discuss it all in detail when this is over."

"Uh, DiNolfo ..." said Liam.

"Yes?"

"After this case is wrapped up."

"Yeah?"

"I'm going to need a vacation and a raise!"

"How does a promotion and two weeks off sound?"

"A promotion?" asked Adam.

"Yeah. I have no Deputies. If you want the position, it's yours. You did a hell of a job on this case."

"Let's get out of here first," said Adam as he cast his brother a worried glance.

"You got it, Deputy Morrow," DiNolfo joked, trying to lighten the air. There was still a very real threat, but they would be able to more easily tackle the task at hand with a lighter heart.

Jack leaned in to Jenna and whispered to her, "Isn't there a test involved in that?"

Jenna shook her head in denial.

"Nobody wants the job. I have a police force of seventeen and they are the only two I would trust in that position. They are the exact opposite of Amos and Earl. It's what this town needs."

Jack couldn't agree more.

Shane steered his father's pick-up truck nervously down Mountain Road until they were outside of the Elkhart Police Station. Blake ran into the police station and spewed out everything he knew to the officer that was sitting at the front desk. Before Blake had even exited the building, police cruiser E3 was barreling down Mountain

Road, towards the entrance of the mine. Sirens filled the warm night air as all available officers were dispatched to the mine to help.

Tristan climbed on the hood of the police car as she continued moving rock and debris. Cole and Frank were directly behind her moving larger pieces of rock. Bridgette was on the ground next to Natalie assessing her wounds, which weren't nearly as bad as her own. She determined that Natalie had some rope burns around her neck and wrists, a bruise on her head, and a nasty scrape on her leg, but as far as severity went, Bridgette, Tommy and Liam certainly took the cake.

"Sit down, Bridgette!" yelled Jack. "You've been shot. You need to sit down and take it easy."

Bridgette grumbled, contemplating whether she should take her own bullet out, so that people would stop telling her to sit down. She wasn't thinking clearly as she pulled up her shirt sleeve.

"Jenna! Stop her!" yelled Jack as he gawked at his sister with wide eyes.

"What the hell are you doing?" asked Jenna as she pulled Bridgette's hand from her sleeve.

"I'm a nurse. I know what I'm doing!" Bridgette insisted as the last of the color faded from her face.

Suddenly, the sounds of approaching sirens filled the mine.

"That sounds like an ambulance!" Joe exclaimed with hope in his voice.

"Sergeant DiNolfo?" yelled a voice from the surface.

"Down here!"

"Are there any injured down there?"

"Yes. We have a rope. They can be pulled up. There is no other way in!"

"Bring them to the access point and we'll get them out!"

"Bridgette, Tommy and Natalie, let's go!"

"I can help!" insisted Bridgette.

"You already have. You've done so much. Now we need you to get that shoulder looked at."

"I'm fine!"

"Bridgette!" Frank yelled from the rubble. "Go with the paramedics!"

"Let's go," Jack said, as he ushered his strong- willed sister to the heart of the mine where the paramedics were waiting for her. Tommy was the first to be lifted out of the mine on a stretcher. He was promptly loaded in the back of the ambulance and was en-route to Grier Mountain Medical Center. Natalie followed behind without a single complaint. She wanted nothing more than to put this experience behind her. As Bridgette was being pulled up to the surface, she glanced back at the body that lay on the ground. A small sparrow was pecking at Angie's skin.

"1 ... 2 ... 3 ... Lift!" said Cole, Jack, Joe and Frank in unison as they began to move a particularly large rock. Dust began to billow, and Tristan's eyes went wide.

"Stop!" Tristan screamed as she saw a large slab of cement start to shift loose. "Get out of the way!"

The slab of cement was sliding from the top of the wreck and was heading right for the spot where Jack and Cole stood. Tristan knocked them out of the way as they watched the slab crash into the black van. The sheer weight of the concrete cut right through the van's bumper, and knocked it clear off.

"You need to be very careful!" yelled Tristan as she climbed back up to the top of the wreckage.

She continued moving smaller rocks and dirt with her bare hands until finally, she saw something that looked familiar. Under the thin layer of dirt, the cracked windshield and the smaller fragments of rock, Liam's exhausted face peered out in shock.

"They're in there?" said Officer Rutledge as he looked at the crippled mine in shock.

"That's what the kid said!" replied Officer Cruz.

"The whole entrance has collapsed! We aren't getting in there."

"There has to be another way."

"What about ..." began Officer Cruz, but he was interrupted by an earth-shattering sound.

It sounded as if the mountain was collapsing through the very earth it stood upon.

"C'mon! Hurry! I know another way!" shouted Rutledge as he ran back to squad car E3.

Cole and Tristan stood on the hood of the car now, removing as much debris as humanly possible. They were so close to freeing Adam and Liam. They couldn't stop now. There were still rocks on both sides of the car, so Adam couldn't open his door, but now, thanks to Tristan and Cole, he could push through the windshield.

"Watch out!" Adam yelled as he prepared to kick the windshield out.

"Liam! Cover your face!"

Adam's size thirteen boot kicked through the windshield, shattering the glass into tiny shards. Cole shielded Tristan from the shower of glass that poured down over them. Adam cleared the window frame of any sharp edges. Liam didn't have the strength to get out himself, so Adam was going to have to lift him. He didn't want him to suffer any further injuries. Liam was in bad enough shape as it was.

"Dad, we've got them!"

Jack ran from the opposite side of the fiery wreck with a worried but relieved look on his face. He took one look at Liam and he just about lost all his resolve. Liam was paper white and had lost a lot of blood. Adam's police shirt was soaked with his brother's blood and Liam was too weak to move himself.

"Frank!" Jack called, not realizing that Frank was already by his side.

"I am going to help lift him," explained Adam. "I need you two to pull him out."

Jack stood on the hood of the car ready to pull his son out by his good arm, but before he could, Frank was leaning his large frame into the car, grabbing Liam around the waist.

"I need you to push up. Do you understand?" Frank asked Liam, looking him square in the eye.

"You're a big guy, so I can't do this all myself," said Frank.

Though Frank was strong, he wasn't invincible. Liam stood at six feet three inches tall and weighed over two hundred pounds. He wasn't a lightweight by any stretch of the imagination. His stocky build and tall frame made this task even more challenging. Liam shook his head in understanding. Frank pulled as Liam pushed, but he could not get him out of the car.

"Adam, get out," Frank urged. "Jack get on the hood of the car." Frank slipped into Adam's seat as he got a better grip of his nephew.

"Jack, put your arms around his chest. Don't touch that shoulder at all."

Jack did as he was told as Frank gave Liam a firm boost. Liam screamed in pain as he was moved. Jack pulled his son out of the car, keeping a firm hold on him. Liam was absolute dead weight. He had lost so much blood that he had absolutely no physical energy left.

Jenna took one look at Liam and ran for the paramedics. If they didn't get him to the hospital soon, they would lose him for sure.

"Come quick! You need a stretcher!" barked Jenna at the paramedics.

As Jack and Liam stepped off of the hood of the car, a horrible rumble echoed through the mine.

"Get him to the stretcher now!" yelled Adam.

Joe and Adam carried Liam quickly to the heart of the mine where the stretcher was waiting for him. Paramedics strapped him down and he was immediately lifted out of the mine and loaded into the back of the ambulance that waited on the surface. Nick, one of the paramedics, now focused his attention on Jenna.

"Sergeant, we have to get you out of here!"

"No! Not until everyone else is out!"

"I insist!"

Nick put the rope in Jenna's hand as he yelled to the top.

"Pull her up!"

"C'mon! We have to go!" yelled Cole at Tristan as she jumped over the rubble in the mine.

The tunnel that Liam and Adam were trapped in had caved in. The ceiling of the mine collapsed upon the beleaguered police cruiser and flattened it like a bug. Tunnel after tunnel began to disappear, becoming nothing more than rubble on the mine floor. The access point that led to Harrow's General Store was blocked by several tons of debris. The only way out was up. Everyone ran to the heart of the mine as they choked on the billowing dust that swarmed around them. Cole grabbed Tristan's hand and refused to let go. She tripped over a large slab of rock and slammed her head hard onto the concrete surface. As blood streamed from her head, Tristan felt Cole pick her up into his arms.

"Go, go! Get her up there!" yelled Jack at Cole as he carried Tristan from the collapsing mine. He passed her off to the paramedic who laid her down on a stretcher.

"Pull her up!" yelled Jack. Rocks fell from the ceiling of the mine as the hole that used to house the Bone Tree expanded. The earth was opening up and it was swallowing the Forest of York down into the mine.

"You're next!" Jack yelled at Cole and Adam as the paramedics hoisted them up.

The rumbling sound that had begun only moments earlier intensified as the ground above caved in upon them. When the smoke cleared, Jack's eyes went wide at the sight before them. Sliding before them at break neck speed, the Bone Tree was crashing down into the mine.

"Move!" yelled Jack as he pushed Frank out of the way.

The tree missed hitting Frank by only a few inches. He would have been dead if not for Jack. The white tree crashed to the mine floor with a tremendous bang as the entire contents of the Forest of York fell towards Jack and Frank. They had to act fast if they didn't want to be swallowed alive by the swiftly deteriorating mine.

"Grab hold!" yelled Nick the paramedic as the rope began pulling upward.

Seven firefighters fought to pull the remaining survivors of the mine accident up on an old fraying rope. Jack, Frank, Joe and Nick held on tight as Ladder 42 pulled them out of the abyss.

As his feet left the ground, Jack watched as O'Mara and Bone Tree were swallowed whole by the collapsing mine of Wilhamette.

CHAPTER 29

June 21, 2000
Emergency Room
Grier Mountain Medical Center
101 Mountain Road
Elkhart, PA
3:14 A.M.

JACK BATTED HIS FATHER AWAY as Angus tried to stitch up a gaping wound on Jack's head. Grier Mountain Medical Center was woefully understaffed for an incident such as the one that occurred in the Wilhamette Mine. The on-staff Emergency Room physicians were needed in the operating room for multiple patients with gunshot wounds and a patient with a particularly nasty stab wound. Angus, though he hadn't worked at the hospital in years, still had privileges at Grier Mountain and he was doing what he could to help out. He and Moira had just returned home when they got an urgent call from Blake saying that they needed to get down to the hospital right away.

"I don't need stitches! I just need to see if everyone is okay!" Jack protested as he received a heated glare from Angus.

"Like hell you don't need stitches! I can see your skull. Now hold still!" Angus barked as he continued stitching up his son's head.

"How are you making out over there kid?" Angus asked Cole, who was being treated for rope burns on his hands. His palms were rubbed raw from moving the rocks earlier and holding onto a fraying rope for dear life.

"I'm fine. Is there a status on Tristan yet?"

"Not yet. Hold tight."

"Lay still!" Angus yelled at his son as Jack tried to get up off of his gurney to see what was keeping the nurse. He had asked Nurse Wendell for a status on everyone over a half hour ago.

"I need to know if they are okay," pleaded Jack with a worrisome look on his face.

"Listen to me very carefully," Angus said in a firm but calm tone. "That is my daughter and my grandchildren in there. I want to know just as much as you do that they are okay. But three out of the four are in surgery. You have to wait."

"Frank Kilpatrick dropped his head into his hands as he simmered in the waiting room. He was desperate to hear some news from the other side of the double doors of the ER, but so far, he had heard nothing. Joe Piedmonte was sitting next to Frank. He laid a heavy hand on Frank's back in a show of support.

"Hang in there, bud."

Despite all his physical strength, Frank was the first to admit that he was nothing without Bridgette.

"What if she doesn't make it?"

"She will."

"How do you know?"

"She's a fighter. You saw her down there."

Frank shook his head as he fought off the nausea that was rising in his throat.

"Is this really necessary?" complained Jenna as a nurse attempted to put a breathing mask over her mouth. Adam already had one over his own face and he was already starting to feel better.

"Absolutely! Lord only knows what you breathed into your lungs down there!" scolded Nurse Wendell as she slipped the mask over Jenna's face. Both she and Adam had come into the emergency room choking from the dust and debris that they had inhaled in the mine.

"Now try to relax and your breathing should get easier."

"Tommy Morrow, you are one lucky kid," remarked Dr. Stern as he continued to stitch up his belly. "Just two centimeters to the right and she would've punctured your kidney."

Tommy Morrow was still unconscious on the operating table, but it was an old habit of Dr. Stern's to talk to his patients while undergoing a lifesaving operation. He firmly believed that on some level they could hear him.

Dr. Stern had gotten Tommy's bleeding under control fairly quickly. Only two hours after the emergency surgery had begun, Dr. Stern was sewing Tommy back together, layer by layer.

"Nurse Beatty, will you please give the patient's family an update?"

"Of course," said the nurse as she removed her gloves and backed out of the operating room with haste.

"Okay, young lady, you're good to go," said Nurse Garrett as she signed Natalie's chart. "Do you have a ride home?"

Natalie had never heard more refreshing words in all her wife. She breathed a sigh of relief to finally be cleared to leave.

"Yes. Mrs. Morrow is going to take me home."

Moira stood by Natalie's bedside, ready to drive her back up to Morrow Manor away from the stress of the hospital. Shane and Blake had already retreated back to the house at Moira's urging. *The less people involved in this, the better*, Moira thought. She desperately hoped that everyone else would be accompanying them soon.

Dr. Franklin hovered over Liam's body as he frantically tried to remove the bullet from his chest. Liam was in critical condition and the doctors were fighting to save his life. What was initially believed to be a shoulder injury was actually a chest wound. The bullet was lodged dangerously close to Liam's heart, and he had flatlined three times already. Nurse Kelly and Nurse Teagues were waiting on standby with the paddles if a fourth occurrence presented itself. Liam's skin had turned a sickly shade of gray from having lost so much blood.

"Don't quit on me!" Dr. Franklin said sternly as Liam's heart rate once again wavered out of control.

"Got it!" Dr. Franklin proclaimed as he removed one bullet from Liam's chest. It clunked loudly against a metallic pan.

"Close him up, Dr. Fields. Hurry."

Bridgette lay on the operating table fully conscious but heavily medicated as Doctors McKenna and Conrad saw to her care. They extracted the bullet with ease as Bridgette groggily told them all about her ordeal. They decided to only put Bridgette under a local anesthesia since she had managed to get the bleeding under control herself. The only thing the doctors had to do was remove the bullet, clean out the wound and stitch her up.

"Are you Jack Morrow?" asked Nurse Beatty as she approached Jack in patient room 3A.

"Yes. Do you have a status for me?"

"I do, sir. Tommy is coming out of surgery now. He will be in recovery for the next several hours, but he is stable."

"Oh, thank God!" Jack vented as both he and Cole breathed sighs of relief.

"Do you have any update on my sister, my son, Liam, or my daughter?" Jack said with worry.

"Your sister is in recovery. Her surgery went very well."

"Oh, thank God. What about Tristan and Liam?" Jack said nervously.

"Liam is still in the OR. There were some complications, but we will keep you updated."

"And Tristan?" Cole demanded.

Why was this nurse being so difficult?

"I'm afraid Tristan hasn't woken up yet. She is stable, but still unconscious."

Frank saw Doctors Conrad and McKenna walking towards him and his stomach tightened unforgivingly. Frank rose to his feet and shook both of their hands.

"Ted ... Carl ..." Frank said warmly. He knew Bridgette's colleagues well from the annual hospital Christmas party.

"Do you have good news for me?"

"Of course we do," Dr. Ted Conrad replied. "She talked our ears off throughout the entire procedure."

A tidal wave of relief overcame Frank's body. The breath was taken away from him as he stood there in a happy state of shock.

"She had the wound under control. All we had to do was remove the bullet and close her up."

Frank was speechless.

"She's in recovery. You can go see her if you'd like."

Finally the words came to Frank as he wiped the tears from his eyes.

"Guys. Thank you. Please lead the way."

"She hasn't woken up yet?" asked Jack with worry.

"She sustained a major head injury. We performed a CT scan and there are no internal bleeds or injury to her skull. Her vitals are stable. We are just waiting for her to regain consciousness. I expect it will be soon."

"Can we see her?"

"Not until your own doctor has cleared you," explained the nurse. Angus looked at Nurse Beatty with a speculative glare.

"He's cleared. Show me to my granddaughter."

"Are we free to go yet?" asked Jenna with an annoyed tone of voice. She had taken her breathing mask off yet again.

"Not yet... Please keep the mask on."

"My breathing is fine ... I have to go."

Adam followed suit.

"We have an investigation to wrap up," Adam reminded Nurse Wendell.

"Officers, I must insist!"

The nurse could insist all she wanted, but she wasn't keeping Adam and Jenna stuck in the hospital. Not with a murder investigation to wrap up and an officer in the OR with a gunshot wound to the chest. With determined fury, Adam and Jenna bolted out of the Emergency Room and into the waiting room of Grier Mountain Medical Center. When they emerged, the tiny waiting room was packed, with very few empty seats remaining. Along with Joe, there were also five off-duty officers waiting for a status on Liam. They had heard what happened through their police radios. Jenna looked at her officers with shock visible on her face.

Officer Craig Fishel stood up from his chair. "We're here to help. Tell us where you need us."

Officers Jamal Burnes, Christina Parker and Will Oakman stood up behind Craig, all ready to assist. Meanwhile, Officer Ryan Sumter saw the shock on DiNolfo's face.

"You didn't think we'd leave you hanging, did you?"

Adam laughed. "It's about time you guys showed up."

Immediately DiNolfo started barking orders.

"Sumter, go wake up the captain and tell him that we need all entry points to the mine blocked immediately."

"Oakman and Burnes, put a police perimeter around the Forest of York."

"The whole thing?"

"The whole damn thing."

"Fishel ... Parker ... This is important."

"Okay."

"Go up to Morrow Manor and ask Moira for the box that is on the dining room table. I'll call her and let her know you're coming. Bring it back to the station ASAP."

"Now what?" Adam asked.

"We wait. I need that box."

Dr. Fields watched Liam's heart monitor as his heart rate began to normalize again. They did it. They removed the bullet, repaired the chest muscle and stitched the skin back together. The operation was a success. Liam's skin was already beginning to pink again.

"Solid work, folks! Someone please alert the sergeant and the patient's father."

As the officers began to disperse from the waiting room, the double doors to the Emergency Room swung open. Dr. Franklin emerged still dressed in his blue scrubs.

"Sergeant DiNolfo?" Dr. Franklin called. Suddenly the officers stopped what they were doing. DiNolfo held out her hand for the doctor and shook his hand respectfully.

"Do you have a status for me?"

"Indeed. Officer Morrow is out of surgery. We successfully removed the bullet. There were some complications, but he is stable now."

The noise that erupted from the waiting room was deafening. The off-duty officers celebrated amongst each other, giving the doctor high fives and patting him on the back. Adam meanwhile felt like he was about to faint from his overwhelming relief. Joe stood up and offered a supporting arm as Adam took in the news.

"Thank you, doctor. Excellent news," remarked DiNolfo as a broad smile grew over her face.

"All right, Officers of Elkhart, do me proud. Let's get this done."

Jack and Cole walked quietly into Tristan's hospital room. As they took in her unconscious body, they felt sick to the bone. She lay there, weak and pale, unaware that she had visitors. The side of her face was badly bruised from the impact of her fall.

"Tristan?" asked Jack.

The nurse encouraged them to talk to Tristan, "She knows you're here. Talk to her."

Jack stood by Tristan's bedside as Cole took the seat on the opposite side. Angus meanwhile continued to talk to the nurse in the hallway. Cole grabbed Tristan's cold hand, and begged, "Please wake up ..."

"Honey, it's Dad. We need you to wake."

Tristan's chest rose and fell softly. She didn't respond. Jack and Cole sat quietly for a moment. Suddenly, Tristan's hand flinched a tiny bit in his own hand. His eyes immediately looked at her face.

"I think she's waking up," said Jack.

"I know what will wake her up," said Cole slyly. Cole continued, "Geez, Tristan, I can't take my eyes off of you for a minute."

Jack looked at Cole as if he was insane.

"What are you doing?"

"Just play along. Tristan, I told you that you needed me to protect you."

Tristan's other hand began to flinch now.

"So stubborn. You're always saying how you can handle yourself. How you're fine," mentioned Jack. It was a long shot, but he hoped he could get a rise out of her.

"You're a stubborn mule, just like your father and grandfather," quipped Cole as Jack shot him a dirty look.

Suddenly, a gasp escaped Tristan's mouth. Jack and Cole looked at her face with excited anxiety. As her eyelids slowly opened, Tristan complained, "I am not."

"Oh, my God! You're awake!" yelled Jack as he hugged her.

"Can't a girl sleep? And Hey! I can handle myself just fine!"

Cole and Jack could do nothing but laugh and breathe sighs of relief. She had them so worried. Jack ran out into the hall to grab the nurse. Tristan glanced over at

Cole with a sleepy smile.

"I thought I lost you again," said Cole sadly as he kissed Tristan on the cheek.

"I think you should know by now that I'm not going anywhere."

"I need to make a phone call," remarked Adam as he and DiNolfo walked down Mountain Road to the station.

"Now?"

"Yes. It's urgent. We got a call earlier today from a detective in Seattle. Angie's husband turned up dead."

"I saw the file."

"I just need to let him know that we got her. Then I think we should go to the O'Maras' house."

"I need the box first."

As Adam and Jenna walked into the station, they were immediately agitated by the sheer amount of noise that was sounding from the holding cells in the back of the building.

"Hello?" Jesse Trafford shouted.

"Is anybody here?" yelled Hunter McCord.

"What the hell is their problem?" DiNolfo asked Officer Conklin.

"They've been yelling just about all damn night. At this point, I'm ignoring them."

Adam rolled his eyes as he went back to deal with the raucous.

"What's the problem, boys?" snapped Adam at the two noisiest prisoners.

"Did anybody get my van back?"

"Nope."

"Well, where the hell is it? Did you at least arrest the person who stole it?"

"Nope."

"What the hell?" Hunter screamed, looking like a madman. He punched a wall in anger.

"Hate to break it to you, but where you're going, you won't need it."

"What?" Hunter screamed, red-faced and belligerent.

"I told you, he's a complete lunatic. He's hopped up on something."

"Damn, dude ... Lay off the white stuff."

"Come on, Adam. We gotta go."

Adam followed after DiNolfo, but not before grabbing a file folder that was lying on top of his desk.

CHAPTER 30

June 21, 2000
27 Caribou Road
Elkhart, PA
6:18 A.M.

THE SUN ROSE RED AND VIOLENT over Elkhart as Adam and Jenna arrived at 27 Caribou Road. Adam walked up the garden path that led to the front door while Jenna followed behind with a cardboard box in her hands. With three firm and steady knocks, Adam announced his presence at the O'Mara residence.

Roger O'Mara woke with a start. There was someone banging loudly on the front door. He looked at his wrist watch.

Only six eighteen ... Who would be knocking this early?

Roger pulled on his robe in a hurry as he rushed downstairs to answer the door. As the door swung open, he was alarmed to see the two officers standing on his front steps.

"What's happened?" Roger asked with great alarm.

"Roger, may we come in? We need to discuss something with you," asked Adam professionally.

Roger immediately opened the door for the officers and let them in. Adam could tell he was nervous. Roger's hands were shaking.

"Is Mrs. O'Mara awake?" asked Jenna as she tried to maintain a calm tone of voice.

"I will get her."

Roger ran upstairs and bolted into the bedroom that he shared with Gwen. He shook his wife gently.

"Gwen, you have to wake up. The police are downstairs."

"What? What's happened?"

"I don't know. They want to talk to both of us."

"Oh, my God. I'm coming."

Gwen pulled on her yellow silk bathrobe, slipped her feet into a pair of slippers and skidded down the front staircase.

"Jenna, what's happened?" asked Gwen in a nervous voice.

"I think we ought to sit down," suggested Jenna.

Roger and Gwen O'Mara sat down on the couch as Adam and Jenna sat next to them like bookends.

"I'm afraid we are the bearer of more bad news," said Adam gently.

Roger and Gwen both caught their breath.

"Angie is dead," said Jenna bluntly.

Roger's face turned a terrible shade of red.

"What? How? When are you going to catch this bastard?" Roger demanded to know.

It took considerable effort for Jenna not to grimace at Roger's comment.

"Angie was killed by police fire," explained Adam.

This was true. Cole's shot had rendered Angie brain dead, but DiNolfo's shot to the chest was the one that took her life.

"Police fire. Why? What is the meaning of this?" Roger continued to scream.

"Who shot my daughter?" Gwen demanded to know.

"Angela O'Mara opened fire on three police officers last night and struck one. She confessed to the murders of Tiffany O'Mara, Courtney O'Mara, April Dearing and Jeremy Macklon. She kidnapped Natalie Piedmonte last night and stole Hunter McCord's van. When Angie fired on Sergeant DiNolfo, she fired back in self-defense."

Gwen could feel her sanity loosening from her grip.

Did she just say what I think she said?

"Wait what?" Roger demanded. "She confessed ... There is no way ..."

"I don't understand," said Gwen in a state of shock.

"She loved her sisters. She was upset when they died!" insisted Roger.

Gwen sobbed hysterically as she spiraled out of control.

"Half of my daughters are dead!"

Roger put his arm around his wife to try to calm her.

"I have something to show you," said Jenna as she put the cardboard box on the coffee table. She gently pulled the jewelry box out of its container.

"Do you recognize this?"

"Yes! How did you get it?" Gwen asked angrily.

"I'm asking the questions," said Jenna bluntly.

"This was my grandmother's jewelry box. Belinda Elizabeth Kendricks. She left it to Bernard in her will because he had a fascination with it. They also shared the same initials."

"Open the box."

Gwen did as she was told and removed a stack of photographs from inside.

"Flip over the first photograph and tell me whose handwriting that is."

"Angela's."

Gwen flipped over picture after picture. As the realization set in her eyes, she said, "This is the day they died!"

"Or were supposed to die. If you notice, my photograph has yesterday's date. This box was delivered to the Morrow Manor yesterday afternoon."

The room was spinning around Gwen and Roger's heads. They couldn't make heads or tails of any of this. They were blindsided. How could it be that their most level-headed child was capable of such violence?

"I need to ask. What was your daughter's relationship with Bernard Kendricks?" asked Adam with a serious look on his face.

Roger sighed. It all came down to Bernard in his mind. Bernard had turned her into the monster she became. Bernard awoke the sleeping dragon that resided in Angie's soul. In Roger's mind, if it wasn't for Bernard, he'd have all of his daughters here today.

"They were cousins," said Gwen plainly.

"And lovers," added Jenna.

"We don't discuss it!" yelled Gwen.

Roger sighed. It was time to let the truth be known. It had lain buried far too long.

"We need to tell them, Gwen."

"I won't allow it."

"May I remind you, Mrs. O'Mara, that this is a murder investigation," said Adam sternly.

Roger scratched his head as he prepared to allow the truth slip off his tongue.

"Bernard Kendricks molested our daughter when she was thirteen years old."

Roger had to catch his breath. The truth tasted strange coming from his mouth. Foreign. He had hidden it for so long.

Roger continued, "I nearly went to jail. I beat the living hell out of him for what he did to her. She was never the same. In fact, she didn't seem to understand that what he was doing was wrong. "

Jenna wrote what Roger said on a legal pad verbatim. Adam noticed that Gwen was no longer crying. Her eyes had glazed over, and she looked like she felt dead inside. The vibrancy that once overwhelmed Gwen's beautiful face was replaced by a cold vacancy.

"She continued to see him behind our backs. She changed as a person, becoming cold and disrespectful. We felt like we didn't know her anymore. Then Courtney happened."

"I'm sorry?" asked Jenna with a perplexed voice.

"Angela and Bernard begot a child together."

Adam's eyes nearly bugged out of his head. Tommy's ex-girlfriend was Bernard Kendricks and Angela O'Mara's daughter.

"So you're saying that Courtney was Angie's daughter ..." said Jenna skeptically.

"Yes. She barely showed. She had Courtney in August of 1979. She was incapable of taking care of herself, let alone a child, so we raised her as our own. We never told anyone. Not even Courtney."

Jenna's mind was blown. She hadn't befriended Angie until senior year. She never once suspected that Courtney was not Mrs. O'Mara's daughter.

"After that, we thought that Angie had parted ways with Bernard. We thought she learned her lesson. She started going out with Hunter, and we thought for sure that Bernard was out of her life for good. We were wrong. She was still seeing him in secret. We wouldn't have known anything had our next door neighbor not said something to Tiffany."

"Joe," Jenna confirmed.

"Yes. When Angie found out Tiffany had told us, she was furious. She attacked her sister on the front lawn. She gave her a black eye, a bloody nose, and ripped out tufts of her hair. She said Tiffany was just jealous. I knew better, though. As soon as Tiffany found out she ran into the house in tears. Tiffany was afraid for her sister. I, of course, forbid that she ever see Bernard Kendricks again."

"Did she listen?"

"She didn't have a choice. I grounded her. She was only allowed out for prom. The night Tiffany died. I always thought it was him. I thought he was responsible for Tiffany's death. After all, she did keep him from seeing Angie by telling us. I never thought it possible that it was Angie seeking revenge on her sister."

"What reason would she have to kill Courtney?"

"She was a reminder. A reminder of everything that Bernard and Angela went through. The sick beginning and the failed end. That's my theory."

"Would you mind explaining something to me?" asked Adam with a dark tone to his voice.

"If you knew that Bernard Kendricks was a child molester, why did you not put up more of a fight that he was teaching at a local school? I understand that you couldn't press charges because it was mostly hearsay, but don't you think it was your responsibility to alert the school?"

Roger looked at Adam firmly. He knew where Adam was coming from. He knew what had happened to his younger sister and that Bernard Kendricks was wholly responsible.

"I did try. The school responded that they do criminal background checks on all of their teachers and somehow Bernard had no record."

"Sometimes the system works, but in this case, it failed us," explained DiNolfo.

"Can you please tell us where Angie is?" pleaded Gwen with a dark mood coming forth.

"Angela O'Mara is inside of the Wilhamette mine."

"Can we see her?"

"No, not yet. We have a crew digging out rubble. The mine caved in, and she is underneath the debris. Once we get her to the medical examiner's office, someone will call you to identify her."

Gwen's resolve failed her. She broke down and as Roger tried to console her, she beat her hands against his chest. She looked ravenous, like a wild beast.

"Gwen, calm down ... Please, calm down," Roger pleaded.

Gwen responded in an indecipherable scream.

"I have another question," Adam proceeded.

"Give her a minute," DiNolfo warned.

"I can answer your questions," Roger admitted.

"A detective from Seattle sent over some information to us. Jeremy Macklon, Angie's husband, was also murdered. It is believed that he was killed at the apartment that they shared after he came back to pick up some of his belongings the night before she returned to Elkhart."

Roger gasped. This was incomprehensible. His daughter was a mass-murderer.

"The detective faxed us over some of the information he found. There were many pill containers tossed about the apartment and medical records scattered across the bed. Do you happen to know what Angela's diagnosis was?"

"She wouldn't tell us, and the doctors refused to discuss it. They said that under the mental health scope, she was considered an adult."

"All that they would tell us is that she had to take her medication. I forget what it was called."

"According to the records sent over to us, Angela Macklon was a sociopath. She was diagnosed with Anti-Social Personality Disorder. Apparently she had been seeing a psychiatrist, but in recent weeks, stopped taking her pills. The detective said he found stockpiles of pills in the kitchen."

Roger couldn't speak. Jenna and Adam watched as the life faded from his eyes. They had raised a monster. They allowed her to come back to live in their house, while she slaughtered innocent women, including her own daughter. Roger felt disgusted and repulsed by the very thought that Angie was his daughter—his own flesh and blood.

"We will give you two space. Please call us if you have any additional information or questions. I am truly sorry for your loss. I have a responsibility to protect the innocent civilians of this town," offered DiNolfo and she stood up from the couch. Roger shook her hand but Gwen wouldn't even look at her.

"Take care," said Adam.

A moment later they were gone.

CHAPTER 31

June 22, 2000
Grier Mountain Medical Center
101 Mountain Road
Elkhart, PA
8:14 A.M.

CAPTAIN JAMES JACOBSON walked through the doors of Grier Mountain Medical Center with an air of importance. Sergeant Jenna DiNolfo and Deputy Adam Morrow followed close behind, all dressed in full police regalia. They took the express elevator up to the eleventh floor and quickly found patient room 1103. Officer Will Oakman was outside of Liam's hospital room, standing guard. He nodded at each of his superior officers as they passed through the door.

"Deputy Morrow," said Captain Jacobson with a confused voice. "What on *earth* are you doing?"

"Paperwork," Liam said as he scrawled his signature on yet another page.

Jenna brought her hand up to her face as she shook her head. She had trained him well. Maybe too well.

"You're in the hospital. It's okay to rest," Jenna suggested.

"I feel fine. I want to go home."

"Sounds like you're getting out of here today," the captain explained.

Liam breathed a sigh of relief.

"Captain wanted to stop by. He had some things that he wanted to talk about with you."

"Oh, yeah? Take a seat," Liam suggested to Captain Jacobson as he pointed to one of the powder blue arm chairs that lined his wall. There was rarely a moment when they were empty. Between family and friends visiting, and his sister, who was allowed to walk the halls now, he had company most of the time. The nurses didn't seem to mind as long as he took it easy.

Captain Jacobson took a seat by Liam while DiNolfo and Adam stood by the foot of his bed. The Captain spoke in a deep voice full of authority and purpose.

"First of all, I want to thank you for putting yourself on the line for your community. If it was not for you and Adam, she might still be out there."

Liam shrugged as if it was nothing and his shoulder ached immediately after. It reminded him that it wasn't nothing. It was an honorable deed. He took a bullet while protecting his community.

"I've nominated you, Adam and DiNolfo for awards of valor. Also, I'm sure you've heard by now. You've been promoted."

"I thought we had to take a test for Deputy. I was beginning to look into it before all this happened."

"Typically, yes. However, seeing as though no one else wants the job, we've nominated you and your brother, if you'll accept. You are more than qualified for the position."

Adam replied, "I've already accepted, Liam."

"It comes with a slight pay increase. Now don't go expecting extra zeroes at the end of your paycheck! It's just a nominal increase," explained DiNolfo.

"Of course I'll accept," said Liam with a bright smile on his face.

He looked so much better now that he had gotten his strength up. Although there was a long road ahead for him, he had come so far in just a day's time. DiNolfo couldn't refrain herself from smiling from ear to ear and clapping. Adam patted his brother gently on the back.

"Okay, photo op!" Jenna said excitedly. "Cap ... You and Adam lean in towards Liam and smile."

They did as she asked, all looking very proud and thrilled that the threat in Elkhart was over. Suddenly, there was a gentle tap at the door. Tristan walked in dressed in blue jeans and a red t-shirt. She looked better but was still very weak and tired.

"Hey, Tris," Liam said with a smile on his face. Jack and Cole entered the hospital room behind her.

"Are you ready to go home?" Jack asked, knowing what the answer might be.

"God, yes! Are they letting me go?"

"Yeah, the nurse will be in shortly."

The captain turned to Jack and reached for his hand. Jack shook it firmly as he looked the captain in his eyes.

"Jack, thank you. You should be very proud."

"I am. We all are."

"We've just promoted your boys to the rank of Deputy and they have been nominated for an award of valor."

"It's an honor, sir."

"Hey, Dad," Liam called. "Will Tommy be getting out today, too?"

Jack's face took on a more somber light.

"No, son. Tommy has a way to go yet."

"Is he going to be okay?"

"I sure hope so," said Jack.

Tommy Morrow was sound asleep when Bridgette and Angus walked into his hospital room. Bridgette had been released from the hospital the evening before and wanted to check in on her family. Tommy's skin was off-color still, but his vitals were remaining strong. Out of instinct, Bridgette pulled back Tommy's hospital gown to inspect his wound. The bandage was stained dark red, and it was time for the nurse to come and change it.

"Press the call button," Bridgette said to Angus. He did so without complaint.

"He's stable, but that wound is having difficulty healing which could be problematic," said Angus.

A nurse entered Tommy's hospital room with urgency in her step.

"Is everything okay?" Nurse Rita Carter asked. Bridgette knew her well.

"Well enough. He is ready for a new dressing."

"Okay, let's take a look."

The nurse agreed with Bridgette's opinion and retrieved new gauze and bandages.

"Is it healing properly?" Bridgette asked her colleague.

"Take a look yourself," said Rita as she pulled off the old dressing.

It was a nasty wound that would leave a brutal scar, thanks to Angie's rusted, serrated, hunting knife.

"He was stabbed with a rusty, serrated knife, so we've been fighting off infection. He has a temperature of one oh three. We are trying to bring the fever down and eradicate the infection."

"Overall, it looks like he's healing well; it's just the infection that has me concerned."

"We're keeping an eye on him."

"Please take care of my boy," Bridgette said with worry in her eyes.

Thanks to the headway that Liam had made while in the hospital, the majority of the case paperwork was already complete. Adam and DiNolfo ensured that all the evidence was bagged, marked and archived, except for the jewelry box, which had mysteriously disappeared. Meanwhile, the captain got the go ahead from the state to permanently block off all access points to the Wilhamette mine. Since they were technically state property, they could not fill them in with concrete until authorization was received. The crater that now stood in the middle of the Forest of York exposed the heart of the mine and all the debris that lay within. Tons of debris, rock and tree limbs covered the mine floor. Angie's body was trapped. It took six hours to excavate the body and lift it to the ground behind Monte's Café. Unfortunately, Joe had lost his shortcut to work, but he was happy to give it up as long as his family and friends were safe.

Roger O'Mara agreed to identify Angie's body. Jenna DiNolfo drove him to the medical examiner's office herself. DiNolfo urged Gwen O'Mara to come as well, but she outright refused. Upon returning home, Roger was so angry that he stormed up to Angie's room with a sledge hammer and gutted the room. He plans on turning it into a play room for Cory. Tiffany and Courtney's rooms still remain intact. Meanwhile, Jesse Trafford was sent to Pennington Prison for five years for drug possession and is expected to be up for parole in 2003. Hunter McCord was sentenced to fifteen years at Pennington Prison for drug trafficking and possession. He is expected to face the parole board in 2007. Adam and DiNolfo raided McCord's trailer and found nothing at first, until they came upon the stove. DiNolfo remembered that McCord said that he kept his money in a cashbox in the non-operating oven. She opened the oven door and it wasn't a cash box that she found, but bags upon bags of drugs. Marijuana, cocaine, meth, the list went on and on. It was a location where he could easily destroy any evidence of his stockpile. There were drugs in the refrigerator, cabinets, under the bed, in the couch cushions. When Jenna and Adam were done bagging and marking everything, the captain estimated that they had lifted over six hundred thousand in drugs from McCord's trailer—the biggest drug bust on Skole County record.

After learning of the large amount of drugs seized from the property, DiNolfo quipped, "What the hell was he doing living in a trailer?"

"It's a good way to keep a low profile, I guess," said Liam, who was also baffled by the find.

Everyone at Morrow Manor was now focused on getting Tommy home, alive and well. Jack no longer cared if Tommy walked at graduation. He just wanted him to live.

CHAPTER 32

June 28, 2000
Morrow Manor
Fox Hollow, PA
6:15 P.M.

MORROW MANOR WAS A FLURRY OF ACTIVITY as everyone got ready for Steeplechase's Senior Prom. Bridgette was dressed in a classic, black evening gown with her red curls falling gracefully down her back. She pinned boutonnieres on Shane and Blake as they waited for their dates to arrive. Jack and Frank stomped down the steps in their tuxedos looking nothing short of dashing. Bridgette squealed with delight when she saw them.

Frank laughed. "We clean up real nice."

"Where is he?" asked Jack nervously.

Frank shrugged his shoulders. "He should have been here by now."

"Relax. They just left. Everything is going to be fine," said Bridgette as she adjusted her brother's tie.

"Aunt Bridgette!" Tristan called from upstairs.

"What's wrong?"

"Help."

"Baby, what's wrong?" asked Jack from the bottom of the stairs.

"Not you. Just Aunt Bridgette. Help me get into this contraption," said Tristan, referring to her prom dress. Bridgette laughed as she rushed upstairs to help her niece.

Blake and Shane stood by the fireplace admiring each other's attire. Blake looked dapper in a black tuxedo that was topped off with a fedora. Meanwhile, Shane rocked a white tuxedo complete with perfectly white sneakers and a pair of shades. To say that they were excited was an understatement.

The front door of Morrow Manor burst open as Joe and Jenna entered the foyer with broad smiles. Joe was dressed in a classic black tuxedo with a navy blue vest. It matched Jenna's midnight blue evening gown perfectly. For the first time in a long time, she let her hair down and her wavy brown hair fell just past her shoulders. The adults all laughed at each other's excitement. They felt like they were going to their own prom, and not the kids'.

"Damn, aren't we the best lookin' chaperones ever?" exclaimed Joe.

"Are the kids on their way?"

"Yeah, all the dates are on their way!"

"Now we wait."

"This is a torture device!" Tristan exclaimed as her aunt helped her into a boned corset that would help her dress lay properly.

"I know what you mean. I feel like I'm being choked."

"Okay, and now for the dress," said Bridgette excitedly. Tristan eyed the gown bag nervously as Bridgette began to unzip it.

Jack could hear the sound of tires over gravel before he even looked out the window.

"They're here!" he said excitedly.

Frank swung open the door to Morrow Manor, beating Jack to the punch. Everyone crowded the porch as they waited for the car to come to a complete stop.

"I thought you'd miss it!" yelled Jack to Adam as he opened the door to squad car E7. Adam had a big smile on his face.

"Miss it? Of course not!"

Liam gingerly got out of the car and walked slowly to the house. Adam meanwhile opened the back door of the cruiser where Tommy was waiting. Everyone applauded when they saw his tired but smiling face.

Adam popped the trunk and retrieved a wheelchair, which he helped Tommy into.

"Welcome home, Tommy!" Jenna exclaimed.

"Good to see you back home," Frank said as he patted Tommy on the shoulder.

Jack, whose nerves were utterly shot, had to try to keep his emotions in check. He finally had everyone home.

"1 ... 2 ...3 ... Lift!" said Adam as Frank and Joe helped him lift Tommy onto the porch.

"Do you want to go inside to rest, or do you want to watch everyone?"

Tommy shook his head.

"No, I want to see Tristan off."

"All right, sit tight. I see the limo coming now."

Blake's stomach lurched as he saw the black limo pulling up the long gravel driveway.

"Jesus Christ ... You look just like your mother," said Bridgette as she admired her niece in the mirror. Tristan took this as a compliment since her mother was always known for her beauty and grace.

"I hear Cole downstairs. It's just about time." Tristan's stomach twisted with anxiety.

Cole was the first one out of the limo wearing a broad smile on his face. He looked incredibly dapper in his black suit and red rose boutonniere. He greeted everyone excitedly as he walked up the steps to the house.

"All right ... It's time to see who Blake is taking to the prom. Finally ..." Frank quipped with a smile on his face.

Blake's cheeks blushed unforgivingly and he couldn't help but grin.

"Will the lucky lady please step out?" said Frank.

Everyone gasped in surprise. Natalie Piedmonte stepped out of the limo wearing a beautiful, lavender chiffon gown with her brown hair pinned high atop her head. Blake waved at her and led her in the house as Cole gave Blake a look.

"Don't get no ideas," warned Cole with a stern voice.

"Hands above the waist!" Blake said to Cole.

"I could say the same to you!" Cole quipped.

Cole shot him a disgruntled look. Blake raised his hands in the air, and waved them around, implying, no problem.

"Shane ... Who are you taking to the prom?" asked Adam.

"Pfft! I'm going stag!"

Frank rolled his eyes at his son.

"I plan to dance with *all* the ladies tonight!"

"Sounds like Tristan is ready," said Jenna as she looked inside.

Bridgette walked down the stairs carefully, trying not to fall in her three-inch heels.

"Hold on, let me get my camera out!" Bridgette yelled as she scurried to the end table to grab her camera. As Tristan came down the steps, she started flicking away.

Cole looked up as Tristan began to descend the staircase. Her deep red strapless gown swayed as she moved. The dark red accentuated the flush of her cheeks and the dark of her hair. He felt like he was seeing her for the first time through new eyes. They may be young, but he knew he could never love anyone more. Tristan smiled at Cole. Her blue eyes sparkled and her dark hair was styled perfectly to mask her yellowing bruises from their ordeal in the mine. Cole thought she looked stunning and had never seen her look so beautiful before.

"If I didn't know better, I'd swear that was Catherine standing right before me," said Jack in amazement. "You look beautiful, honey."

"Thanks, Dad. Hi, Cole," said Tristan reverting her attention to her date, who was still awestruck and silent.

Jenna nudged Cole. "Give her the corsage!" Effectively embarrassing him.

Cole smirked as his cheeks turned red.

"You look incredible," he said to Tristan as she smiled.

"You don't look so bad yourself."

Cole smiled sweetly as he slipped the corsage on Tristan's wrist.

"Okay everyone! Line up for pictures!" Bridgette yelled.

All the kids lined up first in the Morrow living room, followed by the chaperones. Tristan thought that the adults were more excited to be attending a prom than they were.

Shortly after pictures, Blake, Natalie and Shane boarded the limo. As Cole helped Tristan inside, he noticed Jack approached him.

"Don't worry, Jack. I'll take good care of her."

Jack smiled sheepishly as he held out his hand. As he shook Cole's hand firmly, he said, "You always do. Have a good time."

Jack and Frank watched as the limo pulled off with the kids inside. Frank patted his friend hard on the back.

"You've come a long way, brother. Proud of ya."

"Thanks. Now let's go party and embarrass the kids," Jack said with a laugh.

Strobe lights threatened to blind Jack as he walked into the dim gymnasium of Steeplechase Academy. A pop rock song was playing on the radio and the dance floor was crowded with students. He looked for Cole and Tristan, but assumed they were swallowed by the crowd. Shane was standing by the punchbowl chatting with a pair of blonde girls in matching dresses. Blake and Natalie stood nearby and saw the adults as they walked in.

"Oh God. They're here," said Natalie as she ducked with Blake into the crowd.

"This is much nicer than our old gymnasium! Huh, Joe?" said DiNolfo loudly.

"Yeah! This is where the rich kids go," teased Joe.

"Rich. You're real funny. I inherited a money pit," scoffed Jack.

"Where are all the kids?" wondered Bridgette.

"Probably hiding from us," laughed Frank.

"C'mon Joe, let's dance!" said DiNolfo as she lugged Joe to the dance floor.

Cole swung Tristan around the dance floor making her dizzy. She had two left feet and Cole was only slightly better. They were having a good time though, and that's all that they cared about.

"Let's get some punch."

Tristan and Cole found Shane, Blake and Natalie by the punch bowl where they were gawking at someone or something in the crowd.

"What are you looking at like that?" asked Tristan, perplexed at Shane's facial expression.

Shane had a look on his face of sheer mortification.

"Look at them!"

Tristan followed Shane's stare towards the dance floor. Joe twirled Jenna all over the dance floor. Meanwhile, Frank and Bridgette were showing off their moves in the center of the floor, clearly unafraid of the spotlight. Jack had decided to take another chaperone for a spin around the dance floor. Jack twirled Edna Harrow under the strobe lights as her floral dress twirled around her. She had even put in her dentures for the occasion.

"They're so embarrassing!" yelled Shane.

"I think it's cute," said Tristan.

Natalie, Shane and Blake looked at Tristan like she was nuts. Cole shrugged his shoulders and grabbed him and Tristan a cup of punch and found a place to sit down.

"It's the time you've all been waiting for! Time to announce this year's prom king and queen. Drum roll please." The drummer shimmied his sticks on his drum ever so slightly as Vice Principal Irwin began to read the results.

"This year's prom king by popular vote is ... Cole Piedmonte!"

While the audience clapped, Cole looked embarrassed and mortified. Tristan urged him to go to the center of the dance floor against his greatest wish. Principle Irwin slapped a crown on Cole's head as he glared at the crowd. Tristan couldn't help but laugh. She knew she would never be picked for prom queen, and quite honestly, she didn't want to be either. She wasn't nearly popular or vapid enough for that role. She had a pretty good idea who was though.

"And now ... the class of 2000's prom queen is ... Trixie O'Mara!"

The crowd cheered as Trixie rose from the table where she was holding court. She waved at everyone and sneered at Tristan.

"Don't worry I'll give him back," Trixie said snidely.

"Don't flatter yourself, Trixie. It's just a dance."

Cole stood in the middle of the dance floor, clearly not wanting to dance with Trixie. Tristan motioned for him to just be nice and go with the flow. It was only one dance, after all. As the music played, Cole looked like he was being punished, while Trixie looked like she had just won the lottery. After the dance was over, Tristan joined Cole on the dance floor and laughed at how uncomfortable he looked. He eventually forgot about his discomfort though, as he and Tristan danced the night away. Two left feet and all.

CHAPTER 33

June 29, 2000
Morrow Manor
Fox Hollow, PA

PROM WENT OFF WITHOUT A HITCH and though some of the kids were embarrassed by their party animal parents, everyone had a good time. The next morning, Cole packed everyone into his father's SUV to drive to school, since there were no other available cars. Both Jack and Cole's vehicles were trapped in the mine, and he was definitely in the market for a new one. They only had a half day of school, and it was the last official day before graduation. Everyone was eager to hear the results of their final exams. Tommy remained at home with permission from Vice Principal Irwin since he had already finished his exams and was injured.

Tristan had never seen Shane look so nervous before.

"If I fail, will you sing at my funeral?" Shane asked Tristan somberly.

Blake quipped, "Are you sure you want that? She's tone deaf. No ... seriously ... She sounds like a dying cat when she sings."

"I do not!"

"Yeah, Tris. You really do," admitted Cole as he laughed loudly in the driver seat.

Tristan rolled her eyes. "They won't kill you."

"She might," Shane said referring to his mother.

"Aunt Bridgette is not going to kill you. Your uncle might make you paint the barn though."

"In order to graduate you need at least a D," reminded Cole.

"I hope I can swing that," said Shane glumly.

Tristan shook her head at her cousin. Only time would tell if he'd be walking down the aisle tomorrow and receiving his diploma, or if he'd be back for another year of classes at Steeplechase.

"All right, ladies and gentlemen ... The day of reckoning is upon us! I have your final exam scores."

Students groaned loudly from their seats. Shane simply slunk his head and waited to hear his fate. Mr. Kessel read out the names and grades of the students in front of the class for all to hear.

Anderson – 86

Berk – 44

"See me after class, Eddie."

Cosgrove – 79

D'Agostino – 95

Felton – 82

Fries – 79

Gordon – 91

Jacobson – 88

Kilpatrick – 71

"Seventy-one?" Shane yelled as he jumped from his seat.

"Yes. Is there an issue?"

"None! Thank you!" Shane said excitedly as he hugged his teacher.

"Mr. Kilpatrick. Would you please take a seat," said the teacher with a raised eyebrow.

"Moving on ..."

Leaman – 85

Morrow, Blake – 96

Morrow, Thomas – 74

Morrow, Tristan – 99

"Nerd!" whispered Shane to his cousin. Tristan rolled her eyes.

O'Mara – 55

"See me after class, Trixie."

Piedmonte – 100

Richards – 64

Walsh – 73

"That's it, folks. You're free to go."

When Shane got out into the hallway, the relief was visible on his face. He slammed his back against his locker and smiled broader than ever before.

"I really passed!"

"Nice job, bud," Tristan said.

Cole and Blake patted him on the back.

"Thank God Tommy passed, too," Tristan said in relief.

"C'mon let's go home."

They arrived back at Morrow Manor around noon and found all the adults in the yard. Frank was at the grill teaching Bridgette the fine art of not burning chicken, while Jack, Joe and Jenna sat at the picnic table shooting the breeze.

"So you and Edna, huh?" said Joe to Jack just before he broke out into a fit of laughter.

"I was being nice to the old bird," said Jack, getting embarrassed.

"Any chance on you settling down with a special someone anytime soon?" Joe asked Jack.

"No, Joe. My heart is completely unavailable. It is still all wrapped up in Catherine. Maybe someday, but right now, definitely not. Besides, I have enough on my hands."

"That is definitely true. Hey look who it is!" said Joe as the kids arrived.

"Classes are over!" Tristan announced happily.

"That's awesome! I have a happy surprise to announce, too."

"You do?" said Jenna in surprise.

"I sure do."

"Joe's got secrets," Jenna said mockingly to Bridgette.

Bridgette added, "Him and everybody else."

"So what's this big surprise?" Cole asked.

Joe stood up and spoke to everyone, "Well, while I have everyone here, I wanted to tell you all a story."

Everyone's eyes focused on Joe. He was acting so peculiar.

"I've had a gift for one of you in my pocket for the past three weeks, trying to find the perfect time to present it. But considering the events of the past three weeks, it hasn't been easy. So here goes ..."

Joe smirked mischievously as he grabbed a velvet box from his back pocket. He got down on one knee and grabbed Jenna's hand. She had a look of pure shock on her face.

"Jenna DiNolfo, won't you be my bride?"

A look of pure amusement took over her face as she stood up and hugged Joe. Bridgette thought she saw a tear in her eye, but a second later it was gone.

"Of course I will, Joe! Wait until I tell my parents!"

"Your dad already knows."

"Oh my God, a wedding! Dad can they have it here?" Tristan gushed.

Jack laughed. "If they want to."

Joe pulled Jenna in to him and said, "We wouldn't want it any other way. "

Jenna suddenly got a serious look on her face and grabbed Joe by the chin. "But let's get one thing straight. This is a partnership and I'm not picking up your socks or your dirty underwear. Capisce?"

Joe grinned widely.

"Capisce."

"And kids ..." DiNolfo said to Cole and Natalie. They peeked up at her as they both smiled.

"I can never replace your mom. I will never try. But I do love you all, and nothing is going to change that. I promise."

Cole and Natalie leaned in to give their future step-mother a hug as Joe couldn't cold back his emotions any longer. Tears streamed down his face as happiness swelled his heart.

As everyone celebrated, Shane nearly forgot to share the good news with everyone.

"Yo, Tommy!"

Tommy lifted his head. He looked sleepy but happy.

"Yeah, Shane?"

"You passed your finals!"

"Are you serious?" said Tommy in excitement.

"You got a higher score than me," quipped Shane.

Jack gave his nephew a stern look. "Please tell me you passed."

"Of course I did. We all did."

"Hallelujah!" cried Jack, thrilled to have the school year over with. "They are all walking at graduation tomorrow!"

CHAPTER 34

June 30, 2000
Steeplechase Academy
Auditorium
Elkhart, PA
8:15 A.M.

TRISTAN SHIFTED NERVOUSLY as "Pomp and Circumstance" began to play loudly from the speakers in the auditorium at Steeplechase Academy. The graduating class at Steeplechase consisted of seventy-eight graduates, and Tristan was the thirty-second from the front of the line. Blake, who stood in front of her, and Cole, who stood behind her, urged Tristan to settle down.

"I'm not a public speaker!"

"You'll do fine," said Cole. "Just read off of the speech you wrote."

"Imagine everyone in their underwear," suggested Blake.

"That is *not* helpful!" Tristan quipped.

The line began to move and one by one the students made their way down the hallowed aisle where their parents had graduated before them. Tristan watched as Blake proudly marched up the aisle as Jenna, Moira and Bridgette's cameras flashed brightly. Now it was Tristan's turn. After all her hard work, she felt frozen in place.

Cole put a gentle hand on her back and whispered, "You can do this. I'm right here behind you."

Tristan smiled as she took the first step towards the future.

Tristan sat in between Blake and Cole on stage and watched as the rest of the students took their places. The music continued to play after Nathan Zawicky had taken his place.

"What are they waiting for?" Blake said to Tristan.

"You'll see ..." Tristan responded with a broad smile on her face.

Suddenly the double doors of the auditorium sprang open. Dressed smartly in a white button-down shirt and a pair of black slacks, Jack pushed Tommy in his wheelchair up the center aisle. Tommy looked studious in his cap and gown and his broad smile caught the attention of everyone in the room. Jack did not rush up the aisle. He let his son enjoy his accomplishment. He deserved this moment. After all he had been through, he deserved his moment of glory. Tommy's smile beamed as Moira blew him a kiss. Bridgette and Jenna's cameras went off like wildfire.

A tear escaped Tristan's eye as the graduating class of 2000 applauded her brother as he was wheeled up to the stage. Cole felt it too. It tugged right at his heart. Tommy was like a brother to him. As Tristan breathed a sigh of great relief, Cole smiled and squeezed her hand tight.

"I know."

Jack wheeled Tommy to the front of the auditorium and placed him in plain view. Jack backed away out of sight until he was needed again. Vice Principal Irwin walked on stage and greeted everyone.

"Good morning parents and staff, esteemed colleagues and graduates of the Class of 2000. It gives me great pleasure to welcome you to the Steeplechase Academy commencement ceremony. Before we begin with the distribution of the diplomas, we will listen to some words from our Valedictorian, Tristan Morrow."

"That's you, kid," Blake said as he nudged his sister.

Tristan rose from her seat as her panic began to intensify. She approached the podium with shaky hands, but when it was time to speak, she found that she was confident.

"Good morning parents, teachers, alumni and the class of 2000. We've learned a lot this year, but often we question, how much of this will we use in real life? The answer depends solely on you. The other day, I heard my brother Blake say, I will never use algebra in real life, and I told him, he might, if he looks at it a different way. Steeplechase taught us language and reasoning, problem solving, deduction, business skills, and communication skills. I will use the education provided here and put it to greater use. It is up to you to do the same."

Tristan paused for a moment as she took in the crowd. Parents and teachers looked up at Tristan as though she had some wisdom to share.

"Beyond the classroom, there are no practice tests or second chances. You have to use the tools you were given and hone the skills that you excel in. The world is a mystery, but there is no secret that we cannot unravel. There is no problem that we cannot solve. We just have to apply ourselves."

Tristan turned to face her fellow students.

"Class of 2000 ... Stand up. Pledge to your family and friends. Repeat after me: We, the Class of 2000, will strive for greatness. We may not all be Harvard-bound, but we have a bright future ahead of us. It is up to us to continue down this bright path. We have the tools ... Let us use them to build our own path. There will be bumps, but regardless of the challenge, we have the courage, strength and intelligence to overcome them."

Both the audience and the students cheered loudly. Once the noise ceased, Tristan continued.

"Many graduation ceremonies have a feeling of farewell. In Elkhart, we will continue to live amongst each other. Even if you go away to college, move to another town ... Elkhart will always be home. Let us hold each other responsible for keeping our town safe and supporting each other to a new level of success and happiness. Go forth into the world and show the world what Elkhart stands for. I believe in you. Class of 2000, the world awaits you."

As Tristan stepped away from the podium the crowd got to their feet. Her speech was exactly what this town needed to hear. As she took her seat, Cole leaned over to her. "Are you running for mayor?"

Tristan laughed. "God, no."

"That was great."

The commencement continued and awards were handed out for excellent commitment to education, volunteer efforts, and good citizenship. Cole won a $100 good citizenship award for his efforts in helping his fellow students. Shane won a $500 sportsman award for his time dedicated to the Steeplechase gridiron. Meanwhile, Tristan received the highest honor: The Principal's Scholarship for $10,000 for sixteen consecutive marking periods on the honor roll. She graduated top in her class and acted as the president of the Honor Society at Steeplechase. Jack could not be more proud of his children. When he rolled Tommy to receive his diploma, he struggled to keep him in his seat. The last thing he needed was for Tommy to blow out his stitches. But Tommy was so excited that he wanted to jump out of his chair and hug the Vice Principal. The very same Vice Principal that had suspended him countless times for reckless or rowdy behavior.

"Our high school days are over," said Tristan.

"And there are far better things on the horizon," reminded Cole.

As the recession music began to play, Tristan held Cole's hand and departed up the aisle. The future had never looked brighter.

CHAPTER 35

July 2, 2000
St. Mary's Cemetery
Elkhart, PA
10 A.M.

A MURDER OF CROWS lined the roof of 27 Caribou Road as Gwen and Roger O'Mara stepped out into the late morning gloom. The day that they both had dreaded since this ordeal began had arrived. Courtney O'Mara would be laid to rest. Roger escorted his wife to the car with a strained look on his face. As he shut her car door, he cast a weary look at the three birds that lined his roof. Something about them cause him greater unease.

A harsh familiar ache overtook Gwen O'Mara's body as the funeral directors lowered Courtney's casket into the ground. She wished that she could say she felt heartbroken, because even that would be better than what she currently felt. She felt hollow inside. It was a heavy emptiness that wore her down. Her worries and devastation echoed through her, unchecked and unresolved, in the great empty space where her heart used to reside. She wanted to cry as she watched her sweet granddaughter being lowered into the ground, but her tears were all cried already. Roger wept into his palm as he kept a firm grip on Gwen's shoulder.

Tommy Morrow sat in his wheelchair as he somberly looked at his ex-girlfriend's coffin. Tristan and Cole stood by him like bookends, offering whatever support they could give. Jack stood behind Tommy, keeping a firm hold on his shoulder. Tommy was doing better than anyone expected. Jack wheeled Tommy closer to the coffin and Tommy dropped a single red rose into the grave. As a tear slid down his face, Roger O'Mara approached him. Tommy looked up at him with an almost fearful glare. But Roger did not approach him with ill intent.

Roger held out his hand firmly and he waited for Tommy to reach out to him. Tommy shook Roger's hand firmly and looked him in the eye. Roger had a strained look painted upon his face.

"I'm sorry I ever doubted you, Thomas," Roger said with a pained expression.

Roger continued to grasp Tommy's hand for a moment, then shook Jack's hand and departed with his family. Tommy sat where he was and watched the O'Maras leave the burial site with a look of shock and pain on his face.

⚜

Gwen O'Mara walked home from the funeral with a distant stare in her eye. One daughter was laid to rest in a respectful, peaceful way. The other daughter would get exactly what she deserved. Gwen marched upstairs to her bedroom and retrieved the simple silver urn that contained Angie's remains. She would not be laying her to rest peacefully, but in a way that would not only have sent her obsessions into overload, but also her delusions running amuck. Gwen walked alone to St. Mary's Cemetery. The funeral party had dispersed, and Gwen was alone as she walked through the older section of the cemetery. Some stones were toppled over. Others, nature had tried to reclaim. Finally, she approached the twin stones. Both stones were fairly new. Dorothy Kendricks had purchased the plots when she became engaged to Bernard's father, Nathaniel Crowe. The plots were intended for Dorothy and Nathaniel, but instead she lay there with her beloved son instead. Gwen hovered over Bernard Kendricks's grave with a look of pure rage on her face.

"You wanted him so badly. You went nuts over him. Now you can be with him forever! Killed your own daughter over him! Curse both of you to hell! Maybe you'll be happy there!" Gwen shouted as she spit at the grave.

She dug with her bare hands over the space where Bernard Kendricks's dead body lay. She pulled up grass and dirt and kept digging and digging until finally she had dug a one foot by one foot hole.

"Here! Take her! Sick bastard! At least you can't take any more of my daughters!"

Gwen took the lid off of Angie's urn and dumped her into the ground that lay above Kendricks's body. As she covered Angie's ashes in the hole, Gwen pounded the earth with fury. She looked to the sky and screamed.

"What have I ever done to deserve the hell you've given me? What have I ever done? I paid attention. I raised them well and half of them are dead! Take me instead!"

Though Gwen's tears were squelched, the skies were not. Rain began to pour from the clouds above. The droplets ran down Gwen's face and her screams of agony were only drowned out by the sound of thunder. As she continued to scream, Jenna DiNolfo ran from her squad car and lifted Gwen out of the mud and to her feet.

"You've done nothing wrong. This is not your fault."

Gwen moaned, but it was undecipherable.

"Come. I'm taking you home."

As Jenna led Gwen to her squad car, Mrs. O'Mara's wails cried over the thunder that sounded in the distance.

Jack Morrow couldn't seem to get Gwen O'Mara's face out of his mind. She had looked so lost, so deeply disturbed. Who could blame her, really? Jack didn't know what he'd do if he had lost his children or discovered that one of them was a murderer. He knew that Gwen and Roger O'Mara were good parents. They doted on their daughters and did right by them. Was it luck of the draw that his children turned out right? No. That wasn't it, Jack decided. He provided everything his children needed, but most of all he gave them guidance, advice and crucial life lessons. He kept a firm eye on them.

While Tristan would complain that Jack was overbearing, he was that way for a very good reason. He would go to hell and back for all of his kids, especially his daughter. Jack ran a tight ship, and by doing so, he kept his kids walking a very narrow line. Even Tommy, the wildest of the bunch, knew not to cross his father. When Jack wasn't around, Frank and Bridgette were certainly not afraid of disciplining his lot of kids. They were as much Frank and Bridgette's children as they were his own. In town, Joe Piedmonte and Jenna DiNolfo kept a close eye on all of them. But when it came down to it, Jack knew that he raised children that looked out for each other. They didn't want to harm one another. They weren't jealous of each other. They enjoyed each other's company, most of the time.

Jack believed that he would know if one of his kids was hiding a secret like Angela O'Mara. He didn't want to discredit Roger and Gwen's parenting, but he was sure that if they had run a tighter ship, they could have controlled the damage caused by their daughter's delusional mind, and her mentor, the depraved Bernard Kendricks. When Jack heard that Bernard Kendricks had molested Angie when she was only thirteen, he immediately thought of Tristan.

"Are you sure he never tried anything like that?"

"Dad ... For the millionth time. I told you what happened. I didn't let him near me."

"You're very lucky."

"No, I'm not lucky. I just know how to defend myself. When are you going to learn that?"

"When are you going to learn that we will never stop trying to protect you?"

"And that there is nothing wrong with that?" Cole quipped.

Tristan laughed.

"Thanks, guys. And trust me; luck has nothing to do with it. I was trained well."

CHAPTER 36

July 15, 2000
Fox Hollow, PA
Morrow Manor
4:17 P.M.

IT'S AMAZING WHAT A LITTLE TIME will do to heal your wounds. Liam was back on patrol, Tommy was getting around just fine now, and Bridgette had never missed a beat. While the external wounds healed fast, the internal wounds would take longer. Everyone was making significant strides in putting the horrors of June of 2000 behind them.

"C'mon, Tristan. What are you waiting for?" Tommy shouted from the bank of the Croft Lake.

Tristan stood on the edge of the lake with Bernard Kendricks's jewelry box in her hands. She was surrounded by her brothers, Tommy and Blake, as well as Shane, Cole and Natalie. Adam and Liam ventured out onto the deck of the lake house to view the spectacle.

"Chuck it in!" yelled Shane.

"Let's put all this behind us," urged Cole.

"What are you waiting for?" asked Natalie excitedly.

Tristan looked back at the anxious crowd and smiled. She gently pressed down on the clasp to open the jewelry box and removed two photographs from her pocket: an old yearbook photograph of Bernard Kendricks and a photograph of Angie O'Mara. She placed the two photographs gently in the box and slammed it shut.

"Okay. Now we're ready," said Tristan. "Does anyone have any last words for them?"

"You messed with the wrong family!" shouted Tommy.

Shane and Cole agreed with his statement wholeheartedly.

"Rest in pieces?" suggested Blake.

"So wrong," said Natalie as she nudged Blake in the gut.

Tristan shook her head as she prepared to let the past go.

"We cast you away and condemn you to the depths of the lake where our mother's life was stolen from us. You can no longer haunt us, because we are not afraid. Your memory is no more than a nuisance; a bee in our ear that we will forever shoo away. There is light and dark in everyone and everyplace. Our light will snuff out the darkness and it will forever shine over this land and this family. There will be bumps, but regardless of the challenge, we have the courage, strength, intelligence and resilience to overcome them."

As the final word escaped from Tristan's mouth, she launched the metal jewelry box in the air. From the other side of the lake, Jack and Frank raised their shotguns and sent a pair of bullets flying through the blue sky over the lake. With great force, Jack's bullet met the box and ravaged the metallic frame. The bullet punctured through the beautiful BEK monogram, tore through the red fabric inside, sliced through Bernard Kendricks's eye. Frank's shotgun ravaged Angie O'Mara's neck and came out the other side demolishing the frame of the box. As the box tore apart, the Crowe diamond, which was discretely hidden under the velvet lining of the jewelry box, was shattered to a million pieces, each splashing into the water with a brilliant sparkle. The most prized possession that Bernard Kendricks ever owned was banished to the abyss of Croft Lake. Tristan and Tommy watched as what remained of the box rained into the water. While the others cheered, Tommy and Tristan pulled each other in tight. If anyone could understand the true depths of Angela O'Mara and Bernard Kendricks's depravity it was them.

"It's over now," Tristan said softly.

"For good," replied Tommy firmly.

"And guess what?" Tristan asked with a happy expression in her eyes.

"What?" asked Tommy.

"Life goes on."

EPILOGUE

A MURDER OF CROWS lined the roof of 27 Caribou Road, like ancient gargoyles keeping watch from above. They passed judgment on all who entered, and all who strayed. They chased the shadows and they knew the truth of everyone who resided within. It was their duty to know. One by one the trio spread their wings and departed from the cursed house of the O'Maras. Battered wings beat against the unseasonal chill as the birds flew from one house to another, storming through the sky like a black rain cloud. As graceful as swans, the crows alighted on the roof of the Piedmonte residence. Their claws hooked into the roof, and as the sun went down that day, the murder of crows called into the night.

All secrets must come to light. Like a fungus that thrives in the dark, secrets will find a way to the surface. Angie O'Mara proved that not all secrets are harmless. Yet, no matter how you try to squash them, they always find a way out of the dark and into public view.

Everyone in Elkhart has a secret; it just so happened that Angie O'Mara possessed one of the darkest of all. Not everyone in town possessed skeletons so rancid, though. Joe Piedmonte's only secret was that he wanted to marry the girl that got away so many years ago. Jack Morrow's deepest secret was one that broke his heart: His beloved Catherine was torn from him by a depraved lunatic whose obsessions were more real than the threat of a gun to his head. Jack would never love another woman again like he had Catherine. Cole's biggest secret was that though he was the most mild-mannered of the group, he had no trouble defending the people he loved, especially Tristan.

The one person Angie spent her life running from was not Bernard Kendricks, but the girl who loved and obsessed over Bernard. The girl who would do almost anything for him. The girl who gave birth to his child at the age of seventeen. The one person Angie spent her life running from was none other than herself.

Bury a secret, and prepare to have it haunt you well past your dying day.

ABOUT THE AUTHOR
ADDISON KLINE

Addison Kline is an International Best-Selling Author who resides in Pennsylvania with her family. When she is not writing, she is immersing herself in music, reading to her heart's content, traveling with her family, or binging on her favorite shows on Netflix that include Wentworth, Bloodlines and Sons of Anarchy.

Addison is a member of the International Thriller Writers Association and while she loves to write in a variety of genres, Addison always says "mystery is her game." Some of her other favorite sub-genres to write include romantic suspense, psychological thrillers, crime and mafia thrillers.

Some of Addison's greatest influences to date include Edgar Allan Poe, Stephen King, Ray Bradbury, Harper Lee, Gillian Flynn, Emily Dickinson, Jane Austen & James Patterson.

You can follow Addison on Social Media:

Mailing List

http://bit.ly/1KcoNGs

Facebook

http://on.fb.me/1DCZOaO

Website

http://addisonkline.weebly.com/

Other titles by Addison Kline

Stolen Innocents
A Murder of Crowes
Miles Away
Black Horse
Broken Road
Shattered Chances
Breaking Black
Down To You
Mark My Words
Lucy and the Wish

Coming Soon:

Phoenix
Raven
Serving Life
Rebel's Cut
Barred
Cinder
Belle Curve

Made in the USA
Middletown, DE
02 June 2017